Madge Swindells was born and educated in England. As a teenager, she emigrated with her parents to South Africa where she studied archaeology and anthropology at Cape Town University. The author of numerous novels, her work has been translated into nine languages and has reached bestseller lists across the world. She currently lives in Kent.

HOT ICE

Christine Winters and Sienna Sheik were best friends at school, but when they followed their careers the two friends grew apart. It seemed that their worlds would never meet again. But Chris's life is turned upside down when Sienna is brutally kidnapped from her wedding car — she does everything in her power to save her, but fails . . . Later, working for a financial investigation agency, she's given the opportunity to solve the mystery of her friend's disappearance. Suddenly Chris finds herself in the dangerous underworld of diamond laundering, civil war and terrorism. She must use her wit and bravery to uncover the truths surrounding Sienna's kidnapping. It soon becomes clear that once this Pandora's Box has been opened, it is almost impossible to close.

Books by Madge Swindells
Published by The House of Ulverscroft:

THE CORSICAN WOMAN
SUMMER HARVEST
SHADOWS ON THE SNOW
SONG OF THE WIND
SNAKES AND LADDERS
SUNSTROKE
WINNERS AND LOSERS
TWISTED THINGS
RIPPLES ON A POND

MADGE SWINDELLS

HOT ICE

Complete and Unabridged

CHARNWOOD
Leicester

First published in Great Britain in 2006 by
Allison & Busby Limited
London

First Charnwood Edition
published 2007
by arrangement with
Allison & Busby Limited
London

The moral right of the author has been asserted

British Library CIP Data

Swindells, Madge
    Hot ice.—Large print ed.—
    Charnwood library series
    1. Kidnapping—Fiction
    2. Female friendship—Fiction
    3. Suspense fiction
    4. Large type books
    I. Title
    823.9′14 [F]

    ISBN 978–1–84617–619–7

Published by
F. A. Thorpe (Publishing)
Anstey, Leicestershire

Set by Words & Graphics Ltd.
Anstey, Leicestershire
Printed and bound in Great Britain by
T. J. International Ltd., Padstow, Cornwall

This book is printed on acid-free paper.

With thanks to Peter Archer, Jenni Lajzerowicz, Louise Watson and Shelley Power for their valuable editorial advice.

1

Christine Winters, lawyer, economist, voracious gobbler of cases, the company's youngest whizz-kid, who bills her time at two hundred and fifty pounds an hour, glances impatiently at her watch as she calculates the cost of playing truant. The wedding procession is late, but she longs to catch a glimpse of her old school friend, Sienna Sheik, now a bride, so she remains loitering by the traffic lights near the Dorchester Hotel. For days the media have been filled with pictures of the beautiful socialite who will marry a wealthy distant cousin in a private ceremony at the Dorchester and join a lavish celebration party shortly afterwards. It's an arranged marriage. The arranger is Mohsen Sheik, the bride's father, known in London as India's billionaire 'diamond king'.

Chris mops her forehead with a tissue. Is it really this hot and humid or is she suffering from the wine she drank at a boring, but vital, business lunch. Squinting against the setting sun, she sees a long queue of stretch limousines, strewn with flowers, approaching slowly. As they draw near she gapes at the colourful silks and satins, the men's flashing eyes and good looks, their splendid turbans, jewels and bright satin tunics. The women, too, are wearing stunning outfits; each one a bird of paradise! Now she's glad she turned down the invitation to the

1

reception. Nowadays they live in different worlds, but once they were like sisters.

Her heart thumping, Chris watches Sienna pass by in the back of a grey Diamler. She gasps at her shimmering, jewelled, blue and gold gown. How lovely she looks, her glossy black hair hanging loose over her shoulders, half-hidden by a glittering blue veil. Then she catches a glimpse of those well-known, limpid brown eyes looking exceptionally sad and this moves her. Catching sight of Chris, Sienna leans forward to wave, but the car moves on. She gestures madly through the back window, beckoning Chris to the Dorchester.

The lights change to red and half the convoy halts. The bridal car has moved ahead, but is beginning to slow when two cars race forward on the wrong side of the road and stop short with a stench of burning brakes. Shock sends Chris reeling back against the traffic lights. She's surrounded by hysterical screams and blazing guns. Gunmen in grinning masks are belting down the road towards the bridal car shooting at random. Shots come from across the road where eight more masked men are racing towards Sienna. It seems to Chris that she's tumbled into a Matrix movie. This can't be real.

A few guests abandon their cars and flee towards the shops, but most of them sit stiff and upright as if waiting for normality to return. Someone is blowing a whistle. It goes on and on. Blood splatters the road in front of Chris as an armed man falls from a car and lies spread-eagled on the tarmac. The sight of his body acts like a starter's gun and Chris leaps forward in a practiced sprint.

Two gunmen have wrenched open Sienna's door. They are trying to drag her from the car, but she's hanging on as her dress rips and she loses her veil. Time has switched to dead slow.

'Help! Help me!'

Now they've pulled her out of the car, but no one helps. Her guards are slumped over the back seat. The doors of a green removal van, parked innocuously by the curb, slide open. Sienna is screaming and clawing the gunmen as they try to hustle her towards the van.

A voice from the van's shadowy interior yells: 'Move it! Move it! Move it!' A rap nightmare with gunshots as percussion.

Chris regrets the wine as she propels herself forward. Too slow! Why am I so slow? Sienna's silk sleeve is torn away, leaving her shoulder bare.

'Get back . . . back!' a gunman yells.

Chris is panting, forcing herself to leap across the last few metres, hands outstretched, reaching for Sienna.

A last lunge clutches a handful of silk as Sienna is hurled, screaming, into the dark void. The gunmen leap in after her, shooting randomly, and Chris's world begins to spin.

Real life lacks a good director, she decides, as she watches from a vantage point she never knew she had, floating somewhere high above her head.

★   ★   ★

3

Chris opens her eyes and closes them quickly. She feels absolutely vile. Nausea grips her stomach, her mouth and throat are on fire, her head is threatening to explode and she seems to be slowly revolving. Plucking up courage, she opens her eyes again. A man in a white coat is bending over her and there's a strong stench of disinfectant.

'Where am I?'

'You're in the recovery unit of the University College Hospital, Christine. I'm one of your doctors, Tim Rose. We've removed the bullet from your shoulder and stitched you up. It's only a flesh wound. You're going to be fine.' The doctor's eyes glow with admiration. A bedside manner taken to extremes, Chris decides.

'I've done a good job, if you don't mind me saying so. In a year's time you won't even see the scar. Nothing to spoil your beauty.' His hand rests on hers for longer than necessary, while his eyes keep on glowing.

'When can I go home?' Chris can hardly talk her throat is so sore.

'You were knocked out when you fell against the curb, so you have a touch of concussion, but we've X-rayed you and there's nothing visibly wrong. We'll keep you here for a few days, to be on the safe side. Do you remember anything at all?'

'A little . . . it's coming back to me.'

'I'll be up to see you later.'

She thinks for a while. The van's doors had closed in her face leaving a poignant memory of Sienna looking frantic. 'So what happened to

Sienna?' she asks aloud.

'Who? Ah! The bride.' Her male nurse is tall, half-oriental and he looks kind. 'She's been kidnapped. Her father's a billionaire, according to the media. I guess they're after a ransom. Sometimes it helps to be poor like me.

'It's your lucky day, I would say. Even I could do better at that range and I've never handled a gun. You'll be home in a few days' time . . . or so the doctor said . . . as long as you promise not to barge into too many gun fights. We're taking you to the ward now. We're full, so you'll be in tropical diseases, but don't worry, there're no parasites around: they can't stand the cold weather. Well, neither can I.'

He keeps up a bantering monologue in his soft voice with a pronounced London accent as they wait for the lift. Eventually they emerge on the fifth floor where he wheels her trolley along a beige corridor to a two-bed ward with a floral curtain hanging between the beds. Two uniformed policewomen are waiting there. They move towards her as her ward nurse hurries in.

'Just a minute,' she says. 'Dr Rose says you'll have to wait quite a while. Why not come back later. Gently does it,' she adds, as they transfer Chris from the trolley to the bed. For a flesh wound it hurts like hell. The ward nurse ushers out the police.

'Water, please,' Chris croaks. 'How did I get shot?'

'You tried to rescue that unfortunate girl and one of her kidnappers shot you. Don't you remember?'

5

'It seems like a dream, but the pain is real enough.'

'It'll get worse before it gets better. Sip and spit. No swallowing.' He passes a glass and Chris raises her head, with maximum effort.

'You're allowed morphine so ring if you need it. You were given an injection for pain in the theatre, but there's no point in unnecessary suffering. The police want to ask you what you saw, but you don't have to talk to them until you feel strong enough. Luckily, someone handed your bag and briefcase to the ambulance driver. It's at reception. They'll be sending it up soon. By the way, the media were here, too. Your doctor told them to come back later. Your mad dash has made you famous.'

Why famous? She failed and that hurts as much as the wound. Closing her eyes she tries not to remember.

★ ★ ★

The ward is almost dark when she wakes. The policewomen are sitting beside the bed. One of them, young and blonde, introduces herself and her boss, the DI.

'You're quite the heroine,' the sergeant tells her. 'According to bystanders you ran like a professional.'

'You should leave this kind of thing to the police.' The DI speaks with a soft Scottish accent. 'We're trained and we have the right equipment.'

'But you weren't there,' Chris murmurs.

6

'You're lucky to be alive. Tell us all you can remember. Start with the gunmen. What did they look like?' The sergeant takes out her notebook.

Chris closes her eyes and tries to re-enact the ghastly scene. Once she starts, she's surprised how much she remembers.

'I've spoken to your mother, Chris,' the sergeant says. 'She told me that you're a gymnast, an acrobatic dancer and you studied martial arts and kick boxing. Strange choices for a lawyer.'

Chris laughs. 'Being a lawyer means being on the receiving end of a lot of tension. Sport is the best way to work it out of your system.'

Eventually the police put away their notebooks and stand up.

'You have nothing to worry about,' the DI tells her. 'I've organised a round-the-clock police guard to be stationed right outside your ward while you're here,' they tell her as they leave.

And then? she wonders.

The following morning Chris is lying in a state of euphoria, which she knows must be due to the morphine, when the wide-eyed nurse announces that the media have arrived and asks if she can show them in. Chris lifts herself with her good elbow.

'I feel light-headed. Would you pass me the water, please,' she asks the nurse.

The interviewer, young and caring, dressed down in jeans and a black cardigan, with lanky straight hair and a face devoid of make-up, shakes her hand solemnly and introduces herself simply as Jane Irving. The cameraman murmurs

7

'Hi.' He's tall and stooped and resembles an ancient hippie, with his long, grey hair and tired eyes.

'Just what were you thinking, Chris, when you ran to the rescue in the face of armed kidnappers?' Jane asks.

'I thought . . . I suppose I thought I might delay them until help came.'

The real truth was, she hadn't thought at all. There wasn't time. She does her best to answer their questions, but she feels so tired. When she starts to mumble, the nurse ushers them out and she falls into a deep, disturbed sleep.

2

Chris opens her eyes reluctantly at the sound of a voice. Dusk is gathering outside. That's strange. Her night nurse is leaning over her. 'What day is it? I'm losing track.'

'Thursday.'

'Only my second day. Is that possible? It seems as if I've been here forever.'

She has slept since lunch. There's little else to do. She lies staring at the ceiling, pondering on life's ironies: like the promises she's made to catch up on lost sleep, but now that she has the chance, she's bored. She wants to go home, but every movement hurts like hell. It's the torn muscles and ligaments that hurt so much, she was told by her sexy surgeon. She slithers down the bed on her back, hooks her feet under the iron bedstead and sits up. Shit! It's agonising. If this is a flesh wound, what would the real thing feel like? She really doesn't want to know. Swinging her feet to the floor, she stands up cautiously, while Nurse Brendan hovers.

'Don't worry. I can make it to the bathroom.'

Brendan gives the thumbs up sign and smiles sympathetically. She's a sweet and patient woman with kind eyes and a face that invites confidences. She has the sort of beauty that you have to search for, but if you do, it's there, Chris decides. One of these days a clever doctor is going to snap her up.

'Call if you need me. You have a visitor, by the way.' Brendan gives an intimate, knowing smile.

'My mother?'

'No. A friend. I could do with a friend like him . . . he reminds me of someone, but right now I can't think who.'

Chris lingers in the bathroom. Bloody typical, she decides. When she arrived, reception called her mother and asked her to bring books, some night clothes, underwear and toiletries, which her mother had duly delivered to the Sister. She hasn't returned since. So what's new! Mother hadn't visited when she had her tonsils removed, nor when she fell from the trapeze at the circus school when she was twelve. Mum is a bit like a dust extractor: she sucks in love and caring and puffs out recycled air. Sadly, the art of loving has been denied her. Besides, hospitals frighten her. Nevertheless, the ward is full of fruit and flowers from clients and work colleagues and there is an arrangement of exotic orchids from Sienna's father, with a simple message: 'Thank you. I'll be in touch later, but not yet. M Sheik.'

The nurse puffs up the pillows as Chris hobbles back and slithers into bed. 'No, no. I can manage. I must manage.'

'I'll send in Benjamin Searle then, shall I?'

The name is unfamiliar. 'What happened to supper?'

'We didn't want to wake you. I'll warm it up after he's gone.'

'Thanks. Send him in then.'

★ ★ ★

10

If eyes mirror the soul then her visitor is sexy, clever, humorous, sensitive, perceptive and tender. She brings herself up short. 'What have they pumped into me here? I haven't seen a desirable man in months.'

Chris awards him her five-star approval, mainly for his expressive eyes, while accepting that there must be a downside.

'Ben Searle,' the stranger says. He pushes his hand towards her with a tentative smile. 'I lied to the nurse and your police guard . . . said I was a close friend. Sorry, but I need to talk to you. I'm working on an investigation which might have some connection with the kidnapping. To be honest, I saw you on TV. I was impressed with your courage. I'm hoping you can describe some of the criminals.'

What if she could. She's too close for comfort. Would he whip out a gun, or something more silent, like a handy, pocket-sized garrotte? Looking sexy doesn't guarantee a blameless life. She's a close eyewitness to a serious crime and he could be one of the criminals. She glances through the glass panels towards the guard, but his back is turned.

'Do you have some identification?'

'Very sensible of you.' He produces a card which reads: *Benjamin Searle, Financial Investigations Inc.*, plus his qualifications which, strangely, are similar to her own — law and finance. Chris has heard of the company often enough. American-based, they opened their London branch five years ago. They work mainly for governments and multinationals,

11

investigating just about anything to do with politics or marketing. The term 'industrial spying' may not impress them, Chris thinks, but it accurately describes a lot of what they do. Still, anyone can have a card printed.

'Industrial spying,' she murmurs, smiling to herself. Searle reacts fast.

'That's not a word we like to hear, Miss Winters.'

'Oh, please, call me Chris.'

'And likewise, I'm Ben.'

Pulling up a chair, he sits down.

Chris slithers out of the opposite side of the bed. 'Would you mind waiting while I freshen up?' Grabbing her bag and gown, Chris hurries to the bathroom and shuts the door. Moments later she's dialling her secretary's number. 'I'm fine,' she whispers. 'Truly. But I can't talk now. Call this number and ask them to describe Benjamin Searle. He's one of their investigators and he's here. Get right back to me please. It's urgent. And thanks.'

The reply is taking too long. Chris runs the tap while holding on.

'You there, Chris?'

'Sure.'

'His secretary said he looks like Ralph Fiennes: brown hair, brown eyes, about six-foot ... oh ... and married with three kids. She made a point of saying that. Perhaps she fancies him herself. I know I would.'

'Thanks. Well done.'

Chris hurries back to the ward. 'OK. You've

12

passed. So what do you want to know Mr Searle?'

He looks amused. 'Those masked gunmen you saw at close quarters . . . were they foreign? You said they wore masks, but what sort of an impression did you gain?'

'Impression? Fear was about it,' she answers facetiously.

'You were right up close to one of the gunmen. Right?'

She nods. 'One thing bothers me. The one o'clock news mentioned that al-Qaeda were believed to be responsible, but these thugs . . . it's hard to explain . . . they didn't have the sort of arrogance that goes with fanaticism. Quite simply, they were thugs, and they were overly tense and nervous. I felt that they hadn't done something as serious as this before and that they weren't a team. It was a messy job. There was a lot of yelling and swearing in strong, North Country accents. Only four of the eight had darkish skins.'

'Are you sure?'

'Absolutely. One of them, the one who shot me, had white skin and pale ginger hairs around his wrists and neck.' For the third time she relates all that she can remember. 'Any news of Sienna?' she asks.

'Alas, no,' he murmurs without looking up as he scans his notebook.

But that isn't his problem, is it. Kidnapping is strictly for the Force. So what interest does Ben Searle have in the kidnapping?

Chris leans back, closing her eyes. For the last

few nights she has dreamed of Sienna . . . odd fragments of the past and present moulded into a kaleidoscope of absurd happenings which make no sense at all. At school, Sienna had often told her that her father owned several diamond-cutting workshops, but on the one o'clock news on television, he was described as India's diamond king. Of course she's always known that Sienna's family are wealthy, so she assumed that the kidnapping was for a ransom. Yet Ben thinks there's a link with his investigation. So what is he investigating? The diamond industry?

He looks up. 'I told you how useful you'd be. You noticed much more than you realised. You were very quick, too.'

'On the contrary, I took forever to get into gear, ambling off in slow motion.'

'Actually, not so. Shock does seem to alter our perception of time. Three bystanders said you leapt out into the road like a sprinter at the starting gun. They said you'd almost reached the van when you were shot. You were lucky that they missed. Heroic but foolish. What prompted you to make that mad dash?'

'If you must know, I felt disgusted with everyone. The guests were terrified and running out of control, the gunmen were shouting and shooting indiscriminately. People were trying to hide instead of helping. Only two of the gunmen seemed to know what they were doing. The others looked panic-stricken. I thought I had a chance, but no one else helped. Otherwise . . . '

'Don't be too hard on us humans. Most

14

people have never been in a fight. I don't suppose you have.'

'Not true.' Chris looks away and zips up. Why is Searle watching her so strangely with a secretive, brooding expression? She can't have impressed him with her mannish silk pyjamas, one arm in a sling and no makeup. Some women have all the luck, she decides, remembering that he's married.

'Yeah, well, you could say that my life's one fight after the next, on behalf of my clients, of course.'

'So you're a lawyer?' Searle murmurs.

'Entertainment and media mainly. Strangely we have much the same qualifications, so naturally I'm curious about your work. What exactly is the connection between your investigation and diamonds?'

He seems put out by the question, but her obvious interest demands an answer.

'Of course my brief is confidential, but in a nutshell, we use our intellects and our expertise to solve whatever problems our clients may encounter in the financial world or in their marketing strategies. Often it's simply a case of discovering what their competitors are up to. The diamond industry is currently beset with all kinds of problems.'

'Sienna's father, Mohsen Sheik, has the lion's share of India's diamond exports, so you must be looking into all that price-fixing and hoarding . . .'

Ben scowls at her. 'Don't take this any further, Chris. You're too perceptive.'

15

'Sorry I can't be more helpful.'

'You're very helpful. Thanks. Is there somewhere I can contact you? Do you have a card?'

Chris reaches for her bag and gives him one. Regret lingers after he's gone. Is it him or his lifestyle that she hankers after?

★ ★ ★

Not expecting to see Ben Searle again, she is surprised when he arrives with flowers and fruit early the following morning.

'Hello, Chris. I popped in to bring you these . . . '

'And?'

'And I washed the fruit.'

She lets him off the hook. He'll tell her why he's here in his own good time. She pops a grape into her mouth. 'Thank you . . . have some. They're delicious.'

'No thanks. Of course, you're right, I could have sent them over, but I need to see you. It's like this . . . ' Ben glowers at his hands as if wondering where to start.

'We have a vacancy,' he begins, looking up to see if he's offending her. 'The work has its drawbacks, long hours, too much travelling. We're looking for someone rather special. You have the qualifications, but the job requires verve, courage, the ability to think and act fast.' He pauses, gazing questioningly at her. Once again she is struck by his expressive eyes.

'Well, go on.'

'OK . . . courage, intuitive powers, sensitivity,

16

morality. You seem to be exactly the sort of person we're looking for. You're not married, are you?'

'In a way.'

'In what sort of a way?'

'I support my mother and live with her because nowadays she hates being left alone.'

'You'd double your salary! There's a good deal of travelling and it's exciting work. You'd get to use your creative intellect even more than your training.'

'So where's the catch?'

'You're seldom home. The work plays havoc with family life. It can be a bit hair-raising at times, but of course we have strict working boundaries . . . '

'Would you spell that out.'

'OK, while we don't hesitate to make use of computer hacking, we avoid breaking and entering. Naturally, in theory there's a fine line between — '

'I see what you mean,' she interrupts him.

'I thought I'd sound you out. If you're interested we'll proceed through the normal channels.'

'Which are?'

'Our headhunter will contact you. Followed by meetings with the managing partner, discussions and so on.'

'It's exactly what I'd like, but . . . '

Chris takes a deep breath and says 'no,' regretfully. She has her mother to consider.

3

'Why am I so damned secretive,' Chris asks herself feverishly. 'I should have told Ben that Sienna is my friend, so why didn't I? Perhaps because I couldn't bear to explain why I ducked her wedding reception.' She feels so ashamed.

The truth is, the invitation to the wedding had arrived months earlier, but Chris had written back to say that she would be overseas. Lately, a dawning realisation that she lives life by proxy is filling her with fury. Prolonging her friendship with Sienna would provide yet another entry to a world that isn't, and never can be, hers. Most of her work is with the spectacular celebrity classes: film stars, pop stars and their wives, dancers, fashion gurus and an occasional football star. As a successful media and entertainment solicitor she knows their lives in vivid and intimate detail. She attends their parties, visits their luxurious homes, their yachts, their shooting lodges, grabs them between film takes to sign the necessary contracts, listens to their problems, thrills to their scandals, but she returns to spend her evenings at home with Mother. So where is *her* life?

While the City of London's frenetic beat vibrates like a distant thunderstorm, Chris remains a prisoner of *her* conscience. The realisation that she's fallen into the Cinderella syndrome is persuading Chris to get a life

18

. . . any life . . . just as long as it's her life. The problem is, she works all hours and she can't see a way to change her lifestyle.

Her only feeble gesture was to refuse Sienna's wedding invitation. Big deal! Sienna was once her dearest friend, until she went on to Oxford and Chris to London University. Requests to join Sienna in the holidays to tour the Himalayas, scuba dive around the Great Barrier Reef, ski in Peru and many other marvellous pursuits were turned down for purely practical reasons: she couldn't afford the time or the cash. But now Chris lies in bed in hospital, regretting these missed opportunities and wondering if she will ever see her friend again. If only she'd run faster. She should have been there for her, as she had always been at school, although it hadn't been easy in the beginning, she remembers.

★　★　★

Boarding school isn't the great leveller it's made out to be. So what if they all wore the same uniforms, ate the same food and had the same limits on pocket money and sweets. They had eyes and ears, they visited each other on holidays and gossip spreads quickly. Everyone knew that four of their fellow pupils lived in castles, six were to inherit titles, one was a German count. They even had a princess.

Sienna Sheik arrived alone in a taxi, like a nobody. She was a shy, awkward girl of fourteen, who had flown to Heathrow from God-knows-where and taken a train to Bournemouth station and a taxi for the rest of the way. Her school clothes were sent over from the school's outfitters, arriving just before she did. Sienna was short on pocket money, short on confidence and knew only basic English. Their school had a high academic standard, twenty-five percent of the pupils were scholarship prodigies and they all assumed, wrongly as it turned out, that she was one of them. Three days after her arrival, she ran away.

The following morning Chris was called to the headmaster's office. 'Sienna Sheik walked into a baker's shop and stole some bread,' he began fiercely. 'It seems she has hardly eaten since she's been here. I have persuaded the police and the baker to drop charges. None of you students thought to show her where the dining room is and no one accompanied her at any mealtimes.' His voice was becoming more ominous. 'You female students are quite inhuman . . . worse than the boys.'

'Well, who thought up that rule?' Chris retorted angrily. No one was allowed into the dining room singly. Students had to arrive in couples or groups, nothing less was permitted.

'You're forgetting who I am,' he said icily.

Chris kept her mouth closed and after a while he simmered down.

'It's because you are outspoken, and more than capable of looking after yourself that I'm making you responsible for Sienna. From now on, you and she will share a dormitory. Encourage her to speak English, show her the ropes, and look after her.'

'Why me? This has nothing to do with me,' she argued fiercely. 'How could I know she wasn't getting her meals?'

'I'm hoping that some of your . . . let's call it persistence . . . will rub off on Sienna. Make sure that she is not victimised because she's Muslim and dark-skinned, but don't be too obvious about it. Make sure she eats. That's an order.'

'This is so unfair. Why should I be her keeper?'

'You're a natural born fighter, Christine, and you're endowed with a remarkable intellect, but let's see how you succeed with a task for which you have no innate talent at all. It's something you'll have to learn the hard way. Something new for you.'

'What do you mean?'

'I'm talking about caring.'

His critical analysis hit home and hurt. So he thought she wasn't a caring person. 'We'll see about that,' she muttered sullenly as she went in search of Sienna.

★ ★ ★

She found her room-mate behind the pavilion. The boys had cornered a mole, one of many that ruined their soccer field, and they were trying to pulverise it with cricket balls. Sienna had other ideas and stood guard over it, screaming defiance as her legs took the hits.

'Stop it!' Chris yelled. 'Look what you've done. She's badly bruised. The Head's on his way. You guys better piss off.' The mole took the

21

opportunity to escape under the pavilion and the boys moved off in a fury.

'Thank you,' Sienna said, without turning away.

'Listen, Sienna. I'm taking extra gym lessons. Would you like to come along? We could go to dinner afterwards. Evidently we're going to share a dorm' so we might as well get to know each other.'

Sienna looked doubtful, but she came along . . . just to watch.

She was fourteen years old and she'd never been to school. Instead she'd had tutors. Consequently she'd never played any ball games, never been on long hikes, never swum, rowed, sailed, skated, skied, played truant, got up to mischief, kissed a boy or danced. It was like freeing a captive bird long confined. Sienna had to be coaxed out, little by little, but for all she could teach her, Sienna taught Chris much more.

But finally she failed to rescue her friend, and the hurt caused by that failure is ongoing. Each time Chris falls asleep, the scene is replayed in her dreams: Sienna fighting madly, as she'd taught her, kicking out at the thugs, yelling for help, but help comes too late. So where have they taken her? Will she be found? Chris can't bear to think of how her friend must be suffering. Are they treating her well, or is she buried alive in a hole in the ground, terrified and waiting to die?

4

After a week spent moping in hospital and worrying about Sienna, Chris is delighted to be discharged. There's a great world out there waiting to be lived, she tells herself, but she soon finds that nothing has changed. On her very first evening, Chris sprawls on the rug in the living-room trying to read while Mum watches her favourite soap opera without asking Chris if she'd like to watch another channel. Chris swallows her irritation. Once she adored her mother and the intensity of her feelings dominated her young life. Later came the painful realisation that Mum isn't perfect, not by any means, so her feelings are a mixture of love and irritation. She admires Mum's stoic attitude to every setback and her careless acceptance of life's gifts which she squanders without regret, not the least their limited cash. Mother lives life with a light touch. She often says: 'Why should I worry? I'm always lucky. Something will turn up.'

And something always does because Chris is out there in the marketplace fighting to win: for Mum, for her clients, their daily bread, the interest on half a dozen credit cards and her mortgage payments.

Two years ago, compassion was added to her mixed feelings for her mother when she came home late and found her in tears. She quickly calculated. Mum would be fifty-eight in a week's time.

'Why Mum! Whatever is it?'

'It's nothing . . . loneliness perhaps.' Hugging her secret sadness, Mum gathered her book and fled to her bedroom.

Nowadays Chris returns home early, work permitting, with her briefcase full of discs . . . home being her modest, semi-detached house in Finchley. This is exactly why her clients' compulsory social events are becoming the highlights of her days.

Twenty-nine is a trying age for a girl. Thirty lurks in the wings like an aging prompter whispering phrases that no one wants to hear, like: 'It's long past midnight, Cinderella. Perhaps you missed your cue.'

'Shut up! I have a great career, that's enough.'

Chris cuts short her allowed recovery time and goes back to work.

★　★　★

Every measuring instrument screams danger: ozone, pollen, moisture levels, and just plain heat are all over the top as London sweats under the Azores High, an uninvited guest which has moved in and won't leave. In the courtroom, they are mopping their foreheads and flapping notebooks in front of their faces. Occasional thunder and lightning interrupt the dry voice of the opposition barrister as he cross-questions Chris' client. Is it malice, or the storm's sulphurous ozone release that hammers at her temples. There stands her client, wiggling like a snake on a stick, spitting venom in all directions and lying through her teeth. Her fourth ex-husband to be, eyes narrowed with fury, is jotting denials in quick stabbing movements, while his barrister, cunning and patient, spins his web of words. It's only a matter of time before her client blunders into it, despite her warnings.

'Shit!' Chris mutters. 'I'm getting out of this business.' Suddenly she's had enough.

Her barrister hears and glares at Chris. Fortunately the judge is suffering, too. The trial is adjourned.

The storm has moved east, Chris notices when she hurries outside. The sky is an ominous yellowish-grey, but strips of pale turquoise lie along the western horizon. Caught in the sun's rays, the buildings lining the Thames appear gilt-edged, while the still water shines like molten brass. The tube is half empty and she's home by five p.m.

'Hello Mum, I'm back,' she calls, dropping her briefcase on the hall table.

Mum emerges from the top of the stairs. Unbelievably she's fumbling with blouse buttons, her hair and her skirt, and wearing a coy expression.

'Chris, darling, you're early.' Her tone implies that Chris is at fault here.

'The case was adjourned and I have a headache, so I came home.'

A middle-aged man appears in the doorway behind her mother. He smoothes back his longish, grey hair and makes an obvious effort to

25

stand tall and straighten his shoulders. After a few moments of dazed incredulity the scene begins to make sense and it's all Chris can do not to laugh. She doesn't much like the look of him, but he's not *her* boyfriend. He's Mum's. No one speaks as she looks questioningly from one to the other.

'Well, hello Chris,' comes a deep, Shropshire rumble at last. 'I've been longing to meet you. I'm Bertram Loveday. I expect your mother has told you about me.'

Clearly he doesn't know Mum very well.

'Major Bertram Loveday,' Mum adds.

'But you must call me Bert. Everyone else does,' he says too heartily. He smiles, but his eyes look apprehensive. Chris wonders why.

'Not quite everyone,' her mother interrupts him.

No, Mum wouldn't call him Bert, would she.

'We're going to get married . . . ' Mum says happily and Chris smiles, too. She longs for her mother to be happy, but she can't help worrying about Bert's nervousness.

'Eventually,' Bert corrects her. 'But in the meantime . . . '

In the meantime, Chris learns a few days later, Bert is moving in.

★ ★ ★

For Mum's sake, Chris does her best to cope, but as the days pass, the reason for Bert's uneasiness becomes apparent: she is keeping both him and Mum. Mum has no income of her

26

own, so five years back she bought a house large enough for both of them, but the high mortgage takes much of her income.

Chris moves her desk and laptop from the living room to her bedroom. She reminds herself that she's glad for Mum several times a day. Her mother has been so lonely. So why does part of her feel lost, like a buoy that has broken loose from its mooring. She's accustomed to resenting her ties to her mother. Unexpectedly she's free, but it's hard to get to grips with all this freedom.

'I need to get a life,' she tells herself sternly each time she feels like exploding. 'Get a life, Chris! Get a life!'

The following morning Chris calls Ben Searle.

'Good morning, Mr Searle. Chris Winters here. Mother has found a boyfriend and he's moved in.'

'Mazaltov! And thank you for sharing that with me.' She can hear laughter in his voice.

'You don't understand. I'm free, Mr Searle.'

'Ben.'

'Ben. Are you still looking . . . ?'

'Yes. And I'm glad. Hang on a second.' A minute later she is still holding on. A female voice comes on the line.

'I'm Jean Morton, Mr Searle's secretary. Please hold, Miss Winters. Is that convenient, or should we call you back? Ben's gone to make you an appointment with our managing partner.'

'I'll wait.' Cold trepidation creeps from her feet upwards as she hangs on. The seconds loiter while she imagines this coveted job vanishing like a shooting star.

'Hi Chris. You still there? Rowan's attending a three-day conference shortly. He'd like to see you before he goes. Can you make ten-thirty tomorrow morning?'

Only by shuffling around a whole lot of appointments.

'Sure. See you then.'

★   ★   ★

Rowan Metcalf, managing partner of Financial Investigations, has a voice befitting his position; it is deep and authoritative, but the rest of him lets him down. He's short, slight and rather insipid with his ash-blond hair and pale grey eyes. Chris can't help resenting his boring hour-long interrogation, which has turned into a personal eulogy.

'By now you must have grasped that each of us takes full responsibility for whatever we're working on,' Rowan Metcalf is saying, looking pompous. 'I'm only interested in results. If you need to spend three months in Kathmandu, that's your affair. Charge all living costs to your company credit card when you're out of the country on a job. The point is, you have to win. If you fail, you're out.'

This is something Ben hasn't mentioned. Rowan is frowning at her. She has the feeling that he's trying to scare her off.

He tries again. 'Obviously we don't have a hundred percent success rating. What I'm trying to say is that each case is strictly confidential so you have to work alone. You have to be creative

28

when you're planning your strategy.'

What exactly is she taking on here? 'I thought I was going to be Ben's PA.'

'Initially, yes. Ben has to choose between his family and his job. He's undecided, but we all know which choice he will make.'

A pang of disappointment leaves Chris feeling unsettled.

'We've been pretty well briefed by Ben and various headhunters and we've checked around. You have a reputation in the city for intelligence and integrity. You win more cases than you lose. If you have any more questions, keep them for Ben. He'll show you the ropes. Later you'll be on your own. Are you with us?' Metcalf asks.

'Yes.' They shake hands and Rowan relaxes and seems almost human.

Ben arrives to introduce Chris to everyone. 'They all like you,' he says.

Chris interrupts his congratulatory flow. 'Ben, thank you. I'm thrilled to get the job.'

5

Since Bertram moved in, Chris' bedroom has doubled as her office. It's warm and sunny, with high ceilings and big windows, has plenty of space, and it overlooks the garden. It's Sunday. Chris is sitting cross-legged on the floor searching the newspaper for news of Sienna. This morning her mind is all over the place, like an unschooled horse, perhaps because she's tired. There's still no news of Sienna and Chris' fears for her friend are preventing her from sleeping well. Just about every kidnapping film Chris has seen comes to mind in unguarded moments.

Then there's Bertram, whose presence is an ongoing irritation. She can forgive him for his long, grey, unwashed locks, the dandruff on his shoulders, his browning teeth, and even his stained fingers, but does he have to look so damned humble? Even worse, Bertram has laid a guilt trip on her. She feels mean and that's not how she likes to see herself.

'I'll get used to him,' she mutters. 'Madness to resent him. Hasn't he just unlocked the door of my prison. Free . . . at last.'

Forcing herself to let go, Chris concentrates on her breathing. In . . . out . . . Just let your mind go blank . . . don't hang on to thoughts. Let them go. In . . . out . . . But lately a niggling question bothers her. 'Has Mum ever actually liked me?' Sometimes it seems that she's little more than a convenience . . . in Mum's world.

A bad thought . . . let it go.

The sun comes out. She hears Bertram's car being driven out of the carport. Abandoning the floor, she grabs her jeans. It's a lovely day. The starlings are squabbling over their peanut butter sticks, blue tits crowd on to every perch of their seed feeders. The roses need cutting back and the beds need weeding and the bird-bath needs a good scrub, but she has the entire day free to spend in the garden.

Mum is sitting in the living room by the open french windows, reading the newspaper. She looks up and frowns. 'Your jeans have a hole in them. You'd better throw them out.'

'My gardening togs . . . I'm going to potter.'

'No work from the office? This is a first, isn't it?'

This is her cue so she might as well tell Mum everything.

'Listen Mum, I've been offered a new job with more money; in fact, much more money. I've joined a company that investigates business problems . . . fraud, that sort of thing. I'll be travelling at times . . . or so they tell me . . . so I'm glad Bertram's here.'

Mum looks bewildered. 'You've dropped law, after all that expense and hard work!'

'Not exactly. I need law and finance to do this job.'

Mother's face shows conflicting emotions: hurt, surprise and a touch of fury. She puts the newspaper down, folding it slowly and carefully, smoothing each page on the table in front of her.

Then she smiles to herself.

'You've found the perfect way to hit back at me . . . now, of all times.'

'No, you're wrong. Why do you always jump to the worst conclusions?' Her voice is high-pitched . . . a dead give-away that she is hurt.

Mum presses home her advantage. 'Take my advice and stay where you are.'

'Mum, listen. I was offered the job when I was in hospital. I said 'no' at first, but then Bertram moved in and . . . well, let's face it, you have someone to keep you company. You don't need me. Surely you understand. I have nothing except my career, so I have to enjoy it.'

Mum is getting ever more furious. Chris looks away and examines the roses below the old stone steps. They are covered in hips. She'll prune them.

'Don't blame me if you never date. You're anti-social. Blood will out.' Mother's martyred tones signal the start of a familiar tirade. Once Chris used to provoke her, just to glean some news about her father.

'Mum, for once in your life try to see someone else's problems instead of your own selfish needs.'

Chris has thrown down the gauntlet. She's never done that before. She zips up her big mouth, oozing regret, as Mum gives a bleat that squeezes her heart. 'How can a daughter talk to her mother like this?' she gasps. 'You're cruel, just like your bloody father. You're clever like him, too, and at least you never let me down with money. I can't say we're close, but I blame your father for that. All those costly boarding-schools he paid for turned you into a stranger.'

'So the educational trust fund from Grandpa . . . was that fiction?'

'Yes,' Mum admits grudgingly.

In the long, uneasy silence Chris walks to the window to hide her curiosity. Somewhere in Africa lurks the donor of sperm and cheques who can pay, but can't love. She longs to find him.

'You never think.' Mother's accusing voice breaks into her reverie. 'What if it doesn't work out? I mean . . . Bertram and I. You have a lovely job at the firm. It pays well. You are well thought of. Why can't you stay there?'

'Wrong tense, Mum . . . had! I gave notice and they asked me to leave right away. Evidently they prefer an immediate cut-off if someone is quitting, but they paid me three-months' notice. It will help towards the cost of another bathroom.'

Mum isn't listening. 'You can't escape your genes. Your father was off on any reckless adventure with no thought for commitment, disappearing for months on end without so much as an apology, or any idea of when he'd return.'

Bitter drops of information, but over the years they've been guarded like precious gems. 'You get your kicks from danger . . . just like your father.' 'You're damned selfish, like your father.' 'As for running after an armed thug . . . that's your father all over.' Mum only talks of *him* when she's hurt or angry. Chris decides to break the unspoken rule and question her.

'So what does he do?' she ventures gently.

'He's a geologist . . . mainly freelancing for himself. He finds and registers claims, and sells them to the big mining houses. He roams all over Africa . . . and Alaska. He was well thought of, but he liked to be free. I used to sit around for months waiting for him to return to Johannes-burg. I never knew when he'd come . . . or leave.'

'He should be easy to find,' Chris mutters to herself. 'What was his first name?'

'Leave it, Chris.' Two red spots appear on Mum's cheeks and her perfume wafts past on a wave of heat.

'Mum. I have a right to know about him. If you don't want to help me, I'll find out in my own way.'

'Are you threatening me?'

Is she? Chris changes the subject fast. 'You must have loved him very much.' She waits silently, wondering if she should leave, but Mum needs to talk.

'He'd arrive out of the blue in his battered 4×4 to sell whatever claims he'd registered. I worked for the biggest mining group in the city. I used to help him to get a good price. He kept the best claims secret while he saved the cash to develop his own mine. That was his dream. He never spent much. If we went out it was hamburger and chips, but mostly I cooked at home. After two or three weeks, he'd leave.'

'So what went wrong?'

Mum gives her a searching look, almost as if she's wondering whether or not to trust her daughter. 'You could say that my life was ruined because of a tatty leopard.' She sighs and then begins to talk.

*   *   *

'Willem Zuckerman, manager of our mining house, was hosting a big party up at the company's private game camp, near Botswana. He was worried about a marauding leopard that had killed two children, so when he learned that Dan was back, he asked him to track and kill the beast. Dan was a good hunter . . . the best . . . although he only killed for the pot.'

Mum doesn't have to search for words. She must have told herself this story so many times. It sounds rehearsed, like the stories her clients tell her as they rewrite the past, laying to rest any blame they might feel.

'I was furious that we had to join their blasted party on the very day Dan arrived. It was a seven-hour drive to the camp with Willem and his new girlfriend, Marie van Schalkwyk. She was the loveliest girl I'd ever seen and only nineteen, while he was fifty-odd. She had a ring on her finger like a rock. She was half Swedish, half Afrikaans, and she was a slut.

'The moment we arrived, Dan insisted on leaving at once to track the leopard. I begged him to wait until morning and we fought rather bitterly.'

She sighs and straightens her shoulders and Chris realises that her mother is on trial and she is the judge and jury.

'I had to make the best of a bad job and join Willem and Marie at their table. Later they persuaded me to accompany them on a night safari. I'd only been in the country for a year, straight from Sussex. I hated the harshness of the *bushveld* and let's face it, once you've seen one lion . . . '

Mum breaks off. She's not one for quoting clichés.

'Right from the start, things went badly. We'd only been out for an hour when we had to cross a flooded causeway. Kevin, our game ranger, let the wheel slip off the concrete, so he went to attach the truck's winch to a tree across the river, taking his rifle with him, and he never returned. Minutes later we were surrounded by lions. It was freezing cold and damned dangerous and we sat there in the open truck, smelling the beasts, hearing them, as they circled for hours. When one of them actually leapt onto the truck, Willem fainted.'

'My God! What happened?'

'Marie drove it off with a bottle of champagne. She was tougher than she looked.

'Hours later, Dan arrived. He'd tracked the leopard to the river, shot it, and found Kevin's body. He and Marie went to fetch the corpse. They rolled it in a tarpaulin they had in the boot and they winched the truck onto the causeway. When we got back to camp, Willem went into the bar and drank until he passed out, but by then my fear had turned to fury. We fought and I locked Dan out of my rondavel and tried to sleep, but of course I couldn't sleep.'

36

Mum pauses and Chris sees that she has turned quite pale. 'Go on, then,' she urges her.

'Eventually I went to look for Dan and found him in bed with Marie.' Her voice is so matter of fact, but Chris can see the hurt in her mother's eyes.

'To cut a long story short, I never saw him again. When I learned I was pregnant, I tried to contact Dan through his lawyer, but I . . . well . . . He avoids me. I've never seen or spoken to him since.'

'What a bastard! Yet he supported me through school and university.'

She sighs. 'All expenses. Whatever I asked for, as long as it was for you.'

'How unfair. He was the wrong-doer, not you. I should have been your lawyer.'

'Yes,' Mum says woodenly.

Mum has a hunted look in her eyes and Chris knows that this isn't the whole story, but how can she hurt her mother further by probing into her private life. All she really wants is information to help her find her father.

'Mum, at least you've got me and I love you. I'll never let you down, but I need to find my roots . . . it's like a compulsion . . . even if I only see him once. Maybe he'd like to see what he's been paying for. I'd certainly like to see him. That's my right.'

'You had a lot of rights and so did I. He denied us any of them . . . except money . . . and even that comes through his lawyer in New York. I'm telling you now, I don't want you prying into my life. Do you hear me! The past . . . whatever I did . . . is buried. It must stay that way.'

'Well, at least I know my father's name. Dan Winters! It has a nice ring to it.'

'Dan Kelly.'

'Kelly! But . . . I thought . . . '

'No, sorry.'

Chris swallows her hurt. 'Kelly is Irish, isn't it?'

'He's American . . . the best geologist in Africa. Everyone acknowledges that.'

'So where is he?'

'How should I know. Somewhere between the Cape and Cairo. Or maybe he went back to the States. I never knew where he was when I was dating him, so how should I know when I haven't seen him for close on thirty years?'

Their shared hurt brings a sense of camaraderie. 'I'm so sorry, Mum.'

Chris feels strangely deflated as she saunters into the garden. Mum isn't the type to have an illegitimate daughter. She's been knocked badly. Bloody man. She'll never mention him again. She'll forget him. The past is none of her business. But of course he's her business. He's her bloody father, isn't he.

Grabbing the trowel, she begins to hit on the weeds that have spread in the flower beds, punching and pulling and pounding. Damned weeds! Damned grass gets everywhere. But how perfectly awful. Strictly speaking, she doesn't have a father at all. But is that really true? Nowadays unmarried fathers seem to think they have rights. The same rights as married ones. A father is a father, married or not.

The weeds are stunned, knocked out, kaput, dumped in a bucket ready for a bonfire. Armed with an axe, she turns in her bereavement to some fallen branches.

She could laugh when she remembers all her silly dreams. She used to visualise the inevitable grand reunion when Father, looking strangely like Anthony Hopkins, would admit that he'd erred and that he needs her. By now the scene has become so real she can smell his aftershave and feel the stubble on his cheeks as he hugs her close. Variations on this theme have been played out dozens of ways over the years. She sighs and makes an effort to switch off her futile longing. She's twenty-nine, she's never had a father and she certainly doesn't need one now. But all the same . . . There and then she decides that she will contact a South African Missing Persons' Agency and set in motion a search for her father.

6

Chris wakes feeling optimistic. It's Monday morning and the first day of her new job. She's wearing a tailored black suit, black court shoes and a white silk blouse, and she makes the office by eight a.m.

When Jean Morton, strong-featured, fiftyish, with iron-grey hair and a trace of a moustache, ushers her into a single office overlooking Regent's Park, Chris tries to disguise her glee. There's a green carpet, Venetian blinds, modern furniture and, best of all, a lockable filing cabinet and a wall safe large enough to take two dozen files.

Jean, once Ben's, now half hers, is trying to establish her authority and get to grips with who and what Chris is and how much of a threat she is likely to become. She explains how the expenses work and jots down Chris' details for a company credit card. She pries a bit further than she has to, and fills Chris in on company gossip: Rowan is an unknown quantity who seldom socialises in the office, but he brings in most of their business from the many clubs and associations he networks. Ben and his wife have agreed to split, but Ben is depressed since he learned that Annette plans to return to Paris with their children. Janice Curtis, IT, is supposed to be on hand to help everyone with research, but she's built up a three-week backlog doing private work, so it's quicker to cope without her. Jean dismisses them all with a contemptuous chuckle.

Ben arrives at nine-thirty, looking so sad that it hurts.

'Pretty good view from here,' he says as he sits on the other side of her desk. 'We've been having a reshuffle and I grabbed this office for you. Do you have everything you need?'

'Yes, thanks. I like the office and the view. I'm going to love being here.'

She smiles warmly and watches the sadness fade from Ben's eyes.

'It's not a picnic, I assure you. We have to crack this case as soon as possible. The reason for the hurry is that various non-governmental organizations, called NGOs, based in London and America, are about to combine their resources to persuade the public to boycott diamonds. They were very successful with furs some years back. If they aimed their skills at diamonds the resulting boycott would send the industry into a slump. No one wants that. Developing countries would be badly affected, miners would lose their jobs, and, incidentally, it would reflect badly on us. Several demonstrations have taken place in the States recently.'

'Why would anyone want to boycott diamonds?'

'Because most of the civil wars in Africa were financed by diamonds and the resulting cruelty — injuries from mines, limbs hacked off, children forced to be soldiers . . . you know the score — has sickened every right-thinking person. Hence the term 'blood' diamonds.'

'But do all the blood diamonds come from war-torn territories, Ben?'

'No. The point is these diamonds are not legal. They might be blood diamonds mined to finance civil wars, or diamonds that are surplus to a country's quota, or stolen gems. Masses of roughs are stolen from legitimate mining houses every year. In other words, the diamonds are illegal in terms of a United Nations mandate, and since most of them are from conflict zones, the term *blood* diamonds is most appropriate.

'Apart from these problems, we now have a kidnapped bride. I'm sure there's a connection here, although I haven't found what it is. By the way, whatever information we find — that's relevant to a crime — goes to the police, via Rowen. That's how we operate. The police are currently stumped, so let's hope we find something that sets them on the right trail.'

Surely now is the time to tell Ben that Sienna was once her best friend and that her father dominates India's diamond industry, but she can't bring herself to confide until she knows exactly what it is that the kidnappers want from him.

Ben breaks into her thoughts: 'How about coffee? It's a lovely day. They make good coffee round the corner and the pavement tables overlook a garden square.'

'Sounds great. Let's go.'

As soon as they are out of the office, Ben relaxes and shrugs off their work. He asks how her wound is healing and, in turn, she asks about his children. Before long, Ben is telling her of his constant travelling, which is part of their job, and the havoc this plays with a marriage. She senses the anger that Ben is trying to conceal and his sadness at the prospect of losing his children. Chris has the feeling she could immerse herself in his life and never want one of her own. Don't set your cap at Ben, Chris lectures herself as they walk back to the office. He's not the type to let his family go.

★   ★   ★

'OK, let's get started,' Ben says, when they reach Chris' office. 'This is the boring part . . . facts and figures. I'll try to be brief. Stop me if there's anything you don't understand.'

'Sure.'

'A century of brilliant, international advertising campaigns have built up a world diamond market of around $5 billion a year. I'm not talking about rough diamonds. The market is valued as cut and polished stones set into jewellery of some kind, such as rings.

'Prices of diamonds are kept at an artificial peak by a rather canny marketing ploy, which I'll explain to you now. The world's forty-five main diamond producing countries — excluding America — jointly market their roughs through a central marketing organisation in London, which is called the Diamond Trading Company, or DTC. They play the market very carefully, limiting the supply of diamonds offered to the world's markets so that there is never quite enough to satisfy the demand. The way they do this is by a quota system: depending upon the production capacity of an individual mine, each company is given a quota and the remainder is supposed to be held in stockpiles — awaiting market growth, I suppose. Billions of carats are held back all over the world, sometimes even left in the ground, but guarded, and that is why diamonds have kept their rarity.'

He breaks off, gets up and walks to the window restlessly.

'Prices of *roughs*, as rough diamonds are called, offered to dealers are not open to negotiation. Buyers are carefully selected by the DTC. They represent the world's leading diamond traders, and they are each offered a parcel of roughs at a certain price on a take it or leave it basis.'

'I can't believe what I'm hearing.'

'Believe it. That's how it goes.'

'It must be the first time forty-five nations have got together to fix prices and got away with it . . . aided and abetted by a UN backed body.'

Ben frowns at her.

'Am I to believe that you're liberal, green, anti-vivisection and you loathe the IMF?'

'Merely veering towards humanitarianism. I don't like to see the public ripped off.'

'The UN-backed body was set up to stop diamond revenues being used to fund wars and terrorism. OK, let's move on. Not long ago the amount of blood roughs entering the world's markets was estimated to be only four per cent of the total of legitimate diamonds. Nowadays

44

the amount is massive and somewhere along the marketing route the gems become legitimate, complete with certification. Blood roughs are bought cheaply and they sell for top prices in high street jewellers. It's called *diamond laundering*. No one knows how it's done and the profits are massive. Once they know, they will be able to stop it.'

'So we have to find out how it's done . . . that's our job.'

'Exactly. Remember, not who, or why, simply *how*.'

Chris stirs restlessly. 'Tell me about the Kimberley Process.'

'It's quite simple. To stem the flood of blood roughs landing up in the West, diamond producers got together and created a system, known as the Kimberly Process, which is backed by the UN. Each rough must be sold with a certificate, showing which mine it hails from, the country, the carats, and so on. Each of the forty-five producers, as well as cutters and retailers, are issued with a *'licence to trade in gems'*. Breaking the rules by buying or selling an illegal rough leads to their licence being revoked. No one in the industry will trade or buy from a producer or a dealer without a licence. In other words, to break the rules is commercial suicide.'

'Let's home in on this term *illegal*,' Chris says.

'Perhaps illicit is a better description. A UN-backed body has some standing,' Ben argues. 'You can't ignore the ferocity of the civil wars. It's a way to stop diamonds from funding these terrorists.'

'Yes, Ben. But is that really what it's all about? I doubt it. The wars were mainly over by the time the Congo was expelled from the Kimberly Process, for exporting vastly more diamonds than it produces. So what's it all about?'

'I see you've been doing your homework. To answer your question, it depends where you're standing, Chris. For the public and the NGOs, it's all about stopping the wars and the suffering. For the big mining houses it's about keeping out the competition.' Ben is getting impatient. Clearly he doesn't like teaching. Chris decides to cool it.

'Right now, diamonds are being laundered on a massive scale. I have a hunch that al-Qaeda are behind it, using the profits they make from buying and selling diamonds to stockpile arms, just as SWAPO did in the Seventies and UNITA in the Angolan Civil War. That should start you off. You'll pick up the rest as you go along. You seem to know a lot about the industry. I've been on this investigation for over a month and I've got nowhere, other than infiltrating several militant Islamic groups.

'I'm sorry, Chris, but you're about to be thrown into the deep end. I have to fly to New York as soon as I can. Something's come up. It's a family matter. My sister's married a moron. Sometimes I long for the days of the *Shadchan*.'

Chris raises one eyebrow questioningly.

'Traditional Yiddish marriage broker, usually old, widowed and female, but invariably she made good choices, better than most young women do, better than I did. My sister, Sharon, went for looks and forgot about brains. She married into a diamond cutting family and now they're in trouble.' He sighs and gets up restlessly. Soon he's pacing the office.

'I'd better explain about it, since it's relevant to this investigation. Sharon married Jonathan Bronstein, a diamond cutter whose family own Bronstein's, a well-known firm of New York diamond dealers, which has been in the family for three generations. Unbeknown to Sharon or the family, Jon has been buying blood roughs on the cheap from an unlicenced, backstreet Liberian trader. Jon used private funds of his own which he keeps in a Swiss bank. Despite the fact that this was a strictly private deal, the company's licence to deal in diamonds has been revoked, which spells ruin for the entire family, all of whom have shares in the company, including his father, who is the chairman. From now on, they can't buy from or sell to any reputable dealer.'

'What was he going to do with the diamonds?'

'Sell them, of course, and make a large profit which he'd keep to himself. There's always a buyer at a cut price. Jon was caught red-handed by Kimberley Process officials following a tip-off — he must have been boasting to his colleagues — and they are using him to make a point.'

'Can't he appeal against such an arbitrary decision?'

'I'll try to help him.'

'Really! So what can you do?'

'If I could trace the Liberian dealer who sold him the roughs I might be able to prove that they didn't originate in any war area. Jon doesn't know how to contact him.'

'He's a diamond launderer, I assume.'

'No. He merely sells blood roughs, which terrorists — or freedom fighters, depending upon your point of view — smuggle over the border to Liberia. Freeman makes no effort to launder them. That's why they're so cheap.

'Look, there's one thing you should know. Traditionally, all diamond deals are conducted with the utmost secrecy . . . usually for cash . . . and sold again for cash. Only a fool get's caught and that means Jon.'

Ben is getting impatient with her, but she still has a couple more questions.

'I see. Thanks. Tell me, Ben, how do these Kimberley Process guys know one diamond from another?'

'Practically speaking, they don't. There's a new process that enables chemists to analyse minute sediments of water deposits in the diamond's grooves which tells them from which area the rough originated. Of course that's unrealistic in terms of the masses of diamonds that reach the market each year. That's the whole point of the certificates, all diamonds entering or leaving a country must be transported in tamper-proof containers and the certificates of origin must be made out by the mine's management.' Ben hesitates, running his fingers through his hair. 'Jon's such an arsehole.'

He glances at his watch. 'You have an appointment at ten-thirty this morning with David Marais. He's the chairman of Trans-Africa

Diamonds Ltd, one of the top five diamond companies in London. They have mines all over Africa. He's also a friend of Rowan's and he's offered to get his staff to help you with your research.'

'Thanks. I'm astonished that the chairman would bother to waste his time on a PA.'

'No doubt he'll turn you over to his PR department. Good luck. See you after lunch.'

Suddenly the enormity of her undertaking catches Chris with a body blow. How on earth do I start? Where do I look? Chris can't help wondering if she's over-estimated her ability.

7

Chris arrives in London's celebrated diamond quarter with more than half an hour to spare. Looking around, she finds a small coffee bar that's clean and comfortable and the coffee smells great. Choosing a table by the window, Chris orders black filter coffee and a croissant, and settles back to consider her morning.

Talking to Rowan and Ben has knocked away her preconceptions, leaving her with a sense of unease. This is a new ball game. Winning is the code she lives by, but she has to believe in her client's right to win before taking on a case. She needs to be on the side of the angels, but in this business there are no angels, only ruthless greed. Who can say that a 'legitimate' diamond is one produced by members of the London-based diamond cartel? Or that a quality rough discovered by an impoverished African farmer on his own land is illegal, classified as a blood diamond, and therefore not his to sell? Aren't the rules a gigantic hoax to maintain artificially high prices? So who suffers? The brain-washed public who are ripped off? Or the maimed and displaced children of civil wars? Or jobless African peasants who have thrown off the yoke of colonialism only to find themselves up against a new kind of 'ism'?

For a moment she seriously considers quitting, but what about Sienna. Chris longs to uncover some small clue that will help the police to find Sienna and her kidnappers. She feels sure there's a connection and she believes she can guess what it is.

Indian polishers specialise in the smaller, cheaper diamonds, some so small you would need a magnifying glass to see them, which are used to brighten the surfaces of cheap jewellery. In the past forty years these polishers have created a worldwide market for cheap diamond jewellery and they are also the only buyers for these small, brownish roughs which have always been considered the waste product of the diamond industry. What better way to persuade Mohsen Sheik to buy lowgrade, 'blood' diamonds than by kidnapping his only daughter.

But how could someone like Sienna survive such an ordeal? For a second Chris is overcome with images: Sienna crying her eyes out over a dying bird . . . and later, smuggling milk to the dorm' to feed a baby squirrel knocked from its nest by a violent storm . . . and she succeeded in rearing it. Sienna's shocked face when her first love dumped her.

'For goodness' sake, pull yourself together,' Chris mutters as she wipes a stray tear from her cheek. She glances at her watch and pays her bill, before hurrying out into the moist London morning.

⋆ ⋆ ⋆

Trans-Africa Diamonds Ltd is situated at the edge of London's diamond quarter in an eight-storey staid and solid building that looks as if it has stood there for centuries. Chris approaches a desk in the old-fashioned entrance hall, where a uniformed security man directs her to the Chairman's suite of offices. David Marais' secretary, an elegant Chinese woman, shows her into his den and leaves her sitting opposite his desk.

Chris studies the photographs on the wall: rugby teams, cricket teams, rowing and skiing shots. There are several paintings of wildlife and some stunning photographs of wild birds and flowers. Half an hour passes, so she takes out her notebook and jots down the relevant details of her conversation with Ben. Feeling bored and impatient, she tries to imagine what a man with this much power and wealth would look like: red-veined from too much rich living, over-weight, balding and arrogant, with a booming voice and a costly diamond signet ring.

Her image shatters as the man himself hurries into the room. He grins apologetically as he grips her shoulders and kisses her on both cheeks.

'I'm so sorry I'm late. I hate keeping people waiting, but my flight was delayed. I've just returned from Namibia.' His voice is soft, but deep, and there is the faintest trace of a South African accent. As she watches him unpacking his briefcase, she's trying to work out the source of his sex appeal. He's not good looking, his face is blunt and square, but his eyes are crystal blue and a thatch of straight blond hair falls forward over his forehead. Add to that, he's tall and slender, with a smile so warm his entire face is brought into play. A total smile! But does that explain that mysterious power that leaves you weak in the knees. Early fifties, she guesses, feeling strangely drawn to him.

'So this is your first day at FI,' he rushes on, while stacking the files in his cabinet. 'You must be very bright to get in there. Good luck with your investigation.'

'Thanks.'

'OK!' He rubs his hands together. 'Now we can get down to business. Ben asked me to give you the low-down on the industry. Everyone in the industry would like to see you succeed. We need to know just how much of a problem this diamond laundering has become. Let's dispense with formalities, I'm Dave and you're Chris. Is that OK with you?'

He raises one eyebrow and she grins, feeling at home with him. Dave's glance lingers. 'You're a little younger than I was expecting. You packed a lot of studying into a few years.'

'I suppose I did.'

Dave opens a door behind his desk and beckons Chris to follow. The back passage leads to a small elevator and moments later they are descending slowly.

Dave grins at her. 'It's not as bad as it seems . . . there's only three basement levels, but the lift is slow so it seems much more. This building once housed a bank and we're descending to the former vaults. In the Second World War the War Office bought the building. Their essential personnel worked down here on the second basement level, and they housed their documents on the floor below.'

The lift door opens and they step into bright neon light reflecting on the whitewashed walls of a long passage. Dave presses the dimmer switch.

'Of course, I've redecorated and changed all the fittings . . . all Spanish . . . beautiful, aren't they?'

Taking her arm, Dave leads Chris along a well-lit underground passage while Chris dutifully admires the door handles and circular steel light fittings set into the ceiling. She watches as Dave places his index finger over a smooth black patch. He swears.

'You have to find the precise, hidden spot and then . . . bingo.' He winks lewdly and she can't help laughing. The door slides open and they walk into a long, low room filled with benches, with overhead spotlights shining on numbered glass containers. Each bowl is half full of large diamonds. She walks slowly forward, trying not to gasp. Billions of pounds of gems are glistening in the spotlights all around her.

'Use this,' he says, taking a small eye-glass. 'It's called a loupe. Place it in your eye socket like this . . . ' He demonstrates and drops it. 'Damn!' Passing her the loupe, he pushes a velvet card towards her.

Chris stares at the diamond's curious golden sheen. Pushing the loupe into her eye, she peers into the depths. All at once she's lost amongst brilliant shafts of yellow light, like sunbursts of golden prisms. Each slight tremble brings a moving mosaic of uninterrupted brilliance.

She gasps. 'Incredible!'

She puts down the loupe and steps away, unable to clear her mind of the vision of golden light. Dave is watching her curiously and Chris wonders why she feels this strange sense of intimacy. Perhaps he reminds her of the father she never had.

'I feel I must warn you, Chris, as a friend — I hope we shall be friends, so please don't take this the wrong way — millions of pounds are being pocketed by the diamond launderers. They're flooding the market with blood diamonds bought cheaply in Africa and sold at current inflated prices maintained by our costly advertising. Their profits are massive. If anyone gets in their way, they would kill, believe me. It sounds melodramatic, but it's true. So while I'm here, whenever you need me, just call. At the same time, I wish you would ask Rowan to transfer you to something less dangerous.'

'I'm not quitting,' she murmurs.

'I'm getting to like you, Chris, but it's important that you and Ben uncover this laundering network fast. As I said, let me have regular updates on your progress. I may be able to help you.'

'But Dave, our briefs are confidential. Both Rowan and Ben impressed that on me.'

He laughs softly. 'But in a way, I'm your client, Chris. I'm acting for the government of a certain Central African Republic. Let's get down to work and maybe you'll have time to have lunch with me. Look here.'

She touches the smooth rosy sheen of a pile of strangely shaped roughs. They lie in a bowl like red pebbles from a distant planet's shores.

'South American,' Dave says, running his hand through them. 'Real beauties. Every one of them is worth a million, if indeed there were buyers with all these millions. As it is they remain in our stockpile, worthless and not even earning interest until they can be sold. Maybe one of them might go for a million next year.'

'What if you let the gems find their own price levels? Supply and demand is a reliable system.'

'And what if someone pays a small fortune for a diamond ring and the price tumbles soon afterwards? Diamonds must have a guaranteed value.'

A feeble argument, Chris decides, but she keeps quiet.

'Come over here.' Dave pauses in the centre of the room and Chris follows him.

'Namibian, a hundred and twenty carats.' He points to a pure white rough on a velvet dais. Chris ogles at it.

'In the Seventies, this famous diamond, which was on display at a Namibian mine, was stolen by an Ovambo mineworker. Unbeknown to management, he was a member of a West African liberation movement. There was a hue and cry, but it was never found. No one could work out how it had been smuggled out of the mine. Perhaps you know that the miners strip naked and pass through scanning machines at the end of each shift . . . just in case they've swallowed a few gems. Years later, the Ovambo told his story. The diamond was hidden inside a golf ball and sent flying over the tall, boundary fence during a game. Eventually it fell into our hands and we named it *Golfer's Dream*.'

'So you do buy stolen gemstones.'

'Good God, Chris. I feel like a mole locked in with a terrier. That purchase was made long before blood diamonds became a dirty word.'

He takes her arm and walks her to the end of the room, but when they reach the glass shelves he doesn't release her. 'Each stone along this bench has a curious story. This diamond ring was once part of the Russian Royal family's collection. It was given to Anastasia by a relative, perhaps because of a curious flaw that forms an 'A'. Eventually it became known as the *Anastasia*.' He releases her arm and hands Chris a loupe.

'Looks like an upside down V to me. I can't see the crossline.'

'Keep looking. It's has a very old-fashioned cut which does nothing to reveal the true beauty of the stone. We intend to re-cut it soon. Then perhaps we'll destroy the curse.'

'A curse? You're joking.'

'Probably. Do you want to hear the rest of the story?'

'I'll buy it.'

'Once upon a time the ring was bartered to a Cossack officer by an escaping nobleman, to purchase a safe passage to Odessa. This was at the time of the Russian revolution. The nobleman was murdered by the Cossack who travelled to Iran. He found work laying oil pipes across the desert until he died of dysentery. The diamond changed hands a number of times, but

57

each time the owner was killed, or died soon afterwards. Finally the widow of a quinine planter escaped the Congo during the revolution, hiding the diamond in her body. She was raped several times and the diamond was pushed up into the neck of her womb. When she reached Brussels it was removed by surgeons. Convinced of the curse, she sold the gem to our agent, but she died of septicaemia a week later.'

'No more.' Chris holds up her hand. 'I'm not superstitious, but I'm not fond of gruesome stories.'

He laughs. 'All right. Here's a success story for you. This small stone, like millions of others, was formed billions of years ago in an exploding star. Later, as part of a meteor, it roamed through time and space for billions of years until it was caught up in the Earth's magnetic pull. It plummeted into our planet, perhaps a half a billion years ago, and deep in the earth it grew by adding layer after layer, each layer a clone of the original minute speck. There it remained until forced to the surface by a volcanic eruption, which dumped it deep in the Namibian desert where it lay for millions of years, until the Orange River flooded one year and carried it down to the sea, leaving it just off the coast of Alexander Bay. It would have remained there forever if it weren't for today's enterprising geologists who found a way to dredge up the diamonds hidden under the sea.'

Geologists like her father! But this was her secret and Dave would never know about Dad.

'Let's get back to my office,' Dave says when they have exhausted the complicated subject of polishing and marketing diamonds. 'How about lunch?'

'I'd better get back. After all it's my first day,' she says. 'I'll leave lunch for another time, if you don't mind.'

'But I do mind. You can't work without food. My secretary checked with Ben and it's OK. He's too busy to see you right now, so you're stuck with me.' Dave studies her curiously.

Chris has run out of excuses. She walks arm in arm, like old friends, to a small, discreet fish restaurant not far from Dave's offices where he entertains her with stories of the African bush while they eat grilled prawns and drink ice-cold Portuguese green wine.

Eventually she steers Dave back to the diamond industry and listens intently while he reels off facts and statistics.

'Would you mind telling me what this is all about?' she asks when they're drinking coffee. 'You seem to know an awful lot about me.'

'I saw you on TV. I thought you were very brave. When I heard that you were joining FI I asked Rowan about you. I was intending to hand you over to my PRO this morning, but when I saw you again I changed my mind. Beautiful young women don't often walk into my office nowadays.'

She laughs and leaves it at that.

When they reach his headquarters, Dave turns

suddenly serious. 'Be careful, Chris. Don't talk about your work. If you need to ask questions, say you're writing a book about diamonds. Better still, come and ask me. There's little I don't know about the industry.'

Suddenly she feels his hand pressed over hers. She looks up, startled by the gesture and by the strangely intent look in his eyes. I feel good about this, she thinks. I must be crazy.

Chris refuses the offer of a lift home and mumbles her thanks for lunch. She needs a walk to sort out her many impressions. Just what is Dave after? She is well aware of his overbearing maleness and his sex appeal, despite his age. Yet he deliberately set out to give the impression that he is taken by her. She doesn't believe him. Why should she? Men haven't exactly been beating a path to her door prior to taking this job. Dave could have anyone he wants. And why is Ben confiding in him. She will have it out with him, she decides. Nevertheless, she can't completely squash a strange feeling of joy as she walks back to the office.

8

It is seven-thirty a.m. on Friday morning and raining when Chris reaches her office. She switches on the light and feels a surge of joy flooding through her as she glances around. She's been here for only four days, but she's loving every minute of it. Her desk is piled high with Ben's research files and she has pages of notes waiting to be typed. She intends to keep her office ultra functional, no pictures, no art, not even a calendar to spoil the plain white expanse of her walls, but already there's a massive bouquet of flowers in a cut-glass vase from David perched on the filing cabinet.

Ben was amused when the flowers arrived. 'Just shows . . . you never really get to know a guy through work. I thought Trans-Africa was Dave's only interest.'

Today is Ben's last day. He leaves for the States in the morning. She will miss him, but hopefully he won't be away for more than a fortnight. This past week they've worked together for twelve hours a day and already it seems as if they've known each other for years. What a curious, complex man Ben is. To some extent they have learned to size up each other's strengths and weaknesses, as they drive each other to the limit. But it hasn't been all work and no play. Some evenings they have put the work aside and gone for walks in the park and twice they went to dinner and then there are the sad times when he tells her how much he misses his family.

Someone is unlocking the main door. It's Ben and he looks exhausted.

'You haven't slept much,' she accuses him.

'True, but I can sleep on the plane. You can take things easy today. I have a few meetings, but if you don't mind working late again tonight we could finish off the statistics.'

Chris assumes that her acceptance is taken for granted. Not that she has any objection to spending the evening with this sensitive, soon to be eligible, sexy man.

★   ★   ★

By seven p.m. Ben is still briefing her. The sun is lingering on the horizon and long shadows are reaching out across the park. A chill is hanging around and Chris shivers in her summer dress and wonders if she can break Ben's flow to fetch her cardigan. They have been in his office for the past two hours. Clearly Ben has set his heart on a functional office with no personal artefacts or distractions to scatter his concentration, but the desk is littered with bulging files and so is the floor behind his chair. Reference books lie where they have fallen, while notes impaled on spikes gather dust. Ben is overworked and it shows. Chris turns from the window and switches her mind back to their work.

'It's easy to find buyers for blood diamonds, but the prices are low,' he tells her. 'There's a network of agents buying illicit roughs in all the main diamond producing centres. Some of them are Russian, bartering second-hand arms for diamonds. When the Congo was banned from trading, other routes were found. No one knows quite how . . . yet it's working. My guess is al-Qaeda.'

'But Ben, do you have any real proof that al-Qaeda is involved?' Chris wonders if she should be so forthright, but it's too late now.

'Not yet, but you may be luckier. I have a lead for you to follow up. I stumbled on it by accident. You'd better take a couple of notes.'

Chris grabs her notebook.

'When I was studying economics at London University, I joined a local cricket club and discovered that a member of the team was also in my economics classes, a Prince Husam Ibn al-Faisal, to give you his full title. An unlikely friendship evolved, mainly because we found ourselves thrown together time and time again . . . at training sessions, parties, lectures, tutorials and so on. Eventually I got to know him pretty well, although our opposing cultures, class and incomes prevented any deep confidences.

'Prince Husam went on to get his Masters because he was expected to play an important role in the Arab Bank, or so he told me. Yet I bumped into him two months ago at a conference on sisal production in East Africa. I was damned curious to see the prince there, so I checked with the conference organisers and learned that Husam works at an old established South African building society, called the African

Provident Trust, which is, or was, firmly entrenched in white South African culture. I decided to check further and I learned that after the white regime went out, massive influxes of cash from an Arabic investment bank gained control of the building society. That was when they moved the head office to London.'

Ben frowns and pauses. 'It's just a hunch, but I couldn't let go. Since then there have been continuous injections of cash into the company's accounts from the Middle East. Lately, the Provident Trust has been providing funds for various cultural groups to study in the Middle East and it's been spreading its tentacles all over Africa. Sisal in Tanzania is just one of the many projects our prince is taking a keen interest in.'

'But I thought that the Saudis are firmly opposed to Islamic fundamentalism.'

'So did I, but who knows what Husam's views are and he's running the show. He hates to use his title, by the way. While I'm in the States, I thought you should hack in to their computer system and find out about their money flows. Janice in IT will help you. Perhaps aid to Africa could be stretched to include purchasing diamonds. You may find the missing link we badly need.' It's eight p.m. and Ben looks tired. He stands up and yawns and then apologises sweetly. Chris, on the other hand, is in no hurry to get home. She's loving every minute of the briefing. Now, at last, she has something to sink her teeth into. She can't wait to get started. She certainly needs no help from Janice, and why should she restrict her efforts to hacking. She's longing to show Ben just how determined she can be.

'We haven't really finished, but I have to leave early tomorrow morning. Come on. Let's get out of here. We'll have dinner, but it'll have to be brief. I still have to pack.' He shoots a nervous glance her way. 'Fancy cooking while I pack? My place is nearby and the fridge is full of TV meals for one. I have some excellent whisky.'

'Why not! I'll fetch my coat.' Seeing Ben's apartment will give her a chance to get to know him better, Chris imagines.

* * *

She couldn't have been more wrong, she realises ten minutes later, when they have risked the archaic lift to reach the eighth floor of a Mayfair apartment block. Ben's home, with its scarlet, over-stuffed couches, Persian carpet and reproductions of hunting scenes on the walls, seems ridiculously wrong until she learns that it came furnished and he has only been there for two weeks. Ben has left home at his wife's request, he explains, and he's expecting that she will miss him enough to ask him to return, but so far this hasn't happened.

'It's straight moral blackmail, Chris. My wife wants me out of FI. There's too much travelling. Make yourself at home.' He hands her a glass of neat scotch. 'Ice in the fridge if you like it on the rocks. Back in a second.'

Looking around, she sees touches that are pure Ben: a clarinet lying on the table with piles of sheet music; a large case of CDs, jazz and classical; another bottle of pure malt on the mantelpiece; some of his books: poetry, economics, medieval history and aerobic exercises, plus snaps of his family on a recent skiing holiday. There's a photograph of Ben taken at the launch of his book on corporate fraud and another of Ben and his wife at a nightclub. Annette is beautiful, in her late thirties and she looks feminine, but capable, not the sort of woman to let her marriage go to pieces.

Ben returns from the bedroom. He's changed into corduroy trousers and a T-shirt. 'It's too bad I have to leave when you've only just begun,' he grumbles. 'I have a bad feeling about the trip.'

'What sort of a bad feeling? How bad?' Chris asks, feeling troubled.

'The worst. But it's only feelings. They don't mean anything. What I meant to say is that I spent this morning dictating details of my research to date. The tapes are in the filing cabinet. I haven't got far with this investigation, mainly because I only began recently.'

The phone rings and Ben runs his hands through his hair in a nervous gesture she is getting to recognise. He drains his glass. He seems to know who's calling.

'Hi darling.'

Chris goes into the kitchen, but she can still hear Ben's voice.

'Yes, I must. But it's not bloody business. It's family. Come with the kids, if you like.' There is a long silence. 'I don't see anything particularly irresponsible in my statement. We've had

66

holidays together before now . . . Well, I agree, it's hardly a holiday, but the kids would love to see New York and you could do some shopping. Just a suggestion.' Another long pause. 'I don't like them much either, but Sharon's married into the family and she deserves our support. What's that? God how I hate that phrase: 'not my problem'. OK, goodbye. I'll call the kids from the airport.'

Chris busies herself around the kitchen. She finds chicken curry and rice for two and plenty of lettuce and tomatoes. She hunts around for something else and finds onions and chives in a cool box. She makes a salad while the food is warming, serves in the kitchen and puts the plates on a tray. Ben is standing at the window, his back turned. When he swings around, she sees his sadness and she longs to comfort him.

'There's a chance I can hang on to my family by leaving the company, but I'm so resentful. It's straight blackmail and it's hurting. I'm not sure if our marriage can survive this. I feel trapped. I love my work, but I don't want to lose my kids.'

Chris decides to change the subject. 'The food's ready. Where do we eat?'

'There's a small dining-room through that door.' He smiles. 'You're very efficient.'

'It's not difficult to warm a TV meal, Ben. No more silly flattery please.'

She places the tray on the table and feels Ben's hand on her shoulder. When she turns, his expression hurts, so she puts her arms around his waist and hugs him, but she's unprepared for the delicious smell of him, or his taut, muscled

67

back, or the way he clutches her. He holds her very close and a sigh shakes his body.

'It will come right Ben. No woman in her right mind would let you slip through her fingers.' She steps back and sits down. 'The food's getting cold.'

'Thanks Chris. I was in dire need of a hug.'

'So was I. Come on, let's eat.'

'To music? Do you like jazz?'

'Naturally.'

'Clarinet?'

'The best.'

Ben plays a Benny Goodman CD and puts his sadness behind him. Over supper, he tells her of some of his investigations that have gone badly, but hilariously, wrong, like the time when the night watchman's dog trapped him against the wall of the IT room of a pharmaceutical company until the morning shift arrived. 'My first and last attempt at breaking and entering.'

Chris steers the conversation back to their investigation. 'I assume you think that Sienna was kidnapped by al-Qaeda agents?' This is a possibility that Chris can't accept. It's too horrible to accept.

'I guess it's probably connected with the diamond industry, given her father's wealth and power.'

'I was at school with Sienna for four years. We were close friends.'

'Why didn't you mention that?'

She shrugs. 'Perhaps because I've always been a little ashamed of my costly schooling. Sienna and I were thrown together. We became good friends, but after school our different cultures interfered with any real socialising. Sienna went on to Oxford and we hardly kept in touch. She had three years to find a good Muslim husband there. She knew that if she didn't she'd face an arranged marriage. We used to talk about it sometimes. I don't normally stand around watching wedding cavalcades, but I wanted to wave to her and see her wedding dress. Once we were like sisters and I've always missed her. The thought that now she's . . . ' Chris breaks off.

'What a loyal girl you are, throwing yourself at armed kidnappers to save an old school friend.' His hand reaches for hers. 'I'm so glad I have you for a PA, Chris. It's been a wonderful week. Why don't we open a bottle of champagne? In fact . . . ' He leans forward and kisses her cheek, and Chris reminds herself that Ben has been drinking scotch steadily since they arrived. 'I've such a yen for you, Chris. I've longed for you ever since I first saw you. You looked so forlorn and so brave, but so lovely, too. I'll never forget the way you slipped off to check up on me . . . '

Chris pulls her hand away and shakes her head. 'I'm here to work, Ben,' she counters uneasily. 'You're an attractive, sensitive, passionate man and you're not safe to be left on your own. Someone will snap you up so smartly. If your wife has any sense she'll lure you back any day now. But I'm lonely and far too vulnerable to get involved with a man who loves his wife. I think you sense how I feel about you. I wouldn't be able to cope.'

He laughs approvingly. 'That's the neatest

put-down I've ever heard.'

'It isn't a put-down . . . it's the truth. I think that's my cue to leave. Please be careful, Ben. If Jon's Liberian dealer is al-Qaeda you could find yourself in real danger.'

For answer he pulls her towards him and kisses her on her lips.

'Good luck in the States, Ben. I'll be waiting impatiently to hear from you. Meantime, I'll be hacking away.'

'I'll come down and wait until a taxi comes.'

'Don't be silly. I'm going by tube. *Ciao!*'

Ben peers anxiously through the wrought iron gate as the archaic lift descends with clunks and clatters. 'Take care, Chris,' echoes down the lift shaft.

Chris sets off at a brisk pace, hoping that the walk to Green Park tube station will disperse a cloying sense of unease for Ben.

★   ★   ★

The moment she steps from the Finchley tube station Chris feels vulnerable. Someone is watching her. She pauses and looks around. It's misty and drizzling slightly. The streets are badly lit and visibility is poor. Damn. But she knows there's someone out there watching her intently. She should carry some type of protection . . . even a whistle would be better than nothing. Ignoring her intuition she sets off on the ten minute walk to her home.

It's just a feeling, that's all. I've been watching too many spooky movies. I've walked home a

70

hundred times and never been nervous. There's no one here but me.

Abruptly she turns left, away from her home and hurries back towards the main road. So what if it takes her five minutes longer. She's almost running by the time she reaches a narrow alleyway, stretching between two tall blocks. She makes it in a dash. Now she's on the high street where wet pavements reflect a lurid glow from shop windows and neon signs. But where is everyone? Even the restaurants are closed. She slows down and finally pauses, pretending to gaze into a shop window.

Listening intently, she hears a dog barking in the distance, a cat scuffles in refuse bags, far off an owl cries. She feels chilled and depressed. A car passes with a whoosh of tyres on wet tarmac. Nearer the sounds are unmistakable: a crunch of a stone dislodged and then a short skid from a misplaced step. Someone is creeping on rubber-soled shoes on the wet pavement, not more than thirty metres behind her. Then there's silence. She's being followed and it's for real. All the murders she's read about over the past few months crowd into her mind. Does she have anything at all to defend herself? Only a small pair of nail scissors.

Chris peers sidelong into the gloom. The night is full of deep shadows but none that seem to have any living form. Then something moves. A tall figure walks slowly into a pool of light from the street lamp. He knows she's seen him and he doesn't care. He's moving towards her, but suddenly she feels a surge of courage. She's

71

identified the enemy. She knows who she's dealing with. He's just one man and she's a trained kick boxer. She's not helpless. Far from it. She might even send him packing. And then? How would she know who he was? Ahead of her she catches sight of Timmins, the jeweller's, where a night-vision security camera is above the window.

Hurrying forward, she gazes into the shop window, lingering long enough for the camera to get a good shot. The stalker is getting much closer now, bolder, more menacing. He's deliberately intimidating her. She moves on, but not too far, and pauses at the dress shop. He pauses, too, standing tall and undecided in front of the jeweller's window.

Two blocks away, on the other side of the street, there's a seedy, old hotel, which caters mainly for immigrants. Could she make it? She waits long enough for him to be caught on camera before making a sudden dash across the road just ahead of a passing car. The driver hoots, swerves and shouts through the window at her. Footsteps are gaining on her as she reaches the entrance. Thank God the front door is unlocked. Her hasty entrance wakes the security guard who had been dozing at his desk, the lights are on and suddenly she's safe. She struggles to catch her breath.

'Someone's stalking me,' she says eventually in a remarkably calm voice.

The guard gets up and stares into the street. 'No sign of him, Miss. Shall I call the police?'

'No.' She remembers Ben's instruction not to

involve the police unless absolutely necessary. 'I'll call a taxi.'

'You'd best wait in here until the cab arrives.'

Half an hour later she pays the cab and unlocks her front door. The house is in darkness. Mum and Bertram are asleep.

She's soon in bed, but sleep evades her. Who was he? Why was he stalking her? He looked so threatening in his long grey coat, with his face half-hidden by a scarf. Was Ben right in blaming al-Qaeda for the kidnapping? Could she be in any danger? More likely her stalker was merely an unhinged man on the loose. After all, how could he possibly know she would be emerging from the tube station at exactly that time. Perhaps he'd been waiting for any woman to walk the streets alone. Slowly she reassures herself and after a while she even believes her comforting ideas, until she falls into a restless sleep.

9

The IT department of FI is amazingly well-equipped for hacking. Chris has left some highly specialised software running overnight in the hope of discovering Prince Husam's computer password. Arriving at seven a.m., she hurries to the IT room to find that the programme has been completed and there is the password on the screen: 24-05-53. Strange password ... someone's birthday perhaps. Triumph surges bringing goose-pimples to her arms. 'Ha! Gotcha,' she says aloud.

Hyped up and trembling, she enters the Provident Trust's financial records. There it is ... everything she needs, a mass of transactions from every African branch. Sighing with relief, her fingers race over the keyboard. Hardly noticing her discomfort, she sits hunched over the screen. Occasionally she pauses, stretches, makes a few notes, calls for coffee and a biscuit and returns to the screen.

'Just how late are you staying?' Janine calls out some time later.

Chris looks up in surprise. It seems that the day has hardly begun, yet Janine is going home.

'Don't mind me. I'll lock up,' Chris tells her.

★　★　★

Three days have passed since Ben left and Chris has spent hours each day examining the prince's financial records. She's also seen the local branch of an American NGO and listened to their plans to launch a worldwide diamond boycott soon, if the industry can't keep blood diamonds from the market.

Chris has masses of information on Arab investment in Africa, but nothing that indicates large cash payments for illicit diamonds. The hours pass too quickly. Sometimes Chris goes out for a coffee and a snack around six p.m., otherwise she works through, leaving around one a.m.

It is eight p.m. and Chris is alone in the IT room. She stands up, stretches and performs a few karate *katas* until she feels more relaxed. She is about to get back to work when the telephone rings. It's Ben calling from New York and the sound of his voice makes her feel warm and happy.

'They treating you well over there, Chris?'

'Everyone's great. How are you doing?'

'Rather well. I've managed to locate Jon's dealer. His name is Moses Freeman. I have some data for the file. Better switch on the recorder.'

'OK. Ready.'

Chris listens as Ben gives the addresses of Freeman's two sisters, in New York and Johannesburg. 'Moses Freeman is Liberian-born,' Ben continues, reading from his notes. 'He's descended from a freed slave, Benjamin Freeman, who was repatriated to Africa from the United States in the 1820s. Moses converted to

Islam three years ago, and he often wears a fez and robes, but he has retained his family name, which is strange. I have the feeling that his religion is merely a status symbol. His American sister, Lydia Jasmen, is a devout member of a local Christian-African sect . . . she wears a crucifix and a long blue robe, but they seem to get on well together. She owns a house in the Bronx and Freeman stays with her when he's in town on one of his frequent selling trips.'

'How did you get all this so quickly, Ben?'

'Ah. I've been devious . . . '

Chris can hear the satisfaction in his voice.

'When Freeman is about to arrive in New York, he places a cryptic message containing the word 'diamonds', plus a post office box number in the classified advertisements. Dealers interested in buying from him have the opportunity to write to his box. Then Freeman can check them out before contacting them to make an appointment. I had to rope in a friend of Jon's to provide me with a jeweller's background and a letterhead.'

Chris listens in silence, feeling anxious. Ben was never designed for cloak and dagger work. He's too candid and trustful. 'Please be careful, Ben.'

'Sure. I met Freeman in the New York Palace Hotel. He twigged that I wasn't a dealer in no time and gave me the slip. Fortunately I'd arranged to have him followed. He unwittingly led us to his sister's home. I tried to barge in on Freeman, but he was out. His sister made an appointment for me to see him tomorrow morning. Hope he shows up. If not I may have to fly to Liberia and dig him out of his burrow. I got his Liberian address from Immigration.' Ben read it out for the files. 'Apart from Jon's problem, Freeman can help us a great deal. I'd say he knows exactly what's going on.'

'So how're you progressing with the hacking, Chris?'

'I have all their financial transactions for the past six months. I've been analysing them every possible way, but I haven't found anything suspicious. As you said, there are millions of dollars *en route* to Africa. They have masses of cash at their disposal. Most of it goes to charitable groups, schools, hospitals, medical research and so on. I haven't found any major cash withdrawals and I guess they'd have to pay for diamonds in cash. I can see no trace of purchases of arms either.'

'OK. Keep trying. It was only a flyer.'

Chris can hear the disappointment in Ben's voice as she says goodbye. How can she fail Ben? At the same time, if the group has been set up merely to hand out freebies to Africans, what else could she hope to find? Suppose they really are buying illicit diamonds, laundering them, and selling them at ultra high prices, what sort of evidence could she find? Massive cash withdrawals obviously, yet there's nothing shown in their accounts. What she needs is a closer look from the inside. There's nothing more she can do tonight, so she locks Ben's recorded tapes in her office safe and goes home.

Early the next morning, Chris calls the personnel officer at the Provident Trust to ask if the company has any vacancies. All their hiring is handled by an agency, she's told. Next, she calls the agency, but there are no vacancies. She seems to have reached a dead end.

'If you give up now, you might as well quit the job,' Chris tells herself sternly.

'Use your head, Chris. You'll find a way.'

She hurries into Jean's office. 'What would Ben do if he needed to check on someone's routine?' she asks.

'Get a detective maybe. The company normally uses Jeff Jennings at the Browning Agency. Shall I get him on the line?'

'Thanks, Jean.'

'I'm Ben Searle's PA,' Chris explains to the detective. 'I need information concerning the movements of someone and I'm in a hurry. Can you see what you can do in twenty-four hours?'

'I'll certainly have something. Let's have the details.'

After spelling out her requirements, Chris hesitates for a moment.

'There's something else. Someone's been stalking me. I'm not sure, but I think I managed to get him to pause in front of a jeweller's in Finchley long enough for their security camera to get a good shot of him. It was around midnight. I stood there seconds before, so it might follow after a shot of me. Timmins, the jeweller, knows me. He's a friend of my mother's. I need to take a look at this stalker. Is there some way you could perhaps identify him?'

'I'll give it a go. Will tomorrow do?'

'That's fine. Thanks.'

Chris spends the rest of the day rechecking the building society's financial transactions to find out if she has missed anything. Her very last job is to cable FI's Bombay office, asking them to get hold of a review of Mohsen Sheik's company's past weeks' cash transactions. 'We're looking for large and regular cash payments, probably amounting to a million dollars a month . . . or more. Or any sign of a large cash withdrawal.' Surely they would know that his holding company is called Jewelrex, but then she adds the name to be on the safe side.

She works late into the night and goes to bed with a sore neck and burning eyes.

★   ★   ★

The following morning, Jennings calls back before nine a.m. 'OK, Chris, here's his routine. Got a pen handy?'

'Sure. Go ahead.'

'Yesterday, Prince Husam Ibn al-Faisal, manager of the Provident Trust Building Society, drank a sundowner at the Cedar, a club close to his office. The barman said he goes there most evenings and that sometimes he goes on to Shumi's. Yesterday he left the Cedar at seven p.m. to dine at Tramps, another habitual watering hole. At half past nine he called Elle, an exclusive dating escort agency . . . one of the

79

better ones . . . to send him an escort. He's a regular client, but he only asks for good dancers. He took the girl dancing at China White, after which he sent her home in a company taxi and walked six blocks home to his apartment in St James.'

'Is he gay?'

'Just choosy, I think. I chatted up the girl at the escort agency. He had a French girlfriend for a few months, but they split in April . . . there's been no one since then, as far as anyone knows. I took a few discreet pictures which I'm sending over by messenger, together with my report. If I had more time I could get you more information.'

'Thanks. This is all I need right now.'

* * *

After lunch, Chris searches New Bond Street's shops for a dress to wear . . . not just any dress, but something clinging and low-cut, yet demure. Not an easy project, but she finds exactly what she's looking for. Marcasite clips for her hair and glittering black sandals seem absolutely right. Leaving at four p.m., she goes home, bathes, changes and douses herself with costly perfume.

As she creeps downstairs, Chris can hear her mother and Bertram talking in the living room. She reaches for her black coat hanging on the hall stand, hoping she won't be seen, but her shadow falls across the doorway.

Mum is appalled. 'You look like a tart.' She seems deeply hurt.

'That's good. I have to pick up an Arabian prince,' Chris teases.

'Well, don't come crying to me when you get into trouble. Is this the best you can do after all those years of studying . . . a pseudo spy!'

'Mum, this dress is very expensive. It was featured in a top fashion magazine.'

'It looks like a black satin petticoat . . . the sort I used to wear in the Seventies.'

'There's a certain resemblance,' Chris murmurs, gazing in the mirror. 'But it sets off my pale skin and my hair. Don't you think so?'

'I don't recognise you, Chris. You've changed.'

'Change is the only fact of life that's truly inevitable.'

Mother sighs. 'You're a fool. I never thought I'd live to see the day . . . ' Mum is about to burst into tears, so Chris grabs her coat and leaves.

★　★　★

The Cedar's 'mod-Mayfair' decor, as Chris has nicknamed it, is designed to attract rich clients, preferably foreign, and make them feel at home. From every nook, wall panel, floor and ceiling, exotic richness hits the eye with a wallop. Chris shudders as she hurries towards the bar, pausing to open her bag and gaze intently at Jennings' pictures of Prince Husam. And there he is in person, leaning back in a tapestry armchair reading a newspaper with what looks like a glass of neat scotch on the table. Surely that's taboo for him. He is alone, which is fortunate. A surge

81

of adrenaline runs though Chris at the enormity of what she is trying to do.

She chooses an empty table near the prince, but not too near, and orders a glass of Bacharach wine. The prince, absorbed in the news, doesn't seem to notice her. From time to time she glances at her watch and looks over her shoulder towards the entrance, as if anxiously waiting for her date.

Half an hour later, when nothing has happened, she risks another sidelong glance towards him. She takes out the photographs and studies them from behind a menu. Undeniably there are flaws: his eyes are set at different angles. From one side of his face a caring, romantic man stares back, but the other half shows a fierce, nomadic Bedouin. The pictures don't do him justice, Chris decides. He's young and athletic, well over six-foot, with the type of looks that label him Arabic, like his smouldering dark eyes, an imperious nose in an otherwise perfect profile, sensuous lips and long tapered hands. His hair is thick, black and wiry, and cut very short.

She looks up, feeling startled, as a strange man leans over her, puffing alcoholic fumes and the stench of cigarettes into her face.

'You must be waiting for me?' He leers confidently at her, slightly drunk and thoroughly offensive.

'I'm waiting for a friend. Please go away.'

'You don't mean that, darling. You're waiting for the right guy. Well, I'm the right guy.' He takes out a wad of notes, flips through them and shoves them back in his pocket.

So Mum was right. She looks like a tart. She'll never wear this dress again. Leaping up, Chris grabs her coat and bag, but as she turns she almost collides with the prince who has miraculously and swiftly come to her aid.

'Fuck off while you still can,' he says menacingly to the drunk.

The drunk takes a few steps back, looking undecided. Moments later the club's bouncer is escorting him to the exit. They look like buddies as they walk arm in arm through the tables. No one seems to notice the intruder's arm twisted behind his back. It's over in less than a minute.

'That's a very efficient bouncer. Thank you so much. My friend is late. I think I'd better go.'

'You look very pale. You're trembling. Come and sit down with me until you feel calmer, then I'll see you to a taxi, just in case that idiot is lurking outside.'

'Thanks. I think I made a mistake coming here alone.'

'You're right there,' he scolds her.

Wrong century, Husam, but quaint. She almost explains that this is England, not the Middle East, but that would give the game away, since his English is perfect. Instead she says: 'Surely I'm not trembling . . . not for something so trivial.' But she is and she knows why. She was so close to failing. She blesses the drunk, whoever he is.

'The truth is, I was supposed to meet a man from one of the headhunters. He's been trying to interest me in a vacancy at a rival company. We were supposed to discuss my requirements over a drink.'

'He may still come.' Husam looks pleased as he pulls out a chair. He introduces himself and gives her his card.

'I thought you were English,' she lies. 'You sound English.'

'Most of my schooling was in Scotland.'

That explains his slight brogue.

'I have a lot of business friends here,' he tells her. 'Many of them are having difficulties finding the right staff. I might be able to pass on some contacts. That is, if you don't think me impertinent.'

Impertinent! Heavens, no. He's following her imagined script verbatim.

As she gives him a brief CV, his eyes glow with admiration. She's hitting on his hobbyhorse, she learns, which is women's emancipation. He has personally lobbied for his two sisters and his aunt to study law in the States. He would like to drag everyone into the twenty-first century, but meantime his mission and his dream is Africa.

He tells her about his African journeys. From the passion in his voice she realises that this is far more than a business interest. How could diamond smuggling fit with this degree of commitment?

She can't help liking him, but she isn't here to like him, she reminds herself as he glances moodily at her low *décolleté* and looks away flushing.

'Why don't we have dinner, or even dinner and dancing? I have a feeling that you're a good dancer. I know a very exclusive place.'

'I don't think I should do that,' she says demurely. 'But thank you for helping me.' She stands up. 'I must be getting home.'

'Someone's waiting for you at home?'

'Yes. My mother.'

'Wait! I must see you into a taxi.' He helps her with her coat, beckons the waiter and scribbles a note on the menu, which he hands to her with a slight bow. Chris recognises the number . . . it's the headhunter she called that morning.

The taxi is waiting by the time they reach the pavement.

'If you're interested in finding a very rewarding position please contact them after ten-thirty a.m. I know of one that would suit you well. I'll pass the information to them.'

His eyes appraise her, passing from her hair to her cheeks to her lips, and then comes a gentle touch of ownership as he pulls her scarf up around her ears.

'There's a sharp wind tonight,' he says as he helps her into the taxi.

The job is in the bag, she decides as she waves goodbye. But how could she possibly outwit such a discerning and intelligent man as Prince Husam. And if he really does have connections with al-Qaeda . . . what then?

★ ★ ★

The cab driver seems to have found a roundabout way of getting her home. Perhaps he's working up the fare. She is about to complain when his voice booms through a loudspeaker behind her.

'We're being followed, Miss. Did you arrange for someone to follow you?'

'No. Are you sure?'

'Mind if I make another quick detour, just to be on the safe side?'

'I'd be grateful.' She half turns, but his voice stops her.

'Don't look back. At least, not unless you want them to know they've been spotted. It's a white Ford Fiesta, but I can't see the number plate. Know anyone with a car like that?'

'No.' She feels a strange, sinking feeling in her stomach as she struggles to quell her anxiety.

The taxi races through a series of sharp turns in backstreets she's unfamiliar with and then moves to the main road. She glances over her shoulder as the Fiesta skids badly.

'I think I've lost them,' he says five minutes later. 'But there's no mistake they were tailing us. Got a jealous husband or a boyfriend, have you?'

'No. Nothing like that.'

'Perhaps someone's stalking you, Miss. It's a funny old world we live in nowadays. Things have changed for the worse since I was young.'

'I'm sure I would have noticed.' But would she? She hasn't bothered to look. 'Thanks for losing them.'

She's home at last. She gets out, pays, and hurries up the driveway, her key in her hand. Once inside she closes the door and leans against it. But why is she panting? 'You wanted excitement,' she speaks sternly to her distorted reflection in the hall mirror. 'So . . . enjoy!'

10

It is her first day at the Provident Trust. She's working as a 'temp' until she joins the permanent staff in a month's time. That's the rule here, she's been told. Chris feels as taut as a winch, but there's no need to worry, she reminds herself. Prince Husam can't possibly suspect her motive for being here. He's sitting at his desk smiling smugly, feeling he's scored.

'Have you worked as a PA before, Chris?' he asks, after ten minutes of passionate rhetoric on Western leaders' disinterest in Africa's plight.

'No. I worked alone, handled my own cases, mainly media contracts . . . and divorces, of course. Incredible muck-stirring.' Chris actually manages a laugh . . . a little high-pitched, but acceptable.

'Well, a PA has to be around most of the time. We'll work together, make joint decisions, size up the potential of every situation. Two heads are better than one and nothing can match a woman's intuition.' Prince Husam seems to have rehearsed this. He pauses as his eyes lower for the briefest possible flicker towards her breasts. 'I want to tell you a little about my personal philosophy, but why don't we discuss this over coffee.'

His voice is so deep it seems to vibrate . . . beautiful hands, too. Chris pulls herself together fast. She is surprised by the speed at which he moves. Bounding to his feet, he grabs his jacket and there he is, grinning like a schoolboy and ready to go.

They travel in silence. Husam seems to be absorbed by his calculations, his fingers stabbing at the calculator. He stops the cab two blocks away, 'so they can get a breath of fresh air,' he explains.

First stop is the Tanzanian Embassy, where the prince harangues a junior minister for practical assistance for his 'Women Against Poverty' project, which is sweeping through the country.

Husam opens a file and reads rather grandly, gesturing with his hands.

'All over your country, your womenfolk are creating cottage industries backed by funds from the Provident Trust, making jam, straw hats, bead jewellery, herbal medicines, weavings and designing and even making clothes. Women have stepped in to become the breadwinners and save the day for a country where there's virtually no secondary industry and ninety per cent of the men are unemployed. We supplied the funds and the expertise. I've spent two million dollars on this project. What are your plans to help me?'

From the official's nervous blinks and soothing grunts, Chris gathers that this is an old feud and that the government has no plans to help him. He needs land for cooperative shops where produce from his many cottage industries can be sold, and workshops where he can teach new skills. Eventually he runs out of steam. Slamming the file on the desk, they leave.

'What did you think of my approach, Chris?'

'Passionate . . . effective . . . really great.'

The prince beams.

He really is quite manageable, Chris decides, feeling more confident.

By the time they reach *Patisserie Valerie* for a coffee break, after another long walk, Chris is so hungry she breaks her diet to order a toasted cheese sandwich with filter coffee.

Husam is off on his hobbyhorse again. 'The last thing Africans need is charity. Africa is fast becoming a basket case. What they need are secondary industries, jobs and training, all of which require massive capital investment . . .'

Husam has a captive audience and he's making the most of it. By the time they reach the office, Chris feels she's an expert on African development . . . or lack of.

★   ★   ★

They eat a leisurely lunch at Tramps. Fortunately, Husam has a private appointment in the afternoon. He dumps a pile of files on her desk.

'This will keep you busy. Please familiarise yourself with these projects of mine.' He smiles as if humouring a child.

As soon as he leaves the office, Chris hacks into every file in the office, but after two hours of concentration, she has found no mention of any diamond purchases or sales. She is intrigued by the massive investment flowing into African countries from Arab banks. In the past decade, the Islamic Development Bank (IDB) has given, not lent, $1,000 million to thirty-four African states. African Muslims now total 380 million, which is several times more than the Muslim population of the Middle East.

Other private investments are pouring in from various Arabic sources. Most of it goes via Mahe in the Seychelles, where huge banking headquarters have been built around a bay. The bankers have commandeered the entire area, so the government is building a bypass road around the bay. The Pahlavi family, who once ruled Iran, owns an entire island in the Seychelles group, she discovers. Other large tracts of land and homes are being purchased all over Africa, plus dozens of five-star hotels. Zimbabwe, too, is being colonised by Arab financiers. The Provident Trust handles most of the land purchases. It has also purchased millions of dollars of oil company shares and several mines producing strategic minerals.

She finds references to the mysterious T-files, wherever they are, but no mention of diamonds.

★   ★   ★

It is almost four p.m. by the time Husam returns. He has to make a call to his bank. It's private, he tells her, looking regretful. Chris goes into her office, closes the connecting door and switches on the intercom and her tape recorder. Husam is transferring a million dollars to a German-owned bank in Windhoek. He repeats the account number twice and the name of the recipient, which is Moses Freeman.

By now Chris is shaking with excitement as

she recognises the name of the man who sold blood diamonds to Ben's brother-in-law. This is it, then. Here's the proof Ben needed, or at least a hint of it. She can't wait to tell Ben. It seems that this vast shuffling of dollars is routine, for Husam is calm and cheerful when he barges into her office to take her to tea and for a walk through St James's Park.

After tea, Husam decides to dictate letters for two hours. At half past six he informs her that it's time for a drink, so they walk to the Cedar, where Husam talks about his polo ponies back home, and how he pines for the desert, even though he seldom gets the chance to go there. She's getting to know his past life intimately.

Chris glances surreptitiously at her watch. It's eight p.m.

'What do you feel like eating?' he asks politely. 'Fish, or something more exotic perhaps?'

At ten p.m., Chris insists on her right to go home. 'I do have a home,' she says. 'I'm tired, Husam. You're a real slave-driver.'

'I'm sorry. I had no idea.' He looks aggrieved as he escorts her to the pavement, where the doorman flags a passing taxi.

'I wanted to give you a good time on your first day. First days can be tense and scary. I hope you enjoyed yours.' He grabs her hand and kisses it theatrically. 'Am I forgiven?'

'You're such a tease, Husam.' Green Park station, she tells the driver as she steps into the taxi. As they speed out of earshot, she leans forwards. 'I've changed my mind. Turn left here please.'

★　★　★

By day, the London headquarters of Financial Investigations seem more like a hotel than a business: clients are entertained for coffee or lunch, the food prepared in their own kitchen; partners meet to discuss sport, or politics, or the stock market, secretaries quip jokes and pass on gossip in sly whispers as they move from office to office, and the corridors and rooms vibrate with energy. At night every sound seems to echo along the dark, empty corridors. Not that this bothers her, Chris reminds herself.

She switches the light on in her office and examines her desk. Four messages from David lie on top of the 'In' tray. Jean has written a note, too.

Mr Marais has been badgering me. He's desperate to get hold of you. What shall I tell him? I called Jeff Jennings and he agreed to visit Timmins jeweller's and ask for the pix of your stalker. He sent the attached pix to me this afternoon. I'm worried about you. Take care, Jean.

Chris opens the envelope and stares at the photograph of a man she has only seen by dim street lights. She has no idea what a stalker would look like, but this would be the last person she would suspect. The face is full of contrasts: curly, jet black hair, laughing green eyes. He's smiling into the camera. Did he realise he'd been set up for a mug shot? Sensuous lips, a nose that's been broken many times and put together

92

with a hammer by the look of things. Yet there's something about him that signals a tough and ruthless man. She's not sure what it is. Sexy sums him up rather well, too, she decides.

The detective's message is even more intriguing.

Your stalker doesn't appear to be on any police file. I can't find a trace of him, but I've contacted Interpol.

The addendum reads:

Bingo! My Interpol contact found him in the African mug shots. His name is James Stark. He's American and he spent nine months of a ten-year sentence in prison in Equatorial Guinea on charges of distributing alcohol. Conditions were terrible, but after nine months he was rescued by a team of American mercenaries. He's supposed to be an ex-mercenary, too, but I can't find any proof of this. Once he was a remittance man. It's rumoured that his father owned a tyre factory, but when funds ran out Stark stayed in Africa by choice. He takes on anything as long as it pays. Be careful. He seems to be a thoroughly unscrupulous person.

Why on earth should such a person follow her? What could he possibly want? Gazing at the picture of herself, she is ashamed to see how frightened she looks.

She works on, still hoping that Ben will call, but he doesn't. Of course there's nothing to worry about. She forces herself to face her fears and soon realises that they are based on nothing more serious than disappointment. She is longing to tell Ben about the million dollars the prince transferred to Moses Freeman. She'll wait another five minutes, she decides as she prints her report, making a copy for Rowan. So he'll phone her tomorrow. At midnight, she calls a taxi.

Chris is exhausted by the time she has bathed and stumbled into bed. Lying in that curious state of half awake and half asleep she seems to hear Sienna calling from some dark, underground dungeon, and then she is watching Ben walking into the shadows. She screams a warning, but Ben can't hear her. Transient images persist . . . scenes from Arabian nights, fleeting flashes of Husam's eyes fixed fiercely on her . . . a clever man with dangerous connections. Madness to think she could outwit him.

11

Chris wakes in the night with a jolt of fear ... first Sienna ... now Ben. But this is nonsense. Ben will be back in the morning. And later she wakes muttering: 'Bastards ... Bastards ... ' And still later: 'Whoever you are ... I'm coming after you.' But how can she? Chris falls into a deep sleep only when dawn sets the birds singing. Birdsong always comforts her.

She oversleeps and has to skip her usual half hour at FI and go directly to Husam's Provident Trust. She's soon into the swing of things. She might have been working there for weeks instead of days. Lately, she feels more relaxed since she's no longer afraid. Armed with a notebook, she accompanies Husam to a meeting with an Ugandan banker, and on to his gym. In between these chores they take fast walks in the park. Husam has a passion for walking and Chris is considering buying flat-heeled shoes for the first time in her life. The prince has a love of antiques, so they arrange to attend a new French exhibition. A visiting Turkish art collection has to be fitted in, too. Husam adores London and hardly an event occurs without an invitation arriving in the mail. She sorts them and works out his timetable. Evenings he expects her to accompany him to new shows or concerts. He doesn't seem to need sleep.

At noon, when Husam goes to a private

meeting in the company's boardroom with a group of bearded, robed compatriots, she hacks into his correspondence, his past travel itineraries, his work files and his bank details. Husam was in Dar Es Salaam when the US Embassy was bombed. Was that a coincidence, she wonders? She'll never know unless she finds the hidden T-files. Suddenly she's in an excitingly crazy world.

★　★　★

They are on the way back from lunch when Husam says: 'A year back I bought a collection of rare sixteenth-century African maps by Livio Sanuto. They had to be slightly repaired and now we have to choose the frames. It's not far from here so let's go.' He hails a taxi.

'Antique maps are becoming very scarce,' he lectures her in the taxi. 'I expect to double or treble the value of my investment in two years time.'

As if he didn't have enough already.

Chris soon finds herself facing an assortment of frames and masks. She's expected to choose the right colours to highlight the hand-coloured maps. This gives her an idea.

'How can I pick out the best frames if I don't know the backdrop? I mean, where will they be hanging, Prince Husam? What colour is the wall? Do you have antique or modern furniture?'

'I should have thought of that.' He takes her arm and bends his head close to her ear. 'Don't use my title. It's archaic . . . something I don't much care for. Besides, it's a clear signal to rip me off. Just Husam will do.' He steps back.

'Of course. Very sensible. I'll show you round my apartment soon and we'll come back another time.' He waves to the picture framer who is clearly annoyed by yet another delay.

'Look. This is just a suggestion,' Chris begins. 'You have a private meeting with the board this afternoon. I could go and look around your apartment and meet you later at the picture framer's.'

To her surprise, Husam hands over his keys and gives her the address. It's all too easy. Why does he trust her so much? Chris stifles her guilt and regrets.

★   ★   ★

Husam's apartment is disappointingly English. Ugly Victorian furniture clutters the rooms and there's plenty of chintz and velvet, but she reckons that the maps will fit perfectly in old-fashioned, gilt frames. Chris finds his laptop in the bedroom and switches it on. Seeing a document labelled 'T-files', she opens it and reads the daily notes of Husam's work during his previous summer in East and West Africa. As she skips through pages of entries of meetings and expenditure to launch his many projects, she becomes increasingly excited. So this is where the cash projects are filed.

In mid-June, Husam flew to the west coast of Africa. She reads: *I met Moses Freeman in Monrovia, during a trip to Liberia. He sold me a* million dollars of roughs at the low price of twenty dollars per carat, which is standard in the Congo, but cheap at Liberian prices. He tried to interest me in purchasing three excellent diamond pipes in the Congo, but in my opinion prices of roughs will soon drop. Buying and selling conflict diamonds is the only way to get started. Freeman is interested in running the show. I'll check him out.

She moves on to the next document: 24-04-04: half a million dollars transferred to Freeman's Windhoek bank account. At last she's making progress.

After that comes document after document of information on details of Husam's cottage industries, most of which require massive cash injections, and finally, after a long search, there are two more transfers of cash to Freeman, making a total of 2.5 million dollars.

She's jotting down cash payments when she remembers the time. Reluctantly she eyes the list . . . hundreds of millions of dollars. It's too easy. Suddenly she feels anxious. She must leave at once or Husam might guess that she's spying on him. Somehow she'll find a way to come back.

★   ★   ★

Husam is relaxed and friendly enough when they meet up again in the office. 'How about a sundowner?' he asks her around six p.m. 'And I have tickets for a play. I'm hoping you'll accompany me.'

Chris is tired out and determined to change

their routine. 'I have to type my notes and I could do with an early night, so I must go,' she says determinedly. 'See you in the morning, Husam.'

'Not even one drink?' His brown eyes search hers beseechingly.

'Really, Husam. I need the evening off. I haven't spent an evening at home for days. Besides, you're not supposed to drink.'

'When in Rome . . . ' He breaks off as a new threat occurs to him. 'You have a date.'

'None of your business. But yes, a date with an early night. How about tomorrow?'

He brightens. 'Go on then . . . off you go, if you must.'

Oh God! Those eyes. They seem to be beaming a world of love at her. But that's ridiculous. He must be lonely, Chris decides as she hurries to her office.

Jean is working late and this surprises her. Has she been giving her too much work? Surely not. 'You're working late, Jean. This is a surprise.'

'I hung on to see you. For goodness' sake call Mr Marais,' Jean grumbles. 'I'll get him on the line for you.'

'No wait. It's too late. He'll have left by now.'

'He gave me his home number. Listen, Chris. I know this is awkward . . . I doubt he's calling for business, but after all he's deputising for the client. You *must* call him. What if he complains to Rowan?'

'He wouldn't dare.'

Moments later her telephone rings. Chris picks up the receiver.

'Chris, it's Dave. What's going on? Getting hold of you is just about impossible. Don't you ever call back?' He sounds hurt, which surprises her.

'I'm sorry, Dave.' She gestures to Jean that it's Dave Marais.

'Look, I'm sorry I haven't called you back. I'm not free to make calls from nine to five and by the time I get back here, it's too late to call you. I come in early in the morning, well, most mornings, but you're not at work yet.'

'Don't apologise,' he interrupts her. 'Just call me at home in future. Thank heavens you're all right. What are you up to?'

'Ben left me with a project to complete which involves being out of the office all day. Sorry Dave.'

'Well, nevermind. I thought you'd thrown in the towel.'

'Not my style. How could you think that?' She feels annoyed by his inference.

'Calm down. I want to take you to dinner or lunch. Whichever you feel you can cope with.'

'I can't. Truly I can't. I'm not sure how long I'll be involved with this job I'm on.'

'You're moonlighting!'

She laughs. 'Strictly under orders. Don't ask, because I can't tell you any more, except that it's strictly short-term. Listen Dave, this is a bit of a long shot, but I need some background on a man called James Stark, an American. Have you heard of him?'

'Unfortunately yes. Steer clear of him, Chris. He's an ex-mercenary who'll turn his hand to

100

anything that pays. He's a real con . . . spent a while in prison in Equatorial Guinea. It can't get worse than that. More recently he tried to interest us in a long-term contract to purchase Angolan blood diamonds. He's a known liar and cheat, so be careful.'

'Thanks, Dave. I will. Be seeing you soon.'

'Hey there. Not so fast. OK . . . what can I say . . . I'll have to wait. I'll be honest, Chrissie, you intrigue me. I look forward to our next meeting.'

Chris feels surprised. 'I'll keep in touch . . . promise.'

She replaces the receiver and considers the call. Dave is old enough to be her father and he doesn't look the type to make a fool of himself, so what does he want?

Jean leaves and soon she's alone. She works all evening but Ben doesn't call.

⋆ ⋆ ⋆

By midnight anxiety has gained the upper hand. Chris dials Ben's mobile, despite the fact that it's six a.m. in the States. There is no reply. This is more than strange. Feeling thoroughly alarmed she waits an hour before calling Ben's sister.

'Hello. Is that Sharon . . . Mrs Bronstein? Oh, hi. My name is Chris Winters, I'm Ben's assistant . . . '

Sharon interrupts her with a rush of words. 'I know who you are . . . Ben told us about you. Is Ben all right? He didn't even say goodbye . . . Oh God!'

Chris catches her breath as she hears Sharon

101

talking in the background. Something is terribly wrong. Her stomach quails. A man's voice replaces Sharon's.

'Hello there, Chris. I'm Jonathan Bronstein, Ben's brother-in-law. We assumed that Ben was back in London. He's not, then?'

'No.'

'The truth is, Sharon and Ben had a disagreement. He wanted Sharon to sign away the proxy on her company shares in favour of my father. She wasn't keen. She knows Father would vote me out of the company after what's happened. Ben's been helping us. He saw Moses Freeman a second time . . . wait a minute you don't know . . . ' Jon clears his throat noisily, but his voice was still husky.

'I know why Ben flew to New York.'

'Fine! Well, Ben scored. He managed to get a signed, sworn statement from Freeman claiming that the diamonds he sold to me were purchased from a Canadian mine that has not joined the Kimberley Project. Two days ago Ben had a meeting with the executives of the KP. He got back after lunch with the good news . . . we're in the clear.' Jon broke off as if expecting a reply.

'And then?' Chris murmurs into the static. 'Please tell me . . . what's happened to Ben?'

'We don't know. Sharon tried to persuade him to fly to Paris to see his wife, but Ben was adamant that he was going straight to Heathrow. He was about to leave for the airport when a driver arrived with a message from Freeman. He said that Freeman was waiting for him at a downtown cafe and that he had valuable information for Ben. Ben arranged to follow the man. He was going to drive on to the airport and drop off the hired car there.'

'And did he?'

'I didn't check. Look here, Chris, there was a bit of bad feeling between us.'

Chris's mind seems to be in two places at once. Part of her wants to burst into tears and beg this nightmare to go away, at the same time her thoughts are racing ahead of Jon's words. Of course Ben would have called her, or Rowan, from the airport . . . even if he'd taken a day off, he'd let them know. Chris feels disaster creeping up on her. It's a strange, numbing sensation. She becomes very calm, very precise and strangely empty, all at the same time.

'Did you call his wife?'

'She's in Paris. I don't have her number. Besides, what's the point of worrying her?'

'Have you checked the car hire firm?'

'Well, no.'

'I'll call Rowan.' Unthinkingly, Chris replaces the receiver. She tries to get herself under control as she dials Rowan's home number.

'Rowan, listen, we have a problem. Do you know where Ben is? Has he contacted you?'

'No. I assumed he was still in New York.'

Rowan listens in silence while she tells him what she knows.

'I have a few numbers I can try . . . his wife, for starters. You go home now. Call a taxi and charge the office. I'll see you in the morning.'

'Call the New York police, Rowan,' she urges.

'You're right,' he says tonelessly.

An impersonal click terminates the conversation.

★ ★ ★

Chris leaves soon afterwards. Once again she recognises the white Ford Fiesta tagging along behind her. Does he sit around all day and half the night waiting for her, she muses? And anyway, who the hell is he?

It's a bad night for Chris. She can't allow herself to admit that something might have happened to Ben. Positive thoughts can make things happen, she reminds herself, so for Ben's sake she has to believe that he's OK. It isn't easy . . . and then there's Sienna. So far the police have no clues and her fate is still unknown.

12

Chris hears Rowan out in silence as he tries to reassure her and himself. 'We're not Ben's keepers. There's every chance that he's taken a couple of days off to be with his family.' He let out a loud, comforting laugh, a sure sign that he's nervous.

'So there's no news as yet.'

'As I said . . . '

'What about the police?'

'They haven't come back to us yet.'

It's seven a.m. Chris has dropped into the office hoping for news of Ben. She's late this morning, having fallen asleep at dawn after lying awake for hours. She arrives at the Provident Trust half an hour late to find Husam pacing his office looking upset. He tries to hide his shock at the sight of her and this worries her. Did he think that she wasn't coming back? Something's gone wrong.

'I overslept. I'm sorry.' She manages a quick, decisive tone.

He doesn't answer, but his eyes reproach her.

'Don't look at me like that. I work all hours. Last night I couldn't sleep.'

'What's wrong?' He looks as if he had a sleepless night, too.

'It's irrelevant.' She sighs as she sinks into a chair, although her mind is racing over every second of their previous day together. They parted as friends. Surely nothing can be wrong.

'No, tell me.'

'A colleague . . . that is, a former colleague . . . from way back . . . well, he's disappeared . . . or so it seems . . . I'm sure he'll arrive back in the office . . . with apologies all round.' She tries out a smile, but it fails.

'You look so forlorn. Are you fond of him?' His eyes are glittering, but why? With hurt?

'Yes, I am fond of him, but not in the way you're implying. He's a happily married man.' Or was! The thought of that makes her flinch. 'What's bothering you?' She speaks aggressively, feeling unfairly blamed.

'Circumstances have changed. I'm going to have to spend more time in Tanzania . . . on and off, of course. I expect you to come with me.' He waits, but not expectantly.

'Oh, I don't know about that. I don't think so. I'm no jungle bunny.' She manages to laugh convincingly.

His eyes are fixed on hers. There's a message there, but Chris can't work it out. Something is wrong. Is this a ploy to get rid of her? Inexplicably she feels let down, which is silly since she's only days from quitting. Later, he dumps some files on her desk to sort and file, but for the rest of the morning he ignores her. Finally, at noon, he comes in to say he is going to lunch.

'I have a meeting this afternoon. It might take hours. Why don't you go to the picture framer's and order the frames.'

'Just like that? It's you who has to live with

them, not me. Well, all right,' she goes on, since he doesn't comment. Luck is on her side.

She looks around her desk and in her briefcase. 'Damn. I've lost the measurements. I think I'll go back first and measure the spaces again. Best to be on the safe side. I didn't have a ruler so I had to guess last time. We can't have a heavy gilt frame hanging in a small space.'

He takes his keys out of his pocket and puts them on his desk. 'Leave the keys with the security desk on the ground floor. I might be late back . . . very late, in fact.'

Why is he lying? There's no meeting. It would have been in his diary and besides, she would have known about it. Why does he look so uncomfortable. He's setting a trap for me! The bastard! Her suspicions are unwelcome and hurtful, but she might be mistaken, and if she doesn't go he'll wonder why.

★   ★   ★

She makes her pilgrimage to the picture framer and returns to the office. The telephonist confirms that Husam left early and isn't expected back, so she works for a while. Later she gathers her courage together and walks to Husam's apartment, wondering why she feels like a thief.

She's had enough, she decides, waving to the security porter who knows her face by now. More than enough, she decides as she ascends to the fifth floor in the escalator. Who would have imagined that taking on a business investigation

107

could lead to spying in someone's private home. It feels wrong. But why does he keep half of his accounts at home in his bedroom? If he kept them in the office, like everyone else, she wouldn't be here. Chris pauses at the bedroom door, longing to flee, but that won't help her to find where Sienna is imprisoned. Thoughts of Sienna and Ben harden her resolve.

She locks the door from the inside, fastens the chain just in case, and walks across the spacious hall to the bedroom door. Glancing at her watch she notes that it's half past six. Time for cocktails. Then dinner and still later dancing. That was his routine. Would he bring his date back here? Who cares. She'll be long gone.

It's like delving into Pandora's box, she decides, as she sifts through the fascinating contents of folders and documents. Massive amounts of cash are being withdrawn and dispensed with all over Africa. The payments are filed under wages, sundry items, building materials, maintenance, there's no shortage of creative thought here. But what if these workshops and cottage industries don't exist at all? What if it's one big scam and the cash is to purchase blood diamonds?

She pushes that thought away for another day and concentrates on the job in hand, which is copying all cash transactions and putting them on to another folder. This will be transferred to a disc which she has in her bag. There's masses of material.

Glancing at her watch later, she sees that it is half past eight. Good God! She's been there for two hours. She should be out of the flat by nine p.m. If she hurries she can make it. She starts to transfer the data on to her disc . . . just in case.

★ ★ ★

She's startled by someone knocking on the outside door. For a split second of shocked horror she remains as if frozen to her chair, then the sound of someone unlocking the door throws her into a panic. Panting and shaking, she transfers the data, throws the disc into her bag and switches off the laptop. Someone is banging the door against the chain. Thank heavens it's holding.

'Chris. It's me. Open the door.' Husam's angry voice booms down the passage.

Panic-stricken, she races to the bedroom, tears off her clothes and dumps them on the chair. Flinging her bag on the floor, she rumples the bedclothes and the pillows and flings back the quilted silk duvet. 'Fuck . . . fuck . . . fuck . . .'

She grabs his silk dressing gown and puts it on. Stumbling to the door she peers through the opening.

'Oh, Husam. You're so late. How was your meeting? I was waiting for you, I wanted to surprise you, but I must have fallen asleep. What time is it?' Fumbling with the chain, she opens the door. So many emotions flicker in his eyes, but lust wins.

Moments later she's picked up and carried to the bedroom.

He is all those things she had hoped he would

be, but better. He is skilled, and romantic and beautiful, but later he turns his back on her and lies staring at the moonlight shining through the branches of the trees.

'Are you awake?' she whispers. 'What's wrong? It was good, wasn't it?'

'Decadent English girl . . . I thought you were different.'

'I am different. I don't want a commitment, but with you I'm safe. We never had a future. You know how I feel about you . . . but . . . ' She gives up. Words are not the only way to communicate. She wraps her arms around him and holds him close and after while he falls asleep.

★ ★ ★

At five a.m., when he is sleeping heavily beside her, she slips out of bed and tiptoes to the bathroom. When she returns, Husam is sitting up and the television is switched on.

'Come back to bed. You'll catch cold.'

'I must get home before my mother wakes. I'll get dressed.' He bounds out of bed and grabs her wrist. His hand is as strong as a bear trap. She can't free herself as she is pulled to the bed.

'No, Chris, we're going to watch movies.' He tucks the duvet around her and a pillow behind her and she, stunned and shocked, makes no effort to fight him.

'Let's see now. This one is dated September 1st.'

Her first day at work. She watches as he slides

the video into the slot and presses a button on the remote control, at which the screen lights up with a picture of herself, looking formal and dutiful, as she works away at the computer.

'Very industrious,' he murmurs, 'except that you were supposed to be reading the files I gave you. You had nothing at all to do at the computer.'

Everything about him predicts danger. There's no warmth in his glance, merely a blank stare. She is all too aware of her nakedness under his cold scrutiny.

'I have a video like this one for every moment that I was out of the office. Whatever work it is you do, you're not very well trained. Why didn't you look around? An expert would have spotted the security cameras. I want you to know that I don't blame you . . . you have to earn your living . . . but perhaps you will indulge my curiosity. You have a another job, yes? Your boss, Ben Searle, is in the States and you are helping him with his enquiry.'

Ben. Oh God! At the unexpected sound of his name her eyes fill with tears. 'You're talking nonsense. I told you that I worked there for a day. Then I left. I've been doing some typing of my own. You didn't give me much to do. I was bored.'

'But Ben has disappeared and you said you are worried about a missing colleague.' Almost before she realises why, her arms are pricking with goose-pimples. How does he know that Ben is missing . . . unless he has something to do with it? Her fear turns to anger.

'They still take messages for you, or Jean does. She's your secretary, I believe . . . or yours and Ben's. I knew Ben well once. I suppose he told you.'

'Yes, yes and yes . . . to everything.' She tires of the inquisition. 'I'm cold. I'm going to get dressed.'

'Ben had only to ask me. I would have told him whatever he wanted to know. I have no secrets.'

'Oh yes, you do. You like to think you're a saint, but I happen to know better, having gone through your files pretty thoroughly. Don't think I don't know that your aim is to stop the West from honing in on Africa's oil and minerals.'

Her anger has got the upper hand. She longs to stop her flow of rhetoric, but she can't. 'All that high-minded talk about Africa for Africans was based on self-interest. You really had me fooled. It was oil . . . and gold . . . and platinum . . . and all those strategic minerals scattered over the continent. You're as hypocritical as everyone else.' She says much more, but later she can't remember what she said. Panic, rage and a sense of loss have combined to open the floodgates of her emotions. But why is she feeling so hurt? Husam means nothing to her. He's part of the investigation. Nothing more. Who cares if he falls off his pedestal. She already has.

'Tell me why you are buying illicit diamonds. How many cheques have you made out to Moses Freeman? You, who supposedly love Africa, are helping insurgents to fund civil wars, lay mines, kidnap young children and turn them into zombie fighters. Moses Freeman is the reason why Ben went to New York. So tell me . . . how did you know that Ben is missing? No one knows. We aren't even sure . . . I mean we're hoping . . . '

She breaks off and makes an effort to pull herself together.

'I'll tell you why, if you listen. Massive quantities of diamond roughs are removed from Southern Africa on a weekly basis. They are sold in London and most of them are cut and polished in Amsterdam and Tel-Aviv. The Western mining houses refuse to let Africans learn to polish rough diamonds, although this could provide a massive secondary industry leading to thousands of jobs. Even those countries' governments must buy roughs at exorbitant London prices.' He sighs melodramatically. 'I'm trying to change all that.'

There is a long and ominous silence. 'I'm going. Don't try to stop me. If you touch me I'll scream the place down.' She scrambles out of bed, pulls on her clothes, grabs her coat and bag and makes for the front door. It's not even locked. He must have forgotten last night. A woman from the flat next door is picking up her newspaper. She looks amused as she stares blatantly.

Chris backs into the room and shuts the door gently. She returns to the bedroom. Husam is still sitting on the bed. When he looks up she sees sadness in his eyes. It's then that she realises that it wasn't he who set the trap for her, but someone else.

'Who did this? It wasn't you. You trusted me.'

'I was a fool.'

'So who?'

'Naturally I have a security team at the bank. My security chief showed me the videos when I arrived early yesterday.'

That figures. She'd noticed the icy atmosphere.

He sighs. 'You're just doing your job. I assume you're investigating diamond laundering. The problem is . . . you're going to make someone very angry and that won't be healthy for you. Give it up. Go back to law.'

'Is that a threat?'

'It's a warning. Give up your job, Chris. Leave it alone.'

Shock waves send her eyes watering and her fury mounting.

'Husam . . . '

'Don't! There's nothing you can say except goodbye.'

'Damn you. You should have stayed on your bloody pedestal.' She can't hold back her tears.

As her feet pound the pavement, images race towards her. So many good times packed into a week. He'll make someone a hell of a husband, she tells herself. Until he takes his second wife . . . and the third. That thought brings her longing back into perspective. By the time she reaches the office she's shrugged off her guilt, but her anger remains.

114

13

It's well past nine a.m. by the time Chris steps out of the lift on the sixth floor. She pauses . . . hears the lift doors close . . . the hum of its descent . . . Something's wrong. There's a difference. It's the silence, she realises, as she hurries across the marble foyer, past the empty desk to the passage. First on the right is the secretaries' open-plan office. She sees Jean is sobbing into a tissue. Mary Frampton, Rowan's secretary, is standing beside Jean's desk looking distraught. Their ten typists look pseudo-sad, like mourners at a funeral who don't know the deceased sufficiently well to grieve. Chris hovers in the doorway wondering if she should interfere. Then the boardroom door opens and three men emerge. Rowan hovers behind them. Chris steps into the office as they pass.

'Rowan left a message on your desk. Ben has died,' Jean says. Her mumbled words end with a high-pitched sob. Moments later she is holding a handful of tissues over her face, while Mary tries to comfort her. Her words knock Chris headlong into another kind of reality, a state of mind where emotions are banished and cold, hard reason takes over.

'How did he die?' she asks.

'How can you be so cool?' Jean snaps accusingly.

Mary looks shocked. 'Rowan called Ben's

brother-in-law. He was found hanging under a bridge. At first the FBI were talking about suicide but now it's murder. The men leaving now are from the US Embassy.'

Ben . . . dead . . . It was inconceivable. Insane! Chris feels unreality crowding in on her, yet her mind is racing from point to point as she goes through Ben's last call. Ben had been about to meet Moses Freeman. He'd been prepared to go to Liberia if necessary. Did Moses Freeman kill Ben?

She's about to hurry after Rowan and tell him this, but she hesitates. If she reveals her suspicions to Rowan, he'll take her off the investigation, but she's not going to let him do that, there's too much at stake. She has a compulsion to find out who killed Ben. And then there's Sienna captured by those thugs when she should be on her honeymoon . . . or is she already dead, too?

She is right about Rowan. A sealed envelope lying on her desk contains an official letter from their managing partner, relating details of Ben's death and his regrets, ending with the words: *A new investigation has landed on my desk concerning the fashion industry. It's for you, so please return all data concerning the diamond laundering investigation, including your latest report, no later than noon today.*

Chris feels fury mounting until she can't think straight. She slams her door, cancels all calls and forces herself to think rationally about Rowan's decision, but as her head clears, her anger sharpens. Reaching a sudden decision, she calls Jean.

'Is Rowan alone?'

'Hang on, I'll ask Mary. Yes. Look, I'm sorry, Chris. After all, as Mary says, you've only been here for a few days, not long enough to get to know Ben.'

Long enough to love Ben, Chris decides grimly as she murmurs the appropriate words of condolence and replaces the receiver.

★ ★ ★

Black despair grips her and that's something that she fears. Only fury can disperse her mood. She strides into Rowan's office, ignoring his glance of frustrated impatience and rips his letter down the middle. Dropping the halves into his bin, she glares right back at him. 'Forget it, Rowan. I came here to work on the diamond laundering investigation and until it's finished it's my baby.'

'OK. Calm down. Let's talk about it. Want some coffee?'

She feels like a deflated balloon as her anger evaporates. 'It's like this . . . '

'Save it . . . count to ten . . . or ten thousand . . . I have to read this and phone someone. Sit tight and wait for coffee. You need to learn to handle tension.'

For God's sake, it's not tension, it's murder and kidnapping, but she keeps her retort to herself. Right now she needs FI and she needs Rowan.

Coffee comes. Chris ladles in three spoonfuls

of sugar, hoping the carbohydrates will stoke her fury. Anger brings courage, a quick tongue, a sense of invincibility and sweeps aside all opposition. At last Rowan pushes the pages aside and calls through to Mary. 'Tell him we'll go ahead,' he grunts.

'Ben called me,' Rowan begins deceptively softly. 'I'm sorry I didn't tell you at the time. He said he had a bad feeling about the investigation and he asked me to take you off it. In a way you could say that it was Ben's last request, so you might see my decision a little differently. I wasn't suggesting you're not capable . . . '

'Let's not start that again,' she interrupts him.

So Ben had wanted her off the case. He cared. Chris can feel sorrow taking over, clogging her mind. What could be more ludicrous than a sobbing woman in a man's world. She stands up abruptly and walks to the window. It's a while before she can risk talking, so it's lucky that Rowan is saying much the same thing all over again.

'What choice do I have?' he's bleating, but she can see that his heart isn't in it. Finally, in the face of her determination, he caves in and actually looks relieved.

'For God's sake take care. We don't charge danger pay to our clients. We're not supposed to be taking risks. Believe me, I don't have anyone else keen to take this case over, but naturally I'm worried about you. Worried sick, to tell the truth. Have you had any problems? Any threats or warnings?'

'No,' she lies. Now is not the time to tell him

about her stalker and the white Ford Fiesta. Then there is the curious fact that Husam knew about their investigation and knew that Ben was missing. It's like playing blindman's bluff and she's the one who's blindfolded.

'I have to go to New York. Moses Freeman is our only lead.'

'That's out of the question. Are you harbouring some sort of a death wish . . . ?'

She quells him with a scathing look. She's beginning to suss him out. Rowan is a weak man, playing a strong man's role, relying on brains and cunning. She says: 'Perhaps Ben was murdered because he stumbled on to something that would shed some light on this investigation. That's the only possibility that makes any sense. I mean . . . there has to be a good reason.' Her voice is rising ominously, so she makes an effort to calm herself.

'Did Ben have any success? Did he find anything?'

'Ben had a hunch that al-Qaeda is behind the diamond laundering. I'm not so sure. Ben's murder was dressed up to look like suicide.'

'How do you know that?'

'You told Mary. Mary told me. Let's face it, this isn't the way those guys do things. They murder with a flourish, preferably on television, with the intention of circulating their horror story to kids' mobiles.' She shudders. 'Surely the fact that the murder was disguised as a suicide tells us that the person or persons we're looking for are vulnerable to any publicity or probing.'

'We have no proof that Ben's murder is

connected with this investigation.'

'Ben is not the type to get mixed up in anything murky. You know that.'

Rowan nods. 'True! And what about the Provident Trust. Was that a total waste of time?'

'I'm not sure. Prince Husam Ibn al-Faisal is a deeply spiritual man and he has a vision. He sees himself galloping on his white Arab stallion to slay ignorance and poverty. He told me he longs to drag Africa into the twenty-first century. But yes, he does buy illicit diamonds. Masses of cash pass through his hands as aid for various African countries and it's gleaned from all over the Middle East. I have dozens of his projects on file, but there must be many more.'

Rowan watches her curiously. 'I can see that he's impressed you.'

Ignoring his inference, Chris stands lost in thought for a few seconds. 'Just one thing bothers me . . . ' She breaks off.

Why tell Rowan of Husam's dealings with Freeman. He'll try to pull her off the investigation again and he'll block her passage to New York.

'You were saying . . . ' Rowan prompts her.

'Let's not forget Mohsen Sheik,' she improvises. 'His daughter's kidnapping tells us something. My view is that Sienna is being held hostage to force her father to purchase the more inferior grades of blood diamonds.'

'Why him?'

'Because India is the only market for tiny, low-grade rough diamonds. They are polished and exported to brighten cheap jewellery. In the past these roughs had industrial uses, but nowadays the industry uses synthetic diamonds. Indian workshops provide the only market for this so-called diamond waste. Mohsen Sheik controls most of the country's polishing workshops . . . he supplies them with roughs and exports the polished stones.'

Rowan glances sharply at her. 'How do you know all this?'

'At school I shared a dormitory with his daughter. By the way . . . I meant to ask you . . . the police should have this information. Shall I . . . ?'

Rowan was scribbling in his notebook. 'Write it down and give it to Mary. I'll pass it on. It'll save you time. All police collaboration normally goes through me, unless they specifically want to see you. Anything else I should know?'

'Well, yes, there is something. I didn't mention that I cabled our Bombay office. I asked them to send us a review of Jewelrex Company's past weeks' cash transactions, and that we're looking for large cash payments.'

Rowan stands for a while with his back turned, as if deep in thought. 'Good thinking Chris, but be careful. I know I should relinquish the investigation, but it's at government level, so I'm reluctant to throw in the towel. At least not right now.'

'I won't let you,' Chris whispers to herself as she stands up and makes for the door. 'It might help me to know who our clients are.'

'Believe it or not, it's the Republic of Congo. They feel they're suffering from unfair prejudice.

They want the facts before they appeal.' Chris tries not to show how startled she feels. 'Dave Marais claims to be deputising for our client.'

'Yes. He's acting for this government in an advisory capacity.'

She sighs with relief. 'Then I'll be getting along.'

Rowan sends one of his rare, twisted smiles her way. 'Keep away from Moses Freeman. That's an order.'

As Chris hurries back to her office she considers her options. Despite Rowan's advice, her top priority is Freeman, but it might be wiser to do without Jean's help in booking a flight to New York. Chris hasn't yet decided whether or not she can trust her. The last thing she wants is Rowan breathing down her neck again.

14

Chris closes her office door and calls her travel agent. Fortunately there's a cancellation on the six a.m. flight the next day. She has only just replaced the receiver when Dave bursts in unannounced. Jean follows hard behind him looking flustered.

'It's all right, Jean. This is Dave Marais from Trans-Africa. David, meet Jean, no longer a disembodied voice on the telephone.'

'Damn woman wouldn't let me in,' David grumbles the moment the door closes behind her.

'Guests are supposed to sit in our conference room where they get coffee or tea with biscuits . . . even lunch if the kitchen is warned in advance.'

Dave ignores her. 'I can't believe what happened to Ben. It's a bloody nightmare.'

So he knows. The word has got around fast. Chris nods, unable to speak for a few seconds.

Suddenly Chris feels Dave's hand pressing hers. She looks up, startled by the gesture and by the strangely intent look in his eyes. She stares at his hand. He has long, strong brown fingers and there are thick blond hairs around his wrist. This would be great if she felt the need for a masculine shoulder to lean on, but she doesn't. She sets about extricating her fingers.

'I feel useless and frustrated,' Dave is saying in

a husky voice. 'Ben was a close friend . . . one of the best. This investigation . . . well, let's say it's dangerous . . . best left to the police. There's too much money involved. I want you out of here. I can't let you come to any harm, Chris. I think you know how I feel about you. Women always know.'

Chris stems her irritation and persuades herself that Dave means well. He's a man you can trust, even if his views are a little passé. A tough, reliable, clever man and for reasons which she doesn't understand, he seems to be trying to impress her. He's probably pushing fifty, but he's sexy, suntanned, lean and athletic, but she's not paid to waste time in office hours. She decides to cut short his visit.

'You're wasting your valuable time, Dave. I'm not leaving. I've just had the same argument with Rowan.'

'Do you see yourself as some sort of a bionic woman? Invincible perhaps?' He subjects Chris to a keen, searching appraisal, from her feet to her hair. It's disconcerting and Chris guesses that his intention is to throw her off guard. She doesn't bother to answer.

'Look here, Chris. I understand that you crave adventure enough to throw up a brilliant career, but don't you think this detection work is beneath you . . . with your brains?' He smiles indulgently.

What can she say? You have a flattering turn of phrase, David, but I'm not falling for it. Or . . . I owe it to Ben and Sienna. Or how about . . . mind your own bloody business, Dave.

124

Wisely she says nothing at all, which doesn't phase David because clearly he has other matters on his mind.

'Come clean, Chris. You haven't found out a damn thing, have you?'

'Too true,' she replies with a brittle smile.

'So what have you been up to? You've been out of the office for days.'

Chris glances sharply at him. 'I've been doing the rounds of retailers . . . getting to know the marketing side of the diamond business.'

'Anyone helping you?'

'Not really. I took your advice and pretended to be writing a book on diamonds.'

'Have the police contacted you?'

'No. Why should they? I was in London.'

'But I expect you know who Ben saw in New York. He must have told you.' He glances anxiously at her.

'No. Unfortunately not. No doubt his sister will send his notes back to us when the police return them to her.'

'That could take some time.' Dave looks up from studying her desk. His large, grey eyes scan her cautiously. 'Do you reckon you're any nearer to finding the culprits?'

'No, but you've just joined the list of suspects, David.' She laughs at his studied indifference.

'Why do you say that?'

'All these questions.'

He stands, as if deep in thought. How on earth is she going to get rid of him? 'I have another appointment, Dave, and a great deal of work to do,' she says gently.

125

'Listen,' she adds hastily noticing his hurt expression. 'I appreciate your concern. OK, so you're a bit chauvinistic. Out of tune with the times, I would say. It's your colonial upbringing that's to blame, but you care and I thank you for that.'

At last she's got through to him. He grabs her arm and gives her a slight shake.

'Don't be frivolous. This isn't a frivolous matter. Listen to me, for God's sake. Hear me! You're like a little buck in the forest, still wet behind the ears and stumbling around in the dark. These masterminds are putting away millions in Swiss banks. Their transactions are almost impossible to trace, but just suppose you do discover one of the laundering routes . . . they'd put out your light . . . just like that . . . just like they did to Ben.'

Suddenly she's grasped in a bear-like hug that almost knocks the wind out of her.

'I can't allow you to get hurt. You've got to give up this business.'

'Dave . . . please . . . this is my office.'

He pushes her away and strides out without saying goodbye.

So what was that all that about, she wonders after he's gone. He didn't ask her out to dinner after all.

★ ★ ★

It was past eleven before she managed to see Rowan again.

'Mr Marais has been on to me. He wants me

126

to replace you with a man.'

'Dave's the ultimate male chauvinist pig,' she snarls.

Rowan looks embarrassed. 'I told him we'd be open to a sex discrimination claim.'

'Good for you. Listen, Rowan, I need to check on one of Prince Husam's African ventures, namely the diamond cutting workshops in Liberia. Husam has shed a lot of cash there. Seven workshops are supposed to have been set up and there should be large cash payments for wages, for instance, office expenses and so on. I need to know if these workshops really exist, or if they cover for his cash payments, which could really be for buying blood diamonds. Do we — or does our head office — have a man in Liberia?'

'There's a team nearby investigating an oil scam,' Rowan replies without hesitation. 'I can ask them to look into it.'

'Thanks. Here are the details.' She lays her memo on his desk.

'It may take a couple of days.'

'Sure.'

★ ★ ★

Jean waylays her in the passage. 'The public relations officer of the diamond trading organisation has only just called to ask why we haven't replied to their invitation to a diamond exhibition. I told them we didn't receive one, so they've sent one round by hand. *Diamonds through the ages*. All the nobs in the diamond

127

world will be there. Plus, four top fashion houses are combining with a number of European jewellery designers to show jewels and gowns in a fashion show. What shall I tell them?'

'When is it?'

'It's tonight, I'm afraid.'

Just as well or she'd have some explaining to do.

'Tell them I'll be there. Thanks Jean. I wonder how they know we're into diamonds? Oh, by the way, I've been waiting for a call from Bombay. Did it come while I was talking to Rowan?'

'Not since I've been here.'

'Please call our Bombay branch and tell them I'm waiting for a reply.'

'Will do.'

'I'm going to be busy in the IT room for a couple of hours. You can put through my calls.'

'Will do.'

★ ★ ★

As usual, Janice is tied up with some mysterious task which suits Chris perfectly. It's simple to hack into Husam's home PC. She has all his details. She runs through recent 'Sent mail' and finds a note written to Moses Freeman about half an hour after she left the apartment that morning.

Be advised that Ben Searle is a partner and director of the London branch of an American financial investigation company. (FI Inc.). They are currently investigating diamond

laundering. For the time being, I'm cancelling all future diamond purchases. I'll keep in touch on this matter
Prince Husam Ibn al-Faisal.

The full title. Wow! What on earth is the connection between these two men? Is it quite as altruistic as Husam would have her believe? She sits deep in thought, leaning back on the chair rest, gazing at the ceiling. Husam claims that he has established seven workshops in Liberia to create the kernel of a diamond cutting industry. Lately he has sent two and half million dollars to Freeman. So Freeman must be running the show.

'You need help?' Janice's words cut short her train of thoughts.

'Thanks, but no. I'm just thinking of what I should say.'

'Fine.' Janice was soon clicking away at the keyboard.

After some thought, Chris types in the email address of Moses Freeman used by Husam and, using the prince's PC as a base, types the following message.

To: Moses Freeman. Be advised that my PA, Christine Winters, will be arriving in New York tomorrow evening on my instructions. She'll contact you soonest in order to relate a certain message which I cannot trust to the Internet. At this stage we had better communicate via Winters. Our commercial arrangement is too sensitive to be broadcast to

those with ultra-modern technology.
Prince Husam Ibn al-Faisal.

'Oh . . . beautiful! Beautiful! Beautiful!' Chris manages a faint smile, despite her sadness.

'What is it?' Janice pushes her screen glasses up over her head and stretches.

'I've had a sudden brainwave . . . well, part one of a brainwave. Part two will have to come a little later. Perhaps tonight. I'm going to a boring diamond show.'

'Good luck.' Janice gets back to the screen.

Checking her 'In Box', Chris finds a reply from their Bombay office. She has time to write a note to Rowan.

MEMO TO ROWAN METCALF
Investigator: Chris Winters

I've just received this email (copy below) from our Bombay office. Their managing partner requires your authority to put a man into the plant.

Large parcels of roughs recently purchased by Jewelrex Ltd are keeping Mohsen Sheik's staff on overtime. Two days after Sienna Sheik was kidnapped, Mohsen transferred a total of twenty million dollars to a Geneva bank from various bank accounts in Surat and Bombay, held in his and his brothers' names. We feel sure that any 'unusual' cash withdrawals or payments would be ex-Switzerland for confidentiality.

Recent analysis of some of the roughs

130

*procured and brought to us by our informer
shows that they were mined in Angola.*

*We are continuing our investigation into
this matter.*

Back in her office, Chris hums to herself as she
deals with the mail and locks away her files. She
decides to send a request for an interview with
Mohsen Sheik, but she won't hold her breath for
a reply because he's probably being watched.

Well, that's that. There isn't much more she
can do in that direction. It's up to him now.
Chris glances at her watch. Lunchtime. She
could do with a walk in the park to clear her
head. It's a habit she's picked up from Husam.
She buys a brisket sandwich and a bottle of
water and dines on a bench in St James's Park,
before walking around the lake. Some of the
leaves are turning gold, she notices with a pang
of regret. Surely this is too early. She watches the
ducks squabbling over bread thrown by a little
girl and wishes she'd brought some with her.

It is then that her tears come . . . inexplicably
and without warning. An image of Ben appears
in her mind's eye: Ben with his caring smile, the
way his face lit up when he made a smart quip,
the way he ruffled his hair when he sorted out
his thoughts. If only she'd spent more time with
him. If only he hadn't gone to the States. She
should have stayed the night and cared for him
while she had the chance. All those tears that she
hadn't been able to shed when she heard the
news surge up from some unknown depths of
her mind. It is as if Ben is sitting there beside

her. 'Ben . . . oh, Ben . . . ' she sobs. Blinded by tears she stumbles over a clump of grass and makes her way to a nearby bench. Aware of being surreptitiously watched, she dries her eyes, fumbles in her bag for sunglasses and moves on.

'I shall miss you, Ben,' she whispers. Abruptly she decides to cheer herself up by shopping for a cocktail dress. She has absolutely nothing suitable to wear to tonight's diamond show.

15

The weather has changed. The balmy late summer heatwave that has hung around for days has given way to a brisk north wind. Chris' life, too, has been touched by cold reality. She feels disturbed and vaguely frightened, but of what? She pulls up the collar of her coat and snuggles into a corner of the taxi, gazing through the window at a moving scene that's racing her into a hazardous future. She should go backwards ... to the security of a safe job where there were no unknowns and danger had never been encountered. Suddenly London's streets, once loved, seem shadowy and scary. Why would anyone want to kill Ben ... or follow her? But there's that damned white Ford Fiesta sneaking down the road behind them. Or is it? It could be any white car.

'Pull yourself together or quit the job, Chris,' she remonstrates. Perhaps she over-estimated her own courage when she took on the investigation.

The taxi pulls up outside the Goldsmith's Hall in Foster Lane, and Chris hurries inside. Handing her coat to the attendant, she suffers a momentary qualm. She's wearing a halter neck dress of pleated red muslin with frills from the bust to the hem which shimmer and shake with every movement. The dress has cost her a month's salary and she had thought she looked good until she bumped into Mum on the way out.

Mum was explicit. 'Where's your castanets, Chris?'

'You're so funny, Mum.' This is her standard answer. Don't get offended. Turn the whole thing into a joke. Mum's interest in fashion terminated in the Eighties. A little black dress reaching from her knees to her collar bone, with a pearl necklace and a scarf, is Mum's perennial outfit for an evening out.

An attendant offers her a glass of champagne, but she chooses orange juice . . . she's on duty, isn't she . . . and steps softly forward. She hardly recognises the hall, it's so full of glitter, with shimmering curtains and soft lights along the catwalk. The music is almost drowned by excited chatter. She's rubbing shoulders with the celebrity classes: Chris recognises two pop stars, a film star, a model and a famous footballer's wife. Discreetly dressed, middle-aged matrons wearing gorgeous diamond pendants, bracelets and earrings . . . one even sporting a tiara . . . sway through the crowd. Moments later a heavy hand falls on her shoulder.

She flinches, then pulls herself together. Turning, she gazes into Husam's expressive eyes. He's pleased to see her, but furious because he's pleased, and embarrassed because a remarkably beautiful girl is clinging to his arm. Trophy girlfriend, Chris decides, feeling thoroughly spiteful. Husam whispers to his companion. She gives Chris a haughty glance before disappearing into the crowd.

'Come with me.' He links his arm through hers and leads her through throngs of chattering socialites to a showcase of Arabian jewellery. Chris gapes and gasps and longs to own just one exquisite piece. Perhaps her longing shows, for two bear-like guards lounging behind the exhibit move closer to overwhelm her with their belligerence.

'Most of this was designed for Middle-Eastern potentates from the sixteenth century onwards,' Husam murmurs with satisfaction, pulling her closer to him. 'Every piece is a work of art and priceless, but seldom seen. The entire collection was brought over solely for the exhibition. Those damned sultans keep it hidden in their vaults. All these works of art, designed to adorn lovely women such as yourself, lie hidden from view in palace cellars.'

So why is he complimenting me? Chris wonders with a touch of asperity. He should dislike me, but he behaves as if nothing has happened. It doesn't make sense. What's he after?

'Listen,' he whispers. 'I can't believe the terrible news. I'm so sorry about Ben. I always liked him. Don't stay there . . . leave that place. Do you want your job back? This time it would have to be on the level.'

'Dear Husam. I'm so sorry. I'd better go.' She turns away, but his hand restrains her.

'You're so naive, Chris,' he mutters, bending very close to her. 'You're thinking in clichés and that could prove dangerous.'

'What do you mean?' Husam turns away as his

girlfriend approaches and locks her arm with his. Chris is left biting her lip as she tries to figure out his cryptic comment. Nothing makes sense.

★ ★ ★

It's time for the model show. Chris is about to find a seat when she is almost knocked over by an idiot who appears to have drunk too much.

'I'm so sorry. Did I hurt you?' He has a deep voice with an American accent.

'Don't worry. I have another foot,' she says bitterly. She looks up from her sad examination of her soiled satin shoe into a face that is frighteningly familiar. She flinches and steps away. It's him. The stalker!

'At least let me help you to a seat,' he says, taking her arm in an iron grip. She can cause a scene, or she can allow herself to be manoeuvred to a seat. Moments later she is pushed firmly into the second row and to her annoyance he sits next to her, blocking her exit.

Pretty neat exercise and pre-planned, she reckons. He can sit where he likes since the seats aren't reserved. She wonders if she should move elsewhere, but the row is filling up fast and it would be difficult to push past everyone. Besides, she won't learn much if she always runs away.

'I'm James Stark, from Boston originally, but lately I move around Africa. Most people call me Jim. How do you do,' he says, pushing his hand towards her.

She shudders and gives him a frigid nod, and

then decides to touch his hand briefly.

'And you are?'

'You know very well who I am,' she mutters sulkily.

'What do you mean?' His eyes are mocking her.

'This is our second encounter in ten days.'

'Fifth, honey. Maybe you're not as smart as you think you are. How about the Antiques Fair ... Tate Modern ... first night at the Old Vic ... it was a good production, or so I thought. Then there was the night you picked up the prince at the Cedar. Of course, I was wearing a fez, just to fit in, so I'll excuse you for not recognising me.'

She laughs without meaning to.

'Here, have this.' He hands her a programme and glances at his watch. 'They're late.'

'Why have you been following me?'

'To be honest, you intrigue me. You don't look the type to pick up rich Arabs. And then, of course, it's my job. I head up Prince Husam's security team and train his bodyguards. It was no coincidence that I was at the Cedar on the fateful night you walked into my life. I keep an eye on the prince. By the way, I thought your efforts were clumsy and contrived. I guess you haven't done that kind of thing often. New to the game, are you?'

'Why should you care?' Her mind is racing. It sounds good, but he's lying. The night he followed her from the tube station in West Finchley was before she picked up Husam. Who is he really working for and what does he want?

137

She decides to play along and find out.

'I'm surprised you spotted me,' he's saying. 'Most people don't. I have the sort of face that people don't notice.'

She isn't going argue, or to tell him about his great eyes or his sex appeal. She gives him a quick scan. His eyes are green and very expressive . . . teasing eyes. His blue-black curly hair falls forward almost to his black brows, his face is heart shaped, his lips sensual. Altogether he is one of Mother Nature's better efforts . . . Stop it Chris. He may turn you on, but he's to be avoided at all costs.

She asks: 'Just for the record, do you drive a white Ford Fiesta?'

'No. Should I? Prince Husam was very taken by you and I can see why. Might still be, for all I know. So what went wrong?'

'Nothing went wrong. And anyway, what business is it of yours?'

'I like to keep up with the local ladies of the night. Makes my job a lot easier. So who's your next target, Chris? I see you aim high.'

★　★　★

A fanfare of music brings the first model onto the catwalk. She could be Ethiopian with her jet-black skin, sculpted features and tall, meagre figure. Her dark complexion sets off the fabulous, modern designs of diamonds, set on platinum spikes, glowing like stars in the spotlights. She is sheathed in jewels and little else. Breathtakingly lovely though the model is, the jewellery outshines her. The audience gasps and claps.

Chris leans back and tries to fathom out her next move. This is like chess, she speculates. If Jim is what he claims to be, what should her reaction be? And who is she . . . solicitor or soliciting whore? Perhaps he is trying to provoke her into blurting out her motive for hitting on Husam? I'll play along, she decides as she stands up.

'Excuse me,' she says, stepping past him. 'If I were you I'd start looking for another job. Husam and I have an understanding.' Jim is still laughing when she glances back over her shoulder.

At the bar she orders a coke and fumbles in her bag for her wallet. She pulls out her picture of the stalker and scribbles on the back of it.

This man has been stalking me. He's here tonight. When I confronted him, he claimed to be James Stark, your security chief. Is this true? And if so, why are you having me followed?

Calling a waiter she points out Husam to him and asks him to deliver the note.

Dave is standing near the door, watching her. She wonders if he knows how scary he looks when he scowls. Carrying her glass, she hurries across the room to him.

'Hi Dave. Why aren't you watching the show? Have you been here long?' She watches the scowl fade as his charm takes over.

'I don't much care for the company you keep.' He beckons to a waiter without taking his eyes off her.

Chris is in no mood to be polite, but she manages a laugh, humouring him.

'If you've appointed yourself my bodyguard, I must tell you, I don't pay good wages.'

'Don't be fatuous. Jim Stark is a dangerous man and you should keep away from him. I've told you that before.'

'He collided with me, said he was drunk, and showed me to a chair.' Why was she making excuses, to him of all people?

'To be honest, I've never seen him sober. The two of you seemed pretty engrossed. Just take care, that's all . . . and don't believe a word he says.'

'He seems pleasant enough.'

'He's been bumming around Africa for years. He'll turn his hand to anything . . . deals in drugs, arms, diamonds . . . oil . . . anything to make a dishonest buck. It's his sort that gives the diamond industry a bad name.'

How about a stint as a bodyguard, she wonders. Hardly the job for a drunk. Jim looks strong, tough and very dangerous. He's kept himself fit by the look of things. He certainly isn't drunk, although he'd pretended to be when he trod on her foot. Chris has a extraordinarily keen sense of smell and she could swear that he hasn't touched a drink for the past eight hours.

'How is it that you know Prince Husam?' Dave asks.

'He was a friend of Ben's,' she answers

truthfully. 'They were at university together.'

'And Ben introduced you to him?'

'Heavens, Dave. What is this? An inquisition?'

Dave gazes moodily at her. 'You need looking after and I've voted myself the man to do the job. But then I arrive here to find you keeping company with the two most dangerous men in London.'

'Dangerous? How could Prince Husam be dangerous? He's some sort of a philanthropist.'

Dave shrugs. 'If you say so. I can't say more, other than to warn you.'

'You can't throw out accusations without backing them up with the facts.'

Dave looks around to make sure no one is listening. 'Jim Stark has no scruples whatsoever. He's a thief and a liar . . . an ex-con who did time in the filthiest prison in Africa. God knows what he picked up there. Husam is an Islamic fundamentalist, providing money to every terrorist group in Africa. He's believed to be connected to all the wrong people.'

Dave refuses to say more, so she gives up trying to prompt him and walks back to the catwalk to watch the show from a seat near the door. She sees Husam leaving, his beautiful model clinging to his arm.

Moments later the waiter approaches her. 'Madam, Prince Husam asked me to give you this. She unfolds the paper napkin wrapped around the photograph of Jim. Husam's reply is brief.

Ex-security chief as from tomorrow, is scribbled across the picture. *PS. Not guilty. H.*

141

Just before the show ends, Chris sets off for a brisk walk to St Paul's tube station. She has too much aggression to dispose of. The day's baffling events keep repeating themselves like a kaleidoscope of happenings, but it is Husam's cryptic criticism that disturbs her the most. 'You're thinking in clichés and that could prove dangerous,' he'd told her. So what on earth did he mean by that?'

16

September mists transform the night, obscuring the harsh lines of the buildings and muffling the footsteps that are undoubtedly following her . . . again. And like the mist, she drifts haphazardly, jogging lightly. How lovely the night is, a scene by Turner in shades of grey with blurred street lights creating iridescent haloes. She needs to exorcise her fears. Abruptly her mood turns to fear as she hears footsteps gaining on her.

'Miss Winters, wait a minute,' calls a disembodied voice.

'Keep away,' she mutters under her breath. Jim carries yet another more personal danger zone.

'Jesus! What a night for a marathon,' she hears him grumbling hard behind her. 'If you want to go somewhere real bad, why don't I wave down a cab?'

'Why don't you go away?' She turns and backs against the wall. 'OK. What do you want?'

'You have nothing to fear from me, Miss Winters. I merely wish to invite you for a drink. There's this club . . . a friend lent me his membership card . . . perhaps you know of it.' He shows her the card. 'We need to talk. Want to give it a try?' His eyes are firm and discerning. Not the eyes of a drop-out or a drunk. 'In your line of work you might pick up all kinds of useful leads.' He raises one eyebrow and watches her with a quizzical expression.

True enough, although not in the way he means. It was probably Jim who'd told the prince that Ben is missing. No one else knows, except Ben's family. Jim and Husam, she muses. Unlikely partners in crime. Adrenaline is pumping into her veins as her body urges her to get as far away from Jim as she can, but if she quits now she'll never learn anything.

The club is disappointing, not that it matters. They enter a wooden doorway framed with velvet curtains, and emerge in an unimposing dark hall with security cameras strategically poised above it. A machine to slot in members' codes is all that greets them. Jim presses the numbers and a painted arrow leads them to sliding doors where black-clad bouncers lurk. A passage, lit with cheap neon lights, leads to a large, dismal hall, with a stage, a huge central dance floor and tables squashed around the periphery.

Jim chooses a table as far from the dancing as he can get and calls the waiter. 'I guess you'd like champagne. That's what you girls usually drink, isn't it.'

'I'd like fresh orange juice and please cut the play-acting. You know who I am and who I work for. You've been following me for days. You know very well why I picked up Prince Husam. You told him where I was working and you showed him the security shots of me going through his files. You got me the sack.'

'That's my job, sweetie. Most of you girls have day and night jobs. It lets you buy the latest fashions. That's a pretty costly outfit you're wearing.' He's smiling, but it isn't a pleasant smile. He's trying to provoke her.

She bites back her retort. 'I like it,' she smiles sweetly.

'So tell me about Husam,' Jim says. 'Is he good in bed?'

'The best,' she says stoutly, fighting an urge to throw her drink in his face.

'Did you find what you were looking for?'

'No. I don't believe that he's any more dangerous than a modern day Joan of Arc.'

'It's your privilege to believe whatever damned nonsense you wish.' Jim's dry response startles her.

'I thought you two were in cohorts.'

'I run his security, but I don't have to trust the bastard.'

'I must say a few things surprised me,' she begins, trying to lure Jim into responding in kind.

'Such as . . . ?'

'Well, a hell of a lot of money goes through that place.'

'And where does it land up?'

'You don't know?' Chris asks sweetly.

'As I said, I'm just running his security.'

'Then it's best that we don't talk about it.' She changes the subject. 'The band's quite good.' She smiles in the face of his scowl, to show she's inviolate to his moods, in fact, to him. He has hidden agendas, but so does she. Who is he really? The question intrigues her. With the beat of the music trembling in her limbs, she notices his athletic build. The way he looks hardened and tough at times. Then his mood changes and suddenly he's laughing at himself, or at her. His hand is lying idle on the tablecloth — strong, tapered fingers. She longs to reach out and touch him.

'Shall we dance?' she asks.

'Sorry, I don't dance.'

But that's what this place is for . . . a huge empty floor in the centre, a few tables gathered around the outside. It's rather grim, not the kind of place you'd choose for a chat. Jim's not someone who does anything without a reason. So why are we here? She's about to find out, she feels sure.

'My friend says there's a good floor show here. Talk of the devil . . . Here he comes.' Jim has enough talent to look surprised.

'Hello there, Guy. This is a surprise. Where's Melanie?'

Tall, blond and grey-eyed, Guy assumes an anonymous expression.

'I was talking to friends when I saw you come in . . . thought I'd pop over.' His terse remarks sound rehearsed. There is no warmth in Guy's eyes as Jim stands up and they shake hands.

'Meet Chris Winters. Chris, this is my friend, Guy Johnson.' Guy stands around awkwardly, handling a slim briefcase as if it's getting red hot.

At least Jim's putting on a show of friendship, but from Guy's attitude she can see that they're more like office colleagues than friends. And Jim is Guy's superior, she discerns. Guy is nervous, and when Jim claps his shoulder, the gesture is more of a warning than of friendship. Clowns, both of them.

'So you work at the Provident Trust, Guy?'

He looks startled.

'Of course he does,' Jim says quickly before Guy can answer.

'I gained the strong impression that you two work together.'

In the strained silence that follows, Guy seems to have turned to stone. He's hovering beside the chair Jim is offering.

'Sit down, Guy.' It's an order. 'What'll you have?' he asks, signalling to the waiter.

Some sort of a warning is passing between them. Intuitively she senses that the meeting is contrived and too hastily rehearsed, leaving Guy unsure of his script. She's being set up, but she can't think how, or why.

'Nothing for me right now. It's a good band,' Guy says, relaxing slightly. 'Would you care to dance, Chris?'

She shakes her head.

'Don't be shy. Come on Chris. You were longing to dance. Lets me off the hook. Thanks, Guy.'

Yes, but with you, not Guy. Jim is irresistibly sexy, but it seems that he's not available. Chris frowns, thrusts out her hand and allows herself to be led to the dance floor. Guy is a good dancer and he knows how to tango, which is a welcome change. For a few minutes she lets herself flow with the music, but then she wonders why she is being manoeuvred through the dancers to the other side of the dance floor, away from Jim. Abruptly the song ends, the singer takes a bow and Chris mutters her thanks and moves away.

Guy comes to life with a snap, as if someone has pressed his button.

'Say, Chris. Wow! That was great. No, you can't go yet. I won't let you. You're a marvellous dancer. Do you like Arabic dancing? They play a lot of it here.'

Chris glances around for the absent Melanie, but all the chairs she can see are full, so where has Guy been sitting? Strange, she muses. The band comes to life with a series of wailing minor chords and Chris writhes her way backwards towards Jim, partly so he will see what a truly sexy dancer she is, but also to see what he's doing. Twisting round, she sees Guy's briefcase lying open on his chair, while her bag is on the table. How can that be? She left it on her chair.

Guy spins her back and pulls her close, his hand and body acting like a strait-jacket as his breath fans her ear.

'Where's Melanie sitting?' she says pointedly.

'Over there.' He gestures behind him.

Still clutching her in a tight embrace, Guy mutters in her ear: 'Don't get mad because Jim won't dance. His left knee and ankle are held together with pins. It hurts like hell if he tries. He was beaten up in an African jail some years back . . . had to spend six months in hospital afterwards. Let's face it, he hates clubbing . . . a real man's man.'

'What was he doing in Africa at the time?'

Guy shrugs. He seems to think he's said too

much and from then on 'maybe' answers all her questions. The music stops, Guy glances surreptitiously towards Jim. Relief shows in his eyes as he hurries her back to their table. Chris notices that her bag is back on the chair and his briefcase is back on the floor.

'It was a pleasure to watch you.' Jim says appreciatively, looking smug.

Guy says goodnight, takes his briefcase and leaves, but he's too tall to pass unnoticed and she sees his blond hair gleaming in the neon lights as he hurries through the sliding doors . . . alone.

'He's not very convincing. Is he new?' Chris asks.

Jim scans her haughtily, one eyebrow raised. 'Do you always talk in riddles, Chris?'

'He's part of your outfit, isn't he? Of course, he left without Melanie.'

'Very discerning of you, but she went home while you two were dancing.'

Chris takes her bag and goes to the cloakroom, where she tips it upside down on the counter and goes through the clutter she's managed to squeeze into it. Her credit cards are all present and correct, but perhaps Jim has taken down the numbers. Her cash is still there, her keys are untouched, but are they? There's a strange smell of methylated spirits all about. She fingers the keys. They're slightly damp and the smell is unmistakable. How strange. So that's what this evening was all about — copying her keys and the kit was in the briefcase. But why should they bother? It's easy enough to break into FI's offices, although first they'd have to get past security on the ground floor. Maybe they'd already tried and come up against her office safe. Damn! They've duplicated the key of her safe. But all it contains are her reports and transcripts from Ben's calls. Maybe Husam wants to know what Ben knew about Moses Freeman. Is there anything to worry about?

'They'll find out that I have Moses Freeman's addresses. Damn! Husam will let him know and he'll move on and I'll never find him.'

She's spoken aloud. A woman emerging from the lavatory gives her a strange look. Chris dials security at FI's offices.

'Chris Winters speaking. Listen. Someone has just copied my office keys. Yes, that's right. I'm on the sixth floor. Please don't let them get into my office safe. It's the fourth on the right down the passage. If you remember you came there to . . . Yes. Thanks. Any time from now on, I would say. I'll be right over.'

Jim stands as she reaches the table. 'Thanks Jim. I enjoyed this evening.'

We didn't have much time to talk,' he points out.

'I didn't think you were in the mood for talking.'

He grins and holds her shoulders, moving forward to embrace her.

Unable to resist, she closes her eyes as she feels his breath on her cheeks and turns her head. His lips are full and mobile and for a few seconds nothing else exists. Then he steps back abruptly.

'You're wasting your time. I'm not rich,' he mutters. 'Let's get you a cab.'

'Where to?' he asks, as a taxi moves towards them.

'I think you know my home address as well as I do, Jim,' she says sweetly.

★ ★ ★

Her cab sets off along St James's Street, but she redirects the driver into Piccadilly and down Duke Street to their new and imposing office block overlooking St James's Square. By the time she arrives, it's all over. The intruder has been scared off, but he got away.

On the drive home, Chris tries to sort out her muddled impressions and suspicions. Jim has tried to sell blood diamonds to Trans-Africa, or so David told her. He has a criminal background and bad reputation. Suddenly he has a job as a top security officer in the head office of a major bank. Then there's Guy, who clearly works with Jim, or for Jim. How did Jim get this job, she wonders. He's certainly not the drunk Dave takes him for. He's fit and smart. Perhaps that's his cover, but for what? How did he know that Ben was missing? It all points to some sort of a liaison between Husam, Jim and Moses Free-man. And Freeman was undoubtedly involved with blood diamonds and Ben's death.

It's two a.m. by the time she gets home. She's leaving for New York in the morning, but she can sleep on the plane. She packs and sets the alarm, but sleep evades her once again.

Images appear as if on an IMAX movie screen and she's propelled headlong towards them. Ben being strung up. Sienna screaming in the van. Jim's eyes glowing with ironic amusement in the darkened nightclub. She can't see the pattern, but there must be one. She can't give up now, there's too much at stake.

She sleeps fitfully and wakes to pain and to moonlight flickering on her face. She turns away, but her room seems so light. Pain pounds through her temples. Damn! All she needs is a headache when she has to have her wits about her. She sits up and winces as the pressure intensifies, her neck has stiffened and she is feeling nauseous. She must go down to the kitchen where Mum, who is prone to headaches, keeps aspirins in a drawer. Taking her torch, she pushes her feet into her slippers and creeps downstairs, trying to avoid the creaky places, but she stumbles once or twice because she's so dizzy.

Reaching the kitchen, she is about to reach for the light switch when she sees a movement beyond the window. She switches off the torch and peers through the glass. The moon is full, the night sky clear, and patches of white light contrast with inky black shadows. But surely someone is there. Right there outside the window, almost close enough to touch. A tall, thin figure seems to be standing in the shadow under the Laurel tree, not two metres away, and he seems to be staring straight at her. Surely that's not possible. It must be a trick of the light.

She shrinks back against the dresser, seeing

nothing she can hide behind. A split second later, she freezes as a dark shape moves out of the shadow, creeping across the garden path towards her. Fumbling behind her for the drawer, she grasps the carving knife.

Dressed in black jeans and a polo neck shirt, the intruder looks sinister and larger than life as he steps into the moonlight. Dazed by pain, and lack of sleep, she stands helplessly watching him placing his feet down cautiously, step by silent step, as he keeps on coming. His shadow falls across the kitchen floor. Chris claps her hand over her mouth. Who is he? And why is he here?

Then she pulls herself together and steps towards the glass. For a long moment they stand stock still, staring at each other. He's tall, thin, and dark-skinned, with straight black hair, a long, angular face and a prominent nose. He smiles and puts up one hand, as if to hold off any reaction, but his smile is more frightening than his scowl as he backs away towards the gate. And then he's gone.

He hadn't looked like a thug. Quite the reverse. Could he be al-Qaeda? And with Ben murdered, had they turned their attention to her? Thoughts of her mother's safety almost persuade Chris to call the police, but he's gone now and Ben had told her to avoid calling them, if at all possible.

Chris checks the windows and the locks and goes back to bed. There's no point in trying to sleep now. She'll sleep on the plane. She tries to read a novel, but it's hard to concentrate as the night's events keep surging into her mind.

Finally she puts the book away and jots down all the relevant details of her investigation so far. She can't see a pattern, but there must be one. She's stumped for ideas, but she can't give up now, there's too much at stake.

'I'll get there,' she murmurs. But the intriguing question remains: how can she out-fox this clever bunch of crooks?

17

A man is waving a placard bearing her name. Could that be Jon? If so, she can see why Sharon married him. He's a Hollywood version of an ancient Pharaoh and appealing enough if you like florid looks. He looks cheerful, despite Ben's death. A young woman leans over the railing beside him looking grave and trying to smile with pitiful intensity. The strong family features, so right for Ben, make his sister look like a witch. Right now her eyes are puffy with dark crescents beneath them. Chris waves and walks towards them.

Sharon clasps Chris across the barrier and kisses her on both cheeks, enveloping her in an aura of perfume and costly cosmetics. 'Charges against Jonathan have been dropped. He's in the clear. We heard this morning. Ben did that for us,' she says tearfully.

'I'm so glad, Sharon. And I'm sorry for your loss. I haven't been at FI long, but I was very fond of Ben.'

'Ben was murdered because of what he did for us. Oh God! I'll never forgive Jon. Never!' Her body begins to shake as she sobs into a handful of tissues.

Sharon's emotional greeting throws Chris off balance, but Jon steps forward and hugs her as if she were family.

'They were very close,' he whispers. 'I'm in the

dog house over this business. We haven't spoken for days.'

He takes hold of her trolley while Sharon grabs her arm. Feeling manhandled, Chris allows herself to be steered out of the airport and into an alien environment where it is still morning and the mood is bitter. Chris wishes she wasn't staying with the family, but when she called to tell them she'd be in New York, Sharon had all but exploded.

'Visit . . . convenient . . . what sort of talk is this? You'll stay here. Whatever we can do will be too little.'

The motorway is snarled up for the first ten minutes, but once Jon steers his Volvo XC-90 onto the highway to New Jersey, they speed south to Teaneck without interruption. Nevertheless it is a painful drive, punctuated by Sharon's sobs as she looks straight ahead, her swollen face set and controlled, her eyes brave and condemning.

'Did Ben tell you of our role in this nasty business?' Chris asks, attempting to alleviate some of the tension. 'We're investigating diamond laundering. That's why I'm here.'

'The crafty bastard never said a word about that.' Jon breaks off as another point occurs to him. 'So it's possible that Ben's murder has nothing to do with me?' His trauma is lightening, Chris can see from the set of his shoulders.

'My guess is that Ben was murdered because he knew too much, or he stumbled upon something relevant, perhaps when he was seeing Freeman.'

Jon swerves suddenly and steers on to the highway's shoulder. He brakes and covers his face with his hands.

'Not guilty,' he says quietly. 'You hear that, Sharon. Not fucking guilty.' He rests his head against the steering wheel. After a long silence, he straightens up.

Chris has not yet shaken off her own heebie-jeebies. It takes a while to trust her voice not to waver.

'Jon, tell me, do the FBI have any idea where Moses Freeman is staying? Have you let them know how you and Freeman used to arrange your meetings?'

'Good God! Did Ben tell you? No. Absolutely not. I'm out of that mess. I want to stay out of it.'

'But then how will they pick him up?'

Jon doesn't answer.

'So what happened exactly?'

'It was like this . . . ' Jon begins, as he manoeuvres himself into the fast lane. 'It was around seven p.m. That right Sharon? It was around seven, wasn't it?'

'Yes. Perhaps even a little later.'

Suddenly they are talking to each other. Chris sighs with relief.

'A man came to the door wearing a cabby's uniform. He had a note from Freeman telling Ben he would take him to someone who knew all there was to know about diamond laundering.'

'I didn't like the look of him,' Sharon interrupts.

'What's a cab driver supposed to look like? You tell me. They're mainly immigrants from all over

. . . Cuba, Albania, Israel even. The note said that Ben should bring a thousand dollars in cash. I think that's what clinched the matter in Ben's mind. Paying for information was something he knew all about. Otherwise, well, maybe he wouldn't have gone so willingly. He followed the driver in his hired car. He was going to go straight on to the airport afterwards.'

'We never saw him again.' Sharon gives a small, anguished cry. 'Not until I had to go and identify his body.'

★ ★ ★

They sit in silence, engulfed in their gloomy thoughts. Jon slows down in a wide, leafy road in Teaneck, where the houses are costly, yet the locals have managed to hang on to a village-green atmosphere. Next minute they are driving through wrought-iron gates towards a rambling bungalow, set behind a neat garden, where children's play apparatus fills most of the lawn.

Two children run towards the fence and a woman in a striped uniform gets up heavily and walks to the gate. One of them, a toddler with dark hair and eyes, and a marked resemblance to Jon, runs towards them and hangs on to Sharon's legs. A thin, pretty girl of about six smiles shyly at Chris.

'Welcome to our home, Chris.' Sharon gives her another hug and she is drawn into the house. 'Meet Ruth and Barry. And this is Bridget, our Nanny.' Bridget gives a broad, mirthless grin, grabs Barry and strides down the passage.

Chris nods and smiles. 'Two children. How wonderful.'

'There's another on the way.' Sharon flushes deeply.

'I envy you.'

Sharon looks dubious. 'Surely not you. Ben told us you're the ultimate, successful career woman.'

Her words are strangely unnerving. Chris is brought face to face with her perennial problem: whether to compromise and settle for her best option for the sake of raising a family, or whether to wait and hope that chance will bring her ideal man to her door. At times, in despair, she seriously considers becoming a single parent.

'So what's it like being at home as a full-time mother. Ben told me you were a copywriter at a top London agency. Do you miss the buzz?'

'Sometimes. Motherhood is a full-time job, but at times I get lonely. Kids are lovely, but you can't have a conversation with them, at least not yet,' she confides. 'But I happen to believe that my children need a proper home until they reach ten. The plan is that I start writing, but I never have a moment to spare.'

As if sensing her longing, Sharon changes the subject. 'Perhaps you'd like a snack . . . or breakfast?'

'I couldn't eat. Do forgive me. I had lunch on the plane.'

'I expect you'll want to sleep this afternoon, otherwise you'll get jet lag. By the time we sit down to dinner it's two a.m. in London.'

159

'I have to go out on an errand for Rowan.' She glances at her watch to hide her face. She hates lying, but if she tells Sharon that she's going to see Freeman she knows Sharon will freak out. 'I'll see you later.'

⋆ ⋆ ⋆

The taxi arrives promptly at eleven, but Sharon waylays Chris as she reaches the front door.

'You're going to see that Freeman guy, aren't you?' she whispers. 'If you know where to find him, it's your duty to tell the police. Freeman's lethal, Chris. He lured Ben to his death. Please don't do this.'

Chris interrupts her. 'If I find Freeman I'll tell the police at once. Promise. But my duty to Ben is to solve this case.' She breaks off wondering why guilt always switches her into a fighting mode.

'You're mad. What drives you like this?'

'Myself,' Chris mouths quietly as she gets into the taxi. She should have lied. Now Sharon will worry all afternoon.

Trying to switch off and relax, she leans back to admire the neat homes and open gardens. Eventually the lush, middle-class prosperity comes to an abrupt halt. They move off the highway and Chris finds herself in an alien world where skinny youths with predatory eyes hang around in groups, jeering at each other. The taxi weaves through rows of shabby rooming houses where the streets provide a playground for the local kids.

Humidity is high, and even the air seems polluted.

'This is it, Ma'am.' The driver brakes in front of a shabby house in a row of similar buildings. The youths cluster around them.

'Do you want to get out here? You sure you've got the right place?'

'Yes. Thanks. Can you wait?'

'Here's my card. Call me when you're through. If I'm busy I'll pass you back to the office.'

Waves of electrical shocks are running up and down her spine as she mounts the steps. The door is locked, but there are dozens of name plates, some so dusty you can hardly read them. '*Jasmen, for all enquiries*,' she finds at last. She's having second thoughts about going in there, but the taxi is moving away. The boys are watching her curiously. There's only one way to go and that's onwards. She presses her finger on the grimy bell.

★ ★ ★

'Who's there?' The woman's voice is deep and slightly foreign.

'Mrs Jasmen?' she calls. 'I'd like to see your brother, Moses Freeman. He's expecting me. I'm Chris Winters.'

'You'd better come in. Ground floor, first door on the left. Shut the front door properly. This place is full of rogues.'

Chris walks inside and closes the door carefully behind her. Standing alone in the

161

gloomy hall, she fights off a moment of panic. She should have called the police and given them Freeman's address. It's madness to come here. The hall is dark, the air fetid and her stomach is contracting with painful spasms. Steeling herself she pushes open the door and steps forward into a shadowy hall, lit by a dim light-bulb hanging from the centre of the ceiling. A single door faces her. No one opens it, so she pushes it wide and stands blinking in the sudden light and relative opulence.

As the door closes behind her, Chris takes a deep breath and recovers her poise. Briefly she scans the polished wooden floors, zany woven rugs, tribal masks, two good paintings of African wildlife . . . all the evidence of a comfortable lifestyle and a dollop of homesickness. Mrs Jasmen appears to own the house and from the door plaques it seems that she leases apartments. Presumably the house purchase was financed by Freeman's diamond profits.

'Jesus,' she whispers, as the door opposite swings open.

There is nothing welcoming about the woman towering in the doorway. Wearing four-inch heels and a bulky turban, she is well on the way to six-foot-six — a massive figure of a woman with a skin so dark she might be Ethiopian. A jewelled crucifix on a heavy gold chain hanging around her neck gives no sense of comfort, for her fierce eyes blaze with hostility.

Have they found out that she is not from Husam at all? Chris feels deadly cold, but then she notices beads of perspiration gathering on the woman's forehead. She, too, is afraid. Presumably, they have something to hide from Husam, which might give her the edge over them. She decides to harp on finances.

'How did you find us? Prince Husam does not have our address.'

'He must have made it his business to get it, for he gave it to me,' Chris retorts.

She makes a quick decision. 'Mrs Jasmen, I'm merely a messenger. Prince Husam has a number of questions and instructions which I must put to your brother, Moses Freeman. I also bring some information from the prince.'

Jasmen bites her lip. 'We are very private people. We don't expect folks to come knocking on our door. My brother won't be pleased about this.' Her surreptitious glance at the door through which she has just entered, tells Chris that Freeman is out there listening.

'Prince Husam informed you of my coming visit. Mr Freeman needs to hear the information I have for him. It's vital for his safety.'

Her voice sounds normal, which is comforting. Only she can hear her heart knocking against her ribs. She tries to slow her breathing. There isn't much she can do about her dry lips.

18

When Moses Freeman enters the room, Chris flinches and her fear almost gives her away. Hearing her panting breath, she attempts to breathe normally, but it's not easy. Freeman is scanning her with a mistrustful expression. He suspects! Even worse is his sinister appearance. Freeman is a beanpole of a man, taller than his sister and his grey top hat increases his height. He's dressed for a funeral . . . hers, perhaps.

Apart from his long jacket and striped tailored trousers, his hands are cluttered with several large rings, which she guesses are worn as knuckle-dusters rather than for decorative purposes. Heavy gold chains hang around his neck. Freeman's complexion is like his sister's, sooty black, but his eyes are disturbing, for his near-black irises float like beach balls in a silt-stained estuary. Murderers' eyes, Chris decides, but on second thoughts malaria and hepatitis are probably responsible. His grim appearance is heightened by his droopy black moustache and the deep lines around his nose and lips. Fiftyish, Chris reckons. Despite his age, he looks a tough and dangerous man.

'Good afternoon, Miss Winters. Did you have a good journey?' The sound of his voice, so unexpectedly high-pitched, brings goose-pimples to her arms.

'Thank you, yes,' she says, entering a world of

unreality. For a moment she almost believes her role. She has so many roles . . . for Freeman, for Husam, for Jim . . . now why had she thought of Jim? Freeman ushers her to a chair and sends his sister to make coffee.

'So Husam has chosen a beautiful woman to be his emissary. These Arabs . . . ' He leans over her and leers suggestively. His laugh reveals tobacco-stained teeth.

Bastard! Freeman has riled her, but she will fight him obliquely, she decides there and then.

'Apart from being a lawyer, I also oversee the prince's finances. I'm here to report back on how the prince's investment of two and a half million dollars is being utilised. Naturally I need to examine your projected cash flow to determine the cost of each new job created . . . the prince is waiting for these statistics.'

'He said nothing of this to me.' Freeman, who is clearly frightened, takes out a handkerchief and wipes his damp forehead. 'It's far too early for this kind of exercise.'

'It's normal business procedure.' Chris savours her revenge.

'Let me tell you about my dream. I see the day when the sidewalks of our Monrovian streets will be littered with simple workshops, like the diamond quarter of Surat. I see a future where entire families will sit crouched over their wheels, polishing our country's diamonds, working their way out of poverty and Third World status.' His eyes become glazed as his voice rings with conviction.

He's told this story often enough, but he's

reaching the climax, she senses after a few minutes. As for the glow in his eyes . . . is it missionary zeal or fury?

She decides to placate him. 'Prince Husam is very excited about your dream.'

'No longer a dream since the prince got involved.'

Is that the only connection between them? Is Freeman just another tool for Husam to refashion his beloved Africa? No wonder he warned Freeman about their investigation. For some reason, this pleases her. But where does Husam's security officer, Jim Stark, fit in?

'Those greedy mining magnates maintain that Africans have no talent for cutting and polishing diamonds,' Freeman is saying. 'But I say that it is a learned skill, so give the tribesmen the chance to learn it. The prince agrees with me.'

'Yet you also sell blood diamonds in the States.'

Freeman battles to conceal his shock. Obviously he keeps his vocations in separate compartments.

'I have to live, Miss Winters.'

She watches a trickle of sweat weave its crooked path down his cheek.

'I have twelve workshops established in Monrovia. Naturally I've used a great deal of my own money.'

'I don't understand why Prince Husam feels it's imperative to use conflict diamonds. You offered him some excellent diamond pipes which could be purchased at a good price, or so he told me, yet he feels that the bottom might fall out of the market. Why is that?'

Freeman shrugs and laughs. 'There are vast new finds in Canada, my dear. You must know that. Meanwhile, we're both doing what we can to help Mother Africa.'

Is he for real? Chris stirs impatiently and moves to another angle.

'You must understand that these confidences can't be voiced over the Internet.' She glances at him, but his face is expressionless.

'Prince Husam is being pressurised by agents of al-Qaeda to assist them with their diamond laundering network. He wants to know if you are being pressurised, too.'

Freeman laughs with genuine amusement.

'In my opinion, Bin Laden has franchised his Islamic revolution copying American business methods.'

'You mean like fried chicken?'

'Exactly. He's produced a recipe which encourages and inspires every fragmented Islamic group with a gripe. Their diamond laundering is localised and small scale compared with . . . ' Tantalisingly, he breaks off.

'Compared with whom, Mr Freeman?'

Freeman's eyes glitter uneasily. Once again his grey handkerchief makes its appearance.

'Every wall has ears, they have agents all over Africa. Make sure that Prince Husam doesn't come up against these people. That would be a dangerous mistake which could cost him dearly.' Freeman's voice is hardly more than a whisper.

'Is that a threat, Mr Freeman?'

He glances sharply at her. 'No, of course not.

Prince Husam is my benefactor. Please believe me, I know very little about this criminal organisation except that they are dangerous.'

'That's strange! Prince Husam told me that you know all there is to know about diamond laundering.'

'That's not true . . . '

He breaks off as his sister walks in bearing coffee and a ledger which she lays on the table. The rustle of fabric sounds so loud in the silence. Chris notes the warning glances passing between them as she opens the ledger. Then Jasmen sways out of the room.

'Just copy whatever you like.' He sounds furious. 'Do you have paper?'

She nods and opens her briefcase. The silence becomes more ominous as Chris examines the figures. Ten workshops have been set up on the outskirts of Monrovia employing fifty people, forty of which are learning to polish diamonds. Soon she becomes so involved that she hardly hears Freeman get up and leave the room. Shortly afterwards she hears Freeman's voice bellowing from the room next door. He's demanding to speak to Prince Husam.

'Oh God!' Her fear is acting like a winch, tightening her joints and hurting her neck. Should she get out now? Minutes later, Freeman returns looking grim. 'I called Prince Husam. I'm concerned at his interest in the laundering network.'

She shudders and tries to hide this. Has he noticed?

'Unfortunately he's away.'

She exhales silently while Freeman sits and carefully refolds the neat line in his trousers. He admires his shoes and straightens his cuffs.

'Prince Husam asked for more information about the current laundering routes.'

He gives a funny little mock bow. 'I'll do my best.' Adding: 'Perhaps you'd like to take notes.'

'About sixty per cent of the high-quality gems mined in Sierra Leone are smuggled to the Middle East by Lebanese immigrants living in Liberia. It's the same story in every diamond producing country in Africa. Only geography and idealism change. Arab fundamentalists launder diamonds to buy arms for creating unrest in the Middle East. The Russians launder diamonds to set themselves up in the West. Various states support their civil wars with diamonds. Many of the best cutters in Europe sell forged certificates, but that's too costly for run-of-the-mill diamonds. Everyone has an axe to grind. Marketing diamonds is a dirty business.' He leans back, looking smug. 'Many of them are idealists working for a cause. Those who do it for profit only are the dirtiest of all.'

'And who are they?'

Freeman seemed to be working himself up into a temper. Flecks of white show on his fleshy lips. 'I can't answer your question. Let's move on. Would you believe me if I told you that campaign donors to the current US Bush administration have interests in Liberian dia-monds. Could that be why the US government sent troops to Liberia recently!' He goes on at

169

length about the Americans.

Chris decides to cut Freeman's rhetoric. 'Besides the Russian Mafia, the Lebanese, al-Qaeda, and various independent terrorist groups, who else is laundering diamonds?'

'I've told you all I know.'

'You aren't being straight with me. You're protecting someone, or some organisation, perhaps because you're terrified of them, or maybe you're one of them.'

Freeman makes an obvious effort to stay cool. 'Miss Winters, you mentioned a certain warning . . . '

'Yes. Of course . . . you sold illicit diamonds to Jonathan Bronstein and he was caught and banned by the Kimberly Process. His brother-in-law, Ben Searle, flew over from London to see you, to get a certificate of origin for the diamonds. You were successful and Bronstein is off the hook . . . '

'How did the prince get this information?' Suddenly he's looking ugly. Has he guessed who she is?

'Two nights ago Searle was found hanging under a bridge. He was last seen by his family when a stranger, claiming to be your driver, brought a note requesting that Searle should come with him to meet you. He said you had information for him.'

Freeman leans back blaspheming furiously in some foreign tongue.

'Wait!' She raises her hand. 'The police have opened a murder docket and they are looking for you. Naturally, Prince Husam wants your

170

side of the story. He suggests you leave the States at once.'

Freeman turns pale. His eyes are haggard. It's not a pretty sight.

'And you sat here wasting my time. You must leave . . . at once.'

Freeman grabs her elbow, hauls her from the chair and pushes her towards the door.

'Return to London and tell Prince Husam to wait until I contact him. I'll call from the airport.'

Chris finds herself back on the pavement in record time.

He's innocent of murder, at least, she decides. No one could be that good an actor. Freeman was shattered by the news and absolutely terrified.

Chris walks rapidly down the street towards a shop where she feels safe enough to call a taxi. The youths tag along, but she senses that they're merely curious.

19

Chris is feeling pleased as the taxi draws up outside the Bronstein's home. Her trip has been successful. She can shop around tomorrow without feeling guilty. As she steps out and pays, she notices Jon jump up from his garden seat and hurry towards her. He's clearly angry.

'Sharon suspects that you saw Moses Freeman this afternoon. Did you?' Clutching her elbow he hurries her into the house.

Chris is expecting trouble, but not this fast. She takes off her coat and hangs it on a peg in the porch before answering.

'Actually, yes. That's what I came for.'

Sharon joins them looking worried.

'You're mad. Well, that settles it. You're getting out of New York tonight. Don't take this the wrong way, Chris, you're always welcome here, but right now I won't relax until you're safely back in London.' Jon's words sound friendly, but his eyes tell a different story and throw her into a state of anxiety.

'But I've only just arrived, Jon. I have other appointments here.'

The most pressing of which are with Manhattan's department stores. She's promised herself a few hours of shopping. After all, it's Saturday tomorrow.

Jon shrugs. 'Next time! I took the liberty of checking the flights back and I've booked you tentatively on British Airways at eight p.m. You must be there two hours beforehand, so maybe you'd better pack your gear.'

Annoyed by his imperious tone, Chris glances at her watch. 'I can move into a hotel . . . really, Jon, that would be better.'

'I feel responsible for you. I'll only relax when you're back in London.'

'You're not hearing me.' She turns to Sharon for moral support. 'I have work to do.'

'Of course you're staying. Don't listen to Jon. He's over-reacting.' Sharon's voice has a reproachful tinge. 'Besides, I've prepared a special dinner, a traditional Jewish meal.'

'It's not as if it's forever,' Jon argues, trying to placate Sharon. 'Chris can come back in a few weeks time, but only when Freeman is safely locked up.'

Chris longs to tell Jon to mind his own business, but she knows he means well. Freeman is innocent of Ben's murder, she feels that intuitively, but Jon needs facts, not intuition. At the same time she's unwilling to increase the family tensions.

'Listen, Chris!' Jon makes an obvious effort to control his irritation. 'Freeman knows where Ben was staying. Did you give him the impression that you worked with Ben?'

'Absolutely not.' Unless Freeman gets through to Husam, which he will, and probably has. Her twinge of fear is quickly quelled. 'He could find out,' she adds humbly. The reason for Jon's panic hits home hard. 'Oh my God! I didn't think along those lines at all. But listen . . . Freeman didn't know that he was implicated in Ben's death . . . he didn't even know that Ben had died.' Suddenly she chokes on the word and blinks hard while she struggles to recover.

'Freeman turned pale when I told him about the note the cab driver brought. It was weird. He was terribly shaken . . . he couldn't get rid of me quickly enough. He insisted that I leave New York at once.'

Jon's eyes burn with anger. 'If it wasn't Freeman, then who else knew about Ben's investigation? Or where Ben was staying? Or the fact that Ben had seen Freeman and asked a whole lot of questions about diamond laundering? In other words, who or what are we up against? We've only seen the driver.'

Now Sharon looks scared, too. 'Ben was a fighter. He was in the Israeli army, just like Jon. He wouldn't be overcome by that skinny old man.'

'You stuck your neck out by going there, Chris. That's your right, but this is our home and the kids' safety is uppermost in our minds.'

Jon is trying to be reasonable, which makes Chris feel even worse. Suddenly she's overcome with remorse. 'I'll leave right away . . . and I'll take a taxi . . . give me twenty minutes.'

'Nonsense.' Jon calls after her. 'We'll take you to the airport. It'll be a treat for the kids.'

The decision is taken out of their hands when Barry has a nosebleed and throws up. Jon is reluctant to leave Sharon alone, so finally he calls a taxi.

While Sharon is putting Barry to bed, Chris takes Jon aside.

'Listen, Jon. I'm sorry, but someone has to tell the FBI about the note the taxi driver brought to Ben, and exactly how Ben found out where Freeman lives. It's vital. You or I must . . . '

'Leave it to me,' he says distractedly. 'I didn't want to get this diamond business publicised. Later, when they told us Ben was murdered . . . well . . . having left it so late, I didn't know how to tell them the truth.'

Chris packs and goes to find Sharon, who is in the nursery looking upset. 'I brought some London presents for the children . . . '

'Thank you, Chris. I'm sorry. Jon's paranoid about the kids.'

'Who can blame him? Look . . . '

'Here's the taxi, Chris,' Jon calls.

'Say goodbye to them for me.' She hugs Sharon, promises to return soon, and hurries to the taxi.

'Change of plan,' Chris tells the driver, as they leave the house. 'Find me a hotel in Manhattan.' She leans back, exhales with a whoosh, and consciously tries to relax.

Manhattan is jam-packed and finally she has to settle for a costly suite in the tower block of the New York Palace Hotel, where she dines alone in splendour and yawns all the way back to her suite on the thirty-fifth floor. She's been up for twenty-four hours. She places the 'do not disturb' sign on her door handle and goes to bed.

★ ★ ★

175

Chris wakes with a sense of excitement. From her corner suite she has two marvellous views stretching to far horizons shrouded in purple mists. From this height, the streets, the cars and the people, resemble figures in an animated toy town, while the cathedral far below looks like a child's flat building block. She's loving it all and she can't wait to get out there. She'll skip breakfast, she decides, as she dresses hurriedly.

By late afternoon, Chris and her spare cash have parted company; she's used all her available credit and she's had to buy another suitcase. She returns to the hotel to shower and change in time for her reservation at The Four Seasons, where she's booked a table for one. She's running late, but she lingers at the window to watch the sun, a hazy crimson globe, sink over the misty Hudson river. She's crazy about New York and sad to leave.

Chris is dreamily listening to trickling water, admiring the decor and enjoying her Parma ham and melon with ice-cold, dry Californian wine when she looks up, startled by a sense of being watched. She's right. Jim Stark, remittance man, ex-Bostonian, ex-con, currently broke, or at any rate beached on Husam's shores, is staring at her from across the room. He waves and weaves his way through the tables. She feels trapped. How has he found her? And why should he want to find her? And how did he know she is here in New York? Even the Bronsteins think she is back in London. She feels like a hunted fox, but there are no convenient bolt holes to hand, so she pretends not to notice him.

He pauses by her table. 'What a coincidence! If it isn't a certain lady of the night and self-proclaimed spook, sitting here looking so demure . . . no glitter eye-shadow, no split skirt, no deep *décolleté*. Clearly you're not on the game this evening. Taking a break, Miss Winters? Or may I call you Chris?'

'You're being offensive. I don't believe in coincidences. How and why did you find me?'

'May I join you?'

'Only if you answer my questions . . . truthfully.'

He sits down and beckons to the waiter. 'I followed your flagrant paper chase. You were willing me to find you.' He's smiling, but his eyes are derisive and remote.

'I was not. What a cheek! What paper chase?'

'Showering your credit cards all over Manhattan. Fortunately I have a friend working at the bank.'

'How did you know I was here?'

'Your hotel porter was persuaded to tell me.'

'But no one knows I'm staying at that hotel.'

'No one?' He's mocking her. 'You must have told someone, since I know. Besides, you've picked up more tails than a Chinese kite. Even for a zany, untrained investigator you seem curiously unaware of your surroundings.'

He's talking nonsense, of course. She longs to pummel his grinning face into dust.

'You copied my keys and sent a man around to search my office.'

'You must think your files are very valuable for me to go to such extraordinary efforts. What could you possibly know that I don't know?'

The waiter arrives to take Jim's order. For a while they discuss the menu. For an ex-security guard he seems to have extravagant tastes. Does Jim know she lost him his job? she wonders.

'Why are you following me? What do you want from me?'

'I'm merely doing my job. Prince Husam needs to know why FI Inc. are so interested in his bank and his business. Perhaps you'd like to tell me.'

Jim's not as smart as he thinks he is, Chris decides, leaning back and smiling softly. Husam knows very well what she's investigating because she told him, which means that Jim's lying. Besides, he's been sacked.

'I'll trade off,' she replies. 'Tell me who's following me.'

Jim's supercilious smile fades. 'Two men. So far I've only managed to check out one of them.' Suddenly he's serious. 'He's dark-skinned and bearded. Notice anyone like that? When he's not tailing you he teaches Pashto part-time, mainly freelancing, and he translates from Pashto to English and vice-versa for publishers when he gets the chance.'

'That's crazy. Are you sure?'

'Sure I'm sure.'

'And the other one?'

'I don't know yet. Stick around and I'll sort it out for you.'

'But why should I, and why should you want to? Why did you follow me here? Try to tell the truth this time. Husam knows about my investigation. Besides, you don't work there anymore.'

'Thanks to you. It's obvious, isn't it? You're lovely, clever, resourceful and I long to get to know you better . . . much better. I'd hate you to get hurt.'

'That sounds like a threat. I have no desire to engage in silly games with you,' she says primly as she beckons to the waiter and stands up.

'It wasn't a threat. Please don't go. I meant what I said. Look, let's get one thing straight,' he says, leaning towards her across the table. 'I knew you were on an investigation when I watched you hit on Prince Husam. It was clumsily done and I guessed it was a first attempt. I followed you, and found you'd just joined FI. With your qualifications you could only be a financial investigator.

'It didn't take long to find out that you'd been appointed PA to Ben Searle, but he has been showing unusual interest in al-Qaeda . . . going to lectures, buying books, visiting the mosques and talking to Islamic fundamentalists, followed by a visit to Afghanistan three months ago. It seems to me that you're continuing with Searle's investigation.'

So Jim was investigating Ben Searle even before she joined the company. His interest in her makes sense now. If he's not lying this time.

★　★　★

Is Jim waiting for an answer? Chris isn't sure. She isn't concentrating, for Jim, with his

179

brooding dark eyes and his pensive expression, is throwing her off balance. He turns her on and for Chris this is a major disaster. She steers clear of any situation where she's not in control. She's not a power freak . . . nothing like that. It's just that she trusts herself and no one else. Mum's the trusting kind and look what happened to her. She can't think why Jim should have this disastrous effect on her. Perhaps it's his eyes. There's a reckless glint there, a hint of smug assurance, as if he's always one step ahead. He's ruthless and he's crooked.

'This is no job for a young woman, however smart a lawyer she may be,' Jim is saying. 'With Searle dead, you're in the front line. Any normal, full-blooded American male would worry about you.'

'What on earth do you use for a pretext when you're tailing a man?'

'Much the same, darling,' he murmurs in a falsetto voice.

She laughs. She can't help it, and she can't stop either. He's stopped pretending and it's a relief to be off her guard momentarily. 'You're an idiot.'

'How about letting this idiot show you a little of Manhattan's night-life . . . a night on the tiles? Come on . . . how about it?'

Of course Jim doesn't fancy her. A new angle occurs to Chris: what if his security job is merely a cover. What if he and Husam are running a criminal gang? What if he had Ben killed? She must play along, she decides, and sooner or later he'll slip up and she'll learn just how he fits into her enquiry.

'Maybe.' She sits down slowly and tries out a sexy smile which doesn't seem to work too well. Jim raises one eyebrow and gives her an amused look that zooms straight into her psyche.

He knows exactly what he's doing to me. Perhaps it's his ruthlessness that turns me on. Danger always entices me. It's like taking a leap from the top trapeze . . . or a bungee jump . . . that split second as you fall . . . like a death wish . . . I feel it now . . . I'm on a high because he's irresistible . . . and deadly. She decides to ignore his crass pretensions to find her irresistible.

'I'm beginning to have more faith in you, Chris. You always leave yourself an escape route. What do we have to do to get rid of the *maybe*?'

'Tell me more about yourself before I decide,' she prevaricates.

'Where would you like me to start?'

'At the beginning. Why not?'

'OK. As a kid, there were few things I hated more than fish pie and rice pudding. At school we got both every Friday.'

'What school was that?'

He shrugs. 'A special school for gifted children in Washington. They're not short of gifted children around those parts. Later, I specialised in East European languages. My mother was Russian, so I had a head start. My father owned a Chicago-based tyre factory. He met my mother when he took part in a marketing campaign in Moscow. When my parents split, my mother returned to Russia, but my father wouldn't let

181

me leave the States. Not even for holidays. I blamed him for the split, so we didn't get along too well.'

'And was it his fault?'

'I don't have your legal mind . . . You lawyers seem to be able to pinpoint the truth, depending upon your stance, but I can't answer your question.

'When Father died, he left the factory in the hands of a management group. I became a remittance man, bumming around, doing very little, while the so-called management ruined the business and inflation ate into what was left of my income. I made a bit here and there, buying and selling. Still do.'

'But why Africa?'

'That's where my heart is.'

So he has one . . . or so he claims.

'Guy mentioned that you spent nine months in prison in Equatorial Guinea. Fortunately you were rescued.'

'Guy said that?' He tries to conceal his anger.

'It served me right. I was drunk . . . in an Islamic state. I was flung into a hellhole, euphemistically called a prison. By the time I was rescued I was pretty badly beaten up and emaciated.'

'You were lucky to get out in time. Who rescued you?'

'A visiting Imam contacted the nearest vicar, who called in a group of Christian missionaries. They paid good money donated by the faithful to rescue this miserable sinner, along with several others. Three of the rescued prisoners had to have their feet amputated. They had gangrene from the filth we were forced to stand in.'

'Oh, my God! How horrible!'

'An episode never to be repeated.' He shudders.

The shudder is real. Chris could swear to that, but as Jim spins out his tale of bumming through Africa, she decides that nothing else is real. How could he be a drifter. He is far too smart. She will have to accept his silly stories and wait for the truth to reveal itself.

'Lately I decided I needed a better income, so I borrowed the cash to start a security company. Unfortunately it failed, leaving me with a stack of debts, so when I saw the job of security chief advertised, I applied for it. Satisfied?'

By no means, she decides silently. What was it David said? 'Jim Stark has no scruples whatsoever. He's a thief and a liar.'

Chris' legal training and experience has taught her to home in on lies, but despite her patient questioning, she can't fault him. His story is perfect and he can provide lengthy explanations for any part of his background she cares to pick on. And she does, as they visit Jim's favourite nightclubs and dance through the night.

By five a.m. they are sitting in an all-night café on Fifth Avenue with bacon and egg sandwiches and good, strong black coffee. Strangely she's not a bit tired.

'What exactly is your brief,' Jim asks her. He yawns to show that he's only asking out of politeness. 'Obviously it's commercial, yet it has

183

something to do with Arab fundamentalism. Husam, by the way, is a babe in the woods. His only crime is arrogance. He thinks he can make a difference.'

'I came to that conclusion, too. Only later I changed my mind.'

'Has it occurred to you, Chris, that we could save a hell of a lot of time by joining forces?'

The gain would be all on his side, she reckons, so she smiles. 'How could you possibly help me, Jim, since you're out of work?'

He ignores her taunt. 'What did you think of Moses Freeman? Did he wear a top hat? He's got his hands in the cookie jar.'

Chris tries not to show how startled she is. The truth hits home . . . she's outclassed and in danger.

'Who's Moses Freeman? I don't think I know . . . '

'He called the prince right after you left. Now he knows you're a fake, he's hopping mad. Don't go near him.'

'Since you're here, how could you possibly know that?'

'I have a few friends back at headquarters. Strange guy, even for a Liberian. I guess you know that Liberia was created by the Americans, specifically President Monroe, hence the capital, Monrovia.'

'No, I didn't know.'

'When the US abolished slavery, a small number of the ex-slaves opted to be repatriated to Africa, so they shipped them back and deliberately set them up as a ruling class, mainly to serve US interests. Those guys made themselves the masters in no uncertain terms. They built plantation-style mansions and turned the locals into virtual slaves. They even wore top hats and waistcoats, and this habit survived until very recently. Freeman's one of the old school. He's salted away the prince's money all over Central Africa and Switzerland and he's got his finger into so many pies: oil, diamonds, gold, copper, armaments . . . ' He breaks off and smiles his very best smile.

'You're such a novice, Chris. Tell me what your brief is. I can help you.'

She almost falls for it. This is worse than an inquisition. She says: 'This Freeman sounds a real character. I wish I'd met him.'

He looks at her sharply. 'Play it your way. There's no limit to their corruption. Liberia has always been a mess and the current civil war isn't helping. It's lasted fourteen years! The capital's in ruins and the countryside is choked with mines.'

For some reason Jim badly wants to know what she's investigating. Is that why he copied her keys? But what possible interest could it be to a man like him? Yet she has to admit to herself that she has no real idea of what kind of a man Jim is. There's a barrier, like a *Star Wars* shield, all about him . . . invisible, but impenetrable, and she senses that it has been there forever.

Dawn is breaking in a purple and scarlet extravaganza that covers half the sky, but Chris is

185

only conscious of Jim's arm around her shoulders and his breath on her neck. She's trying to fathom out how she could lust over a man she neither knows nor trusts.

20

It's seven a.m. on Monday morning and it's raining in London. FI's offices are deserted. Chris, who returned from New York the previous evening, sighs with relief as she locks the door behind her. She can work without interruption and avoid Rowan for a while. Hopefully her report will deflect some of his fury, depending on how well she writes it. Checking the email, she finds an intriguing note from their Bombay office . . . another plus for her report. Humming quietly, she starts typing.

PROGRESS REPORT

To: Rowan Metcalf
From: Christine Winters

Despite your lack of enthusiasm, I decided that a trip to New York to see Moses Freeman was essential. Freeman was my only contact and I felt that he might be persuaded to supply the answers to a number of queries, if he trusted me.

Hacking into Prince Husam Ibn al-Faisal's PC, I sent a message supposedly from the prince, informing Freeman of the coming visit of the prince's PA, (namely myself), in order to discuss confidential information that could not be trusted to the Internet. Freeman seemed convinced of my credentials and answered most of the questions freely.

The diamond market: 328,000 carats are mined daily worldwide, according to Freeman, but these figures reflect only legitimate diamond roughs. It is claimed that illicit roughs that filter into high-class jewellers account for only four per cent of the total. The true figure is much higher, according to Freeman.

Stolen and illicit gems: Theft is commonplace in the diamond industry. For instance, hundreds of millions of dollars of roughs are stolen from De Beers' mines each year. Russian criminals steal up to forty per cent of that country's newly mined roughs, and so on. Every diamond producer has similar problems.

Blood diamonds: At the height of the civil wars over $1 billion rough diamonds were leaving Africa each year. Each country's quota under the Kimberley Process limits them to sell only a specified proportion of their production. The surpluses are supposed to be stockpiled, but most of these countries are desperately short of foreign currency and ex-quota diamonds, together with stolen and blood diamonds, are known to be infiltrating the legitimate market and all are referred to under the same label, i.e. blood diamonds. There's big money involved for the launderers, particularly when one accepts that the real extent of laundered stones must be far higher than four per cent. (*Naturally no one's counting.*)

Ben's theory: Ben felt that al-Qaeda is behind the purchasing and laundering and that Freeman is one of them. This is a possibility and is one of the two lines of enquiry I'm following up on.

However . . . Freeman hinted at the existence of a large network of buyers (or agents), spread throughout Africa, providing a ready market for roughs not valid under Kimberly Process rules. This information came via a slip of the tongue. Freeman refused to identify them, but I feel sure that he knows who they are.

Mohsen Sheik: I have not yet succeeded in seeing him, but by hacking into Sheik's London office, I have learned that exports of cheap polished roughs to England have doubled over the past month, which seems to back my theory that Mohsen Sheik is being coerced into buying large quantities of low-grade roughs.

In conclusion: My research confirms that the traditional routes for blood diamonds, i.e. Liberia, Antwerp, Switzerland and Tel Aviv have not seen any increase in stones offered. Yet any seller of stolen or conflict gems can find a buyer in every African city. Somehow these stones acquire the necessary certificates and mysteriously enter the mainstream of diamonds destined for high-street jewellers in the main centres of America and Europe. I don't know how yet, but I have a number of leads.

Chris is about to send her memo to Rowan when she notices that she has received another email from the American FI team currently stationed in Nigeria and working on an oil scam. It's a report from someone called Andy Benson and it reads:

To Chris,
Re. the diamond cutting and polishing workshops supposedly initiated by Prince Husam Ibn al-Faisal

I flew down to Monrovia and spent Friday and Saturday there. It seems that your suspicions are confirmed. No one has heard of diamond cutting establishments being set up. No business licences have been issued. No new employers have been registered in this field. There have been no advertisements for staff, property agents have not heard of land purchased or rented, likewise no builders have been called to alter existing properties. Of course these workshops could be set up in anyone's front room, but local jewellers and manufacturing jewellers have not heard of such a venture either. The Lebanese jewellers

*who buy illicit stones for sale in the Middle
East keep their fingers on the pulse of the local
diamond industry and they are convinced that
no such development is on the cards. There's
no reason why these workshops should have
been kept under wraps and the only
conclusion I can come to is that they do not
exist.*

Andy.

Chris staples the email to her report and adds
her comment:

*Either Prince Husam has been duped and
defrauded of two and a half million dollars,
or else he and Freeman are using the cash
to purchase illicit diamonds cheaply around
the west coast of Africa. This is precisely
the kind of information I have been
searching for. Freeman could be just one of
many agents operating in the main diamond
centres for Prince Husam's supposed
organisation, and if this were true it would
seem that Ben's theory is correct. I have a
very good idea of who would have set up
this network of buying agents for the prince,
but as yet I have no idea how the stones are
laundered.*

Chris glances at her watch. It is just past
seven-thirty. Rowan seldom arrives before eight.
She decides to leave her report on his desk and
work in the IT room for a while, where he might
not find her. Entering her password, Chris sees

191

another email has just arrived from David Marais:

Once again you've taken flight and no one seems to know where you are. 'On holiday,' your watchdog insists. I don't believe her. Hope you haven't forgotten our dinner date on Monday evening and that you're back in time. Let's meet at our usual place at nine p.m. Impatiently, David.

Surely she didn't make a firm commitment? In fact, Chris clearly remembers saying 'no', but why not go anyway. David might have some news for her. It seems so long since she last spoke to him. So much has changed since then. Dear David! Why can't she fall for one of the good, straight, reliable guys?

She types a short note back: *Make it ten p.m. and you're on. I have to catch up on some work.* Once that's dispatched Chris turns to a pile of mail.

The phone rings. It's Jean.

'Rowan's looking for you. Are you taking calls?'

'Yes, but don't tell him where I am.'

'I have James Stark on the line.'

Then comes Jim's voice saying: 'How about dinner tonight?'

She pauses for too long.

'I prefer New York's weather right now. I suspect a cold front's about to hit me over here.'

'Sorry, I can't make it tonight, Jim.'

'I wasn't suggesting 'making it'. Just dinner.'

'I have a prior engagement,' she says primly. Jim and his innuendoes. Is this trumped up attraction for real? And if it's not, what on earth is he after?

'Tomorrow then?'

'Lunch tomorrow,' she says firmly.

'Whatever you wish. Meet you at Green's. One o'clock.'

'Yes. That's fine.' An impersonal click terminates the conversation.

Wow! Talk about sulky.

★ ★ ★

Sharp at ten, Chris receives a stern request via Mary to see Rowan at once.

Rowan is a natty dresser, and this morning he's excelled himself in a tailor-made mohair suit of steel grey, a blue and white striped shirt and a dark blue silk cravat. Rowan is strictly traditional in his tastes, but he always looks as if he is on the catwalk and wherever he goes an aura of costly aftershave surrounds him. This morning his face registers the utmost disapproval as he sits motionlessly in his leather chair, watching her with his pale grey eyes.

Two can play at that game. Chris gazes back silently as the seconds pass. Rowan cracks first.

'I've read your report, Chris. It's good, although I don't approve of your methods. What are you trying to prove? Surely you realised the risks you were taking. After Ben's tragic death I would have thought you'd be more circumspect. I'm sure you remember that I specifically told you not to see Freeman.'

'There was no other way forward. You and I

both know that. What else could I do? I'm sure you remember that when I arrived, you told me I had a totally free hand. You said that only results counted.'

'I know what I said.' Now he looks intensely irritated and Chris guesses that he's torn between a desire to get the case solved and his abhorrence of publicity. It won't look good if his staff go down like ninepins.

She tries to humour him: 'Listen, Rowan. My friend has been kidnapped. Ben . . . '

'Please don't get sentimental. I shall express my utter disapproval of your methods of procedure in writing. After that it's up to you.'

'Thanks.' So she is free to do what she likes.

'I'll be straightforward with you, Chris. A great deal rests on this case. Our original client was a Central African government acting through David Marais. At the same time, a powerful American NGO initiated the self-same search with our American head office. There was no point in duplicating the work, so it was a toss-up as to who took the brief: our US colleagues or us. Finally, because of Ben's reputation, it landed on our desks. Quite honestly, we can't afford to fail. Because of Ben's death, the Americans want it back.'

'Screw them! All the more reason . . . '

'Yes, yes,' Rowan interrupts her. 'There's something that puzzles me, Chris. Ben was on this case for three months. According to what he told me, he was getting nowhere fast. What changed the situation so much that Ben became a danger to these criminals, whoever they are?

Something that Ben or you uncovered must have led to his death. Freeman and the prince are the only new elements in your investigation, so one of them must be involved in some way. It looks as if our suspicions of Prince Husam are very relevant.'

And Jim, Chris thinks with a shiver.

'Is there another factor you haven't told me about?'

She shakes her head. 'It sounds logical when you put it like that, but I had hardly got the job at the Provident when Ben disappeared. Freeman turned grey with fear when I told him about the note that lured Ben into the taxi. I'm convinced that he didn't know about it. Besides, why would he incriminate himself?'

'He was arrested, but never charged. He had an alibi, so they deported him. That's all I know. Are you sure you've come clean, Chris?'

'There is something else . . . another lead . . . someone has been following me, even to New York. He says he's the head of Prince Husam's security. It's too early to comment, but I'm playing along.'

'Good God! But that's madness.' Momentarily, Rowan loses his equanimity as he leans across his desk, his eyes searching hers. 'What drives you, Chris?'

How can she explain, even to herself? Her motives are confused. She has to prove herself worthwhile, but to whom? Certainly not Rowan, nor her colleagues here. Or is it to herself? Not really, she surmises, standing up. 'I can't answer that, so I'd better get back to work.'

'Sit down. You don't have any appointments now, do you? How about coffee?' He rings through to the kitchen. 'So tell me about yourself.'

'There's nothing to tell,' she says stiffly. Rowan has absolutely no right to ask. He's prodding for flaws. Just look at his eyes gleaming and intent.

The coffee arrives while she sits in stubborn silence, trying to ignore a throbbing pain that is starting up just above her left temple. Unbelievably Rowan is fetching a file from his cabinet. It's marked *Personnel* and she guesses it's hers. Sipping her coffee, she watches Rowan going through the forms. He won't find much there.

'A brilliant record. You've excelled in everything you've ever tried.' He says admiringly.

'Not everything,' she mutters, thinking of Sienna.

'I see that all your sporting activities are aggressive by nature. You like fighting.'

She shrugs.

'I often sense your aggression directed against me, yet you know nothing about me. In a way, I'm your Rorschach test.'

Chris is unwilling to enter into this crude probing, but she's curious. 'What's that?'

'It's a basic psychological test whereby the viewer is presented with a shaded page of ink blots which he — or she — can interpret in any way they choose. Some see a small boy being beaten, some a loving mother, others see murder and violence or a starving youngster. It gives an idea of what's going on in the person's mind. Men are your enemy, Chris.'

'Some of my best friends are men,' she answers facetiously.

'Think about it, Chris. As for me, I've already deduced that there was an early problem with the man in your life. Perhaps he abandoned you, a father, perhaps, so now you despise him, but you also want to impress him. Yet he has long since faded away and become all the men in your life. You want to show them how good you are while knocking them down.'

'Don't take up psychology, Rowan. You're way off target,' she lies, lurching to her feet. She knows she's flushing.

Rowan is smiling in a silly, superior way while toying with his pen. 'It's not worth risking your life, because this person, whoever he is, isn't around to see you win.'

'Fuck you, Rowan,' she swears silently, but all he hears is '*Ciao*,' as she sweeps out of his office.

21

By nine p.m., Chris's headache is affecting her thought processes. She should cancel dinner with David, but she knows that she won't do that. Sometimes it's hard to understand the need that drives her to near-collapse. Her failure to discover anything to date is an ongoing mental ache which is expressing itself in a variety of physical symptoms. Whatever had led her to believe that she could do this job? She can't help remembering what Ben had said: 'You need more than intellect and training, you need intuition.'

The taxi draws to a halt outside the restaurant and Chris climbs out, but before she can pay the driver, David grabs her elbow.

'The taxi is taken care of. You're late. I was beginning to think I'd been stood up . . . but you're OK. That's the main thing.' Today, David's shrewd, blue eyes are beaming with concern, but he looks harassed. Taut lines around his lips and bags under his eyes show his tension. A speck of blood gleams on his cracked lips. He has lovely lips, she notices, full and sensual.

'I'm sorry, David. So much work piled up while I was in the States. You know how it goes.' Fumbling in her bag, she finds her lip balm and, opening it, she runs it around his lips.

'Keep this. It'll stop the splitting. I have plenty

more. Do you have a cold?'

'Sort of. Hey there . . . you sound a little croaky, too.'

He looks down at her outstretched hand as he takes the lip balm and slips it into his pocket. 'Thanks!' He's smiling, but his expression changes as he swings her round to face him. 'Jesus! What are you doing to yourself? Shadows like moats . . . your cheeks a delicate shade of apple green and you've lost weight. For God's sake, Chris. This job is killing you. Get your priorities in order. Nothing's worth ruining your health. It's only money.'

She doesn't answer.

Still clutching her arm, he guides her into the restaurant, which is bright, light and minimalist. The head waiter behaves as if they are visiting celebrities and recites a long list of the evening's 'specials'.

Chris only replies when he has left and they are alone. 'You're wrong, David. It's not only money, it's Ben's murder and Sienna's kidnapping. It's just that . . . well . . . I'm not getting anywhere.'

'So you reckon there's a connection between Ben's death and Sienna's kidnapping?'

She pulls herself up short. Blabbermouth! 'I don't know. What do you think?'

'No connection. Mohsen Sheik's not talking to the police, or so I've heard, but you can bet he's had a demand. Take my advice . . . forget that angle. Of course I'm concerned. Ben was my great buddy.' David blinks hard. 'But you're also someone I care about and I don't like to see you looking so exhausted. Give yourself a chance. What is it . . . a couple of weeks since you joined FI? Early days . . . plenty of time.'

Not for Sienna! This time Chris keeps her mouth shut. 'You're probably right.'

The waiter is back with glasses of sherry and an expectant expression. From his toadying Chris assumes that David is a good client. He leaves, but David seems unsure of how to begin. He fiddles with his glass.

'If you have any suspicions or evidence of a connection between these crimes and your investigation, we should contact Scotland Yard. Do you?'

She shook her head.

'Two heads are better than one . . . let's have a think-tank. What do you think is going on?'

'Believe me, David, I wish I knew, but to be honest, I haven't the faintest idea what's going on, so I can't tell you anything. I thought I'd get the sack, but Rowan suggests I keep trying.'

'Surely you have some clues or guesses. What about the fabled women's intuition?'

'I feel I'm playing blind-man's bluff.'

He glances shrewdly at her. 'Has Rowan told you who the client is?'

'You mentioned something about being the go-between.'

'Exactly. We're liaising with the Republic of Congo, but that's only because we are very big diamond exporters from that country.'

'Are you? I didn't know.'

'Now you do. I wish you'd let me help you, Chris. Ben and I used to compare notes over a couple of drinks and we'd usually come up with the answers.'

As he talks, Chris is reminding herself that she has no right to confide. Not to anyone, not even David, who is becoming her friend.

'I'll bear that in mind.' She searches for a hint of duplicity, but sincerity beams from his blue eyes. Despite her habitual distrust of men, Chris is beginning to warm to David. He's sincere and straight, which is more than you could say for that fly-by-night Jim Stark.

She says: 'You must know why Ben went to New York?'

'Sure I do. He did a great job there. Jon was lucky to get reinstated. He's as guilty as hell.' David frowns disapprovingly. 'Bronstein's not the only fool around. Several Liberian dealers have large clientele in New York. They travel there three or four times a year.'

'Sometimes I wonder if the entire laundering scam is the work of thousands of freelance agents, each responsible for several thousand dollars worth of diamonds,' Chris says guilelessly, to gauge David's reaction.

'Add a few noughts,' David says. 'Well, that's my theory, too. So we'll close your brief, shall we?'

He smiles teasingly and once again she can't help admiring his charm, which has a lot to do with his lovely smile. As if sensing her thoughts, he reaches out and squeezes her hand.

'Listen to this: I was in Monaco last week when a certain delegate from West Africa produced a parcel of excellent roughs. He said it was legit'. He claimed he was the Foreign Minister. Natty dresser. And he had two beautiful women in tow. Twins. Very dark and luscious. Spanish, they told me, identically dressed in ivory lace. He looked very pleased with himself escorting them to all the best places, but someone told me later they were the hotel's resident whores. He offered me a bargain price for his diamonds, but naturally I couldn't take the parcel.'

'Yet you bought the *Golfer's Dream* diamond, smuggled out of Namibia, which, strictly speaking, belongs to De Beers.'

For a second, David's eyes are sharp with anger, but he quickly recovers and becomes his usual charming self. 'You're quick off the mark, Chris,' he protests charmingly. 'Nowadays it makes perfect economic sense to obey the rules. We need to keep conflict diamonds out of the United States. America is the world's largest diamond market and if we can keep the illicit dealers out, we can hang on to the carefully created image of a diamond standing as a symbol of love and purity. Which reminds me . . . '

He turns and gazes challengingly at Chris. 'You should be more careful about the company you keep. You've been seen around New York with that criminal, Jim Stark.'

'Goodness. Are you spying on me, David?' She is furious and she's sure that it shows.

'Not spying on *you*, but . . . well . . . the truth is, we keep an eye on Stark. Anyway, it's just what I was told. Let's face it, you weren't exactly discreet.'

'Why should I be?' It's part of my investigation, she almost adds, but then decides that she isn't making excuses to David or anyone else.

'I told you Stark was imprisoned in Equatorial Guinea. What I didn't tell you is that he was rescued from prison by a gang of mercenaries. The worst! The guys who lop off limbs and lay waste to entire communities. They and he are in cohorts. We're pretty sure they're making a fortune buying and selling illicit roughs.'

Exactly my intuition, she thinks silently. She smiles sweetly. 'Now you're talking, David. Tell me more.'

'It's only a matter of time before we get proof of this. He's bad news, Chris. Dangerous. I wish you'd give up this investigation, or let me help you.'

'But I am letting you help me. You're helping me now, David.'

'You play things very close to the cuff,' he says stiffly.

'Oh David!' She reaches forward and takes his hand and tries out her most appealing smile. 'It's not that I don't trust you, it's just that I don't have any leads. I don't even understand how you mining managers actually know that diamonds are being laundered. Or just what the statistics are. Do you?'

He looks startled and then pleased. His left hand slides forward and comes to rest over hers. He really is rather pleasant company, Chris considers. She makes up her mind to charm him and get to know the real person behind the barriers he's erected around himself.

David lets go of her hand and leans back as the waiter approaches. Suddenly Chris realises she's hungry. She hasn't eaten all day. She orders Prawn Avocado, followed by Lobster Thermidor. Why not! And then Zabaglione. David is rich and doubtless has a huge expense account.

★ ★ ★

They dine sumptuously and drink too much good wine, exchange backgrounds and joke about their immediate rapport. David even suggests that he could fall in love, given a little encouragement. Diamonds are forgotten as the conversation ranges from subjects as diverse as the drought in Zambia to their shared enthusiasm for skiing.

It's almost midnight when Chris says: 'David, I must go. It's been a lovely evening. Thank you so much.'

'Why so early?'

'I don't want to miss the last tube.'

'I'll take you home,' he says as he stands up.

'No . . . ' She kisses his cheek. 'I like walking and I want to catch the tube. I hope I'll see you soon.'

'Bet your life . . . '

He's frowning as the waiter brings her coat. The frown intensifies as he walks her to the pavement. Ignoring his scowls, she refuses a taxi and his offer to walk with her to the tube station, and sets off at a brisk pace.

Why does she always feel handcuffed by

affection, she wonders. Worse than handcuffed, more like strait-jacketed. David is a great guy, but excessive affection makes her feel claustrophobic. She soon throws off her irritation and enjoys the misty night, the tingling cold on her cheeks as she takes deep gulps of cool, autumn air.

22

Chris is only a few hundred metres from the restaurant when she realises she's being followed . . . again. Someone is stalking her, keeping pace with her steps, trying to disguise their tread. Her stomach clenches painfully, but then she pulls herself together. After all, this is a busy area and she has only to walk into an open shop. She turns first right through misty streets and repeats this manoeuvre until she returns to Piccadilly Circus, but the footsteps doggedly follow hers. Has her stalker been waiting all evening outside the restaurant?

On impulse she flags down a cab and asks the driver to take her to Green Park tube station. There are only a few people waiting on the platform, mainly youngsters engrossed in gloom. She finally feels she's safe as she steps into the tube and the doors close behind her.

By the time she reaches Finchley West, Chris is the only person left in the carriage. She hurries outside to find that the mist has thickened. Pausing in the doorway, she searches the pavements on either side of the road. The neon lights at the entrance glow with a purple haze against the grey landscape that's bleak enough for a Dickens movie. Despite her determination not to succumb to foolish fears, she shudders. 'It's the cold,' she murmurs.

Turning up the collar of her warm coat, she

shrinks into it, pushing her hands into her pockets. A siren wails as a police car races along the road, disappearing into the gloom. There are no loiterers to be seen, so Chris sets off briskly for the ten-minute walk home.

Soon the motion sends her bag slipping off her shoulder. She pauses mid-step to catch hold of the strap, and precisely then she hears the scuffle of a footfall and the skid of a stone accidentally kicked. 'Damn! How the hell . . . ?' But he knows where she lives and he has a car, doesn't he . . . a white Ford Fiesta.

Chris slips off her shoes and bolts for home, but despite her speed, the stalker is catching up. Breathless and exhausted, she glances over her shoulder and sees that it's not one, but two men who are running after her. With a jolt of panic she sees that she isn't going to make it. She sprints forward, but suddenly stops as she hears a yell, a grunt and the sound of falling bodies. Two men are rolling on the ground and even from this distance she can hear their panting breath and the dull smack of flesh on flesh. One of them yells: 'For God's sake . . . you're breaking my arm!' She creeps back and aims her torch at the heaving hump of men.

'Get back . . . damn it . . . get back . . . ' Jim's voice. He's fighting mad and bent on killing an unknown, swarthy man with a beard. The stalker is pinned face down, his arm twisted in a half-Nelson. Jim drags him towards the lamppost and knocks his head hard against it. The stalker screams.

'Don't . . . don't . . . just don't,' Chris yells,

but Jim is slapping the man's face from side to side, with amazing speed and force.

'Stop! You're killing him.'

'Don't interfere,' he gasps. 'Who the hell are you?' he mutters, in the same terse tone. 'Why are you following Miss Winters?' He jerks the man to his feet.

Panting badly, the stalker tries to run for it, but yelps as his legs are kicked from under him. He falls heavily and sprawls beside her, where he lies, gasping for breath.

Chris bends over him and tries to pull him to his feet, but he clutches her collar and jerks her head towards his.

'Your friend's father . . . ' he gasps.

Jim grabs her and pulls her back.

'Stop it. Just stop it,' she shrieks. She makes an effort to calm herself. 'I have to listen to what he has to say.'

Chris pushes Jim away. 'It seems that a friend sent him.'

Jim swears as she helps the man to a sitting position.

'I was hired to protect Miss Winters,' the stalker wheezes.

'Who hired you?' Jim asks.

Chris has already guessed who.

'He's lying.' Jim is fumbling in the stalker's inside pocket. He brings out his wallet and opens it.

'What are you doing?'

'Looking for some sort of identification. A private dick, or so it says here. Of course, this doesn't mean a thing.'

'You can check in the morning.' The stalker is recovering his breath. From the look in his eyes, it's fury not fear that's giving him strength. He stands shakily and scans her with hostile eyes. 'You've been trying to see the father of an old friend.' Adding quickly: 'Don't name him, please. I have to speak to you privately.'

For a moment Chris is too taken aback to speak. 'But you've been stalking me for weeks,' she manages to say at last.

'I'm sorry. You weren't supposed to know that I was following you. I was hired to protect you, because of what you did. There's three of us. We work in shifts.'

'Bullshit!' Jim interrupts him. 'What the fuck are you talking about? You'll have to do better than that.'

'I know who hired him, Jim.'

'So what exactly did you do to deserve such costly gratitude?'

'I can't divulge . . . ' She shrugs.

Jim is furious. 'Get lost,' he tells the man angrily.

'I'm sorry if I alarmed you,' the stranger says, making an obvious effort to regain his dignity. 'Here's my card. If you need me, please call.' He scribbles on the back of it and pushes it into her hand.

'Let me see.' Jim reaches for the card.

She pushes it into her pocket. 'No, Jim. It's confidential and it's for me.'

★ ★ ★

The stalker is limping badly as he hurries to the corner and moves out of sight.

'What a monster you are. You really hurt him.'

'I would have got the truth out of him if you hadn't interfered.'

She frowns at him. Jim is a trained fighter, that much is clear. The stalker, or detective, or whoever he is, never stood a chance.

'Listen to me, Chris. This isn't a game. Maybe he's one of the men who killed Ben, maybe he isn't, but I don't trust the bastard, or anyone else . . . and neither should you.' He breaks off, frowning as he catches sight of her expression.

'For God's sake . . . you can trust me . . . what's got into you?'

'Can I?' If only she could, but she still has the picture of Jim taken outside Timmins Jeweller's in the High Street. Jim was following her *before* she picked up Prince Husam. Why is he always around? His claim that he was checking on her for the prince simply doesn't make sense and she doesn't believe that he finds her irresistible either.

He swears and then tries to control his anger. 'Not very skilled at this game, are you, Chris. The first rule is: don't fall for your suspects. You'd better take me off the list.'

'I wouldn't be such a fool.'

He pushes her into a shop doorway and glances furtively over his shoulder along the street. Then they are clutching, fighting, mouth on mouth, her legs around his thighs. Oh God. This can't be happening. Lust is swamping her reason. She pushes him away. 'Not like this. No, never.

'Don't follow me again,' she says, pushing her coat and skirt down. 'I can look after myself.' Cheeks burning and wet with frustrated tears, she hurries towards home. She hears muttered curses and Jim's voice floating through the mist. 'Stop fighting this. Dinner tomorrow.' A command or a request? Soon there's nothing but the sound of her footsteps and a dog barking far away.

★   ★   ★

Chris wakes from her sensual dream and ponders. Jim is the enemy and she's a fool, yet she never felt such longing. One touch of his hand and her body thrills with a pleasure she's never before experienced. But something is terribly wrong. Jim knows too much and he's keeping an eye on her for reasons of his own, using sex as his excuse.

After a while she remembers the stalker, so she gets out of bed and finds his card in her pocket. It reads simply: *Hamid Khan, Private Investigator*, plus an address in the city and a mobile phone number. *We must talk . . . outside . . . white Fiesta . . .* is scribbled on the back in pencil.

She glances at her watch. It is three a.m. Will he still be waiting?

★   ★   ★

He's there. She had half-hoped that he wouldn't be. Lit by the overhanging street lamp, the car seems to beam a warning through the mist: 'Go back. This is how Ben was trapped.' Chris has trouble putting one foot in front of the other. Hamid Khan gets out and hurries around to open a door. Should she run for it?

'I'm sorry to keep you waiting. I didn't read your note at first.'

'Get in,' he says impatiently. After a slight hesitation she stoops and sits. The door slams on her.

'You look frightened. Please don't be,' he says, fastening his seat belt. 'I am also a trusted friend of Mohsen Sheik.' Khan leans forward to turn the key, the engine purrs and the next moment they are gliding south through the thickening mist.

'Well, you know who I am . . . by now you probably know me better than anyone . . . what time I get up . . . where I go . . . Being a detective is the ultimate in voyeurism, I suppose.' Even she can hear that her voice is pitched too high. She can't stop gabbling as she becomes increasingly aware of her helplessness. 'Where exactly are we going?'

'Nowhere. I thought that if we kept moving there would be less chance of being seen.'

'Why should anyone bother?'

'Wouldn't you think that the criminals who kidnapped Sienna and killed Ben Searle are extremely interested in who you see and where you go? You've shown yourself to be resourceful, brave and clever. You hoodwinked Moses

Freeman. What next? they might be wondering.'

'How do you know all this?'

He shrugs. 'I was told. We have a New York office.'

By now she has gone beyond fear to a curious state of lethargy. He is driving slowly which is comforting. After he turns the corner, he slows and begins to talk and as he does some of her tension lessens.

'You have been trying to see my client, but regrettably this is not possible. It could endanger his daughter's life.'

'That's understandable. I'd feel the same way.' She clears her throat and makes an effort to get her voice back to a reasonable pitch.

'My client feels anxious for you, too. He feels that you should drop this investigation. You are involved with dangerous criminals who have too much to lose to allow you to penetrate their defences.' His voice, deep and expressionless, tells Chris nothing.

'But it's not about diamonds anymore. It's about murder and kidnapping. It's poor Sienna imprisoned somewhere against her will . . . ' She breaks off. 'You might be one of them. How do I know who really sent you? Anyone can get cards printed.'

'I was told that if you ask I should remind you of the time my client came to the school unexpectedly and found you two girls were wearing each other's dresses.'

Chris remembers that day so well. As the school concert loomed she and Sienna arranged to meet two school prefects at a bar in town and go dancing later. Neither of their parents were expected, because they hadn't been told about the concert. Sienna borrowed a revealing, backless, halter-neck red silk dress from Chris. With make-up, earrings and her hair piled on her head, she looked at least eighteen. Chris borrowed Sienna's embroidered evening jacket. School macs hid their dresses, but their plans were ruined by the sight of Sienna's father's grey Daimler sweeping past the bus stop. He braked and ordered them into the car. Once inside the school they were obliged to take off their macs. Mohsen had only accepted the silly excuse that Sienna was rehearsing for her role as Blanche in the coming school play, *A Streetcar Named Desire*, when she recited part of it. Their dates wouldn't speak to them for weeks.

Chris swallows hard and pushes the memory away.

'Has your client had any proof that Sienna is still alive?'

'Yes. They send regular proof. I pray that we soon find Sienna and deal with these evil criminals.'

The way he spoke made Chris glance sharply at him. He was trying to disguise his anger, but it showed in his taut lips, the gleam in his eyes and his trembling hands. He wasn't a private detective. Perhaps he worked for Mohsen Sheik. The cards were a fake she felt sure. She would check later.

'How much do you know about the kidnappers?'

'Only that they are not Moslems.'

'How can you be sure?'

'Any number of small details. Our criminals don't use a rope, they prefer a knife or a gun. Besides, they appear to have no market or marketing agents in the Middle East. They steer clear of that area. Doesn't that tell you something?'

Chris shivers again.

'Does Mohsen Sheik know who they are?'

'No, but he feels sure that Moses Freeman does and that Freeman is afraid of them. It's well known that while he was in prison in Swakopmund in the Seventies, serving a sentence for terrorism, Freeman recruited fellow convicts into his scheme to steal and sell diamonds in order to earn funds for his liberation movement. By the time Namibia gained its freedom, the group had become an extremely profitable concern. That was when Freeman opted out . . . or was pushed out. Since then he's had every opportunity to become a big name in illicit diamond dealing, but he is content with a modest living. In our opinion, Freeman values his life more than money.'

'With good reason, it seems.'

'Yes. Freeman was arrested in New York just after you left, but his alibi was foolproof, so he was deported to Liberia. We tried to locate him there, but he fled the country. We don't know where he is. He can lead us to these criminals, although he's not associated with them. Do you have any questions?'

'None that you could answer, it seems.'

'I'm sorry. My client would prefer you to ask

me for any details you need to know about his company and keep your Bombay office off his back. You can use me as your go-between. You have my mobile number. Call day or night.'

Sudden anger surges. 'You've been frightening me. Are you connected with a certain bearded Pashto translator, who followed me in New York?'

'As I said, we work in shifts,' he says briefly.

'All I want is to be left alone to do my job. Stop following me. You're no fighter, so your protection doesn't add up to a damn thing. If you find out anything relevant . . . like what the hell's going on, please feel free to contact me.'

Kahn looks her over with his expressionless velvet eyes and forces his lips into a humourless smile. 'You're right, Miss Winters. I'm sorry I bothered you. Here you are . . . home. Go well.'

She turns on the pavement and walks back. 'Look, I didn't mean . . . '

The car shoots forward leaving her standing on the pavement. 'Who gives a damn,' she murmurs, feeling shabby. She can't get her rudeness out of her head as she goes to bed.

Only when she is relaxed enough to feel sleepy does she consider the implications of what Khan told her. If she knew where Freeman was imprisoned, she could investigate those men who served time with him. But right now, she must face up to the truth: the only way forward is through Freeman and she will have to find him. But Freeman knows that she tricked him. 'It can't be helped,' she whispers. She has no other leads.

23

'The only way forward is via Freeman and I *must* find him.'

Chris senses that she is losing an argument she should never have begun. She marvels at her own stupidity in confiding in Rowan. Now he will block her because he never takes chances. She may take chances as long as she doesn't tell Rowan, which leaves him in the clear. A novice to the age-old profession of information gathering, Chris is learning that her natural instinct to go out and fight for what she wants is no longer valid. Will she ever acquire the guile, the patience and the discipline to do this job well?

'Absolutely not,' Rowan is saying quietly. 'Let's not go through this again.'

From his tone she gathers that their meeting is terminated. She's blown it! It's not Rowan she's cross with, but herself. What sort of a wimp is she? Why did she ask him for permission to travel to Johannesburg, thereby neatly transferring responsibility for her safety onto Rowan's shoulders. Of course he'd say 'no'. What else could he do? She doesn't need his permission. He laid down the ground rules at their first meeting: no questions, no restrictions and only one rule . . . win! She's not winning and failure makes her insecure . . . but that's *her* problem, not Rowan's. If she doesn't find Moses Freeman, she might as well resign. He's the only one who knows what's going on.

Chris's resolution springs to attention. 'That's it then! Look. I'm sorry, but this investigation means a lot to me . . . for Ben . . . for Sienna . . . so I'll just carry on and see where I get.'

'And stick to normal business procedure.'

What's normal about this business? Chris asks herself when she's back in her office. She sits quietly, trying to clear her head of silly regrets. She has to go. She'll book the first available flight. This is one call Jean can't do for her, she realises, reaching for the receiver.

⋆ ⋆ ⋆

She's in luck at last. There's a last minute cancellation on a business class evening flight to Johannesburg. She must pick up her ticket at the SA Airways desk, Terminal One, later. She books into the Sandton Sun Hotel for one night only because she's not sure of her plans, she explains to the agent.

Jim's next on the list. 'I'm sorry, I can't make lunch or dinner, Jim. Something urgent has cropped up.'

'Whenever you say that, I get a sinking feeling. What's going on this time?'

'I can't talk right now.' She tries not to throw down the receiver, which is burning her hand. Why is everyone trying to manacle her?

'Chris . . . listen . . . I'm thinking of pushing off . . . for a while at any rate. I'm pining for the sun, cheap booze and the beach.' There's more than a question in his tone.

'Why not? If that's what you want.' She ignores a surge of disappointment.

'We could meet tomorrow.'

'I'm not sure. Probably not.'

Replacing the receiver, Chris notices that her hands are shaking. Jim knows that she's going away and he probably guesses her destination. The truth is, Jim isn't what he claims to be and this scares her. How can she feel like this without trust. But it's not love, is it? It's only lust.

A last minute hack into Prince Husam's private mail would be helpful, Chris decides. A quick check from their IT room assures her that there is no further correspondence between Husam and Freeman.

'I'll be gone for a few days,' she explains to Jean as she hands her two A4 pages of single-spaced instructions. She spends the rest of the morning shopping for lightweight trouser suits and cotton shirts.

Telling Mum is the very last hurdle, to be tackled as she leaves.

'But Africa!' Her mother looks suspicious and shocked. 'What am I supposed to do if you disappear? You never think about me. Where would I find you?'

Mum was becoming a practiced martyr, Chris thinks and then feels guilty for her disloyalty. 'Johannesburg, for starters, but I'll be moving around. Of course I'll keep in touch.'

'I suppose you intend to look for your father while you're there.'

'Only if I come across him in the course of my investigation.'

'At your company's expense!' Mum's face is screwed into lines of malevolence. 'Don't lie to me. You've been searching for him this past month. You've no right to pry into the past . . . poking your nose into things that don't concern you.'

'He's my father, so he concerns me.'

'He'll break your heart. Don't say I didn't . . . ' Her warning is muffled as Chris softly closes the door.

Guilt moves in like a cold front, chilling her. How does Mum know that she's searching for her father? Has she read her mail? And why does Mum always try to lay a guilt trip on her? A surge of anger keeps her feet pounding the pavement as she hurries towards the station.

It's almost a month since she contacted a Johannesburg Missing Persons' Bureau in order to trace Dan Kelly, but apart from the fact that he is listed on the American Register of Chartered Geologists, no one seems to have heard from him for over four years. Goldfields reported buying a claim from him in October, 2000, and that was the last trace the bureau could find. So Chris lavished her savings on searches in Australia, Canada and the Far East, but without results. When last heard of, Dan Kelly was prospecting in Botswana, but since then he's disappeared.

When she's sitting in the tube, Chris calms down enough to think clearly. Is she clutching at straws? Does she really believe that Freeman will point her in the right direction? Does she have the guts or the brains to solve this case . . . or find Sienna? What exactly can she do in Africa that she can't do in London? Find my father, whispers a guilty voice at the back of her mind.

★   ★   ★

Chris sleeps for most of the night as the jumbo jet flies into the Southern Hemisphere and on to Johannesburg. At seven a.m., after strong coffee followed by breakfast, she stumbles down the mobile steps and stands blinking on the tarmac, dazed by the glare, the space, the warmth of the crimson sun rising through oyster-grey vistas and the sparkling air. Fumbling for her sunglasses, she follows the passengers towards the airport building.

This is her first shock. Rising four storeys in granite and glass, Chris marvels at the sheer beauty of the architecture, like a potent symbol of the country's riches and power. She shows her passport, retrieves her suitcase and sails past customs into a gesturing mob of taxi drivers touting for business.

By now the sun is burning her skin, the glare has intensified, her shirt is damp and she's longing for a shower. A faint headache is the only indication that she is six thousand feet above sea level.

'Sandton Sun Hotel,' she says, settling back to enjoy the drive. Soon her taxi is speeding across a vast, flat plain, criss-crossed with modern highways, fly-overs and glaring road signs.

Modern factories line the route, but shortly afterwards they are speeding past mile after mile of small, square, concrete homes, with clusters of corrugated iron shanties here and there.

'This is Soweto,' the driver tells her with a grunt of disapproval.

Straight as an arrow, they speed on, but the view remains constant and then, far in the distance, she sees the first peaks of Johannesburg's tower blocks, as if part of Manhattan has been dumped in a dusty plain. The homes became larger and more conventional, the gardens greener, there are trees and lawns with the occasional glint of blue from swimming pools. Strange, flat hills covered with stubbly brown grass appear from time to time.

'Gold mine dumps,' the driver tells her.

He swings left and soon they are by-passing the city, as the highway cuts past farms and occasional industrial complexes to reach the northern suburbs. Here swimming pools are the norm in modern, ranch-like homes set in lavish gardens, with high walls and wrought iron gates.

'Here's your hotel,' the driver says, pointing ahead at a magnificent soaring structure in granite and glass. Moments later the taxi halts at the entrance, three uniformed porters rush to carry her luggage and she enters a vast, cool, sumptuous foyer.

Sumptuous, she soon discovers, describes everything she sees and touches. The hotel and the shopping centre surrounding it resemble a modern Aladdin's cave, with every possible luxury item: from handmade silk carpets from

222

the Middle East and China, and fashions from Europe to ski equipment, and antique African jewellery.

Chris longs to spend the day wandering from shop to shop, but she has a job to do. Returning to her room, she looks in the telephone directory for Tweneni, but there is no such entry. Not a common name, obviously. Perhaps Grace has retained her maiden name, but there is no Freeman listed in Soweto either. A call to directory enquiries proves equally unhelpful. Damn. She will have to drive out there on the off-chance of finding Grace at home.

Twenty minutes later she regrets coming so early. The taxi isn't air-conditioned and the heat is suffocating. She has left her sunglasses behind and the glare hurts her eyes. Glancing at her watch, Chris sees that it is noon. Staring out of the window she watches the air shimmer above the brown grass and parched earth. She leans forward to speak to the driver. 'Why is it so dry?'

'Rain in summer only, but it hasn't come yet.' Chris vaguely remembers from school geography lessons that they are in a summer rainfall region.

'And all those green lawns?'

He laughs contemptuously. 'Those whites can afford to waste water.'

'But it looks as if a storm's brewing.' Along the eastern horizon, dense purple-black clouds are jostling, writhing and piling up for miles into the stratosphere. 'Is that normal?' she asks.

'In summer, yes. Maybe the rain will come. Who knows!'

She shivers and looks away.

223

The comforting, middle-class homes of the northern suburbs have been left behind. They are driving into a meaner, harsher environment where thin, ragged urchins use the roads as playgrounds. Soon they are racing through mile after mile of uniform streets, where the houses are all exactly the same, square boxes of cheap, pale bricks with wire fences around. The sameness is depressing and it goes on and on, mile after mile, with occasional huddles of tin shanties put together on any spare piece of ground.

'This is it,' the driver says.

'Can you wait? My friend might be out.'

'Pay me first.'

'No. Just wait a moment while I try the bell.'

The driver swears as she gets out and slams the door. Too bad! This is the worst possible place to be abandoned.

There's no bell, so she knocks, but there's no answer. After waiting for a few minutes, she walks back to the taxi. 'She's out, I suppose.'

The driver calls to a neighbour sitting on her doorstep and speaks to her in their language.

'Mrs Tweneni is at work,' he translates, which seems strangely brief after their long, loud conversation. 'She gets back around seven. There's nowhere for you to wait and you wouldn't be safe alone here. This is no place for white people.' He starts the car.

Returning to the city, Chris spends the day contacting the chief geologists at the various mining houses. Presumably some of them would know of her father, a few might know him well.

'Don't take it badly,' a Goldfields' geologist tells her on her third appointment. 'Kelly was always a secretive guy. If he told anyone where he was working, every other prospector would be snooping around to see what he'd found. Must be something special to keep him hidden for so long. Let's face it, he's been missing for quite a few years.'

'Four,' she snaps.

'Four is it? In this game, that doesn't mean a thing. Don't worry. You're here alone, are you? There's very little a woman can do alone at night in this city. Don't try window shopping after dark. If you like, I'll show you around.'

'Thanks, but I'll be working,' Chris counters. 'I'm researching a book on diamond smuggling.'

'I can tell you a thing or two about that. South Africa is the draw for most of Africa's gangsters . . . Nigerians, Tanzanians, Namibians and the rest. They're well organised and sophisticated, and they swept down like a poisonous tide when the new South Africa was created. They've thoroughly infiltrated the mines in Botswana and Namibia. We're still hoping to win here.'

The geologist is warming to his favourite theme. Chris stays as long she can, but he has little more to add that's relevant. Nevertheless, she leaves in a thoughtful mood. Perhaps the diamond laundering is the brainchild of an African Mafia network. Either way, it makes no difference. Her brief is to discover how the diamonds are laundered, not the nationality of the launderers, she reminds herself.

* * *

It's time to visit Grace Tweneni in Soweto. Chris buys a sandwich and calls a taxi. Soon they are driving past suburbs into the city, while she marvels at the magical Transvaal twilight. By the time they reach the outskirts of Soweto, dusk is falling, but there's still no relief from the heat. Storm clouds are battening down, clothes and hair crackle with static electricity and the pressure is intolerable. Chris feels restless and uneasy.

Soweto's streets are pitch black. People hurry by, no one lingers except gangs of predatory youths who stare as the car passes. There's the sound of a jazz band far away and nearer she can hear shouting and a cat howling.

They reach number 55 in Fifth Street, Block Nine. Lights are shining in the windows, so she pays the driver and walks up the gravel path. Chris has a moment of absolute panic. Murder statistics for Soweto are second only to those of Colombia. So why is she standing alone in the dark in the second most dangerous place on the planet?

24

Facing the modest square home, Chris Winters has a moment of clarity: *don't go in there.* But Chris is citybred and pragmatic. She's well-known for her get up and go attitude. She has come to see Grace Tweneni in order to get her brother's address and she intends to do just that. There and then! That's how she operates. Intuition is something she tries to ignore. But still she hesitates. A dull rumble of thunder reminds her of the coming storm. Pulling herself together she walks up the gravel driveway and raps the knocker.

Grace Tweneni is wearing a nurse's uniform, which is some small comfort in the face of her obvious hostility. Tweneni is a powerful woman and almost as tall as her brother. Chris finds her large, glittering eyes and her habit of staring without blinking thoroughly bizarre. After some hesitation Tweneni opens the door wide enough to let Chris slip through. Chris finds herself in a modestly furnished living room, which is larger than she had expected, with a good deal of clutter lying around.

'I'm Chris Winters.' Chris says, holding out her hand, which the woman ignores. 'Thank you for seeing me. I'm looking for your brother, Moses Freeman.'

Grace turns away, ignoring her, which disturbs

Chris. 'He told me that you would always know where he is,' she persists. 'I need to contact him urgently.'

'What would a white woman like you want with my brother?' Her voice is deep, more like a growl.

'My employer, Prince Husam, sent me. He and your brother have a mutual business interest in Liberia. I'm in charge of checking the progress of the prince's African enterprises. Tell me, do you know where your brother is?'

Her question is ignored. 'Why are you searching after him? Why don't you wait for him to call you?'

'Because it's urgent. The prince has promised to invest certain sums in their joint venture and quite honestly we no longer know which bank your brother is using.'

Rather than placating her, this information seems to infuriate Grace. 'He's not in South Africa.' Triumph glitters in her eyes.

'That isn't a problem.' Chris counters. 'If you'll tell me where he is . . . '

'You came here alone?'

'By taxi.'

'And the taxi is waiting for you?'

'No. I have a mobile. I'll call for a taxi when I leave.'

'Clearly, you are not from Johannesburg.' She laughs unpleasantly and Chris feels the need to explain.

'I arrived from England this morning. If you'd just let me have his address, I can be on my way.'

They seem to be going nowhere.

Grace smiles, but her smile is eerie, and Chris senses real hatred.

'Sit down. You'll have to wait. Moses calls me every evening around this time. I must clean up. The kids make a mess.'

Chris tries not to stare as Grace moves around picking up books and tapes and dumping them in the next room. Clearly she has children, but Chris is unwilling to try her hand at small talk. She's been snubbed enough. She wonders where the children are.

Half an hour later the telephone rings, startling them both. Grace grabs the receiver and embarks on a loud complaint. Her gestures suggest that she's talking about Chris. At last she simmers down and listens intently. 'Ow!' She exclaims several times. Ten minutes later she replaces the receiver.

'You want to know where my brother is?' she says, looking ferocious. 'He's in prison in Windhoek awaiting trial for fraud, theft and diamond smuggling. He was set up by you. You told the prince that there are no workshops. You put my brother in prison.'

'No! Good heavens! That's insane. Do you think I would come here if it were true? It has nothing to do with me.'

'You pretended to be the prince's assistant. You went to see Moses and forced him to show you all his bookkeeping. Then you lied to the prince.'

'No. I certainly didn't.'

Grace Tweneni is looking murderous and

229

she's moving far too close. Chris backs towards the door.

'They may deport him to Liberia to stand trial. That would be the end for him. You're not welcome here.'

'All right, I'm leaving, but you're completely wrong. I didn't report anything of the kind to the prince. I'm sure that the New York fraud squad looked into his affairs. Perhaps that's why he was deported from America.'

'We shall see. Sit down. You can put your mobile away. You won't get a taxi to come here so late. Those drivers are afraid of getting hijacked. I'll call someone local for you.'

Her offer comes as a welcome surprise to Chris. She slides a chair slightly nearer to the door and sits down. Ignoring her fear, Chris acknowledges that she has achieved her objective. She knows where Freeman is and with luck she will be able to speak to him in prison. All she has to do is to get out of here. She watches sidelong as Grace dials a number and spends a long time gesticulating, her voice trembling with emotion. To get a taxi? Perhaps the driver is her lover. At last Grace switches off her mobile.

'It took a long time to call a taxi,' Chris murmurs uneasily.

'They didn't want to come, but finally they agreed.' Chris sits in silence for the next five minutes, while Grace continues to tidy the room.

★   ★   ★

The car arrives and hoots and the two women hurry outside. Standing on the pavement, Chris exhales. Thank God I'm out of there. Still, it doesn't look like a taxi, there's no meter, but after all, this is Soweto, not London. To her surprise, Grace gets into the passenger seat in front. Perhaps she guessed right and he's her lover.

'Get in. He's dropping me off,' Grace explains.

The taxi twists and turns through the dark streets. The houses become smaller, the roads narrower and soon they are driving into an area of deep poverty. There are no lights, but in the car's headlights she sees tin huts adjoining each other in a jumble of shapes and sizes. Only candles and oil lamps flicker through open doorways. The people are cooking on open fires and paraffin stoves.

Unease is making Chris feel very sick. 'Surely you should have made for the motorway,' she tells the driver.

'He's taking me to my sister's first,' Grace replies.

★   ★   ★

At last the car stops abruptly in a crowded open square in the midst of the shanty town. Poorly dressed locals surge around the car. Grace gets out and beckons and six men rush towards them waving batons. They look like mobsters. Two of them sport handguns in holsters. Chris struggles to throw off a strange feeling of apathy as her world becomes increasingly unreal. The feeling intensifies as she is dragged from the car by two men and her hands are tied. There's no point in struggling. There's nothing she can do against six men and surrounded by a hostile mob.

Don't panic. Panic will harm me. I mustn't show fear. Be calm. No one will help me. I'm alone. So I'll have to help myself. Panic and guilt are synonymous. Stay in control!

The crowd watches in awe-struck fascination. She's the star performer in a horror movie. Or is it a snuff movie? One of the men steps forward.

'Grace Tweneni has laid a charge that you gave false information about her brother, Moses Freeman, leading to his arrest and imprisonment, but you were lying. You are to be tried here tonight by the People's Court. You're an informer. If the charges against you are found to be true you will be punished by the People's Court.'

The fact that he speaks good English gives Chris hope. Perhaps they'll listen to reason.

'There's not a word of truth in this accusation. It's absurd. I came here to see Moses Freeman. Call the police,' she says.

'Around here we are the police. We keep this township safe from skellums, even white skellums. You'll see. If you have something to say, keep it for your trial. You'll get a fair trial.'

A fair trial! Here . . . in the dark . . . with all these people waiting for the show . . . and Grace shouting her head off. They'll kill me.

A hard knock between her shoulder blades propels her towards a clump of trees where she's pushed behind a queue of prisoners. She stumbles twice. Her knees are so wobbly she can hardly stand. Breathing is hard, too. She fights to bring herself under control.

She remembers reading in law school of the infamous kangaroo courts that sprang up in South Africa's slums in the bad old days. The people got together to try to bring law and order to their crime-ridden streets where white police were seldom seen. Since then the authorities have tried to stamp them out, but with limited success.

The 'court' consists of a table and chair placed at the side of the yard where four people are sitting. Two paraffin lamps hang from a post near the table. Other lamps hang from the surrounding trees. A woman is dragged before them. Questions and answers go on and on, but Chris can't understand a word of the proceedings. The judge speaks briefly. Screaming and fighting, the woman is dragged to the centre of the yard, stripped forcibly to the waist. She's knocked headlong to the ground. Three men step forward and savagely beat her with wooden canes. Chris watches in horror as the blood spurts from her back and her screams intensify. Then it's all over and she's free to go, but no one helps the victim as she crawls to the edge of the crowd.

Soon it will be her turn. She has to get away. Chris steps slowly backwards, but collides with a guard holding a knife.

'You will be necklaced,' he whispers. 'You will dance. It takes a long time to die.' He points to a pile of tyres and cans of petrol strategically placed under a tree, lit by the flickering lantern.

Fear comes like blast from a bomb, knocking her on to her knees. She almost blacks out. Using strength she never knew she had, she blocks the scream that's rising in her throat. Instead she sinks back against a tree and closes her eyes.

Surely necklacing is the foulest torture ever devised. With their hands tied behind their backs, the victims leap and fall about in their efforts to shake the petrol out of the tyres, which hang like flaming millstones around their necks.

How many more to go? How long before they drag her to the centre of the yard? As her eyes adjust to the gloom, Chris sees a thicket of trees and shrubs behind her. She sees a man, shackled and tied, being lead to the yard. A quiver of excitement runs through the bystanders. Whatever he's done, Chris doesn't hold out much hope for him. The interrogation is short. Two men force a tyre over his head. He struggles and sinks to his knees as fear sucks the strength out of him.

Chris glances around. The guards, fascinated by the macabre spectacle, have stepped forward for a better view. She steps slowly backwards towards the sheltering trees, but part of her is with the victim in the yard. She can't look . . . it could be her . . . how can she run and leave him burning? She hears the trickling sound of liquid pouring, a strong stench of petrol wafts towards her. Then comes a whoosh as the petrol ignites. The accused man begins to scream. For Chris his screams never end.

Nearer comes a gasp of awe from the crowd. They inch forward to watch the macabre dance, and so do the guards. Chris backs towards the shelter of the trees. She expects to hear shouts and gun shots, but she only hears screams. She turns and flees headlong towards the bushes. It's dark and she's like an animal, bounding, falling, picking herself up. Fear drives her on. Heedless of roots and branches, she runs for her life. Soon Chris hears shouts and whistles behind her and the sound of pounding feet. She flees through the dark woods with no idea what lies ahead or where she's going.

The guards are gaining on her, so she changes direction, moving away from the commotion, racing along a narrow path, unable to shake off a sense of doom. They know the terrain intimately. She doesn't. Then, on her left, she sees lights shining from far away. Perhaps a motorway. Safety seems to lie that direction, so she changes course again.

A long time later she reaches a clearing. It's some sort of a makeshift football field, by the look of the goal posts. She is about to cross it when she sees a light flicker from behind a rock. A torch perhaps. She lurches back into the trees and hears a strange bird call, but surely no bird ever sang that melodiously. The sound sets her heart hammering and her skin crawling. She must get away from here. She turns back, hurtling from bush to bush . . . panicking, falling, hurting herself, but she's beyond caring. Several more shots ring out, but they're in the distance.

Half an hour later, her clothes in shreds, Chris pauses to take stock. Her path is hampered by a strong barbed wire fence. It takes a huge effort of will to stand still and listen. She seems to have left her pursuers far behind. She tries to catch her breath and stop panting as she saws the rope that binds her wrists on the rusty wire spikes until the strands fall apart. Pulling the wire aside, she tumbles through.

Not far away is a small rocky hill, like a vast pile of stones. She might be able to see the motorway from there. It's steeper than it looks and the stones are loose so she keeps on sliding back. Panting and cutting her hands, she reaches the top at last, and she pauses to look around.

The first gunshot is thunderous. It shakes the night like a thunderclap. A second shot follows. She slithers down and runs headlong over the ground. She's lost all idea of time or direction. She only knows that she must keep moving on.

A sudden streak of lightning transforms the darkness into daylight. She's standing in the middle of an empty field. How can that be? The thunder clap is almost simultaneous and a strong smell of sulphur chokes the air. Then the clouds break. A solid mass of water drenches her and churns the dust to mud in seconds. Visibility is nil. Which way? Another flash lights the scene in lurid purple-white light. On the other side of the field stands a house, a garden, a child's swing and a gate. It looks so safe that she bursts into tears. Crouched on the ground in the rain, she rocks backwards and forwards as her tears turn to rasping sobs of anger and relief.

Later, after she has been hustled into a hot bath by the farmer's wife, Melanie, and dressed in the woman's pyjamas and dressing gown, she sips a mug of sweet rooibos tea, gnaws her buttermilk rusks, and tries to think up a suitable story, while the farmer, Steve, tells her how lucky she is to be alive. She doesn't need to be told. She can't stop remembering those terrible screams, the stench of burning flesh, the cruelty.

She has blundered out of Soweto by the most direct route, moving east into farmland, they tell her with the help of a map. Their neighbouring farmer, plagued by stock theft, took pot shots at her, not aiming to hit at all, not now in the new South Africa, they explain carefully, but just to warn her. He'd phoned to wake the neighbours, which was why Steve was looking for an intruder when he found her outside their garden fence.

Chris tries out her story. She's a writer. She came to research a book on diamonds. She brought the address of a friend's former maid because she'd promised to look her up, but she couldn't find her. So she hailed a taxi, or what she thought was a taxi, which took her to the square where they tied her. She couldn't see their faces so how could she identify the guards? Fortunately, she managed to escape.

'You will never know how fortunate you are,' Steve repeats. He is shocked and upset.

The police soon arrive, but they seem to find her story unbelievable.

'Why does it seem so strange to you?'

The Inspector shrugs. 'These kangaroo courts try to do an honest job. The punishments are harsh, but they're helping to keep down crime. They have never picked on tourists. They deal with local, petty criminals, but now they're guilty of murder. We turned a blind eye to floggings for rape and theft. What did their so-called magistrate look like? Can you describe him?'

'No. It was pitch black. They had a few lanterns, but I was pushed behind the trees.'

'What was the address you were given?' the sergeant cut in.

'I don't have it. It was in my handbag.'

'Passport . . . money . . . ticket . . . all lost?'

'Everything.'

'Don't worry. We'll take you to the British Consul tomorrow. Can't you remember any part of the address?'

'Not now. Perhaps when I'm not so shocked I'll remember. Or else I could contact my friend.'

'Were you molested or hurt in any way?' the Inspector asks, looking embarrassed.

'No. I was chased and shot at, but I wasn't attacked in any way.' Chris fields his questions agilely.

Eventually the police take her back to the hotel dressed in Melanie's pyjamas and dressing gown, with her bundle of tattered clothes in a carrier bag. They will collect her in the morning and take her to headquarters, they assure her.

At last she's alone and back in her room.

Shuddering, she throws herself on the bed.

Not now. Don't think about it now. Don't remember. This is no time for delayed shock. The here and now is for keeping your wits about you.

She bathes, changes, packs, retrieves her private papers, credit cards, traveller's cheques and passport from the safe in her room and pushes them in her pockets. She's lost her handbag containing loose cash, that's all. She can buy another bag. She has to leave at once, or she'll be delayed here for days while the police make their ponderous investigations. Freeman might get bail or be deported. This is her last chance to find him.

Leaving cash for the porter to launder and post the night clothes back to Melanie, she checks out and takes a cab to the airport, where she paces the departure lounge, half expecting to be discovered and escorted back to the city 'to assist with their enquiries'. She's witness to a murder trial and this could prove time-consuming. By six-thirty a.m. she's boarding the early morning flight to Windhoek. She pauses on the steps and looks around. The first grey light of dawn is breaking on the eastern horizon. By the time the plane takes off, the sky is a backdrop of crimson and mauve, so beautiful that it brings goose-pimples to her skin.

As the plane takes off she relaxes and closes her eyes, but all at once she is reliving the night's drama. She jerks into wakefulness.

Not yet! There's work to be done. She pushes

239

the tormenting images out of sight into the bog at the bottom of her mind. It pays to get tough with yourself from time to time, Chris decides. She can't afford to sleep, so she turns her attention to writing her report.

25

Chris feels light-headed as she steps off the plane into the glare of the African sunlight, not dizzy at all, but not really there . . . as if she's watching herself on a digital screen. She passes through passport control, retrieves her case, hires a car at the Avis counter and buys a map at the airport bookshop, but still she can't shake off a sense of unreality.

It is ten a.m. by the time she emerges from the airport and walks across the Avis car park towards her car. The air is so hot it scorches her lungs. Chris resorts to short, shallow gasps. Her eyes burn, her lips crack and the mucous in her nose turns to stalagmites that pierce her tender skin. It is the hottest, driest day she has ever experienced. Perspiration trickles between her shoulder blades, her hair is sticking to her scalp and forehead and she's longing for some ice-cold water.

There is only one road outside the airport with a sign pointing towards Windhoek. Ten-foot high wire fences line the road on either side, but she wonders why, since there is nothing beyond but flat gravel plains with no sign of life except the occasional thorn bush. Then, out of the shimmering haze, a herd of Kudu races towards her. She brakes, sensing a massacre as they near the fence at breakneck speed, but suddenly they're airborne, soaring in a high arc, to land in the road only a few feet ahead of her. A split second later they leap gracefully over the next fence and disappear into the haze. Long after they are gone, Chris can still hear their pounding feet and remember the strength and beauty of each of them as they sailed overhead. Dazed and disbelieving, Chris starts the engine and drives on.

Windhoek is a curiously diverse city, where modern high-rise office blocks contrast with the graceful lines of traditional German architecture. At least the Holiday Inn Hotel holds no surprises, welcoming her with it's familiarity. Chris books in, showers, changes into a beige safari suit and finds the prison on the map. Fortunately, it's not far away.

★   ★   ★

How can she convince Freeman that she had nothing to do with his arrest? That's the problem uppermost in her mind as she drives towards the prison. And who shopped him? Who wants Freeman put away that badly? Clearly it must be the same criminals who set him up for Ben's murder. That makes sense. Perhaps she will be able to convince Freeman that it's in his interest to help her to expose this criminal gang. Only then can he look forward to a safe future.

She is stopped at the gate by a guard, directed to a car park and led into a small annex where the shutters are barred and it's surprisingly cool, despite the lack of air conditioning. She fills in a form giving brief personal details and her reason

242

for visiting Moses Freeman. Her bag is searched, she empties her pockets and passes through a metal detector. She is directed to a swing door. Chris retrieves her bag and walks into an adjoining hall.

It's like wading into pea soup. Trying not to gag at the fetid air, she joins a long queue of prisoners' relatives and friends sitting on rows of benches. After half an hour, she wonders how long she will be able to take it. By the look of things she'll be here all day. It's a dismal place. The women look tired and unhappy. Several of them are carrying babies on their backs. Time passes, the seconds tick past ever more slowly and the children's wails intensify. There is no water and Chris longs to go out and buy some, but she's afraid of losing her place in the queue.

By three p.m. Chris is worrying that she might pass out with the unaccustomed heat and her lack of sleep, but shortly afterwards she is called out of the queue by an officious warder and taken to a large, bare room where she stands between two tubular railings, with armed guards watching every movement. The room is split in half by a steel mesh partition, with benches and chairs on either side.

Every detail is impressed on her mind: the prisoners sitting in a row behind the grid, looking emaciated in their khaki shorts and T-shirts. So many melodramas are being played out here, as the guards, bored and sweating, watch impassively. A young man is lead back to the cells, while his visitor, who is probably his grandmother, wipes her eyes and stumbles away.

The clank of the boy's leg irons and the old woman's sobs will haunt her, Chris knows.

It's her turn. A guard is beckoning to her. She walks forward and sits in the vacant chair facing the grid where she waits . . . and waits . . . She knows she's been pulled to the front of the queue. Is that because she's white? She feels guilty. Hearing the clanks that precede each prisoner, she looks up and sees an old man in regulation shorts and top, shuffling towards her. Can this be Moses Freeman? Without his jewellery, top hat and sideburns, and with his beard and hair shaved off, he looks old and nondescript . . . until he catches sight of Chris. Then his rage is awe-inspiring. Taking his guards by surprise, he lurches forward and hammers his fists against the grid. A tirade of words brings phlegm flying from his mouth. His eyes look wild, his nostrils expand as he shouts obscenities at her. A baton crack on his right ear dazes him, but nothing can quieten him. Yelling with rage, he is dragged back to the cells.

'He doesn't want to see you. Move along, Madam,' the guard explains unnecessarily.

All this way for nothing. She won't get another chance. Now what? She has no clear idea of how she can go forward without Freeman's help.

A female guard is waiting to collect her.

'Come this way, please, Miss Winters, the governor wishes to see you.'

★ ★ ★

244

Still longing for a glass of water, she is deposited on a hard wooden bench outside the governor's office. She can feel the sweat trickling down her back and her hair is damp and falling over her forehead. She must look a sight. She tries to smooth her hair into place.

Half an hour later she is shown into a cool and pleasant room where white sun-filter curtains flutter in the blast from the air conditioning. Raffia mats on the floor fill the room with their pungent odour.

'Miss Winters, I must apologise for making you wait ... ' Whether the prison governor notices her distress or not Chris can't tell. Perhaps he does, for he searches around the room until he finds what he is looking for, a fridge disguised as a filing cupboard. He's not sure which way the door opens, but he soon finds out.

'Got it. Please sit down. There are only two options — Coke or cold water?'

'Cold water, please.'

This isn't his office, so he isn't the prison governor. He's not an African either, but he's swarthy. She admires his beautiful hands while he fills a glass and hands it to her before placing a jug of water beside her.

'You're not used to this kind of heat. It can lead to kidney failure if you become dehydrated. Be careful. Drink a lot of water while you're here ... as much as you can, and keep a bottle of water in your car.'

He is a lean, sinewy man in his mid-thirties, she guesses. The deep lines on his face suggest years in the African sun. He's ugly, but he's got good eyes, clear and decisive and very shrewd. His hair is blue-black, the kind of black you see in Spain and parts of France.

'I apologise for the scene you witnessed. We wanted to see Freeman's reaction when he saw you. Tell me, Miss Winters, why does he think you betrayed him?'

Chris sighs. 'I don't know. I really need to see him. I came all the way from London for that reason. I had no idea he'd been arrested until I arrived in Johannesburg.'

'To see his sister in Soweto.'

It's a statement, not a question, and Chris tries not to show how startled she feels.

'Tell me, Miss Winters, why did you risk your life by going to Soweto at night to see Moses Freeman's sister? What is your connection with this man?' Suddenly he is watchful and very hostile.

'Why should I answer any of your questions. I don't even know who you are. You're not the prison governor, I'm sure of that.'

'No, I'm not. I've borrowed his office because it's cool. He does himself proud, don't you agree?'

'It's a pleasant room. Who are you?'

He shrugs. 'You have a right to know who's questioning you.' He flashes a South African police badge in front of her. It is quickly withdrawn, but not before she's read: *DI Petrus Joubert, Gold and Diamond Fraud Squad.*

'Now please answer my question.'

Chris turns the question over in her mind. Ben

246

had warned her to avoid the hindrance of a police investigation if possible, but in this case it seems wise to try to enlist the detective's support. After all, they are both on the same side.

She produces her card. 'I'm here to investigate diamond laundering on behalf of our client, the government of the Republic of Congo.' She sits back, hoping to see his shock, but his dour expression doesn't change.

'I didn't know what you were investigating. I assumed it was Freeman's alleged fraud.'

'No.'

'May I have your passport, Miss Winters?'

She passes it to him and Joubert leaves the room. The next ten minutes pass slowly as Chris worries if she'll get her passport back. He returns looking more relaxed. He even smiles as he hands over the precious document.

'I'll save time by telling you that I know what happened in Soweto. Why did you slip out of the country so sneakily?'

Chris considers the question. They must have questioned Grace Tweneni. How else could they know that Freeman had been arrested and that she would come straight here to see him?

'I had to move fast. Freeman might have got bail, or been deported. How bad are the charges?'

'Before I answer that, tell me what you know about Freeman.'

'Freeman has received two and a half million dollars from an Arab bank in order to set up diamond polishing workshops in Liberia. Naturally, I first thought that he was a man with a vision who was longing to move his country into the twenty-first century. Later our New York office checked in Liberia and found that there are no workshops.'

'And you passed on the information to Prince Husam.'

'Actually, no. He isn't one of our clients.'

'Of course.' He smiles cynically. 'Freeman is a man with a vision. I'll grant you that. His vision is himself as a millionaire, living it up in the South of France with his loot in a numbered account in Geneva. He has a family house in Liberia where his wife and four children live in style, but he spends most of his time in his Monaco apartment with his beautiful Portuguese mistress. Millions are involved. He could get life. The Liberian authorities are trying to force his extradition and since we are fellow members of the African Union we may have to comply with their wishes.'

'But why does he blame me for his arrest?' Chris asks suddenly.

'He is convinced that you informed Prince Husam Ibn al-Faisal that there were no such workshops.'

'I didn't. To tell the truth, I assumed that he and the prince were in it together, using massive cash withdrawals to buy illicit diamonds.'

'It's an interesting theory.' He shrugs. 'We all know that Africa's raw materials should be used to create skilled jobs for the people, rather than making profits for multinationals. Apart from the investment Freeman received from the prince, he was also given a substantial grant from the Liberian government. They can't wait to see him behind bars.'

The DI drains his coke and puts the glass down with a crack. He's on a short fuse, Chris decides. Or is there more to it?

'Listen! This will surprise you. Moses Freeman was once my colleague. In Namibia he is thought of as a patriot, so that might help him. He was a renowned Freedom Fighter and a genius at raising funds.' He changes his tone abruptly. 'Of course, that was a long time ago.'

She listens carefully. He's smart and he's on her side, for reasons she doesn't understand. She says: 'I didn't suss him out at all. I'm embarrassed. I knew he had his hand in the till, but I thought it was small time.'

'Unfortunately Freeman has a large circle of ex-comrades in Namibia. Your life could be in danger. Please be very careful, Miss Winters. The sooner you return to London, the better.'

'So what's new,' she says sadly.

'Arab bankers have been good to Africa,' Joubert is saying. 'Millions of Arab dollars are invested annually all over the continent. The money is helping us to create a strong middle class.' He sighs. 'OK, let's get back to you. Freeman is under the impression that you were working for Prince Husam.'

'I did, but only for a few days. It was part of my investigation. Later, I pretended I was working for Husam when I saw Freeman in New York.'

'How did you get the job . . . just when you needed it?'

'I can't disclose . . . '

'Nevermind,' he interrupts her curtly. 'I don't suppose a beautiful woman like you has any difficulty landing a job with whomsoever you wish to investigate.'

She frowns at his obvious disapproval.

'Let's get down to the nitty-gritty. So what is so important that you risked your life to see Freeman? Surely not for diamond laundering?'

'I can't disclose . . . '

Joubert swears. 'Trust me. I might be able to get some information for you when I question him.'

'OK. A friend has been kidnapped, another, Ben Searle, was murdered. Ben was my boss and he'd been working on this investigation for three months.'

'But you have Scotland Yard.'

'True, but any small lead that I come across might help them to find Sienna, the girl who's been kidnapped. Moses Freeman knows exactly who is responsible for laundering most of the blood diamonds that are finding their way into Western markets.

'A reliable informer told me that when Freeman was in prison he conscripted fellow convicts to be his agents. I need their names. When Namibia gained independence, Freeman opted out of the organisation, but it carried on purely for the profit motive.'

'It makes sense. I think I can help you. Just names. Is that all you want?'

'That would be better than nothing.'

'I might be able to persuade the governor to let you examine prison records for the period when Freeman was imprisoned in Windhoek.'

Chris brightens. 'Are they computerised?'

'Of course, but no print-outs, I'm afraid. You'll have to write the names down. I don't want any records lying around.' For a few moments he sits staring at Chris as if in a trance. Then he snaps to attention. 'Our prison records are in a centralised office . . . I'll arrange a permit for you. How about tomorrow morning at eight?'

'I'm truly grateful.'

'They're just names. No addresses. It'll be a hell of a job to trace any of them after this time lapse. By the way . . . I must warn you that the information you gave me will go to the Johannesburg police. They're annoyed with you.' He looks worried and this throws her.

'Yes, but I had other priorities.' Chris doesn't intend to reveal her need to put as much distance as possible between herself and Soweto.

'Good luck. If I get anything from Freeman I'll call you later at the Holiday Inn Hotel.'

'But not tonight. Tonight I'm catching up on my sleep. I haven't had much lately.'

'That sounds like an invitation for tomorrow. How about dinner?'

She smiles. 'I'm in your debt. Please come to dinner as my guest. Shall we say at seven p.m.?'

'On the condition that you let me buy the drinks.' He looks bashful and apologetic and then aloof as he calls a guard to see her off the premises. What a strange, complex man he is,

251

Chris thinks as she drives back to the hotel.

Chris is beginning to understand that an investigation is like knocking a domino over so that it hits the next one . . . and the next . . . until you move right down the line. She can't wait to get hold of the list of Freeman's fellow convicts. Surely one of them will lead her to further disclosures. So what then? That's where the truth lies, she answers herself. And you better believe it.

26

Chris is waiting outside the prison archives with her laptop and a bottle of water before they open. The head librarian goes out of her way to be helpful and she is given a desk to herself in an air-conditioned room. Thousands of men were imprisoned in Windhoek prison during the five years Freeman spent there, from 1975 to 1980. Their crimes were murder, breaking and entering, robbery with violence, theft and rape, but overwhelmingly the charge sheet states: political sabotage. To her surprise, illicit diamond dealing is also high on the list.

Although Mohsen Sheik's detective was positive that this is not a Muslim organisation, Chris can't be sure he is right, so she is typing the name of every man whose sentence is related to diamonds. It is a long and boring job and Chris works straight through until her neck aches and her eyes burn. She finishes at four p.m., just before the archives close for the day.

Stepping outside is like walking into a sauna. Driving due west towards Windhoek, the sun remains poised dead centre over the road, creating mirages of blinding, reflective pools just ahead. After ten minutes she has a headache so she pulls on to the gravel verge, takes out her notebook, and jots down a few ideas.

After a while she begins to think about Jim and the way he had been on the night he tackled the stalker, who turned out not to be a stalker after all. Jim had excited her almost beyond control. But he had lied to her. Yet knowing this and despite David's many warnings, she still lusts after him and she despises herself for it.

It's an effort to switch her mind from Jim and consider her progress. She has a hundred and fifty names so far. If her theory is right, any one of the names in her laptop might lead her to the criminal gang. But how on earth is she to start on this mammoth undertaking? Then she has an idea. She will check the names against the local newspaper's files. Some of them might have been in the news.

The sun continues its fall towards the horizon. It's lying along the road, as if melting into a large crimson blob, blinding anyone foolish enough to drive due west. The air becomes slightly more bearable, and the landscape even lonelier. But suddenly she's not alone. A group of Herero women, tall and magnificent in their floral crinolines, bright blouses, with scarves over their heads, sway in unison towards the prison. A handful of karakul sheep appear in the midst of the stony plateau behind her. Chris puts down her notebook and gazes at the vast plains shining like gold in the setting sun. A strange twilight suffuses the land. Glancing along the road, she sees the sun disappearing rapidly. Suddenly it's gone, leaving a pale green tinge to the sky. She blinks, waiting for her eyes to recover before driving on. The karakul have vanished into the evening mist, there's not a person or animal to be seen, only these vast plains of flat, infertile soil under the darkening sky. Chris starts the engine and drives back on to the road feeling strangely moved.

At the hotel there is a hand-delivered, sealed envelope in her key locker. She walks to the balcony, orders a fruit juice and opens the envelope. The message reads: *I'll be in your hotel bar at seven. I have news for you. P Joubert.*

She's looking forward to getting more information. She badly needs a push in the right direction, she considers sadly as she goes up to her room. The hotel pool is large, brightly lit and it glitters invitingly. From her balcony, she can smell the chlorine and hear the splashes. Chris hadn't thought to pack a bikini, but she finds one at the hotel's shop near the pool. Rushing back upstairs, she showers and changes and spends the next hour in the pool making up for days of tension. She feels great by the time she has showered. She has only packed one outfit for dinner, a sparkling blue top and navy silk trousers. She gives herself a critical check in the mirror. Better than yesterday, but not quite back to normal yet. Spraying perfume around her, she hurries down to meet Joubert in the bar.

★　★　★

They sit on the balcony overlooking the pool. The starlight is magical, almost like moonlight. It tarnishes the swarthy skin of her companion and shines on his blue-black hair. Chris has never seen stars so big and bright before. It seems as if

255

she's viewing the sky through a wide-angle telescope.

'So this is what you really look like.' His eyes are level and shrewd and a gentle warmth lingers. 'Now I can guess what a bad time you had in Soweto. You must take more care, Miss Winters. We fight a war here between the haves and the have-nots, and it takes place in dark alleys and lonely places. Make no mistake, everyone is on one side or the other. There's no such thing as a noncontender in Africa.'

'I'm sure you're exaggerating.' She feels resentful. He is spoiling the magic of the night.

'How did it go today?' Joubert asks.

Reluctantly Chris drags her mind back to work. 'I have the names of one hundred and fifty men who were convicted of crimes related to diamonds during the time Freeman was incarcerated here.'

Petrus' eyes reveal his scepticism. 'I'm curious to know why you're so sure that these ex-convicts are somehow connected with your diamond launderers. Think of the organisation that's needed and the cash outlay to buy the diamonds. I'd put my money on al-Qaeda.'

'You might be right. That's what my colleague . . . ' she breaks off feeling unwilling to talk about Ben.

Petrus leans back and watches her with a quizzical expression. 'I have some information for you which backs my intuition. I decided to squeeze our friend . . . '

She gasps momentarily.

'Remember Soweto! Don't you want to hit back?'

'No. How can you fight cruelty with more cruelty?' She shudders.

Petrus is openly laughing at her. 'Don't worry. A couple of shocks are good for depression, I've heard.'

He grins to show he's only joking, but Chris isn't convinced. 'I'm sorry. Please carry on.'

'Moses Freeman is a bitter man. He needs to hit out at someone within reach and you are the one he chose, but he's had time to think things over. He's come to the conclusion that you didn't betray him after all. How could you know whether or not the workshops exist since you have never visited his country. Freeman believes that Prince Husam is linked to Bin Laden and that they are cooperating on diamond laundering and have set up an extensive network of agents all over Africa in order to finance local coups.'

She shrugs. 'It's a good theory.'

'Well, my job is to investigate Freeman, that's all. I'm leaving for Liberia early tomorrow morning to search for any signs of business activity. If I don't find any, Freeman's in big trouble.'

'I don't understand why anyone would want to shop Freeman. He's small fry.'

'Exactly my next question to him. Freeman replied that he knows too much. If he hadn't had a very public alibi in New York — he was in a snooker tournament and up to a hundred people saw him there — he would have been arrested

257

for murder and I doubt he would ever have left prison.'

'He told you that?'

'In a roundabout sort of way.'

'He seems to have said a great many things.'

Her implied criticism hits home. Petrus flushes deeply.

Chris has the feeling she's offended the inspector. She wonders what to say next, but nothing comes to mind. Their forced small talk is worse than a long silence, she feels. Eventually she tries to explain: 'Our worlds are so different. I sense that you are a good man forced to do things you don't like. I do apologise for being suspicious and over-critical.'

He smiles sadly. 'I don't often drink much, but tonight's one of those nights when I need to get drunk. It's the interrogation . . . Unless I drink, I have nightmares all night . . . sometimes for weeks. I can't stand their pain. It's a part of my job that I hate, but there's no other way to get information out of men like Freeman.'

She listens in growing horror while he tells her of the torture school he once attended as part of his training before he joined the fraud squad.

'Listen,' he says. He reaches out and clasps her hand, holding on too tightly. 'It was nothing serious. Believe me! A couple of shocks. Freeman raved a bit for a while. He said: 'Do your worst. What does it matter? When I get out of here that fucking accountant will put out my light.' This 'accountant' is someone Freeman fears greatly, but I couldn't get his name. Maybe that will come in handy.'

By the time they examine the menus, Petrus is on his third double vodka and Chris is feeling uneasy. Despite her misgiving, she enjoys his company. Petrus is clever, romantic and a fabulous dancer. He even sings to her, translating the songs the band are playing into English.

★ ★ ★

Much later, when they are having coffee on the balcony and the staff are stacking the tables and chairs around them, Chris says: 'I've been wondering about your roots, Petrus. I'm not familiar with your name. Are you French, or Portuguese perhaps?'

'My roots . . . ' A burst of hilarity surges out of him. 'Only a dumb girl from London would ask such a question. At a guess I would say Xhosa, Malay, Dutch, French, for sure, because of my name, and just about every nationality whose ships ever put into Cape Town's harbour. Come on. One last dance. Then I must go. It's past three a.m. and I leave for Liberia at six.'

'Thank you for helping me, Petrus,' she says as he leaves.

'Good luck,' he turns away, but moments later he turns back. 'Look here, Chris . . . ' He takes out a card and scribbles on it. 'Don't lose this . . . at least not until you quit Africa. This is my private mobile number. Try to keep out of trouble, but if you get in a fix call me . . . day or night. I can always get through to the police wherever you are.'

259

She examines his face gravely. She can see that he means it and she finds his promise comforting. He steps forward and hugs her. For an age they stay that way, swaying slightly, and then he releases her, turns and hurries across the foyer. She is left with a strange empty feeling at the way so many good friends pass by and are never seen again.

27

The *Namibia News* library opens to the public at nine, but Chris had telephoned the previous afternoon and so she is let in at eight. She settles down in comfortable air conditioning with her laptop and her bottle of water. This is so easy. She has only to type in each name and the computer does the searching. She can even dream of the hotel pool: cool, fragrant and inviting, where she guesses she'll be swimming by noon. Her dreams crash when she reaches 1980. Before that year there is nothing at all.

'That's when we computerised,' the librarian tells her, looking smug. 'Prior to the Eighties, we only have old newspapers for records . . . different name, different format. You'll find it tough going, but you can search back as far as the First Word War, if you like.'

'The Seventies will do me.'

Page by dusty page, Chris doggedly reads every word of every column, checking each name against her long list of prison inmates. The old pages are mellow with age and dust and she is soon plagued with sneezes and burning eyes. By the end of the day she has only reached back to January, 1985. At this rate, it will take her three days at least, she reckons.

By the end of the second day Chris has reached back to June, 1979. She's just about given up hope, when she comes across a name that seems familiar: *Herman Visser*. Her hands are shaking as she checks on her list. There it is. A name, at last! She turns back to the report, which came from the newspaper's Swakopmund correspondent. He vividly described the wrecking of a company-owned diamond dredger, *Rainbow's End, en route* to Walvis Bay from Port Nolloth during a bad storm. *A Dutch deep sea diver, Herman Visser, is missing, believed drowned, together with the boat's skipper.*

So he's dead. That's that. Her disappointment is so great, Chris feels like packing up for the day, but she forces herself to skip through the rest of the report which goes on to describe how the remainder of the crew managed to swim to shore. And then:

Ulf Skoog, first mate of Rainbow's End, in a statement to the police, explained that Visser had worked a ten-hour diving shift prior to the accident and was in a state of exhaustion when the dredger foundered. He said: 'The hull was ripped right open on the rocks and we foundered too fast to release the lifeboat. Visser was washed off the deck and I saw him go under. I never saw him again.'

At first police suspected foul play, because the vessel was completing its last day at sea, prior to delivering a large cache of diamond roughs to Walvis Bay.

Geologist, Dan Kelly, 35, who has . . .

Dan Kelly! But that's her father's name. Is this really her father? Chris flinches at seeing his name in print. Her heart is pumping wildly. Can this be true? How many geologists of that name can there be in Namibia? Mum told her he'd been prospecting for diamonds in Namibia prior to '75 which was when she had last seen him. It must be him. But why . . . ? What did he have to do with Herman Visser? Chris finds she is gasping for breath as her eyes skim the column . . .

Geologist, Dan Kelly, 35, who has an off-sea concession near Walvis Bay, was repeatedly questioned by police about his former mining partner, Herman Visser, but affirmed that he had not seen Visser for over two years.

There is nothing else. Chris leans back and rubs her eyes. She feels stunned. Surely that was her father's age in 1979. It must be him. So what age is he now? Sixty-one, she calculates. Two years older than her mother. Everything fits. It takes her a few minutes to pull herself together and continue with her work.

It is half past four and near to closing time before Chris finds Visser's name mentioned again. The dateline is January, 1977. The report reads: *Herman Visser, an accountant from Holland* . . . Chris feels quite shocked. So he was an accountant, not a deep sea diver by profession. And what was it Freeman had said to Petrus? '*Do your worst. When I get out of here that fucking accountant will put out my light.*' Two coincidences! She reads on:

263

Herman Visser, an accountant from Holland, was today sentenced in Windhoek to two-years' hard labour for diamond theft and smuggling. Visser, and his ex-partner, Dan Kelly, a well-known American geologist who is currently diamond dredging off Walvis Bay, suffered defeat in a controversial court case two years back, which deprived them of a rich diamond mine into which they had sunk all their capital. The judge took this into consideration when reducing Visser's sentence.

There is more, but none of it is relevant. At least she knows where her father was in the Seventies.

Chris drives back to the hotel in a daze. She showers and goes down for a swim, but the pool has lost its enchantment as she monotonously notches up the lengths in a swift crawl. If Herman Visser is involved, and if indeed he is the accountant whom Freeman fears so much, does that mean that her father is involved in this scam, too? Another thought occurs to her. Can she honestly use company time and cash to search for Dan Kelly? She has to admit that with Visser dead she has only two leads: her father and Ulf Skoog.

So far she has only reached back to 1977. There are three more years to go in the morning. More names might crop up, and more news of Visser.

★　★　★

That night Chris is too anxious to sleep well. By six a.m. she's back in the pool trying to relieve

264

some of her tension. She arrives at the library at five minutes to eight. The moment she's let in, she hurries to the archive department where the dusty old newspapers, clipped into wooden frames, hang from chains and hooks. It's quite an effort to pick up each frame and push it on to the reading shelf above the hooks while clouds of dust rise around her. There are no seats here and she has to stand as she reads. It's boring work and if there's one thing Chris can't stand it's being bored.

She almost misses the names because they appear in a quasi-legal column, which is written in a racy style by a lawyer whose pen-name is Courtroom Commentator. She very nearly skips this one, because the heading, *Cherchez la Femme*, does not seem relevant to her search. The column is dated September, 1976, and comments upon a court case, won by Wanee Hendrickse, a black fisherman, against a Windhoek farmer, Piet Van As. The writer has made no attempt to be politically correct, perhaps a sign of the times and the place.

The hazards of love are nowhere better demonstrated than in the diamond fields of South West Africa, where today, a young coloured fisherman, Wanee Hendrickse, was declared the legal heir of the late Piet Van As, who owned the karakul farm, Morgendauw. All of which tells us nothing about the true significance of the court decision.

At this stage, Chris's concentration is wavering, but the next sentence brings her attention back

265

fast and sets her heart pumping.

The real story began three years ago, when freelance prospector, Dan Kelly . . .

'My father!' She mutters. 'God! What next?'

. . . when freelance prospector, Dan Kelly, discovered an exceptionally rich diamond pipe on the farm, Morgendauw, near Buffelsfontein. He approached Piet Van As, the owner of the farm, who indicated his willingness to sign away all mineral rights for a price, but the wily farmer wouldn't sign until the full amount was paid. Kelly raised the cash by taking in a partner, Herman Visser, an accountant from Holland.

'So they really were partners.' Feverishly, Chris reads on.

The two men hocked all they owned and pooled their total resources to pay Van As and buy the equipment they needed. Sadly, by this time Van As was dying and incapable of managing his affairs, so they were obliged to obtain the consent of the old man's nephew, Jan Van As, who had lived and farmed with his uncle since his father died ten years previously. Jan had been told he would inherit the farm and there were no other relatives, as far as he knew. Although the ninety-nine-year lease was signed, the two men kept wraps on their diamond find until such time as Jan was proved to be the legal heir. The two men capitalised the farm, proceeding with the utmost secrecy. Six months later, when they were ready to start mining, Van As died and his estate was declared intestate.

This is where the story becomes interesting.

Somehow, news of this massively rich diamond pipe leaked, and a cunning Johannesburg mining manager, Willem Zuckerman, came sniffing around the village. When he learned about Van As' neglected, bastard son of eighteen, Zuckerman sank half a million rands into financing Wanee's legal fight. Sorry to disappoint you folks, there was nothing philanthropic about Zuckerman's actions, for Wanee had signed away all mineral rights long before the first lawyer was consulted.

Yesterday, the court found Wanee to be the true heir and the two miners, embittered and broke, were sued for trespassing by Zuckerman as they tried to salvage their equipment.

And how did Zuckerman find out about this treasure trove? Cherchez la femme, the saying goes. It was a woman who did the dirty on Kelly, or so they're saying in Buffelsfontein.

Zuckerman, she ponders. The name is familiar, so when did she hear it before? She can't remember and it probably isn't relevant, so she puts the question aside. Feeling desperately sorry for her father, Chris copies, files, and searches back to 1975 but there is no further mention of any of the names on her list.

Chris mulls over what she knows so far as she returns to her hotel. Freeman, once an idealist, conscripted prison inmates to join his group in order to buy and sell rough diamonds to raise funds for his liberation movement. Later the group became so profitable that one or more of his agents forced Freeman out and from then on they hung on to their profits. Surely Visser was exactly the kind of man Freeman would recruit. He knew diamonds and he was crooked. Being an accountant must have proved useful, too.

But how can he be the accountant that Freeman fears so much now, when he is dead, Chris wonders. Ulf Skoog saw him go under. Or did he?

Ulf Skoog is not on her list since he didn't do time with Freeman, but there might be something . . . She types in the name, presses 'search' and to her surprise she's rewarded with any number of mentions. In 1982, three years after the wreck, Skoog set up a boat maintenance business in a hangar adjoining the dry dock with a capital investment of half a million rands. Now how did a first mate save half a million? After that there are many minor mentions: Skoog wins a yacht race, Skoog awarded a medal for life saving at sea, Skoog buys a share in a Botswana mine, Skoog buys an off-shore diving concession. Only three years after the wreck Skoog was in the money. There might be something here. She decides to pay him a visit.

And then there is her father. Surely he must have some insight into what went on at that time, if she could only find him. Perhaps he kept in touch with Visser until he died. *Or perhaps he's involved,* says a small unwelcome voice in the back of her mind.

28

Leaving at daybreak, Chris boards a Vickers Viscount prop jet, which crosses the rocky peaks of the Auasberg mountains and hundreds of square miles of featureless, flat gravel plains on its descent to the desolate Skeleton Coast and Swakopmund, where she disembarks at eight a.m.

Chris hires a 4×4 at the car hire counter and sets off through thick sea mist to the delightful old German town, where she books into the Swakopmund Hotel. She feels damp with perspiration as she follows the hotel porter to a front room overlooking the beach. It's light and cool with Venetian blinds, a high ceiling, air conditioning, a fridge and television. After a shower and a change of clothes, she feels ready for a new start.

Driving south towards Walvis Bay is a forbidding experience. Chris tries to shut out the desolation, but goose-pimples tingle down her arms. To the east, sand dunes rise and fall as the wind pummels the sand. To the west, boulders and jagged black rocks are constantly pounded by massive waves, sending spray soaring far into the air. The salt spray drifts in the mist and soils the windscreen. Switching the windscreen spray on time and time again, she wonders if the water will last to the next garage. Occasionally she sees a dead seal deposited by the tide with a handful of jackals scrapping over it. How can they live?

They are so thin they look two-dimensional.

Walvis Bay is little more than a support town for its huge, bustling harbour, where ships of all nationalities crowd the berths. At a glance she sees Japanese, South African and Russian fish factories, a US naval vessel and several local cargo boats. Adjoining the harbour are rows of factories, workshops and ships' chandlers. A cluster of small stone bungalows, built on sand, houses the local population. The mist drifts around the buildings carrying the stench of salt spray, fish entrails, rotting seaweed, ozone and engine oil. Worst of all is the noise. The roar of the surf, the crash of the waves on the rocks, ships' sirens, the clatter of pallets being loaded, cries of hungry seabirds and shouts of the dockers merge into an unbearable roar.

Beyond the buildings there is only sand, hundreds of miles of sand, with tall dunes continually changing shape in the wind.

Chris sighs as she thinks of her poor father spending years dredging for diamonds in this maelstrom of surf, sharks and deadly currents. It seems to Chris that this is the worst place in the world.

★ ★ ★

Having inspected the town and the docks, Chris is hyperventilating with tension as she parks her car outside the police station. She decides to walk around to calm herself. She's passing a nearby churchyard, but there is no sign of anything green, not a tree or a blade of grass.

271

The tombstones stand half-hidden by sand.

'My poor father,' she whispers again. Tears are stinging her eyes, but this is crazy. Is there some psychic, emotional thread that binds her to a man she's never even seen? What sort of a father would ignore his own daughter for her entire childhood? It doesn't say much for his character. Once again Chris wonders if Kelly is mixed up in the diamond laundering scam. When she finds him, it might be better not to tell him who she is, at least until she's found out more about him. But he knows her name, doesn't he. She sees a broken tombstone lying in the sand. *In loving memory of Sarah Vaughan*, she reads. That name will do nicely.

Entering the cool, shuttered police station she notes that sand has taken the place of dust. She leans against the sandy counter and waits. After a while a sergeant saunters over. He's nearing retirement age, and his white skin is piebald with red and white patches where sun and sand have done their worst. His stern blue eyes classify her as a probable lawbreaker.

'What's your problem?' he asks.

'I'm looking for Ulf Skoog. I believe he lives around here. Do you know him?'

'Sure. Everyone knows him. He owns a boat maintenance business in the harbour. You'll find it down beside the dry dock.'

His face shows no expression. 'What's your interest in Skoog?'

Chris changes her story to fit the facts. 'I'm writing a survey on Walvis Bay for a shipping magazine based in Cape Town. I want to include

272

an article about Skoog.'

'That should please the locals.'

'And I'm looking for Dan Kelly, too,' she says, her mouth drying.

'I haven't seen Kelly for years. I heard he went to Angola at the end of the civil war . . . registered a claim on a former Unita-controlled diamond field . . . He put in months of work and heavy spending, but he and his team were shot up by a squad of rogue troops. The team lost their equipment and some of them were wounded. Ask Ulf. He should know. He's looking after Kelly's boat. Good luck with your survey, Miss. Are you going to put my picture in?'

'Why not!'

★ ★ ★

Dread dulls her mind. Surely nothing's happened to her father. Suddenly she's scared of what she might find out. She dawdles past the ships at their berths and the gigantic cranes loading crates of fish and lobsters and unloading fresh produce. The mist is clearing away, she notices. She watches a tug, siren blaring, surge out of the harbour towards a factory ship waiting to be brought in. Seals are bobbing around the ships, seagulls hover and there's a strong smell of ship's oil and ozone. Pulling herself together, Chris moves on.

Beside the dry dock is a large corrugated shed. *Ulf Skoog, Maintenance*, is painted across the front. Peering inside, she sees men are crawling over the boats like ants. The hangar smells of varnish, sweat and diesel oil. Someone is welding at the far end and sparks are flying. It's a wonder they don't all go deaf here, Chris thinks. No one looks up . . . they seem to be working against the clock. Looking around she sees a glass-enclosed office built over a locked room which probably contains stores. Could that be Ulf up there? She mounts the steps.

'I'm looking for Ulf Skoog,' she calls. 'The police sergeant sent me here.'

The Dane, who looks exactly like an ancient Viking, with his blond beard and long, tatty hair, laughs down at her. 'I'd like to find him myself. He'll turn up one of these days if he's still alive.'

Sensing that Ulf is a ladies' man, she smiles coquettishly as she reaches the top. 'Tell me about him.'

'Well, let's see, he's tough, wild and loyal. The best man to have at your back in a fight. The ladies never get enough of him. So what's *your* interest in me, young lady?'

Chris repeats the story she told the sergeant. She rather likes it, but Ulf frowns.

'That's strange,' he says. 'Dickson didn't tell me about it. You know Dickson, of course. He's your local stringer and advertising rep.'

'It's still on the drawing board,' she ad libs, wishing she'd done her homework. 'I'm here to find out how much scope there will be.'

'You mean how much advertising you can pull in.'

'Of course,' she says. 'I'd like to do a story on Dan Kelly while I'm here.'

274

'For a shipping magazine?' Ulf looks incredulous.

'I freelance for a mining magazine in my spare time.' She is falling deeper into the mire of her own making.

'Ah, yes. Well, Kelly's disappeared. He does that from time to time. He's always going for the big claim, but he never seems to strike lucky. Occasionally he sells out a claim to one of the big mining houses. When he's broke he comes back here and starts dredging until he's earned enough capital to finance a few more months' prospecting. He's not getting any younger. He can't keep this up forever.'

'But surely you know where he is. You look after his boat.'

Ulf frowns. 'He might have gone back to the States.'

Chris tries not to show her dismay. 'When did you last hear from him?'

'Four years ago. He owes me a packet for rent and maintenance. I'll give him three more years, then I'm selling the dredger to cover my costs.'

She's reached a dead end. She says: 'I'm also intending to write a follow-up story about the shipwrecked dredger, *Rainbow's End*, which foundered in a storm in 1979.'

Ulf glances suspiciously at her. 'Never heard of it.'

'But you were on the boat, Mr Skoog. You were lucky to reach land safely. I guess you're a good swimmer.'

He scowls at her, looking at a loss for words. Chris decides to prod further.

'There was a huge cache of diamonds on the boat. Have any local scuba divers been treasure hunting?'

'They wouldn't be that daft,' the Dane mutters.

'How about Visser . . . Do you think he died when the dredger was wrecked?'

'Of course.' All the friendliness has gone from Ulf's face. He's watching her with dead eyes. He could be truly dangerous, that's obvious. Perhaps it's time to leave, but he's her last lead, so how can she quit now?

'Well then. Let's concentrate on you, Mr Skoog. I thought a double-page spread story with a photograph of you standing in front of your business would do nicely. This is a well-equipped business. It must have cost a packet to get established. Did you inherit your wealth?'

Skoog nods, but keeps his mouth shut, as if he can't trust himself to speak. Eventually he says: 'I'm busy. Come back tomorrow. Ten suit you? Now if you'll excuse me.'

She's hardly out of the office before Ulf picks up the telephone and prods the keys. No doubt he's calling Dickson to check her story. Chris leaves in a hurry.

★　★　★

Chris needs to speak to a few old-timers in the town and what better place than the dockside bar. The moment she steps across the threshold it becomes clear that she's broken an unwritten

276

code. The conversation lulls, heads turn and the mood is hostile.

Tough! They'll survive, but will she? She's gagging on the stench of cheap brandy, German beer, strong tobacco and hand-rolled grass. The barman glares at her.

'This is not a good place for women, Miss. It can get rough in here.'

She ignores this advice. 'I'm looking for Dan Kelly. Have you seen him around here lately?'

The pub is dead quiet now since everyone is listening, so she appeals to the clientele. 'Kelly was dredging for diamonds here for years. Some of you must have heard of him.'

The barman looks furtive. 'What's your business with Kelly, Miss?'

She changes her story slightly. 'I'm writing a series of articles on famous wrecks . . . like the *Rainbow's End*.'

'Can't be famous. I've never heard of it,' the barman says quietly and the men murmur their agreement. They are all sure that they have never heard of this particular dredger.

'And Dan Kelly?'

'I haven't seen Kelly for years. I heard he went back to the States.' The speaker is an old man, his face deeply lined by the harsh climate, his accent recognisably German.

Chris has trouble concealing her disappointment.

A dark-skinned man smelling strongly of fish interrupts them: 'Can't be true, since his boat's still in dry dock. Ask at the boatyard. Ulf's looking after it.'

'That's not his boat, mate.' The barman interrupts quickly. 'He sold it some time back.'

He's lying, Chris decides. Ulf should know who owns the dredger. Why are they all so anxious to put her off?

'How about Visser . . . do you think he really died?'

'Listen Miss,' the fisherman mutters, drawing her aside. 'Just leave while you still can. This is a rough crowd.'

Judging by the grumbles, this is sound advice. She leaves, but pauses outside. Everyone's arguing, but since she can't understand Afrikaans there's no point in hanging around. There's a reason why no one wants to resurrect details of the wrecked dredger and it surely has to do with the diamonds, but she can't begin to understand why they are deliberately hampering her search for Kelly. Perhaps that means that he's still alive. The thought cheers Chris as she walks back to the car park by the church.

Chris starts the engine and drives north towards Swakopmund. The mist has cleared and it's as hot as an oven. She longs to get back, order an ice-cold fruit juice and jump into the hotel pool. Meantime she has a half-hour drive ahead of her, so she forces her mind back to business.

Not only Skoog, but all the men in the bar were clearly anxious to keep that story under wraps. They probably wrecked the dredger and shared the treasure. Whatever! It's not her problem . . . unless it has something to do with the diamond laundering gang. It's Skoog she's after.

Suppose Skoog were the gang's local agent. Suppose he bought and dispatched blood diamonds . . . what exactly would he need to do this? Masses of cash, for starters, plus some means of disposing of the diamonds the moment he purchases them. She'd love to hack into his bank account, but right now she doesn't have the equipment. Perhaps Skoog was flying the diamonds out of Namibia. Of course. Why didn't she think about this before? She rams her foot on the brake. Next job must be to find out if Walvis Bay has a local private airfield. How about an armed carrier service? Would there be such a business in Swakopmund? Brakes squealing, she skids to a halt and turns the car back to Walvis Bay. Her longed-for swim is drifting further into the future.

29

Chris speeds back to Walvis Bay post office and finds the address of the town's only armed courier, Fidelity Guards. Much to her surprise the boss's PA is friendly and helpful. Some women behave like hamsters let out of a cage if they see another woman who isn't either old or plain, but Muriel, who runs the office, is a woman who likes chatting.

'I write for a shipping magazine based in Cape Town. We're planning a survey on Ulf Skoog and his business,' Chris explains. 'His twentieth anniversary is coming up soon . . . ' In next to no time Muriel is chatting on about Skoog.

Ulf is their biggest customer. 'And when I say big I mean *big*,' Muriel explains, pausing for a fit of coughing. Smoking and the harsh climate has wreaked havoc on her complexion, but she has fine brown eyes and a great smile.

'We collect the cash for wages from the bank and deliver it to him every Friday. He has so many fingers in so many pies you just can't keep up with the money that guy's making.'

'He must have a massive wage bill.'

Muriel's lips purse showing fine lines over her upper lip. 'I guess so, but we just deliver the cash boxes from the bank.'

'Listen,' Muriel calls as Chris is leaving. 'If you're looking for business I'm sure the local safe supplier would support the survey. They've just concluded a massive sale to Ulf. I heard the manager boasting about it in the Ladies' Bar.'

Ladies' Bar! This place is archaic. Chris drives out to the airport where Skoog keeps his Cessna, according to Muriel. After chatting up the pilot, she learns that Skoog pilots his own aircraft and frequently goes off on trips into Central Africa.

'Why don't you pop in to the Cessna suppliers,' the pilot suggested helpfully. 'I'm sure they'd be keen to advertise in your survey. Ulf's their best customer.'

The pilot is anxious to please. He suggests handguns, rifles, motor boats, 4×4s . . . it seems that Ulf is a big spender. Chris begins to wish that there was such a survey. Her commissions would be impressive.

By the time Chris turns back to Swakopmund, her suspicions are beginning to look more like reality. It takes massive cash resources to set up a network of agents strategically placed to buy all the spare diamonds available, but they've had twenty-five years to do just this. Chris strongly suspects that Skoog is one of the agents. His relationship with Visser goes back at least to '79, according to the media, but he probably knew him long before, since it was mainly his evidence that led the Coroner to declare that Visser had died at sea. According to the newspaper records, Skoog launched his business three years after the wreck. Perhaps he got a handsome payout.

But it's all guesses. She has no facts. Chris drives back in a mood of black despair. Where has she got? Bloody nowhere. So what if Skoog buys diamonds. Anyone can do that, *but how are*

281

they laundered? That is the genius of the scam and her job is to find out.

All these unknowns are unsettling Chris. She parks and walks into the hotel foyer, throws her keys onto the reception counter and hurries out to the pool where she orders a glass of iced wine with soda water and sits moodily gazing towards the sea. The sun has set, but the sky is brilliant with changing colours, from rose to cerise to purple with slashes of palest turquoise and oyster-grey lying low along the horizon. A flock of flamingoes passes like a pink haze. Cormorants follow in arrow formation, almost merging into the gathering mists. She sees a school of porpoise leaping high as they, too, move south. Sometimes, Chris ponders, you get these unsettling evenings in Africa when a soft, balmy breeze feels like a caress, when perfume from tropical flowers acts like an aphrodisiac, and the distant sound of a guitar and a man's voice singing a love song throws you right off balance. If only Jim were here.

Forget it, Chris tells herself. Her longing is unwelcome and absurd. She drains her glass and walks back to reception. 'Any messages?'

There are three pushed into her pigeon hole. One reads: *We're practically neighbours. Room 215 on the 2nd floor. How about dinner? Seven suit you? Jim.*

Joy and annoyance fight for precedence. Joy wins, but it's spoiled by a sense of unease. Why is Jim keeping tabs on her. Is he part of the scam and is she getting too close for comfort? Chris calls up to Jim's room, but he is out, so she scribbles a message saying: *Make it nine p.m. Meantime I'll be in the pool.*

The second message is from the porter: Phone DI Petrus Joubert. He says it's urgent. Chris walks outside and calls him on her mobile.

'Are you all right?' Petrus asks.

'Of course. I'm fine. This is a nice hotel. I like Swakopmund.'

'Be careful, Chris. I called you because we received a message from London, from the chairman of Trans-Africa Diamonds. Somehow he's heard about the Soweto incident and he claims that Freeman has organised a contract on your life, from prison. I've put out feelers, but no luck so far. The chairman insists on a 24-hour guard for you and he wants you back in London fast. On the next plane, he says.'

'How did he find out about the contract?'

'He's well in with the leaders of the African Union.'

Chris is too stunned to ask anything else.

'I've put in a request for a guard for you, but I have no authority in Namibia. I'm back in Jo'burg . . . just arrived. Take care, Chris. Better still, leave Namibia. Freeman's influence is restricted to his political pals and they're all local and mainly broke.'

'Thanks. I appreciate your help, Petrus. I'll take care and leave as soon as I can. Go well.'

She replaces the receiver.

How has David found out? He'll probably tell Rowan and then she'll really have problems. She might be recalled, or possibly even sacked. Damn! Big Brother is becoming a pain.

The third message is in a hand-delivered, sealed envelope. It's from Ulf Skoog who writes: *I've located Dan Kelly. Come to my office tonight . . . I'll wait for you.*

Chris hesitates, tapping her fingers on the counter. Her safari jacket is sticking to her back with sweat and her hair is plastered to her forehead. Perhaps she has time for a shower. She glances at her watch and sees that it's already half past seven. It will take an hour to get back to the docks. Just how long will he wait? She decides to go as she is. She scribbles a message for Jim.

Something's come up. I have to drive back to Walvis Bay. I hope to be back around eleven. Don't wait to eat. I'll see you later.

Chris feels uneasy as she hurries to the car park. What if he's lying? Perhaps she's wrong to ignore the contract, but whatever cash Freeman could provide would hardly impress a man like Skoog. Nevertheless she pauses and turns back to reception. Maybe one person in this world should know where she is. She scribbles a postscript on her note to Jim.

Ulf Skoog has news for me. He has a maintenance workshop in Walvis Bay docks. I'm going there now.

For the third time that day she's driving back to Walvis Bay. It's almost dark. There's no twilight here, she notices. The sun sinks and minutes later it's night. The road is full of bright green eyes as scavenging jackals are caught in her headlights . . . how can there be so many and how can they survive in this desolate place?

It's still so hot. Now that the sun has set the earth is belching up the heat of the day. The surf thunders frighteningly close and she can see patches of phosphorescence sparkling in the swell. There's a strong stench of rotting seaweed mingled with ozone and the nearer she gets to Walvis Bay, the stronger it gets.

By the time she reaches the docks a thick sea mist has rolled in and she can't see more than four metres ahead. The guard tells her to be careful and waves her through. Large black shapes turn into piles of railway lines, crates and cranes as she drives past slowly, trying to follow the road. At last she sees a blurred purple ball ahead, which turns out to be a security light above the entrance to Skoog's maintenance shed.

★ ★ ★

Skoog comes out to meet her. 'I'd just about given you up,' he says. 'Too many thugs roam the docks at night. I was beginning to worry. What kept you?'

'I only received your note when I got back to the hotel.'

'Did you have a good day?'

'Not bad.'

'You'll have to drive into the yard or they'll break into your car. Follow me. He shines his torch to show her the way around the corner of the shed to an unlocked gate set in a high wall topped with razor wire. She feels uneasy as Skoog padlocks the gate behind her. A quick getaway is now out of the question.

Skoog has smartened himself up. He's wearing clean white cotton trousers, a navy silk sweater and white trainers. She hopes she won't have trouble with him. He offers her a drink. She says she'd like a lemonade, hoping he won't drink much. She's feeling increasingly uneasy.

'I've had a few messages of congratulations this afternoon,' he says with a wry smile. 'I've been hearing about my twentieth anniversary and your proposed feature. Funny that Dickson knows nothing about it.'

'I haven't told him yet. There's no point until I can work out what kind of advertising support we can expect.'

'And . . . ?'

'Oh, not bad. Safes, aircraft, armed courier, rifles . . . Looks good to me. You spend a lot of money Mr Skoog.'

'Ulf . . . please.'

'OK, Ulf.'

'The pilot was very taken by you. He said you did a thorough job in delving into advertising possibilities.'

That's one way of putting it. She smirks into her glass.

'Look here!' She puts down her glass and grabs her bag. 'I've had a rough day. Can we go and find Kelly, please.'

286

'Sure.'

There's something odd about his eyes. He won't look at her. Perhaps he's trying to hide his fury. Or is it a gleam of pure triumph?

'So where is Kelly?' She asks, as he leads her to the back of the shed.

'Kelly's got a holiday shack a short way up the coast. He's there now. I didn't know that when I spoke to you, but I asked around. Sometimes he needs a break from the *bushveld*. It's tough out there.'

She fights down a shaft of terror that threatens to engulf her as the door opens on to stone steps leading directly to the sea. Thoughts of escape are quickly squashed as she tries to negotiate the slippery wharf in the thick night fog. She would have to go through the warehouse to reach the docks. Her car is locked and Ulf knows the terrain whereas she does not.

'Kelly might not be there.'

'I told him I was bringing along a woman who wanted to meet him.'

'And he said?'

'He said OK. Bring her along.'

It sounds as if Kelly is one of the gang. Her stomach flips.

A powerful-looking Ovambo stands astride the wharf. He appears to be waiting for them. His skin gleams in the security light and the whites of his eyes are brilliant. He is watching Chris furtively and something about his expression reminds her of the guards in the township's kangaroo court.

30

Ulf's cabin cruiser is painted white and navy with a thin crimson line around the watermark. It rocks insanely at its berth beside the wharf. The Ovambo reaches forward, grabs Chris and lifts her over the gunwale. She is pushed into a padded seat beside the wheel. The boat gives a lurch forwards like a nervous horse. They turn and surge out into the open sea. She can't hear her own voice as she attempts to question Skoog, so she gives up.

They appear to be in the middle of nowhere, in the pitch black night, when Ulf abruptly stops the engines.

'Where are we?'

'Right over *Rainbow's End*, or what's left of it. You've been asking about it and here it is. This buoy marks the spot. Plenty of reefs here. That's why the sea is always rough.'

Chris looks around nervously. There's nothing but darkness in every direction. There's no sign of land or any lights, but as Ulf switches on his powerful searchlight she sees how thick the mist is. It writhes in weird shapes, like ectoplasm, as it drifts over the water. The boat is rocking more gently now as most of the swell has subsided. In the silence she can hear the roar of the surf on the far-off shore.

'Take a look here.'

Chris leans over the side and stares far down

into the green channel lit by the searchlight. A dark shape moves across the green.

'Can you see the shark? There are always sharks here. Great Whites! They can cut a man in half with one snap of their powerful jaws.'

She watches, fascinated, never having seen a shark outside of an aquarium. It's at least five metres long and half a metre in diameter.

Suddenly, at a signal from Ulf, the Ovambo grabs her hands and ties them together behind her back. She screams and fights, but Ulf has dropped a slip rope around her waist. The tribesman lifts her with effortless ease and tosses her over the side. She takes a deep breath and grits her teeth hard.

She hits the water with a splash that hurts, but the shock of icy water is worse. She can't swim with her arms tied behind her back. She's falling into total blackness, but she can see a tunnel of green light from the searchlight some way ahead. Curbing her impulse to swim towards the light, she kicks away. Hurry . . . hurry . . . she's screaming at herself. She knows she has only seconds before she breaks surface. Bending her knees hard up to her chest, she pushes one leg up and through her arms. The effort is almost beyond her. She's rolling, somersaulting, out of control, behaving like an injured seal, while desperately hoping that the shark is keeping away. One leg is through. The next one proves more difficult. She is blacking out by the time she succeeds. She breaks the surface and gasps for air.

The cruiser is surging away from her. They've

dumped her in the sea to die. Her screams are cut short as the slack in the rope ends with a violent snap that sends her soaring in the air. Then she's pummelled against the surface of the water as her body bumps behind the boat. In seconds she's bruised all over. It takes all her strength to grasp the rope with her bound hands, pull it towards her and shift her body into a water-skier's classic first posture, knees pulled to her chest, feet first, trying to keep her head above water.

The searchlight almost blinds her as it beams towards her, lighting the sea. She can see nothing but the glaring light. Glittering drops shower around her, as they haul her nearer to the boat. She goes under, but suddenly she's pulled to the surface and for a few desperate seconds she can only choke and gasp for air and try to stop her shuddering sobs.

Don't despair, says a voice in the back of her mind. Most of the crew swam to the shore from the capsized *Rainbow's End*. If they can do it, so can you. Just get free of this damned rope.

Ulf is shouting at her. 'Talk or you'll stay here as shark bait.'

She hears a high-pitched scream that ends in a sob and realises that it's her own. Yet part of her is calculating the odds, as if she's two instead of one. They can't let her go. Not after this. She'd go straight to the police. They have to kill her.

'Who are you? Who sent you? What do you want? Answer me truthfully and you'll be OK.'

She keeps her mouth shut.

The Ovambo jerks the rope hard, pulling her

up, and then throws out slack. She sinks deep into the water. Clearly he's well-versed in this routine.

Holding her hands ahead of her, she kicks herself under the boat. Now she's pinned against the bows by her own buoyancy. There's no danger of surfacing as she struggles to loosen the slip knot, but it's swollen with water and stuck fast. She can't loosen it. She claws at it desperately, knowing she only has seconds left, ripping at the strands with her fingernails. At last she loosens the knot and pushes herself out of the loop.

She has to breathe. Moving towards the stern, her feet propelling her forward in a strong breaststroke, she surfaces briefly and gulps in air, filling her lungs before ducking down under the stern to saw the ropes binding her wrists against the propeller blades.

She can see the searchlight moving round the boat. They're searching for her. If they catch her they'll never let her go. The quicker she talks the sooner they'll shoot her. If they start the engines now, she'll be mincemeat. The light has moved away and from the way the boat is angled she guesses that both Ulf and his boatman are leaning over the bows. At last the rope is cut. She unravels the strands with her teeth.

She can hear their footsteps moving back towards the stern. The hardest thing she's ever done is to slip quietly away from the boat, into the dark sea. She tries to hold back her fear. Sharks can smell fear, like dogs, she read somewhere, but her panic is rising again.

291

The crew got back, didn't they? Not one of them was taken by a shark. That means something. The thought cheers her and sustains her as she silently treads water fifty metres from the boat.

The searchlight is circling slowly around, but she can see it coming in time to dive deep enough not to be seen. At last, with a powerful surge, the boat leaps forward, leaving evanescent gleams of phosphorescence in its trail. The sound fades away. Now all she can hear is the roar of waves on the rocky shore and it seems to come from all directions.

She's heard that splashing sounds like a fish in distress, so she swims breaststroke, a smooth, easy pace, making no splashes. If she doesn't succumb to hypothermia, she can keep this up for some time. As her eyes adjust to the dark, she sees the red and green signal lights at the entrance of Walvis Bay harbour, shining dimly through the mist. She turns gratefully and heads towards them. The crew did it, so you can do it. You're a strong swimmer.

Don't think of sharks. No panic . . . No fear . . . Sharks can smell fear. Keep your mind blank. You're meditating. Concentrate on your breath. In . . . out . . . you're moving into a trance.

The swim back seems to last forever. She passes through periods of calm when she counts her strokes, concentrates on breathing, checks her direction and fills her mind with the need to keep going. Then come the bad times . . . the panic times, when she's sure she can see a dark fin circling her. Tensed with terror she waits for the first bump that the shark always makes before coming in for the kill. Last of all, comes the pain which drives away all other sensations. Every muscle locks into cramps so painful she thinks she will die. And then, when she can't go on, she falls into a trance-like state and her mind floats far away, watching her punitive efforts without much interest.

The mist thickens and now the lights are totally obscured. She has nothing but the roar of the surf to guide her in. When she finds herself in a maelstrom of foaming sea, surging backwards and forwards in currents too strong to fight, she gives up the battle and blacks out.

31

Petrus leans over the bed and shakes her softly. 'Did you tell me everything?' he is asking for the umpteenth time.

The DI is willing her to stay awake, but Chris closes her eyes. She wants to escape from his inquisition and sleep is the only way. With Sarah Vaughan dead, she should slip out of Namibia fast, before Ulf and his boss, whoever he is, work out that she's still alive. This is becoming a habit, she thinks, remembering Soweto.

'Wake up, Chris. I know you're faking. You damn near landed up dead that time. I need to make a few arrests fast.'

Chris smiles absently and brushes her tangled hair off her forehead. 'It's so hot . . . oh, all right . . . but I can't even remember what I told you.'

'Not much that's relevant.'

'How long have you been here?'

'A few hours. No one knows who you are. I'm holding back until I know what's going on.'

'Thanks, Petrus.' She struggles to sit up. 'So what are you doing here and how did you find me?'

'I had to question someone local. Can't tell you much, but I was here when Stark contacted the local police for help in finding a certain abducted female. Thank God I was here. Your hired car was found wrecked and abandoned in the desert. A boy on a motorcycle stumbled across it, so I checked with the car hire company and found it was the one you'd taken. Then I checked the mortuaries . . . and I was damned glad I didn't find you there . . . lastly I checked with casualty.

'OK . . . let's start again.' Petrus looks tired and she guesses he's been up all night. When she tries to sit up she realises that her hands are covered in dressings. She thrusts them under the blankets, hoping Petrus won't see, but he's flipping over the pages of his notebook.

He reads: ''Feeling under the weather this evening, I went for a swim in my underwear, somewhere near Walvis Bay.' No clothes were found, by the way. 'I was caught up in strong currents and swept out to sea. Eventually I managed to swim back to Walvis Bay beach where I passed out.''

'So how did I get here?'

'You were seen by a passing motorist lying prone on the sand wearing only a T-shirt, bra and panties. Your fingers were raw. Fortunately for you he brought you straight here. A truly amazing story.'

'I'm a strong swimmer.'

'I have no doubt of that, but I sincerely hope you don't expect me to believe the rest of it. Who are you trying to protect?' The question is slipped in slyly while he observes her with a swift, sidelong scan.

Even to Chris her story sounds absurd. It was the first thing she thought of when she regained consciousness.

'Look, Petrus, I'm only protecting myself

. . . or rather my investigation. Someone tried to kill me . . . he thinks I'm dead. He and his accomplice, that is. They'll come after me if they know I'm alive. If you arrest them for kidnapping and attempted murder, I might lose the chance to find out who is running this laundering gang. Right now I have a lead. I need time . . .'

'What if I agree to go along with your wishes and use my influence to see that this person is not arrested?'

'Not now . . . believe me . . . I can't tell you yet.'

Petrus is embarrassed, his cosmopolitan features are at variance with each other, his European nose pinched with displeasure, his Slavic eyes narrowed to slits, his African eyebrows knitted. He stops biting his beautiful lip and stands up abruptly to pace the ward.

'Jesus . . . I hate having to pressurise you, but I must,' he says with a furious smile. 'We're working along similar lines, but we . . . that is the diamond branch . . . are cleaning up this entire area. Diamonds are filtering down from Central and West Africa to Walvis Bay, which has become a major depot for accepting and dispatching. I'm in charge. I have very little doubt that we'll arrest Ulf Skoog in the normal course of our duties. You'd be far better off trusting me. Then I can give the order to lay off him for a while.'

'How did you know it was Skoog?'

'Someone told me.'

Chris sits up and considers the situation. Petrus makes sense, but can she trust him? It's crazy to trust anyone in his situation. After all, he's not a free agent. Yet Petrus has helped her, surely she can believe him. He's smiling so warmly at her that she is quite disarmed. 'OK . . . this is what happened.'

★ ★ ★

An hour later Chris is reaching the end of her nightmare story, but she's exhausted now and she can hardly talk.

'It took hours to swim back and I'm sure there was a shark following me . . . ' She shudders. 'Just when I thought I would pass out with hypothermia and exhaustion, something took over and my mind drifted away from the pain. It's been tough having to remember.' She laughs shakily. 'I was numb with cold . . . that was my only comfort . . . I guessed I wouldn't feel it when the shark bit me.'

Petrus swears. His features harden and he looks what he is, a tough cop who has made himself as ruthless as the men he hunts.

'I'll lay off Skoog for the time being, as I promised, but you must keep me up to date with what's going on your end. Remember, Chris, it's possible to play things too close to the cuff and foul up for everyone else. You're holding back on the reason why you went out on Skoog's boat in the first place. You weren't screaming for help. Who, or what did you think you were going to find?'

'Visser, of course.' Chris feels bad about lying to a friend.

'Do you think he's still alive?'

'Possibly.'

'The police went into it very exhaustively at the time.' He frowns at her and Chris can see that he doesn't believe her. 'If it's true, Skoog would never tell you, nor anyone else . . . '

'By the way, Visser was an accountant,' Chris interrupts, hoping to throw Petrus off course. 'Do you remember what Freeman said? 'That fucking accountant will put out my light.' He could have meant Visser.'

'I always thought he might have survived the wrecking.' Petrus says moodily. 'If so, he got away with a fortune. Scuba divers have been searching for those diamonds for twenty-five years. Nothing has ever been found.'

'I fancy he wrecked the dredger and killed the skipper. The diamonds probably set him up with his scam.'

'Your theory has far too many suppositions, but OK . . . it's possible and we've got a deal. Eventually you'll have to come back to testify at Skoog's trial. I can't wait to get the bastard under lock and key, or better still, see him dead. By the way . . . your friend has been waiting to see you . . . he's been in and out all day. He's down at reception. I promised to let him know when I left.'

Chris's stomach does a double back flip. Jim makes her feel vulnerable. It's not his doing, she feels, but has mainly to do with the way she lusts after him. If he knew, she would die of shame. Falling in lust with her prime suspect was not on the cards. Instinctively she reaches out and catches hold of Petrus' hand, drawing him close.

She wants to tell him that Jim is another unknown factor . . . not a friend, nor a security guard, but something far more devious, but how can she? She has to play along. Sooner or later, Jim will slip up and reveal his hand.

'Thank you, Petrus. Go well,' she whispers.

★　★　★

She falls asleep as Petrus leaves and wakes later to find herself alone, other than a uniformed police guard leaning against the glass partition between her ward and the passage. Glancing over her shoulder to the window, she sees that it's dark outside. She fumbles for a light switch.

There is a note beside her bed which reads: *Stay put. I've packed your gear and booked you out of your hotel. I'm organising a private flight out of Namibia. We leave before dawn. Back soon. Jim.*

Who asked him to help? For a moment Chris entertains dreams of fleeing back to London. She could call a taxi and wait at the airport for the early morning flight. She could even ask Petrus for police protection. But if she can't take the tension, she'll have to quit her job. Jim is just one of the many unknowns who must be fitted into the picture. He is the most dangerous of all, she senses.

Pushing away her fears, Chris rings her bell and a nurse hurries in.

'Hello, Chris. I'm your night nurse, Val. You won't remember me, but I was here when you came in. How do you feel?'

Chris vaguely remembers a tall Herero woman holding a glass of water to her lips.

'Not too bad,' she answers. 'What happened to my second visitor?'

'He stayed for a while. He's coming back . . . or so he said. Did you see his note?'

'Yes, thanks. What time is it?'

'Two a.m. You've slept on and off since they brought you in yesterday morning. Do you have any pain?'

Chris sits up cautiously. 'No, but I'm thirsty and my throat's raw.' She stands slowly. 'Apart from an urgent need for a shower, I'm fine. I guess I should wash off the dried salt water.'

'We did that when you were brought in. Don't you remember?'

'Not really.'

'Are you hungry?' the nurse asks.

'A little.'

'Soup and bread . . . that's all we can run to at this time of night.'

'Thanks . . . sounds great. It's about all my throat can cope with. What happened to my hands?'

'You tell me. It looks as if you've been picking oakum in prison. They still do that sometimes.'

'What's oakum?'

'That stuff you were tearing at with your hands . . . rope! When it's unravelled it's used for caulking boat hulls. Been working in a boatyard, have you?'

'Something like that.'

Val laughs. 'Some might believe you,' she tosses over her shoulder as she leaves.

Jim will be here soon. The thought panics her. Typical of him to take over when he thinks she's too weak to argue. She sits up, raging inwardly, while she gobbles her supper. Pushing her tray aside she slips out of bed and stands at the window gazing towards the Namib, where the tall dunes are clearly silhouetted against the starlit sky. These are the dangerous hours, these hours before dawn, when she must leave behind all pretence of safety and follow her intuitive insight, hoping that the truth will find her, if she gives it half a chance.

32

Jim looks furious. 'I thought you'd be pleased.' He's told her that three times. It's four a.m. and they are late. He is pacing the ward, shooting exasperated glances her way.

'I've a pilot and a private aircraft ready and waiting to take you to a place you never dreamed existed ... sheer paradise ... Northern Botswana. You can recuperate in safety, far away from everyone, for a long, or a short stay ... it's up to you. Come on! What do you say?'

Unexpectedly Jim reaches out and clutches her hand. Like a handcuff, she thinks, trying to pull hers away, but it remains in his powerful grasp.

'You're a donkey. What exactly were you thinking of when you put out to sea with Ulf Skoog in his motor launch? I searched your room after you stood me up for dinner. It was clever of you to leave a message.'

'Not clever ... a last minute panic attack.'

'It's always best to trust your intuition. So ... tell me ... '

'I can't tell you much.' She pauses, searching carefully for the right words. 'There's another man involved ... someone who is completely innocent ... yet he might know a great deal. Skoog promised to take me to him.'

'I don't suppose that Skoog knows where Dan Kelly is?'

She gasps with shock and pulls her hand hard. 'What's going on Jim? How do you know about Kelly?' For a moment she feels nauseous. 'You've been talking to Skoog. You know him.'

'Wrong. Listen carefully. We don't have much time. It was midnight by the time I realised that you were missing. I drove to Walvis Bay and tried to find your car in the docks. Eventually I learned that there is only one locked garage in the harbour and it belongs to Skoog. I found a couple of crane drivers working overtime nearby who told me that Skoog had put out to sea with his boatman and a red-headed woman.'

'More auburn than red,' Chris mutters.

'He told me you'd left a couple of hours back, which upset the hell out of me. I called Petrus for a police helicopter and I was still waiting for it when Skoog came back without you. Almost simultaneously the helicopter arrived with Petrus and a medic. We searched the locality for hours, but in the dark . . . ' His voice is hoarse as he turns away.

'You thought I was dead.'

'Yes.'

'Skoog's a sadistic bastard. He wanted to make me talk. Basically, this is what happened . . . '

Chris tries to relate how she sawed the ropes binding her wrists on the propeller blades and then freed herself from the rope knotted around her waist, but at the memory of her fear, her eyes brim over with tears.

Jim is livid. 'You're too vulnerable for this type of work. You've got to give it up. I'll get Skoog one of these days. I promise you that. We only stopped searching for you when we heard that a woman answering your description had been taken into casualty. Jesus! That was a bad night.'

Chris leans her face on her knees. 'We both care for each other, Jim, but you're a stranger to me. I don't understand what you're doing here.'

'I came to find you. I was in the States, so I only just heard about your ordeal in Soweto when I returned to London. I flew straight over.'

'But how did you know where I stay . . . oh, don't tell me . . . my credit card.'

'By the time we got to the hospital you were out for the count. Petrus arranged for a guard and we went back to the station. It was the sergeant who told us you'd been asking around for news of Dan Kelly . . . '

'Petrus didn't tell me that.' So Petrus knew she was holding back. She feels uncomfortable about it.

'Petrus called the *Namibian News* librarian while I was buying you a few things to wear in Botswana and checking you out of your hotel. By the time I met up with Petrus again, he knew about the court case that ruined Dan Kelly and Herman Visser . . . plus the rest. So we had your two leads . . . Kelly and Skoog. Tell me, Chris, what makes you think Kelly will talk any more than Skoog did?'

'Kelly is not necessarily a crook, nor one of them.'

'If he's not, he's a bad judge of character.'

Chris doesn't answer. She's considering Jim's reply. She suspects all of them, her father . . . Jim

. . . even Petrus. Everyone's heard of bent cops. If only there were someone she could be sure of. If only she could trust Jim, but the fact remains he was following her long before she met Prince Husam and he lied to her about the reasons for this. She leans back and closes her eyes.

★ ★ ★

'Get up, Chris. It'll soon be light. Skoog must have heard the helicopter searching for you and he might come snooping around.'

Playing for time while she considers her reply, Chris gets out of bed, opens her case and takes out the plastic bag lying on top. Three pairs of shorts, six T-shirts, trainers and socks. They are plain and functional, in greenish khaki, chosen and bought by Jim. He's packed her camera, too, and her spare bag. She opens it. There's her cash and the credit cards she'd left in her room the evening before. She could be in London by nightfall. And then what? She came here to do a job and it's not yet done. Reluctantly, she's beginning to suspect that Jim is the very criminal she's looking for . . . and he's keeping tabs on her to find out what she knows. Her suspicions are so unwelcome that she pushes them away, but she can never entirely eliminate them. The best way to find out about him is to stick around, but surely London is safer than the African bush.

'I don't know if I'm coming, Jim.'

'I don't understand you . . . you need to get out of Namibia at once. You have a big advantage right now. They think you're dead. For God's sake get a move on.'

'It's your lies. I want to know what's going on. Why, for instance, does Petrus trust you?'

'Perhaps he's a better judge of character than you.'

'You're a liar . . . '

All the danger signs are evident, the taut stance, the fixed stare at nothing, lips pressed so hard they are white.

'Tell me who you work for. I have to know. It's obvious that you have massive back-up.'

He groans with exasperation. 'That's not the sort of question you should ask me. It's classified. You have to take me on trust.'

'Otherwise it's no go between us,' she says, braving the icy chill.

'Well, it's not really classified. Nevertheless, I wouldn't like it to get around.' His glance warns her of the severity of her fate should she open her mouth.

'I work for a Christian NGO. They're a huge outfit in the States. I cover Africa. In fact, I'm in charge. After all, they bailed me out of prison in Equatorial Guinea and saved my life, so the least I could do was to join them. My job is to analyse the spread of Islam versus Christianity in various African countries and do what I can to improve the odds.'

'But that doesn't explain why you followed me long before I saw Prince Husam. Don't argue,' she snaps as Jim opens his mouth. 'I have your picture and the precise date when you gazed into the jeweller's window in Finchley.'

'Very efficient of you.'

'Is that all you have to say? And while I think of it, why on earth were you working for the prince in the first place? And how did you know that Ben was dead before Rowan knew? It was you who told Prince Husam.'

'Some of the guys in our New York office were keeping an eye on Ben for me. I'm so sorry about Ben. He was infiltrating various Muslim fundamentalist groups and I needed to know why. I thought I'd find out what he was doing through you. Later, of course . . . ' He breaks off and gives her a sad smile. 'You must know there's a fight on for Africa's soul.'

'Or its strategic minerals,' Chris murmurs.

'Well, that, too.'

'And the prince? Ditto, I assume.'

'Exactly. Chris . . . listen . . . I told the pilot to consider the trip cancelled if we didn't get there by daybreak.'

'Oh my goodness! I still have to pay to get out of here. That'll take time.'

'It's taken care of.'

This is no time to argue. Moments later Chris is in the bathroom throwing on shorts and a T-shirt. To hell with underwear and make-up. That can come later. Suddenly optimism is seeping into her psyche through every pore.

★   ★   ★

They arrive before dawn at a private farm ten miles outside Swakopmund. The karakul farmer who greets them looks as if the desert air has sucked him dry, leaving only his amazingly

307

youthful blue eyes gleaming from the wreckage of his face.

Breakfast is laid out on the balcony table overlooking a small dam: melon and ham, orange juice, eggs and toast. Chris seldom eats in the morning, but she discovers she is hungry.

As the sun's first rays light the horizon in gold and rosy splendour and the birds set up their shrill song, they take off in a four-seater Auster, from a runway behind the house, piloted by the farmer.

Hour after hour they fly over Namibia's flat plains. It becomes hotter and more of an effort to keep alert. Eventually Chris slips into a heat-induced torpor and wakes much later when Jim touches her arm.

'Swallow,' he says. 'We're coming in to land.'

By mid-afternoon they have changed flights twice, eaten a late lunch at Maun and they are following a broad, gravel road towards Kasane, near the Botswana and Zimbabwe border, in a four-seater Bell helicopter. They soar over dark forests and glades shining emerald green in the sun, with occasional flashes of blue from water holes. Cresting a hill, their plane banks to the north. Before them lie tree-tops stretching in every direction. Soon the forest falls away steeply to the broad, Chobe river. Far off along the riverbank stands a huge and graceful hotel, designed like a Spanish *hacienda*, facing across the wide expanse of the waterway, looking towards the Caprivi Strip on the opposite bank, which separates Botswana from Angola.

Jim is in a hurry to make the hotel before

sunset. They skim over tree-tops, sending buck and baboons fleeing in all directions. Dishevelled and covered in dust, they climb out on to the hotel's helicopter pad and wave goodbye to the pilot.

'Hurry,' Jim calls, leaving their luggage to a porter. Arriving breathless at reception, they find that the hotel's paddleboat is about to leave for the sunset champagne cruise. The pretty receptionist issues two tickets and assures them that their luggage will be left in their rooms.

So that's what all the hurry was about, Chris realises, smiling to herself.

'Let's go,' Jim says. They reach the gangway as the steamer leaves the wooden wharf.

'Jump,' Jim yells, clutching her hand.

The steamer, built like a nineteenth-century Mississippi steamboat, chugs softly downstream, passing close beside a herd of elephants who have waded into the deep river water to bathe, the mothers prodding their squealing infants ahead of them. Hippos surface to protest as they pass too close. Fish eagles line the banks, perched on every tree-top. Chris wonders why they wait there until the boatman takes a bucket of fish and flings the contents over the water for the birds to swoop and catch while the tourists' cameras click.

She knows she will never forget the sound and smell of Africa. Strangely it's so familiar . . . like coming home.

It is dark when they return, happy, tired and full of champagne. They swim in the hotel pool and dine by candlelight on the balcony overlooking the river.

'Oh Jim, it's so beautiful. Thank you for bringing me here.'

'Likewise. We both need a break.'

★　★　★

Why do her fears only surface at night when she's vulnerable? Chris wonders, as she lies awake in bed. She is plagued by suspicions that Jim is not what he seems or says. Be careful, Chris, a voice whispers in her head.

She lists what she knows about Jim, but it doesn't amount to much. Jim is the most exciting man she has ever met. He has a charm that cuts through all defences, but he's also a very private person, hiding his true personality. An undercover man. She has tried, but failed to draw him out.

Unable to get back to sleep, she continues to analyse Jim. His eyes, beaming with affection and humour, tell her that he finds her alluring, but has he any idea how desirable he is with his lazy smile and his startling green eyes?

She longs to be close to Jim and feel his strong, muscular body pressed against hers. She's running out of control and she has never felt like this. The thought that he's just a few steps away, beyond a connecting door with the key on her side, is driving her crazy. Intuitively, Chris knows that she is in danger of losing herself to this man, but she senses that his allegiance lies elsewhere. Finally she gets up and tiptoes into his room. He's asleep. This disappoints her as she climbs softly into his bed.

'What kept you so long?' he asks sleepily, 'I've been longing for you.' He pulls her close against him and sighs contentedly. She feels brain-dead, just a mass of thrilling sensations, her ego has descended to her loins and nothing else exists. Jim is a skilled and sensitive lover, she learns, and at some time during the night he whispers that he loves her.

33

She lies on her side, facing away from Jim, acutely aware of his arm flung around her waist and his breath on her neck, while she tries to fathom out how she can lust over a man like him. I don't even like him and I certainly don't trust him. So why does he turn me on, even when we're arguing? I shall ignore his intensely offensive maleness and his crass pretensions to find me irresistible.

The sad truth is, even now, after a night of incredible sex, Chris still desires him. She closes her eyes and indulges herself, remembering how they had fallen into an exhausted sleep, but he had wooed her tenderly in the night and once again the intensity of her reactions had stunned her. Even now, she must be sending out signals, for his hand moves over her belly and he pulls her closer into his lean frame.

Despite their passionate sex, Jim remains inviolate and she guesses that she will never truly know him. His barriers seem impenetrable.

Don't be a fool, she tells herself. You walked into this job open-eyed. You knew it wouldn't be easy. You've always got your kicks from danger. That's why this man excites you so . . . because he's deadly. But what does he want from her. Play along and you might find out, she argues.

★ ★ ★

It is their fourth night at Chobe. Chris wakes in the cold pre-dawn knowing that Jim is not beside her. She sits up and listens intently. She hears Jim creeping down the stone steps to the pool. Someone calls quietly. It is someone Jim knows well, she can tell by his tone of voice. She'll ask him when he gets back, but he will probably lie to her. Or he'll say that it's classified and she must trust him.

All the old familiar worries that she can cope with during the day seem unbearable in the night. She worries because she's wasting time. Admittedly she has not yet recovered completely. She's covered in bruises and her hands are tender, but she's well enough to work. Even a day wasted is too much when Sienna is still imprisoned and living in fear of her life.

She had contacted Jean on her arrival at the hotel and asked if there was any news of Sienna, but the police seem to be completely stumped. She asked Jean to check with the various banks for any credit card purchases by Kelly. It is confidential, the banks told Jean. They can't release that kind of information, but Jim always succeeds. How does he do it? Finally she called Rowan, who used his influence to get the police to lean on those damned inflexible bankers. Yesterday Jean had called back. The information had come via the Johannesburg head office. Dan Kelly uses his American Express card in Maun fairly regularly. He bought provisions a month ago. So he must be prospecting locally. It's time to search for him. He's her only lead left.

It's almost dawn when Jim returns. She hears

something heavy being scraped along the floor to his walk-in cupboard. He pushes it in and shuts the door before climbing gently into bed.

'Who were you talking to, Jim?'

His body stiffens. He's annoyed that she's awake.

'Why, no one.'

'But I heard you talking . . . in a foreign language . . . I couldn't place the sounds at all. What language were you speaking? It sounded a bit like Arabic.' She switches on the light. 'Don't stare at me like that.' Chris is beginning to lose her temper.

'Like what?'

'Like a stranger. I'm going back to my room.'

'It was an old friend from prison days,' he says, pulling her back to bed. 'Don't be a cuckoo. He gives me information from time to time and we were speaking in Swahili.'

'Don't try to soft-soap me.'

Jim is always on a short fuse and his glance dares her to argue.

'I didn't want to raise your hopes, but I put out feelers all round. My informer tells me that Kelly was seen yesterday approximately forty miles south-east of Ghanzi. You won't find a more desolate spot, but some traders were passing. Nothing's secret in Africa.'

'So how far away is that?'

'Over 400 kilometres as the helicopter flies.'

'Can a small helicopter go that far?'

'If they stock up with petrol. But it would take three hours to get there, although that's not the end of it. You'd be facing a long search once you arrived. We'll drive there.'

Chris snuggles back into his arms. They make love again, which goes a long way towards wiping away her doubts and confusion.

★ ★ ★

Early the next morning, after Jim has left for Maun, Chris takes his bedroom keys from his dressing gown pocket and opens his walk-in cupboard. The suitcase is a reinforced, fibreglass trunk, which she hasn't seen before and it feels as if it's stuffed with lead. She hauls it out, wincing as she hurts her swollen hands. It's locked, of course, but the key will be in his wall safe, and she knows the combination because she set it for him.

As she retrieves the key she begins to tremble at what she might find. Jim could come in at any moment, but she can't stop now. The lid falls open revealing a fortune of rough diamonds. For a moment she can only stare, as if in a trance. Is Jim an agent? He must be . . . or perhaps he's running the show? She fastens the lid and locks the case. It's heavy and it's all she can do to haul it back to the cupboard. One more lunge. Then there's a cracking sound as a hinge breaks and diamonds cascade over the floor in all directions.

Jim will know that she knows. She can't disguise the broken hinge. She should have listened to David. She straightens up and looks around. He'll be back soon. For a moment she contemplates staying and having it out with him. 'Idiot,' she tells herself. Jim's not going to give her the answers on a plate, particularly since it will probably involve Prince Husam, too.

She must hurry. If she calls the helicopter company who ferried them to the hotel, she could be picked up within the hour, but an hour is too long. Jim's been cheating her since he first followed her, pretending that he loves her while he spies on her. It would be wise to leave fast. At that moment the phone rings. She picks up the receiver.

'Hi, Chrissie. I'm on the balcony, river side. It's beautiful down here. Come and join me . . . monkeys on the lawn . . . elephants by the river. What's your order?'

'Orange juice,' she mutters. 'I have to wait for my nails to dry.'

She calls the helicopter company and arranges to meet them on the pad of a hotel further up the river. It's half a mile away, but Jim won't think of looking for her there. It doesn't take longer than three minutes to throw a few things into Jim's haversack. She jots down her needs: a first aid kit, water, sun barrier cream, sunglasses, hat and a large scarf to keep the sun off her neck, a compass . . . it will have to be Jim's . . . a knife, a torch, matches and a packet of biscuits. If she doesn't find Kelly, she'll return to Maun, and fly on to Gaborone, where she can pick up a flight to London. When she's finished packing she finds that her haversack is too heavy to carry, so she sheds some of the water.

★　★　★

316

Within twenty minutes she's airborne and they're heading for a certain spot south-east of Ghanzi, where she hopes to find Kelly's camp. As they near their destination, the pilot begins the search, taking a circular route over the featureless gravel plains. Hour after hour they search the barren landscape, which is monotonously flat except for an occasional row of dunes stretching for hundreds of miles towards the sea.

Chris spends the journey wallowing in guilt. She's lost the plot and lost control and wasted almost a week of her time, all because her knees turn to jelly and her stomach churns at the sight of Jim.

34

They have been searching for hours, occasionally sighting ostriches, strung out in a straight line, racing over dunes and plains. There's the occasional oryx standing alone, as if lost, but mainly they see sand ... hundreds of square miles of sand, of a pale, washed-out hue, almost grey. Even the sky looks bleached by the sun. Can this be planet earth? Chris shudders to think of her father endlessly prospecting through this awful barrenness. When they land to refuel from the spare tanks, the pilot says: 'This is it ... the last of the petrol. One more hour.' Her heart sinks as they climb back into the helicopter to continue the search.

Chris has been glancing surreptitiously at her watch. The pilot said an hour, which means they have ten minutes left. Her anxiety has become a physical lump in her throat. Kelly is her last chance to follow her leads to the diamond launderers. More important still ... she longs to find her father ... and he's so close ... she can't give up now ... but she may have to.

'Look,' the pilot says. 'Do you see that smoke?' She can't see a damn thing. Despite her sunglasses, her eyes are sore and burning from the glare. When the pilot swoops low, they see a shimmering images of a man standing beside an orange blur. 'Is he for real?'

'Heatwaves,' the pilot calls. As they swoop and

soar over the fire, they scatter the burning embers and set up a mini sandstorm. The man is shaking his fist.

'This is him . . . must be,' she calls excitedly.

'And if it's not?'

They put down at a safe distance. Chris opens the door and the heat blasts her.

'Mind the blades,' the pilot yells. Bent double, Chris runs to a man who is shaking the sand out of his gear and kicking bits of smoking wood into a heap.

For Chris, there is a brief moment of impact as their eyes meet. It is like nothing she's ever experienced before, part recognition, part dismay, for he is staring blankly at her. She wants to scream: *Look at me. Don't you recognise your own genes?* Disappointment makes her speechless. She stares for too long. Kelly looks old for his age. His white hair is so short you can hardly see the stubble, his skin is like old leather and then there's his limp. He seems to collapse slightly when he stands on his right leg. Great eyes . . . youthful, alert and very blue, but right now they're blazing with fury. She likes what she sees, except for the limp . . . and the scowl. Surely he should suspect that she might be his.

'Dan Kelly, I'm . . . ' She has her story ready to trot out . . . Sarah Vaughan, journalist . . . but must she lie to her father the very first time she meets him? 'You *are* Dan Kelly?'

'So . . . ?'

She waves to the pilot who drops her haversack on the sand and slams the door. As the blades begin to turn, her father looks stunned and then horrified as he gazes from her to the pilot. The next moment he's running towards the aircraft, waving his arms, shouting. The helicopter soars over the nearest dune, and they watch it disappearing into the blue haze.

Kelly walks back slowly. 'You probably think I won't go off and abandon you here, but you're wrong. If you have any communication with that pilot, call him back now before it's too late.'

His voice is deep, his accent American, as she's guessed it would be. As he speaks he is thrusting his gear into a haversack.

'I don't.'

'Who the hell are you? And what the hell are you doing here? As if I don't know.'

What does he mean by that? 'I need information.' Perhaps lying is her best option. He's hardly in the right mood for a happy reunion. 'I'm Sarah Vaughan.' She pushes her hand towards him, but he turns away and stares at the sand looking frantic. He reminds her of a cornered animal and she wishes she hadn't come. How can Kelly be a crook? He's too vulnerable.

'I'm not here to harm you,' she stammers.

'You won't get the chance.'

'Look here. I work for FI in London, that's a company . . . '

'I know the company.'

'You do?'

'Do you think I'm Rip Van Winkle?'

'God! I seem to have got off on the wrong foot.'

'Any foot would be wrong. You have no right

to do this to me. Do you have any business cards?'

'No.' Another lie. She has, but they give her name and she's not ready for that yet. First she must find out if Kelly is involved in the laundering.

They are glaring at each other like two fighting cocks waiting for the first lunge. Chris sinks to the sand and sits cross-legged. 'Even the sand's hot,' she complains, stirring uncomfortably.

'How did you find me?'

'A colleague back in London checked on your credit card purchases. You've used the card in Maun and round about Ghanzi, Kalkfontein and Tshwane. I guess right now we're nearly dead centre of the triangle. You used your mobile in Kalkfontein. They have a radio mast there. You've been seen around this area. I hired a helicopter . . . of course, we were lucky to spot you. It was the smoke.'

While they talk, Kelly is moving around packing up his gear. It goes into a haversack that looks as if it weighs a ton. She can see how he got those bulging biceps and thigh muscles. She can't help comparing him to a statue roughly hewn out of stone. As for his neck, he could hang millstones from it. Perhaps he has. That might account for the pain in his eyes and the way his mouth folds into a slash when he's not talking. Yet he has a certain charm and he looks straight . . . like someone you could trust.

'What exactly are you investigating?'

'That's confidential . . . I mean . . . for the time being.'

'Listen here, Miss Vaughan. You've put me in an unenviable situation. There's no transport. Mobiles don't work here. We're completely cut off. I've brought only survival rations, not much water. I've no camp. I roam the territory prospecting for just about anything. There's no shelter . . .'

'I get the picture,' she says sulkily. 'I've brought my own food and water.'

'What sort of provisions have you got?'

'Two packets of biscuits, six litres of water.'

'It'll be three days before we reach the nearest village.'

'That's OK. I'm on a diet.'

'When I hand you back to civilisation, that might sound funny. Right now it's tragic.'

'Oh come on, Kelly. You're making a big deal out of very little.'

'Possibly, but you've made a mistake if you think I'm altering my schedule in any way, or discussing anything with you. Please remember that people die in this sort of heat . . . kidneys pack up through lack of water. It's sudden and it's fatal. Drink plenty of water, Miss Vaughan, but ration it out. We'll stop for water every two hours . . . that's if you're still around.'

He shoulders his pack, picks up his rifle and gazes around. 'Keep up, because I won't be looking over my shoulder, but I won't deliberately abandon you because that would be murder.'

'I know a lot about you, Kelly,' she calls at his retreating back.

'You're wasting your energy,' she hears, like a sigh in the wind.

'Fuck you.' Tears evaporate fast in the desert leaving a salty crust, she discovers.

★ ★ ★

They have tramped for hours across the harsh gravel plains of the flat highlands and now it's late afternoon and she feels as if she might pass out. Her limbs are heavy and inflexible, her head aches, her eyes burn and she's as thirsty as hell. Thank heavens for the canvas boots and thick socks she bought in Maun.

So far the frosty tension shows no sign of abating. On the plus side, the terrain is subtly altering. They are moving through a wide valley between gently sloping dunes, following a line of green made up of thorn trees, fever trees and patches of thin grass. She guesses that they are following the course of an underground river. Furthermore, they aren't alone: goshawks are circling overhead, there is a hum of insects and the call of many different kinds of birds. Around them lie the spoor of jackals and she guesses there must be water somewhere around.

After two hours Kelly pauses and squats beside a thorn tree. She notices that he leaves the shadiest part vacant. She almost laughs. He's not the ogre he makes himself out to be.

'It's beautiful here,' she says, collapsing beside him.

'You're pretty tough for a London girl.' He digs a piece of dried meat out of his haversack.

323

'Ostrich *biltong*. Have some.'

She takes it, smells it and hands it back. 'No thanks.'

'Then eat some of your biscuits.' She isn't hungry, but she fears that her thirst will never be quelled, not if she drinks all six litres she's carrying. Five and a bit she reminds herself.

'Listen, Kelly, Is this tension ever going to end?'

'Not unless you tell me why you're here.'

'OK. This might come as a shock to you,' she says, choosing her words carefully. 'I'm investigating a gang who are engaged in illicit diamond trading. It's a scam and it wouldn't be criminal, not in Britain anyway, if it weren't that murder and kidnapping are involved. Huge profits are being made.'

'And they've put a girl on to this?'

'I'm not investigating the gang, or their crimes, but their method of laundering the gems. Business fraud . . . that's my job.'

Kelly gives no indication that he's listening. He's stretched out on the sand with his eyes closed. She decides to carry on anyway.

'I've found that it's like knocking down a row of dominoes. One clue leads to the next.'

'And what led you to me?' he mutters.

Chris conceals her satisfaction. If Kelly's asking questions he must be interested. 'Herman Visser and, later, Ulf Skoog.'

He doesn't believe her. She can tell by the way he's looking at her. He props himself on his elbow and leers at her. 'I can tell you a more probable story. FI is contracted to one of the big mining houses and you're the fall guy chosen to follow me around and find out where my claim is.'

'What claim? What are you talking about?'

'Nevermind.'

'Look . . . I need to know if Visser really is dead. Are you in touch with him?'

She breaks off. In the distance, but coming closer, she hears the unmistakable drone of a helicopter. Jim's coming after her and she's endangering her father. She looks up. The tree isn't much shelter and anyway he'll see their footprints. 'Do you have a gun?' she asks.

'Please stop this absurd charade.' His mouth sets in a tight line as he gets to his feet, shoulders his pack and limps away.

'I was only asking . . . I need information and I need it fast. Listen, just tell me about Visser and I'll make my own way to the nearest village.'

'I warned you . . .'

Soon Kelly is a distant blur, shimmering in the heat. Who needs a father, she wonders, hating his retreating back.

The helicopter is moving away, zigzagging towards the west, but they keep up the same impressive pace, with pauses for water every two hours and once Kelly reminds her to eat four more biscuits.

★ ★ ★

By early evening, the sun has become her enemy and there's no escape anywhere. Chris turns to watch the crimson globe falling against a turquoise backdrop. She feels exhausted. Visser and the laundered diamonds are far from top priority right now. She just wants to drink and drink. She sinks on to a hump of sand to watch the sun disappear. Dark as blood, it is losing shape and melting over the horizon, and then it's gone, leaving a pale, translucent green in its wake. After hesitating, Kelly joins her. It's then that they hear the drone of the helicopter coming closer.

'You don't often hear helicopters around these parts,' Kelly says.

'I'm not surprised.' She drains the rest of her second bottle of water. She deserves it.

'That's it,' she says, flinging down the plastic bottle. Kelly retrieves it and thrusts it in his pack.

'We don't want to spoil the desert, do we.'

'Fuck the desert and fuck you.'

'Why me?'

'Because you won't tell me about Visser.'

'Give me a good reason why I should tell you about him and I will. As far as I'm concerned, selling diamonds is not breaking the law.'

'Does that mean that Visser is alive and selling diamonds?'

There's no answer, but she tucks that knowledge away without commenting. 'My colleague, a dear friend, who was running this investigation was murdered recently. My best friend from school days, Sienna, who is Mohsen Sheik's daughter, was kidnapped on her wedding day. I was standing watching her drive past in her father's car. I tried to get to her, but I was shot.'

'You were shot. So this is where the fairy

326

stories come to an end. Where were you shot and where's the scar?'

'Ah . . . ' She is whipping off her T-shirt, stung by his disbelief. 'Bloody apologise,' she says, thrusting her shoulder towards him, careless of her braless state. 'Now do you believe me?' She swings around. 'Damn you, Kelly.' She pulls on her shirt.

'OK. I'm sorry.'

'Now tell me about Herman Visser and the wrecked dredger.'

'Is Visser implicated?'

'Do you care?'

'I suppose I do in a way, although I lost touch with him years ago. I don't understand how you got on to Visser in the first place.'

'Same place I got on to you . . . in the newspaper archives.'

'But why Visser . . . why pick on him?'

'I was looking for anyone I could find who was in prison at the same time as Moses Freeman.'

'You're talking in riddles. Who is Moses Freeman?'

It took a while to explain and by then it was dark.

'We sat too long,' Kelly says. 'We might as well camp here.'

Making camp consists of eating three biscuits, drinking water, lying on the sand and trying to sleep, but sleep evades Chris. Thoughts of spiders, scorpions and jackals keep her alert. Even worse is her anxiety about her father. Kelly seems to be protecting Visser. Why should he do that? Some sort of a misplaced sense of loyalty perhaps. Or maybe they are still partners. She can't accept that Kelly might be one of the gang . . . if she did, she would never have told him so much.

'Are you asleep?' she asks after a while.

'No.'

'So tell me about Visser. What happened after you and Visser lost out with your mine?'

'I went back to diamond dredging off Port Nolloth. There were good pickings in those days. Visser joined me, but he was angry . . . deeply angry. Foolishly he got into illicit diamond dealing and he was caught almost immediately. He got two years' hard labour, although finally he served only eighteen months.'

His face was emotionless, but Kelly's voice gave him away. He was grieving. He still feels for the man.

'Visser was a changed man when he came out . . . bitter . . . tough . . . vicious. He took a job dredging diamonds on *Rainbow's End*. It's rough work, especially for someone like Visser with his big ideas. There's bad currents that can throw you a hundred yards on to sharp rocks. The suction pipe is powerful . . . hard to hang on to. At times it whips you around like a rag doll and when a rock is dislodged it can thump into you hard enough to break your ribs. I guessed Visser wouldn't last long at the game.'

'And he didn't. He died,' Chris says, watching Kelly's expression.

'So they say,' he admits after some hesitation.

After this Chris tries to get him talking again, but she can't get another word out of him.

There is something else worrying her: should she tell Kelly who she is? She's hurting because her father didn't recognise her. Not even a glimmer of intuition. Nothing. He doesn't particularly like her, she senses. He certainly doesn't trust her. Suddenly it sinks in that if her father had wanted a daughter he would have come looking for her. He'd always known where she was living. If only she hadn't searched for him, she could have hung on to her hopes and dreams. As it is . . .

She tries to swallow her disappointment and get some sleep.

★ ★ ★

She wakes to the sound of a helicopter hovering close by and lurches to her feet.

'Keep still. They haven't seen us,' he shouts above the roar. The plane moves on. A beam of light, like a kite's tail, drifts over the sand.

'Someone is very keen to find you. Is he a friend or an enemy?' Kelly asks. 'And is he connected with Visser?'

'I don't know,' she says in a quiet voice. 'I have two lines of enquiry. Two entirely different sets of potential crooks. One of them might be for real, but they're both keeping tabs on me. The trouble is . . . I don't know who to trust.'

'Two heads are better than one. Why don't you

tell me how far you've got? Perhaps I could help you.'

'That's what they all say,' she says miserably. Curling into a foetal position she tries to get some sleep.

35

There is something different about the veld, there are far more birds, the bush is becoming denser with shrubs, tufts of dried grass and a few sparse trees. They are moving into more fertile territory.

Uncomplaining, Chris plods along Kelly's trail, but her outward passivity is entirely false. She feels like an overheated boiler threatening to blow. They've walked for twelve hours, but Kelly hasn't said a word all day. She guesses that he regrets his confidences of the previous evening, consequently she's getting nowhere. She feels light-headed and resentful, her legs ache abominably and as the day draws to a close her temper rises.

'We camp here,' Kelly announces, pausing beside a small copse of thorn trees. He hesitates, gazing around at the spoor. Then he pulls out an axe and lops off a tangle of leaves and thorns surrounding the lower branches of the nearest tree. 'If you get scared, climb up this tree.'

'It's full of thorns.'

'Dead right.' He lights a fire which is blazing within seconds. 'Stay here. Keep the fire going.' He points to a pile of dead sticks under a thorn tree. 'By the time I get back you need to have enough burning embers to fill a couple of buckets. I'll shoot us some supper.'

She examines the tree. The thorns are almost

as long as her hand: big, thick, villainous barbs that could cut through flesh like a razor. Better than being eaten by some ravenous beast, but Chris hopes she won't have to face the choice.

★   ★   ★

Kelly is gone for over two hours. Not that it worries her, but she might have been frantic with fright. He's still getting back at her for daring to be there. Except for the firelight, it's pitch black under the trees, but for every dancing flame there's a moving shadow right behind her and she's surrounded with thick bushes that rustle and creak. Fear puts her on a high and tonight she's soaring. The moon is close enough to touch, each sound strums within her heart. She feels vibrant with life and part of everything. The soft warm wind carries the musical chimes of frogs and the incessant strum of cicadas. Then she hears the high-pitched call of hyenas, not far off. She knows she will never forget this magical night in the veld as she crouches close to the fire.

Kelly returns eventually with a half-grown wild boar slung over his shoulder which he has already skinned and gutted. He sets up a rough trestle by stringing some branches together, skewers the boar and hangs it over the flames.

'Were you afraid?' Kelly wants to know.

'Fear puts me on a high. I was flying.'

'You, too?'

Naturally, me, too, she ponders, but when is she going to tell him he's her father? She no longer expects a happy reunion. Perhaps she won't bother. By now she dislikes him. He has no right to be so mean. Not to anyone.

Kelly is making himself comfortable with his head on his haversack. He says: 'Wake me when the meat's cooked.'

'Kelly . . . are you awake?' she asks, some time later.

A muttered curse is her only reply.

'I read an old newspaper article . . . perhaps you saw it in the local newspaper. It claimed that a woman told Zuckerman about your mine . . . the one you lost in the court case. Was the woman Marie van Schalkwyk?'

He groans and turns, lifting himself on one elbow. 'Why don't you stick to diamond laundering? It's a great story.'

'I'm interested.'

'Ask Zuckerman. Yes, why don't you?' He glares at her.

'I don't know him. For God's sake . . . ' She's about to blow her top. She knows this and she tries to reason with him. 'What's wrong with you? Do you have a touch of paranoia? Senile dementia brought on by years of loneliness?' She can feel her pent-up rage getting the upperhand. 'Or are you deliberately riling me? I can't believe that you think I'm a spy from a mining company!'

'That's exactly what I think.'

'But Zuckerman . . . for God's sake. He was fifty-plus then. He's pushing ninety now, if he's still alive.'

'How do you know that?' He asks in a voice that's throbbing with temper. 'They didn't put his age in the newspaper. Now I know for sure where you're coming from.'

This is the moment when the boiler blows. Her pent-up fury is impressive. 'Do you . . . do you really . . . ? Well you're right . . . I have inside information, but not from Zuckerman. I've had enough of you, Dan Kelly. You and your sanctimonious, holier-than-thou attitude to people. You think you're a great guy, but you're not. You're cruel and hard and you've ruined two people's lives with your stupid phobias. I came here to find you, but I wish I'd never bothered. You're not my father . . . never will be. You're the sperm donor . . . nothing more. No wonder you live alone. Who'd want you around? You're the villain of the story . . . not me. My mother never harmed you, and neither will I. God! When I think of all those years I've longed to find you . . . imagined our reunion . . . all those nights alone in those rich schools you paid for . . . and what do I find? A mean-minded, pompous bastard like you. I'm ashamed that you're my father. Fuck you, Kelly.'

She has to break off. There's a lump in her throat so big she can't swallow, let alone talk. She pulls up her knees and rests her arms on them, it's as good a place as any to hide her face.

Kelly doesn't answer. After a while Chris raises her head and stares at him. He's gazing at her with horror in his eyes. She might be a suicide bomber about to blow. Chris turns away to hide her sadness.

Kelly swears softly to himself. After a while he gets up and walks away.

★ ★ ★

The embers die down and Chris sits alone in the dark, too sad to think about danger. Reality intrudes with snarling and the crackle of paws on dead leaves. Something is after their supper. She snatches some sticks and puffs at the dying embers. The tinder is dry and flares up. Whatever is out there recedes when she grabs a long stick and thrusts it into the flames. She'll have a weapon ready if it lunges at the meat.

Much later, something big and heavy blunders through the bushes. It's coming towards her. It better look out. She's in a mean mood. She grasps the burning stick and hurls it towards the sound.

'You'll start a fire!' Kelly says, stamping out the embers. He retrieves the stick and throws it on the fire. 'I'm sorry. Christine . . . '

'Chris.'

'I'm sorry . . . what more can I say?' Moments later she's being pulled to her feet and hugged tightly, just as she used to imagine when snuggling under her duvet at school. She can even feel his wet cheeks, but something's missing. Her feelings aren't there. Who is this man? Do I want to know him? Then she cries, too, but silently, deep inside.

'You're not the only one to dream of a reunion,' Kelly is saying. 'For years I longed to see you, but I couldn't face your mother. She always made me feel murderous.'

Chris scans him. He looks contrite.

'You're quite a girl, Chris. I've been secretly admiring you. You've got guts and you're smart. Obviously there's more of my genes in you than anything else. June was a city girl. We couldn't go into the garden without her complaining about ants and spiders. I always knew you'd come and find me . . . if you wanted me. I'd given up hope by now, of course. Then, when you came looking for me, I didn't even recognise you . . . that hurts. I should have. Your mother used to send photographs to my lawyer and you looked like me . . . my hair . . . my eyes.'

'It's all right. Calm down, Kelly. It's cool. Meeting like this, I mean. How could you know?'

'The truth is, I couldn't see further than my damned mine. Not for the wealth, believe me. The claim I lost because of your mother was worth millions, but it was the spite that hurt the most.'

'Mother would never . . . ' She breaks off as she remembers the guilt in her mother's eyes. What was it Mother had said? *'The past . . . whatever I did . . . is buried. It must stay that way.'*

'The meat's burning. Throw some water on the flames, Chris. We should eat.'

They are both behaving as if their fight never occurred, she by putting on her very best face, perfected for dealing with difficult clients, he by showering her with glances of the utmost approval.

'I have some whiskey in my pack . . . to

336

commiserate, or celebrate. What'll it be?'

'Celebrate,' she says firmly.

Kelly digs into his pack and passes Chris a flask. 'It's rye whiskey. Great stuff. When I saw you climb out of the helicopter I thought to myself: How the hell did Zuckerman persuade a lovely girl like her to do his dirty work?'

'For goodness' sake forget Zuckerman. He's probably in a wheelchair.'

'I hope the bastard's dead.'

Catching sight of his expression, Chris believes him.

'You see, Chris, honey, I've found a claim even better than the one I had back in 'seventy-five. I'm keeping the place secret, even though I own the mineral rights. It's all tied up by a top lawyer. One day it will be yours, naturally. That was always my plan.'

Chris tries to look pleased. A diamond mine in the middle of a desert is not on her list of priorities.

'We'd better clear the air. I wasn't lying to you. June betrayed me. She gave everything to Zuckerman.' Kelly's voice is rough with emotion. He is gazing intently at the boar, his knife poised in his hand as he plans the first cut with his Swiss army knife.

She says: 'I'd like to hear the truth for once. You'd better start at the beginning.'

'Right after we've eaten.'

A flat stone, brushed clean of earth and resting on embers, is their warming tray. Kelly is piling slices of pork on to it. Chris is famished and the meat smells great. She burns her fingers

337

grabbing a piece and tucks in. 'I've never tasted anything so good.'

'Hunger helps, but I've never found better meat than wild boar, particularly when it's *braaied* in the bush and eaten under the stars. It took a while to find one.' For a while they eat in silence. Chris cleans her hands on some wipes she brought along. Then she rolls up her spare clothes to make a pillow and lies down, sensing she's in for a long night.

Kelly passes her the flask again. 'Don't fall asleep on me, Chris, honey.' He takes a long time getting started and Chris senses his reluctance.

'I don't want to turn you against your mother.'

'I've already heard Mum's version and it didn't turn me against you.'

'From what I can see of you, June's done a great job rearing you. Of course she had good material to start with.'

Except that I was never at home, always at boarding school, perhaps that's why Sienna and I grew so close. We only had each other. But this is not the time to think about Sienna and it's not something she can discuss with Kelly. She lies back and gazes at the sky, but she's seeing Sienna's face, rapt and excited, just as she always looked when they played truant for a shopping expedition, or the movies, or to meet guys at the local pub. Chris tries to shake off her terrible sadness. Staring wildly at her father she struggles to make sense of whatever it is he's saying.

★   ★   ★

'Way back in the early Seventies, I gambled the last of my cash to buy a concession to dredge diamonds off Port Nolloth. I was almost skint, so I converted a fishing boat into a dredger and I did the diving myself. I used to dive for seven months, October to April, and in winter, when the sea was too cold and the storms too rough, I tramped all over the northern territory . . . Botswana, South West and Angola. I struck lucky fairly early on by discovering one of the richest diamond pipes I'd ever come across, situated on a karakul farm. I kept the location secret while I sold my off-shore concession and the dredger for a million dollars.'

So her father lost everything . . . not just the mine. Perhaps he had the right to feel bitter.

'It wasn't enough, so I went looking for money and I was introduced to Herman Visser, a Dutch accountant who had come to Africa to make his fortune.

'Going anywhere with Visser was hazardous. He had some sort of hold over women . . . they flocked after us . . . he had the looks . . . blue eyes, blond hair and the physique, but it was something about his eyes that pulled the girls in. His eyes were full of secret humour. He seemed to look at the world with amused tolerance and you had the feeling that he and you were buddies and whatever you were up against wasn't all that serious. Ask women what the big draw was and you never got the same story twice.'

Kelly is lost in the past. His eyes have a trance-like glow, he looks happy. Chris guesses

339

they were good times for both of them, until they crashed.

'He'd inherited over two million dollars. I had a million, plus the know-how and the mine, so we teamed up on a fifty-fifty basis, but while our negotiations were going on, the old sheep farmer, Van As, became comatose. He was dying of cancer, so we signed up the mineral rights with his nephew, Jan.'

'If only I'd been there. I wouldn't have let you do that.'

'Geologists aren't lawyers, hon. We worked hard, bought and installed the equipment we needed and began excavating. We'd been developing the mine for five months when we heard the rumour about Van As having a bastard son in the village. Visser and I went looking for the boy. His name was Wanee Hendrickse, he'd never been to school and he worked as a labourer on a neighbouring farm. We offered the boy a good sum to sell us the mineral rights, on the off-chance that he might become the heir, but his mother kept upping the price. There was no real proof that he really was Van As' son. Finally I drove up to Johannesburg to see my lawyer and ask him how I could clinch the deal with Hendrickse.' Kelly sighs as if regretting that move.

Chris stirs uncomfortably. Is this going to be like her divorce cases? Is she going to be nagged for a moral judgment? Will Kelly try to get her on his side?

'I arrived on Friday and drove to the mining house where June, your mother, worked. As soon

340

as Zuckerman heard I was back, he insisted that we accompany him and his girlfriend, Marie, to the company's game park for the weekend. A leopard had mauled a couple of kids and it was essential to kill the beast right away, but no one had been able to track it. My appointment with the lawyer was on Monday, so we locked my papers, with all the details, in June's safe for the weekend.'

'Mum told me a little . . . how you shot the leopard, screwed Marie and broke Mum's heart.'

'In a nutshell . . . yes. I heard later that she woke up Zuckerman in the night and told him everything. There and then the two of them drove back to the city, where June handed over my file. The bastard flew straight out to the site with a geologist. Hendrickse was signed up before noon. A red racing car did the trick. It was so much less than we had offered. Then Zuckerman got a team of top lawyers together to sue for the karakul farm on behalf of the boy.'

'Did you love my mother?' Chris asks.

'No, but I never lied to her either. She'd been in love with me ever since we met. A geologist's life is less than exciting. Pretty women don't sit around in the bush, but whenever I went back to the city, which was four or five times a year to sell a claim, she was always waiting for me. She was so loyal and it was so easy.'

'So you just took and gave nothing in return.'

'Not true. I'd asked June to marry me, but she made a few impossible conditions: I had to give up prospecting, she wanted to go back to England. I couldn't live like that, but June wasn't fond of the bush. She picked the wrong man.'

That sounds like Mother, Chris reasons. She always wants to be in control and she hates the countryside. She doesn't even enjoy our garden, but that is not for Kelly's ears.

'When I reached the city I learned what had happened, but I didn't worry too much because I didn't think Zuckerman could win,' Kelly is saying. 'So we got on with mining the first level.'

'My poor mother,' Chris interrupts him. 'She got a lifetime sentence for a moment of jealous spite.'

'Do you want me to continue?' He sounds cold.

'Yes.' Watching Kelly now, she begins to understand her mother's jealous fury. Kelly is still an attractive man. He must have been highly desirable. Mum probably knew that Marie would leave Kelly if he lost his shirt.

'I couldn't believe my good fortune when Marie followed me back to the cottage I'd bought near the mine. You can't imagine the effect she had on men . . . it was something one can't describe. She had the looks and the figure, but it was more than that . . . some sort of a magic she let loose so that you couldn't think straight when you were near her.'

'And then?' Chris urges, sensing an unhappy ending.

'One day I came home early to find she was in bed with Visser. So there we were . . . the three of us . . . at each other's throats. I owned the cottage, but I couldn't stay there, so I found lodgings in the village nearby. We carried on with the business. We didn't have much choice, we'd both sunk every cent we owned into that mine. Then . . . out of the blue . . . we started to get reports about the case drawing to a close with the odds in Hendrickse's favour. He won and within a week, we were out on our necks. We lost everything.'

He has told his story in a detached tone. Now he shrugs and grins.

'I went back to dredging. I knew I would eventually get back where I was, but Visser took it badly. When he got into trouble, I knew it was my fault.'

'So what happened to Marie?'

'The day Hendrickse won the case, she moved back to the city, married Zuckerman and they sold out and moved to London. Visser took it badly. He was in love with her.'

'And Visser?'

'You read about Visser's fate.' He breaks off and sighs. 'Enough questions. We have a hard day tomorrow, Chris. You'd best get some sleep.'

'Thanks for telling me, Kelly. Are there any scorpions, snakes or man-eating lions around?'

'Sure! But they know I've got a gun. I'll take first watch and I'll keep the fire burning.'

Curled up beside the fire, feeling safe, Chris falls into a deep sleep.

36

Night cloaks the bush under a brilliant star-strewn sky, but in the east comes a glimmer of oyster-grey. All at once a francolin gives its *kraa-kraaa-kraa* call to announce the dawn. The birds begin their chorus, proclaiming their space, until the air hums with their noisy song. Grey turns to red, sending a strange, mystical glow over the land.

'Welcome to the morning,' Kelly says, as Chris wakes in the chilly dawn.

'Morning? But surely . . . why didn't you wake me to keep watch?'

'You need to sleep more than I do.'

She sits up cautiously. 'I'm stiff all over,' she says, trying to smooth back her hair. She reaches into her pack for a precious 'wipe' and cleans her face and neck.

'I'd do anything for a shower.'

'Your wish will be granted this afternoon, with luck. We're moving towards a camp I have on the outskirts of Ghanzi. The shack is primitive and so is the shower, but it works.'

'Sh! Hang on . . . listen . . . isn't that a helicopter?'

'It's been searching around for the past hour. I'm surprised you didn't wake before.'

Chris wonders why Kelly sounds different. Twisting her head, she watches him quizzically. His eyes are laughing, his grin is wide and happy.

Chris smiles to herself. 'You've shaved. You look much younger without that white stubble.'

'I feel lighter. Now that I know who I am . . . '

'Who are you?'

'I'm Dad. Don't interrupt. Now that I know who I am, you will do as you are told and eat this nutritious oryx *biltong*.'

'Yuck, Kelly. It stinks,' she yelps as a piece lands in her lap. 'I'm sure that's what I smelled last night.'

'Could be. I left it hanging in the Acacia thorn tree. Birds and beasts alike are wary of those thorns. I have little stores of dried meat all over the place.'

'How disgusting. But where is the rest of the boar?'

Kelly gestures towards his larder up amongst the thorns. 'I saved you a piece.' He digs into his haversack. 'This should keep you going for a while.'

The drone of the helicopter is nearer now. They listen in silence for a while. The aircraft circles half a kilometre away and then moves westwards until they can no longer hear the engine.

'How about moving on?' Kelly suggests, as if he is giving her a choice.

'Sure.' Sighing, she picks up her pack.

★   ★   ★

'Who is it who wants to find you so badly?' Kelly asks, as he sets up a punishing pace.

Chris takes a while answering. 'It could be Jim

345

Stark. We must avoid him.'

'He's not a friend?' he asks guilelessly.

'It's not that simple, Kelly . . . Dad. I'm not sure about him at all.' Chris tries to calm down and hide her anxiety.

'I think it's time you confided in me.' Kelly's deep rumble seems to lend a sense of security. 'Just let me get the basics under my belt.'

Chris hardly knows where to start, but half an hour later she's given Kelly a rough idea of her progress in the investigation.

'So to recap, Chris, you came to Africa hoping that Freeman would reveal his hand and tell you who runs the laundering scam,' Kelly says.

'Sort of . . . yes.'

'He wouldn't play, but Joubert helped you by giving you access to police records. You hit on Visser mainly because he was there at the time, he'd been convicted of theft and later his death seemed highly suspect . . . to say nothing of the missing diamonds. They were rumoured to be worth at least ten million pounds.'

'Yes, and there's something else. Freeman fears for his life from someone he described to Petrus as 'that bloody accountant.' '

'There's nothing here that will convince the police. So tell me about your tenuous link between Visser and Skoog.'

'I only know what I read in the newspaper: Skoog became very wealthy three years after the shipwreck. Then there was the strange way he described Visser's death at the time. I can't believe he would watch his exhausted friend go under without trying to save him, or at least throw a lifebelt.'

'Good thinking.'

'When I started to investigate his business methods I found out about the armoured cars that deliver the cash to Skoog, and how Skoog always pilots the plane himself on his trips to the interior. His schedule fits my theory. Add to that the fact that he tried to kill me, and I'd say he's guilty.'

'He's certainly guilty of something. So shouldn't you be back in your London IT department, tracking the money routes to find where Ulf Skoog's cash supply originates?'

'That's next on the list.'

'Look here, hon. You're a lawyer and you have a business degree. You're highly qualified, but not as a cop. This is police work. You have no experience of sleuthing and you keep running into danger. You're supposed to be using your financial and legal training in order to solve these problems, and as I see it, your brief is to find out how the gems are laundered. Not who . . . nor why . . . just how.'

Kelly doesn't even turn around, which is lucky because he doesn't see her expression. He keeps up his punishing pace, while telling her how to run her business and the investigation and soon he'll be telling her how to run her life, when he knows nothing about her, or anything else. But why tell him about the investigation if she doesn't want his help? Chris sighs.

'Yes, how? That's the million dollar question,' she answers, putting away pride. 'I can't help hoping that I will find out who is running the show, or any small fact that might lead to Sienna which I could pass on to the police. She was my best friend for years. She still is, I suppose. The thought of her imprisoned somewhere . . . '

She breaks off and sighs.

'I should have gone back to London, but I was hoping you might point me to Visser. Then Jim arrived and . . . '

'What's Jim got to do with it?'

'He followed me to Walvis Bay. I was ill, so he took me to a hotel at Kasane for a few days.'

'Sounds to me as if he's in love. Are you in love with him?'

She ducks that question. 'But what if he's not, Kelly? What if he's running the show, not Visser. I must tell you something else. On our last night at the hotel Jim went out and came back much later dragging a heavy suitcase. I broke it open the next morning while he was out and a fortune of diamonds spilled out all over the bedroom floor. I left in a hurry, I can tell you.'

'Well, he couldn't have been recruited by Freeman, he's too young.'

'True, but he might be a buying agent.'

'Then why is he always in London? You seem to suspect everyone.'

'Anyone who lies about their feelings just to keep tabs on me.'

'But what if he loves you?'

'Then why does he lie?'

'Well, I don't know Chris, but there is such a thing as being sworn to secrecy.'

'Maybe you're right . . . I'm no good at this. I

even suspected you.'

Kelly smiles at her. 'I think you're on the right track with Visser. Herman Visser was very much alive last time I heard from him and that was years after the wrecking of *Rainbow's End*.'

'Wow!' Chris collapses on her back on the sand. 'That's fantastic. Why didn't you say so? This news makes everything so worthwhile. I was worried about wasting company money. Can we have a water break?' She takes a swig of water and shakes what's left longingly.

'Don't lie in the sun like that, Chris, you'll spoil your skin. Pull your hat over your face.'

'Whoa there, Kelly. Are you trying to make up for lost time?' She sits up and peers at him, shading her eyes with her hand.

'Drink your water.' Kelly looks concerned and slightly embarrassed. 'We have to move on. I think we're being followed.'

'I can't think of a more unlikely place to follow someone.' She shudders all the same.

'It could be a hungry lion, which is not a problem because I have a hunting rifle and a gun. People are more difficult to deal with, especially lovesick young men.'

'Oh, come on, Kelly . . . '

'Dad!'

'Dad it is, but stop teasing me.'

'I have good ears for the bush . . . years of practice. The helicopter landed and took off again some time back. After that it stopped searching and made off in the direction of Maun. Some time later, I heard jackals snarling as they were chased off the remains of our *biltong*. Since then there's been a steady trail of disturbed cries … birds mainly … some distance back, but moving in our direction … keeping up.'

'Let's go.' She jumps up, fired with adrenaline.

'I was going to tell you about Visser,' Kelly says. 'I never thought that he had died and as it happened I was right, but this will have to wait until we get back. It's too hot to talk and we have a long way to go.'

★ ★ ★

This has been her worst morning by far. The sun hangs overhead, intent on sucking her dry. Chris feels dehydrated, her tongue is swollen, her nose is sore and her throat is on fire. Her legs are so weak she can hardly walk and every breath hurts. The sun blazes down, baking her, and the sparse thorn trees give little shade. The sand is so hot it burns her feet through the soles of her boots.

By the time they reach Kelly's camp, at four p.m., her limbs have turned to lead and her mouth is parched. Each step forward requires a massive effort of will. She stumbles through a gate, only vaguely aware of having arrived, and sees before her a cluster of whitewashed rondavels with thatched roofs and a large dam glittering in the sun. It must be a mirage.

'Well done, Chris. We've arrived.'

'Thank goodness,' she croaks. 'Water, please.'

'All the water you want … and a cold shower.'

Chris flops down on a bench under a tree and closes her eyes.

Kelly goes inside and returns with a jug of cool water with slices of lemon in it. He brings up a table and hands her a glass.

'It's all so civilised.'

'We're only five miles from Ghanzi. This place suits me fine when I'm prospecting in Botswana,' he replies. 'I like it here.'

The water soaks in and Chris revives enough to look around the camp. There are four fairly large whitewashed rondavels built in a crescent with a connecting wall, plus two more thatched roofs supported by pillars; one covers a large sink and a shower, the other a *braai* area. The washroom has a bamboo fence low enough to peer over. Beyond a thicket of thorn trees is a large shed made of corrugated asbestos sheeting and there the land has been burned and flattened into what looks like a rough runway.

'I can't believe it.' She laughs. 'You're so well organised.'

'Go on, have a shower. There's a *vlei* full of water over there. I pump it into one of the tanks when the rainwater gets low. Don't worry. I've plenty to do out back. Call me when you've finished. No one ever comes here. Enjoy yourself. Just don't try to swim in the *vlei*, you never know when the odd crocodile comes visiting. I've put out a soap and a towel for you.'

Chris strips off behind the bamboo frame and turns on the water. It's divine. She sings as the cool flood cascades over her, streaming over her body, her face and her hair . . . soaking into her pores . . . reviving her.

351

'Well, well, you had me really fooled this time, Chris.'

She yelps, loses her balance and lands half-crouched in the grass.

'Jim!'

'Your past lover inconveniently turns up to save you, only to find that you're shacked up with someone new. Or maybe he's not too new. Pretty ancient, I would say.'

'No, he's not new at all.' Sullen and resentful, she glowers at him.

'Why the hell did you run away?'

'Because I found the diamonds, which proves you're involved, which is what I've always suspected.'

'How did you manage to break the case?' he asks mildly.

'It broke with the weight of the diamonds.'

'Are you all right, hon?' She hears Kelly calling from the doorway.

'Hon?' Jim apes him. 'So you're into the stars and stripes.'

She grabs the towel and wraps it around her. 'Get lost Jim and stop following me.'

'You should have told me about you and Kelly.'

'And you . . . and the diamonds?'

'I sold a certain group some equipment. They paid me with diamonds. I came to Kasane to collect them. End of story. I found Kelly for you . . . remember? If I'd known what was going on, I wouldn't have. Just how long have you known this old guy? Don't you prefer someone your own age?'

His eyes switch to a spot just behind her.

Looking around she sees her father watching them with a quizzical expression.

'It seems you know my daughter. I'm Dan Kelly. Who the hell are you?'

Jim seems to have lost his tongue as his sullen leer vaporises. He stares from Kelly to Chris as if hypnotised, his face brick red, his eyes smarting. Pulling himself together, Jim produces a polite smile.

'James Stark, sir. How do you do.' He holds out his hand.

'OK, James. I'm about to find us some food. I'll need enough glowing embers to *braai* a small buck. You'll have to do it, Chris is exhausted. You'll find a bricked-up grate and plenty of wood round the back. Don't set light to the thatch. I presume you're staying for a meal? You must be hungry. It is you who's been following our trail, isn't it?'

'Yes, sir. Certain facts led me to believe that Chris might be in some danger with you.'

'What sort of facts?'

'The transfer of mineral rights at a price far below their value to Visser,' Jim says, leering at Chris.

'If you want to know why, I'll tell you over a meal. Just make sure the fire's good enough.'

Kelly walks off, shouldering his rifle and the two of them watch him in silence.

'You didn't say that Kelly was your father,' Jim

begins hesitantly. 'How come you didn't know where your father was?'

'My parents split. I'd never met him until a few days ago.'

'Listen, Chris. I've been poking around my contacts for you. I haven't found much, except that this diamond laundering is big . . . very big. It involves several African governments and it's all controlled from London. They . . . whoever they are . . . have very substantial resources. They could put you out of the picture just by clicking their fingers. Life means nothing to them.'

'Are you one of them, Jim?'

Jim's eyes are so expressive. He can switch off his warm, concerned expression like switching off a light, which shows how false it is. Right now he looks as cold and hard as steel.

'I've given you good advice. And take it from me, your old man is involved. You're the last person who should be on this investigation when Kelly is in it up to his eyeballs.'

'He certainly isn't. Go to hell, Jim. No one wants you here. You weren't invited. I wish you'd leave.'

'I'm staying because I'm hungry and I promised to get the fire going. Besides, I want to hear his silly excuses.'

Chris is furious and hurt and just a little worried about Kelly. Of course he's not involved, how could he be? He's her father, after all. Jim goes round the back to light the fire while Chris sits around feeling gloomy. After a while she goes inside and pokes around her father's rondavel, which shows no sign of being lived in. She feels so tired. She curls up on a camp bed on the balcony and falls asleep.

37

Chris wakes to the sound of someone calling her name. When she opens her eyes she finds it is dark, but there is a security light fixed in a tree outside and she can hear the throb of a generator coming from the hangar.

A delicious smell is coming from round the back and she can hear voices. She follows the scent to a *braai* set up in the middle of a grassy patch, surrounded with sliced-off tree trunks for seats. Jim is laughing. He has a glass of wine in one hand and a long pair of tongs in the other. He's pulling off pieces of venison and setting them on a large grid perched on bricks with a few embers beneath.

Kelly is opening another bottle of red wine. So they've got through one already.

'Oh, hi, Chris.' Jim looks round and grins at her. 'Feeling better? Kelly's a very good shot.' Perhaps this explains their sudden camaraderie. 'Straight through the brain, in the dark. The buck didn't know what hit him. I don't know how he does it.' He gazes admiringly at Kelly.

'You can't beat Africa,' Jim goes on. 'Just look at the sky. You don't get a sky like this anywhere else in the world.'

'Alaska's pretty good,' Kelly says quietly. 'But I agree with you. The African bush has always been home for me.'

Chris feels a twinge of envy at their instant

rapport. How dare Jim tell her Kelly's a crook and then treat him like a buddy.

'Dad,' she says, feeling mean. 'Jim thinks you're one of the gang I'm investigating.'

'Hon, I keep telling you that you're not investigating this dangerous gang, merely their methods of laundering diamonds.'

'Are you hearing me?' she demands, her voice rising ominously.

'Yes. Jim said something of the sort to me, but things are not always what they seem. I've told Jim more or less what I told you about the run-up to the court case. I'll tell you about Visser when we've finished eating. Let's not spoil this superb venison.'

How matter-of-fact they both are, for all the world as if eating and drinking are all-important and her father's guilt or innocence is of little consequence.

'Tuck in. Plates and cutlery over there.' He gestures towards one of the tree stumps. 'Jim, how about unravelling a potato for Chris or she'll burn her fingers on the foil.'

'Talk about an over-protective parent,' Chris mutters. Just what has she let herself in for?

'Well,' Kelly says half an hour later, thrusting his paper plate into the bin. 'We're all tired. We don't have all night so here goes . . .'

Just make it good, Dad, Chris prays silently.

*   *   *

'I came to Africa in the late Sixties with a yen to make my fortune. A few miners were dredging off-shore with huge boats. Due to my financial circumstances, I was forced to pioneer a much smaller dredger, which was little more than a fishing boat and only suitable for summer conditions. In winter, I prospected all over Northern Botswana and Namibia.'

Chris grieves for her father. What a life! He's still trying to make his fortune and he hasn't got far yet. Her father's such a tough man, but now he's over sixty, how will he cope?

'As you've both heard, I struck lucky early on by discovering one of the richest diamond pipes I'd ever come across on a karakul farm in northern Namibia. You also know how I lost it. It was my own damn fault. But I always felt bad about Visser. I was responsible for his loss.'

You didn't force him to turn to crime, Chris thinks sullenly. All this guilt is an indulgence.

'He took it badly . . . went off the rails with one illegal scheme after the next. When he landed up in prison, I knew it was my fault. If he hadn't met me, he'd have succeeded somewhere else. He had a good business brain. Then came the shipwreck. I never thought Visser had died. He's an excellent swimmer and a skilled scuba diver, but I couldn't believe he would kill the skipper.'

'Even if the skipper died accidentally, Visser is still responsible, since he deliberately wrecked the dredger,' Chris points out, sounding aggressive, even to herself.

'As I'm sure he did, Chris. The fact is, prior to the shipwreck it was known that several valuable diamonds had been recovered from another dredger belonging to the company. Once a week, all the diamonds were transferred to *Rainbow's End* to be shipped to Walvis Bay. This time, it was rumoured, she was carrying over ten million pounds of roughs. It was winter, a time of treacherous seas and thick fog with visibility down to fifty metres most mornings. As you know, the dredger capsized and although the skipper was lost, the rest of the crew managed to reach the shore.'

'They must be damn good swimmers. The cold water nearly killed me and it was summertime.' Chris shudders. The memory is still too real to bear.

'Yes, strangely they all made it. Even young Dirk Vorster, who couldn't swim. I wouldn't have him on my boat for that very reason. Clearly, Visser had brought the boat in to shore and they'd waded to the beach. Then he took it out alone and wrecked it on the rocks. At least, that's my guess.

'A lot of cash changed hands, but not right then. They were smart about it, but within five years every member of the crew had come into a sizeable cash sum and they all had a viable reason for it. The skipper's body was found, but not Visser's.'

'It sounds as if the skipper was the sacrificial lamb. They needed at least one corpse to convince the authorities,' Jim says.

'True. Perhaps the skipper didn't want to join their conspiracy. He might have threatened them with the police. At the inquest, Visser was presumed dead mainly because of Skoog's evidence. Skoog got his so-called inheritance about three years later, but I'd like to know who left him the cash. Ulf never knew his Swedish father, least of all the uncle who was supposed to have left him the money. His mother worked in a local fish canning factory.'

'And you kept quiet,' Chris accuses Kelly.

'Yes. I wasn't aiming at ruining Visser twice over. He never blamed me, but it was my fault he'd lost his considerable birthright. It was years before I heard from him again.'

Chris shivers. Visser is out there somewhere . . . a clever, ruthless man, backed by unscrupulous government ministers. But ruthlessness can't give him the diamond certification he needs. How does he do it?

'Five years later,' Kelly is saying, 'a lawyer purporting to be the nominee of an old friend of mine, called on me and asked me to sell my marginal diamond claims to him.'

'What claims are these?' Chris asks.

'Mines that aren't viable at current prices. When I find a likely deposit, I register the claim in my name and put it up for sale. If the mine isn't viable I can't sell it, but I hang on to it. This costs me nothing. At the time I had quite a few. Anyway, I refused. I didn't know the guy and I didn't like him.'

'Do you remember his name?'

'I could never forget it. It was the same as Marie's . . . Schalkwyk.

'Then I got a call from Visser. I had no doubt at all that it was him. He went on about old times, romancing a bit, and he told me that

Schalkwyk was his lawyer. He wanted the claims, so I said he could have them for nothing.' Kelly looks around apologetically. 'Put yourselves in my shoes. Try to imagine losing a fortune for someone.'

'He took a legitimate business risk, just as you did,' Jim says. Chris blesses him silently as she drains her glass.

'Strangely, he didn't want them for nothing, he wanted to buy them. Finally Schalkwyk drew up some documents which stated that all my claims were part of our original partnership, which we had never actually terminated. Visser bought me out of the partnership for a trifling sum which I didn't want and never received.'

'But Dad . . . why did you go ahead?' Chris scowls at him. 'You knew it was a scam.'

'Not necessarily. Thousands of abandoned claims are being mined nowadays simply because modern mining methods make them viable and prices have risen dramatically. Visser convinced me that he could make a small profit, so I gave them to him. I didn't want to mine them. I was glad to have something to give him.'

'But that wasn't the end of it, was it, sir?' Jim, who had been lying on the grass as if asleep, is wide awake all of a sudden.

'Far from it. I was coming to that. A year later I found a pretty good diamond pipe in Northern Namibia on a barren karakul ranch. They are the worst kind. They need five square miles to support one sheep in that kind of territory. I signed up the mineral rights and offered it to Visser for next to nothing.'

Chris frowns. 'This is looking bad.'

'I can see you don't understand, Chris. But look at it from my point of view. I'd ruined Visser and set him on a path that led to prison. Now he was trying to make a new, legitimate start by mining a dozen sub-economic claims. I wanted to improve his chances, so I gave him this one, which I'd registered under the name of *Shimpuru-64*. I felt I'd gone a small way towards repaying him. The claim was worth about half a million, but in time and with care I felt he could retrieve his loss. It was the best I could do to clear my conscience.'

'I do understand. Truly I do . . . ' Impulsively Chris hugs her father. 'Payback time is over, Dad. You've paid everyone. Now it's time to look after yourself.'

Jim walks around filling their glasses. There's a great atmosphere. The sensuous moon breaks from behind the trees. An owl shrieks overhead and small birds sheltering in the trees twitter uneasily.

★ ★ ★

Kelly breaks the spell. 'Now Jim, it's your turn to do some explaining. You're James Stark from the Starkwell Tyre family. Am I right?'

'Yes,' Jim says uneasily. 'How do you know that, sir?'

'I studied with your uncle and he married a friend of mine, Julia, your Aunt.'

'Good heavens! That's amazing.' Jim is looking increasingly uncomfortable.

'I used to be very fond of Julia and we kept in touch once a year . . . a Christmas card with scribbled note . . . that sort of thing. When you were imprisoned in the West African Republic five years ago, I made it my business to find out if you were Julia's nephew, or another James Stark.'

'Sir, this is classified.'

'But James, I already know and my daughter should know, because she has been sleeping with you for the past week to find out what your angle is, no doubt convincing herself she's a regular *Mata Hari*.'

Chris gave an agonised gasp. 'Dad. Stop it.'

'It's not like that at all, sir,' Jim says aggressively. 'Your daughter and I . . . '

'Nevermind that.' Kelly waves his hand. 'As a matter of fact, Julia asked me to get up there and try to see you. That's what I was doing when I received a visit from a US Embassy official. It was all very hush-hush. He told me that I must not interfere under any circumstances. Your task, he said, was to get yourself into prison by any means, locate the leader of the opposition, a possible future democrat who had been there for a couple of years, change his views about the US and organise your escape with him, which you did. After that, you hung around long enough to help organise his coup and you were shot in the ankle. I notice you still have a slight limp.'

'Sir, I strongly protest . . . '

'Don't worry.' Kelly interrupted him. 'It won't go further than Chris and me. After that episode, they made you a major. You have always been,

363

and you remain in, one or other of America's intelligence services.'

Chris frowns and tries to sort out her confused reactions.

'Is this true? So what about that Christian NGO?' Chris feels hot with anger.

'It's real, but it's a part of something bigger,' Jim mutters.

'Well, my boy, here's to a job well done. But what on earth do you have to do with my daughter and her investigation?'

'That, too, is classified, sir,' Jim says, suddenly very sober and very annoyed. 'I can tell you a little. Your daughter's job and mine overlap slightly. I didn't know what it was Ben Searle was investigating prior to his death, but I could see he'd attracted the attention of Islamic funda-mentalists. Our US office was keeping an eye on him. Unfortunately we failed to save his life. It's not public knowledge yet, but we know that he had met with Lebanese diamond traders, domiciled in Liberia, who were funding Muslim fundamentalists in the Middle East. Ben leaned on them. I think he was looking for Freeman. The Feds know who murdered him, but they haven't caught them yet.'

'And you, my boy?' Kelly's tone of voice demands an answer.

'Currently I'm assessing Africa's strategic mineral deposits, including oil and diamonds, that are in foreign, that is non-Western, hands. I wanted to know what Chris had to do with all this, and to be honest, I didn't want her hurt, for purely personal reasons.'

'So that's why . . . ' Chris closes her mouth firmly. Why ask when everything is crystal clear.

There isn't much left to say. Everyone is tired. The party breaks up and they go to bed: Kelly on his futon up in the loft, Jim on a campbed, on the balcony behind the mosquito wiring, and Chris on a convertible couch in the living room.

★ ★ ★

She wakes with a sense of being watched. She sees Jim staring down at her, his face lit by moonlight . . . a sullen stare.

'How long have you been there?'

He shrugs. 'It's never long enough . . . '

'What?' She's drowsy with sleep.

'It's hard to find the words . . . I've never doubted my vocation . . . never longed for something other than my work . . . until now. I have a feeling that it will never again be enough . . . that I'll spend my life wondering if I should have quit now.'

'Don't talk. Talking won't help.'

'We have a few hours before morning. Let's go outside.'

There's only one embrace. It lasts until the first light of dawn shines through the trees.

'I love the part of you I know, Jim, but I could never be part of your world.' She breaks off. Words are unnecessary. They both know the score.

'There's one thing you can be sure of . . . I love you,' Jim whispers. 'I tried not to let this happen. I'm no good for you. I chose this life and there's no room for anyone else. Particularly now . . . I'm being transferred to Chechnya.'

She longs to punish him with her tears, but that would be cruel. Instead she props herself on one elbow and, bending over him, kisses him on the mouth. His compelling eyes are gazing up at her, willing her to let go.

'Dear Jim, I love you, too. Remember that. I've loved you since we met. Even when I'm hating you, I still love you.'

'I have a month before I go and a good deal of overdue leave. Why don't we grab that? I'll help you finish your enquiry and we can go to the Caribbean, or Asia, anywhere. You choose. Come with me.'

'Yes . . . anywhere . . . or maybe back to Kasane.'

Later she says: 'I must go. Dad's getting up.'

'Take care. I'll see you in London.'

He picks up his clothes and walks towards the shower. Feeling heavy with sadness, Chris goes inside and snuggles under her blanket, pulling it over her head to avoid hearing the helicopter.

38

Jim has gone and there's an empty feeling deep inside Chris, which she intends to ignore by working twice as hard.

'Dad, about those claims you passed on to Visser ... how close is the nearest one to us now?' They are having breakfast under the trees: porridge and tinned milk with some canned orange juice.

'Over four hundred kilometres away to the northwest, about twenty miles due south of the Shimpuru Falls in northern Namibia. This is the rich mine I told you about: *Shimpuru 64*.'

'Does it still have the same name?'

'Probably. Changing it would mean a lot of paperwork for nothing.'

'Have you been there since you gave it to Visser?'

'No. It's quite a way north. I don't prospect there anymore. Too many mines still lying around. I've already injured one leg. I don't want to lose the other.'

'How did that happen, Dad?'

'It's a stupid story. In 1995, a 24-carat pink was found near a place called Luo, on the Chicapa River in Angola. It fetched $10 million in New York. I was panting to get there. After hostilities ceased I went up on a prospecting trip and registered a claim along the same river. I was well established and finding some good stones

. . . already thinking of bringing in a team, when rogue UNITA forces came out of the bush and attacked. I escaped with a wounded thigh. Fortunately I managed to drive to casualty in Saurimo. A nightmare journey, I can tell you.'

'You're such a toughie, Dad. Promise me you won't take chances like that again.'

'All right.'

'Can we fly up to *Shimpuru-64*?'

'Is there a good reason to do that?'

'Yes, but I'd rather not say right now.'

'OK. We can go right after breakfast.'

           ★   ★   ★

It is eight a.m. and already hot. Chris watches Kelly pull back the sliding iron door and gaze with pride at his old Cessna. Chris tries to share his enthusiasm, but the plane looks past its sell-by date.

Kelly shoots her a rueful glance, part amusement, part apology. 'It's good for another few thousand miles at least.'

Chris shrugs and climbs in and they take off, almost scaling the trees at the end of the short runway. Then they are up and away, her stomach lurching as the plane rises over thermals and falls into troughs. Below, all she can see is sand, under a hazy sky with no hint of a cloud, as usual. They are moving north at 260 kph but there is no change in the boring view, other than the occasional sparse tree.

'Get ready, we're coming in to land,' Kelly calls two hours later. 'I can't imagine what you expect to find here.'

'A derelict mine,' she replies.

Moments later they are bumping over the uneven surface of the sand, skidding to dead slow and taxiing towards a tall fence. Chris ventures out into a hot blast from a furnace. 'It's like being roasted alive in a convection oven.'

'So let's try not to be here long,' Kelly says.

Overhead the saffron sun shines from a jaundiced sky. 'How strange everything looks,' Chris mutters.

'That's because there's a sandstorm moving our way. All the more reason to be quick.'

Hurrying towards the fence, she sees large notices pinned to it. Closer she sees a skull and crossbones. Underneath is written: *Warning. This area is mined.* There are other signs in various African dialects. Searching with her binoculars Chris can see no sign of activity.

'You said this is was a karakul ranch.'

'Used to be. The farm became part of a massive land redistribution scheme. The farms were given to local tribesmen, together with the karakul. Most of them ate the sheep, took the roofs off the houses to make shanties, and abandoned the land. Of course, one must also realise that the bottom fell out of the karakul market. Furs went out of fashion because of the anti-fur campaigns, but I don't think anyone gave up eating lamb chops. For some reason, this mine has been abandoned, too. The farmhouse is five miles away to the west.' Kelly is looking depressed. 'We'll fly over it on our way back. Seen enough?'

'Sure.' Chris switches off and rubs her arms, which are prickling all over. An idea is starting up . . . a thought so preposterous that it makes her shudder. But what if it's true? As for tracing Visser . . . Dad has made it easy for her.

As Kelly predicted, the farmhouse is derelict, stripped of its roof and abandoned. There is no sign of anyone, or any karakul. Once there had been a garden, but now nothing remains. They fly on, too depressed to talk, and by one o'clock they are back at Kelly's camp.

⋆   ⋆   ⋆

It's time to leave. The quickest way home, she learns, is via Maun and Gaborone. Kelly promises to collect her suitcases from the Swakopmund Hotel and Kasane and send them on. He will fly her to Maun.

'Where's your coat, Chris?'

'In Swakopmund Hotel and my anorak's at Kasane.'

'I'll find you an anorak. Wait a minute.'

He bounds up the stairs like a youngster. He's quite a guy, Chris decides. 'It'll be too big,' she calls after him.

'Better than catching pneumonia,' he says as he runs down the stairs. Now put it on.'

It's huge and she feels absurd.

'I don't think . . . '

'Humour me, Chris. Now look here . . . ' He opens the front and shows her a hidden pocket. Put your credit cards, cheque book and money in here and wear it all the time. You don't know

370

about the unemployment in Africa. Carrying a handbag is a great temptation to those who are hungry, so keep only a little cash in it for your daily use.'

'Anything you say, Dad,' she says, teasing him.

'I'll miss you, Chris. So where do we go from here?'

'Same as every other family I suppose. I visit you. You visit me. We email each other and call sometimes . . . spend holidays together. I'll miss you, too. It's been great.'

'Whatever I have will be yours one day.'

'Shh, don't talk about money.'

'You could join me.'

'I don't think I could live in the wilderness. I love my life and my job, and I love London, but Dad, my life will never be the same again, and I'll see you often, promise!'

'I guess so.' Dad looks so sad that she throws her arms around him and hugs him close. 'Love you, Dad.'

'That goes without saying.'

★ ★ ★

Hours later, Chris is still feeling sad about leaving Dad, but she's prickling with excitement, too. She can't wait to get back to London where she can test her hunches. She has to find out whether her father's marginal mines are part of a portfolio of mines owned by an established mining house and whether or not Visser is in control.

She calls Rowan from the Business Class

lounge to let him know she'll be back in the morning.

'I hope to finalise this investigation in the next few days,' she tells him. 'I know how it's done. See you tomorrow.'

She boards the British Airways plane at nine p.m. and settles down for an agonising flight. She knows she won't sleep, she's too keyed up. Hunched in a blanket she considers her options.

What if she's right and she gives her findings to Rowan? Rowan will hand the information to their clients and to Scotland Yard, but will the police act fast enough to save Sienna's life? Chris suddenly realises, with a pang in her stomach, that it's not a crime to sell ex-quota diamonds . . . at least, not in Britain. Kidnapping is another matter. Naturally the kidnappers would get rid of all traces of Sienna as soon as they realise their scam is exposed.

She will have to find Sienna herself before releasing the details, but as Dad keeps pointing out, she's not a trained sleuth. She only knows law and finance. Chris is far too overwrought to sleep much. Longing for morning, she takes her notebook and drafts her report.

To: Rowan Metcalf
Re: Diamond laundering investigation

I'm very close to the end of this enquiry. I have the 'how' worked out, but only a suspicion as to the 'who'. In the meantime, here is a summary of my recent findings.

A series of agents in every diamond

producing African country act as receiving depots, not only for blood diamonds, but also for stolen and ex-quota diamonds. (Some African government officials, resentful of the low quotas allowed to them under the rules of the Kimberley Process, are selling their surplus stocks to these agents.)

For some years, the perpetrators of this scam have been buying unprofitable African mines for a song and claiming quotas for non-existent mining production. Instead of engaging in costly capital investment, labour and mining costs, they buy blood diamonds for very little, only $20 a carat in Central Africa, and claim quotas for their defunct mines. In this way, the roughs, which include conflict, ex-quota and stolen diamonds, are shipped to London accompanied by the necessary certification.

This is not breaking the law. I doubt it would be classed as fraud, because the rules have been created and imposed by a cartel of mining houses, although they do have United Nations backing.

This buying organisation was originally created in 1978, in South West Africa (now Namibia) by Moses Freeman in order to raise funds for a West African liberation group. Later, when the scam became highly profitable, Freeman was evicted by other members of the group who preferred to keep the profits for themselves.

I believe, but have not yet proved, that it was Herman Visser, a Dutch accountant, who pushed Freeman out, took control of the group and still runs it, although it is rumoured that he has changed his name and nationality.

This scam would not be possible were it not for the peculiar structuring of the diamond industry.

In my view, the mining houses' grip on African mineral resources has resulted in two major rip-offs: first to be defrauded are the local population who are deprived both of the benefits of the cash earned from their own mineral resources (since the roughs are shipped directly to London and sold there) and of the opportunity to set up profitable secondary industries by cutting and polishing the gems and manufacturing jewellery, plus all the jobs and revenue this would bring to these depressed communities.

The public, too, are conned — by a century of advertising — into believing that diamonds are the only true symbol of enduring love. Inflated prices are maintained by holding back much of the mining houses' production, which is either stored or left in the ground.

I hope to finalise this investigation within the next few days. Chris glances at her watch. It's only four a.m. The night is lasting forever. It seems hours later when the sun rises and they soar over the Alps.

★ ★ ★

Feeling dazed with lack of sleep and the long journey, Chris sleepwalks through passport control and customs and emerges into the public area to see her name in big black letters, stencilled on a placard, swaying on a stick. The driver wears a green peaked cap, a raincoat and glasses.

'Hello. That's me. Thanks for coming.' She follows the driver to the exit. 'Is it raining?'

'Damp,' he says. 'Did you have a good trip?'

She shrugs. 'Over long.'

'Where's your luggage? Is that all?' he asks, indicating her haversack.

'That's all.' She's blessing Dad for her anorak. After the Namib, London feels like Alaska.

She must remember to thank Rowan for sending a taxi. He doesn't usually think about little details like this. She follows the driver to his BMW, which is new and elegant. The driver is new, too, she realises. He sounds Irish. Their company's personnel always use the same taxi service, where they have an account, and most of the drivers there are Caribbean. The driver holds the door open, but he looks tense and glances around nervously.

Something's wrong. Chris springs to full alert when she sees that there is no two-way-radio for the driver. This is not a hired car. Various thoughts flash through her mind in rapid succession. It's not too late. She can still get out of this. But finding Visser won't necessarily lead her to Sienna. Perhaps this is the right way. She thanks him and steps inside.

The driver gets in and the car moves forward as two men leap out of a neighbouring car, and run swiftly towards them. They scramble in and sit on either side of her.

'What's going on? What are you doing?' One of them grabs her arm, pushing up her shirt. She tries not to panic when she feels a sharp pain, as a needle is jabbed into her muscle. There's a burning sensation which swiftly fades. She feels only a shaft of fear and then nothing.

★ ★ ★

Her head is pounding and it hurts like hell. That's the very first thing she becomes aware of. She stiffens and lies very still, listening. She remembers getting into the car, but did that really happen? She remembers the jab of a needle in her arm. Was that a nightmare? She reaches up and feels the lump. Her arm is badly bruised. It's real. Panic surges. Where is she?

Someone is breathing heavily only a few yards away. This scares her. Opening her eyes she sees nothing at all. She tries again, but nothing changes. It's pitch black . . . the sort of darkness Chris has never experienced. There's always a glimmer somewhere around. Thoughts of victims buried alive set her shaking. She wants to scream, but she controls the impulse. She feels too scared to make a sound, but she can hear her breath gasping. She keeps still and tries to breathe quietly. The air smells stale, but not damp, as if she's in the basement of a centrally heated building. She runs her hand around her body. She's not injured, she's lying on a mattress which is on the floor in the corner of a room, she realises as she runs her hands around the wall.

The heavy breathing stops abruptly. Whoever it is, knows she's awake.

'Chris. Chris . . . ' She hears the merest whisper.

'Yes,' she whispers back.

'It's me . . . Sienna.' A girl bursts into a flood of tears. 'Are you hurt?' she sobs.

'No.' Her heart lurches. 'Do we have to whisper?'

'No,' comes the quiet reply. 'No one comes here at night. Oh, God. I never wanted to see you here.'

'Don't cry, Sienna. I've been so worried about you. We'll get out of this. I promise you. Do you know where we are?'

'In a basement somewhere in London.'

'Are we alone?'

'Yes, always . . . at night.'

Sienna can't stop crying. Chris stands up and topples. Perhaps it's the darkness that makes her feel disorientated, or the remains of the injection. She crouches on her hands and knees and crawls towards her friend.

'Everyone's looking for you. It's only a matter of time before they find you . . . us.' Putting her arms around Sienna, she clutches her shivering body and rocks her to and fro. She's lost a lot of weight. She feels so frail.

'You're skin and bone, Sienna. The sooner we get out of here the better.'

'There's no way out,' Sienna says, sounding so desolate. 'No windows. No locks or handles on the door, no air-conditioning vents big enough to crawl through. A rat couldn't escape from here.'

'We'll find a way. Promise. Please stop crying. That doesn't help at all.'

'I'm crying because you're here,' Sienna says between her sobs. 'You're here because of me.'

'No. That's not true. We'll talk about it in the morning. My head aches so badly.'

'We'll die here.'

'None of your morbid fatalism, Sienna. Your father's looking for you. So are the police. We have friends, too. I have a close friend in American intelligence. He'll be looking for us. However long it takes us, weeks . . . months . . . we're getting out.'

But that might be too long. They have to keep Sienna alive to force her father to buy their cheap diamonds. But there's no such qualification for her. How long has she got? she wonders. Just as long as it takes them to find a way to dispose of her corpse.

39

Bright neon light floods the room bringing terror. Chris bounds to her feet, instantly alert, backing against the wall. She listens, but there are no footsteps. She blinks several times as her eyes adjust and she takes in her surroundings. Walls and ceiling are all white, the floor plain cement. There are no windows, but there is an inset steel door that appears to slide sideways along the wall outside their prison cell. She's seen doors like this before. There's a washbasin and tap set into one wall and at the top of this wall a small air-conditioning unit. No escape route here. Two mattresses lie on the floor, two buckets stand beside them. Nothing else. Chris looks around for a possible weapon, but there is none. Other than breaking down a wall, there's no way of escape. The walls look thick and she has no weapon or tool . . . not even a penknife.

Across the room, Sienna is curled up foetal-style on her mattress, facing the wall. Chris makes an effort to stop shaking and hide her fear. Sienna sits up and turns towards her. She is so thin, she's almost unrecognisable. Her skin is sallow, her hair hangs dishevelled and unwashed over her cheap, outsize pyjamas, supplied by the kidnappers, Chris assumes. Deep brown shadows surround her sunken eyes and she looks defeated. Chris remembers Sienna as she once was . . . her eyes shining with joy and affection. It's as if someone put the light out behind them. Dead eyes! But Sienna has been alone here for two and a half months, enduring total darkness every night. She looks dazed and pathetic and Chris' heart goes out to her. No wonder she has lost hope. Sienna looks fearfully over her shoulder and pushes herself hard into the corner, burying her face in her hands.

'It's me, Chris, Sienna. Don't you remember how we spoke in the night?' Chris kneels beside her friend and puts her arms around her, hugging her tightly. 'Everything's going to be all right.'

'Chris,' Sienna mutters. 'My best friend . . . I know I'm dreaming.' She turns to the wall and sobs quietly to herself.

I've got to get her out of here . . . fast. *Somehow.* God knows how, but I'll manage, just like I used to years ago. Chris can still hear the headmaster's voice, authoritative, but slightly ironic, saying: *'I'm making you responsible for Sienna. From now on, you and she will share a dormitory . . . show her the ropes, and look after her.'*

'I thought you were dead,' Sienna sobs. 'Chris. I'm so sorry. I saw you were shot and I thought you had died. Is it really you? It's my fault you're here and there's no way out. You followed me, didn't you? You followed the van to find me. I knew you would if you could.'

But that was two and a half months ago. Sienna has lost track of time and no one could blame her?

'I've been investigating these criminals . . . I

had just about caught up with them, but they caught me first. They brought me here.'

Chris sits close beside Sienna and stares into space, but her mind is going over every possibility. Air comes in through a vent in the ceiling, but it's far too small to use for an escape. There are no windows and she reckons they are underground. She has to know all that Sienna has learned about this place and she has to know it fast, but her friend seems to have lost her grip on reality. She's fantasising. Sienna needs a crash course in facing up to reality.

'Sit up and talk to me. I need to know everything you've learned about this place.' Sienna shrinks into the corner and curls up in a ball. After a few moments of shocked incredulity, Chris grabs her and forces her to her feet, hating herself as she manhandles her friend.

'We're going to get fit. We have to be fit to survive. Start walking up and down. Come on. We'll do it together.' She pulls the tottering girl across the floor and back again. Sienna pushes her away and throws herself on her mattress, so they start again . . . and again.

★   ★   ★

At ten a.m. the steel door slides open. A man stands there holding a large handgun which points directly at her, not Sienna, Chris notices. He says: 'Bring your buckets and hurry up.'

They walk in single file down the smooth, white passage to a door at the end where a woman in floral overalls waits for them. She's

381

sweating, perhaps with fear, and Chris can smell her sweat. She looks sixty, but Chris reckons she might be forty-odd. Her face is deeply lined, with brown sun spots on her skin. She takes a cloth out of her pocket and wipes her forehead as she follows them into the washroom. The door swings shut and the three of them are alone. Chris looks around at the three showers, a row of six toilets, and a row of hand basins leading to a large sink.

'Hurry up,' the woman says in a strong Middle Eastern accent.

Sienna goes into the toilet.

'Wash your bucket in the sink,' the woman tells Chris.

'Can I shower?'

'No.'

'Why not?'

'Because they've turned off the water.' *They*, not *we*, Chris notices.

'This is not a good job for you.' Chris smiles at the woman, trying to reach out to her. 'You will be blamed for what they are doing. Are you Turkish?'

A flash of anger shows in her eyes, but she doesn't reply.

'Yes, I can see that you are. You're a long way from home. Why get mixed up with these evil people?'

'I am Armenian,' she says, pointing to her chest dramatically. 'Turkish!' She spits on the floor to make her point.

'My name is Christine,' Chris says. 'My friend is Sienna. What is your name?'

382

Her eyes narrow suspiciously. 'Marta,' she replies. 'No more talking. Hurry.'

Despite the steady hum of the air conditioning, which has a larger inlet vent here, the air smells dusty. So where are they? A crazy suspicion is becoming more believable every moment. She hugs it to herself as they are escorted back to their cell, where two plates of porridge and bread wait on the floor. The steel door closes silently.

'Will they come back later?'

'At four this afternoon. They'll bring another meal. It's always the same.'

The toilet fittings are old and shoddy. It's possible that this is one of London's many underground offices, created by the War Office to protect top officials working in London throughout the blitz. Her suspicions are becoming stronger each moment. She nibbles at a piece of bread and leaves the rest.

It was David who had boasted about his three basement levels that were built as bank vaults and later converted into safe living quarters during the war. What else had he boasted about? His Spanish door and light fittings. They looked just like these. But she'd suspected this, hadn't she . . . ever since Kelly described Visser and his fatal charm. There's something else, too. Only Rowan knew she was returning on the British Airways flight from Gaborone. Rowan might have told David, if he called, but he wouldn't tell anyone else.

But still, she can't be sure. Her suspicions seem unreal . . . insane!

★ ★ ★

Their first day together ends with the flick of a switch. Stygian darkness falls upon them. Chris gets up and sits beside Sienna on her mattress. 'I have a torch in my bag. They left it there, but they took my mobile . . . naturally. I'll keep the torch for emergencies, except that I have to see what time it is.'

'Seven p.m. Thank goodness they let me keep my watch. The lights come on at six. I'm stiff all over,' Sienna complains.

'You'll soon get back to normal. Now start talking. I want to know everything.' Sienna seems to grow stronger as she talks. She even manages to poke fun at her guards. She is fed twice a day and taken to the washroom by Marta. Once a week she gets a shower. Then two armed thugs carry a chair in and take her photograph as she holds up a newspaper showing the date.

'So to recap, Sienna, there appear to be no exits, other than the air-conditioning vent in the washroom, and that is too hazardous, although I might attempt it if we get desperate.'

'Aren't we desperate?'

'Far from it. We are about to attack the weakest link in their chain, which is, of course, Marta, the Armenian woman. She's frightened of them, and of us. She's resentful. She hates her job and I guess she's an illegal immigrant, so she's underpaid and scared of being caught and sent home. She has no love for her employers. They've bullied her into doing this, probably

384

because she's dispensable and I'm sure she knows this. At least that's how she seems to me. We must play upon her weaknesses.'

'She has every reason to be scared, but you make it sound so easy. It won't work. She'll tell them.'

'Be positive, Sienna. People are looking for us. My friend, Jim, is in intelligence. We must try to get a message to him, via Marta. Your father has a team of detectives looking for you. The police have been looking for you ever since you disappeared.'

'They'll never find us. We'll be locked up here for years.' She starts to cry and it takes a long time to comfort her.

'Sienna, listen to me. They will find us if we send them clues. Marta will be our messenger.'

'But we don't know where we are?'

'I think I do, but I must be sure. It's up to you, Sienna. I want you to relive your drive here, every second, from the moment when they threw you into the van on your wedding day until you arrived here. Will you do that?'

'If you think it will help. There isn't much to remember. Will it take long?'

'Does it matter? We have until morning before the lights switch on.'

'OK. Let's go.'

As Sienna relives her terrible fear and her nausea, Chris tries to work out the probable route the kidnappers took when the van raced off with her friend locked inside. 'Blank your mind. Meditate. Concentrate on your breathing. Relax, Sienna. Relax . . . '

Sienna's breathing is becoming deeper . . . is she falling asleep?

'It's your wedding day, Sienna. You are driving to the Dorchester. Your car stops at the traffic lights . . . '

'It was so damned hot and I was so thirsty.'

'And then . . . ?'

It is surprising how much Sienna remembers once she begins.

'I fought . . . my poor dress . . . it was shredded.'

'You fought well.'

'I was reaching out to you . . . but then they shot you.' She gives a short sharp cry. 'You were spinning around . . . then they slammed the doors. They tried to hold a pad of ether over my face. I fought them off. I was screaming and shouting. The driver slammed on the brakes and we all fell on the ground. I pushed the pad into my dress.'

'That was well done. What was the van doing?'

'A U-turn.'

It took a long time, but they had all night. Slowly she coaxed Sienna into remembering.

She had heard a brass band and marching feet as they swung to the left.

'Buckingham Palace, clearly . . . it must have been,' Chris says.

'So many twists and turns. I started to feel so sick.' Sienna describes them all and her nausea which led her to vomit over the floor.

Chris starts to get excited when Sienna describes someone shouting through a loud-speaker and people clapping, while the van stopped three times and curved to the right and then to the left.

'It has to be Trafalgar Square. So you're driving down towards Charing Cross,' Chris says excitedly.

'I didn't think of where I was going. I was so sick. I think it was caused by the ether stuffed down the front of my dress, but I know I heard church bells ringing.'

'St Martin's in the Field! Now we're getting somewhere.'

'We're driving down a slope. I was prone on the floor, lying in vomit. I slid forward, but then the van went up an incline and I slipped back. There were men shouting quite close beside the van. They seem to be unloading crates. I screamed. 'Help me! Help me!' One of the goons kicked me hard.'

'Smithfield market. I knew it. I knew it.' Chris jumps up with excitement.

'The van turned left . . . its brakes were squealing . . . down and round and down . . . a door clanked open and closed behind us. It was the most terrible sound I had ever heard.'

'Underground parking! Everything points to the basement of Trans-Africa Diamonds, I've been here before. To think that I was just one floor above you and neither of us knew. You're a star, Sienna. I know where we are. It's just as I suspected.'

'How will that help us?'

'Thank God they only took my bag and mobile and never thought to look inside my anorak. There's a special money pocket inside. We'll send a message and this is how we'll do it.

Chris shares her meal with Sienna. The following morning, when the goon escorts the Armenian woman to collect their plates, Sienna's food lies untouched on the floor.

'She has a fever,' Chris tells Marta. 'She didn't eat yesterday either, but I ate her food. She needs a doctor.'

'No doctor. Not possible,' the woman says in her deep voice.

She follows Chris to the lavatory, leaving the gunman guarding the passage outside their cell where Sienna lies prone.

'I'm afraid, Marta. What if Sienna dies. Later, when the police find me, you could get life imprisonment for murder.'

'This dirty business . . . what has it to do with me?'

'You look after us. You're responsible for us. The boss will say it was your fault.

'We're grateful to you for looking after us, Marta. You should have a better job. Here's a hundred pounds. Please buy us aspirins and something for the flu and keep the change for your extra trouble.'

That is the first of many whispered messages, carefully worked out by the two girls at night.

'I have no more cash. Please take my credit card, Marta. Here's the number . . . cash one hundred pounds . . . Sienna needs some items from the chemist . . . I've made a list . . . don't take more than this amount or the machine will keep the card . . . of course my salary will go in at the end of the month.'

Whatever she takes, Jim and the police will trace the cash withdrawals. They will know that she is being held somewhere in London. Marta might even cash the money nearby.

A few days later, Chris' card is retained when Marta returns to the cash dispenser and attempts to obtain a large amount of cash, although she never admits to this.

'Nevermind, I can give you a cheque . . . take it to my bank . . . A thousand pounds for you, because you are kind to us . . . '

She signs the cheque, *Christine TAD Winters*, hoping someone might pick up the TAD as being Trans-Africa Diamonds. Jim would, she knows, but will he see the cheque? Will the bank cash it?

Presumably they do. Marta is absent for several days. When she returns she is wearing a new dress and her hair has been cut and shaped. She keeps glancing at herself in the washroom mirror.

'Sienna's father is a millionaire, did you know that, Marta?' Chris whispers in the washroom. 'I was promised a fortune to find her. When the police free us I shall be rich.'

Marta watches Chris through the mirror. 'You will never be free. Never! How could you get out of this place?'

What cold eyes she has.

Marta stays away and the girls become desperate. Chris is suffering more than Sienna.

She has always been active, now she is becoming claustrophobic.

When the Armenian woman returns, she is more furtive than usual. Her pockets are stuffed with fruit which she gives to them.

'I need more money,' she demands when they reach the washroom. 'You must give it to me. My son is in trouble. He has to get out of Armenia. He's on the run from the police.'

At last! Chris has been waiting for this for weeks, guessing that Marta's demands for cash would soon become excessive.

'I have no more money, but I know how you can get half a million pounds. That is the amount that Sienna's father has offered as a reward for news of his daughter. You must go to him. Here is his name and London address. I have written it all very clearly for you. If you can't find him, then go to this address, or call this man.' Chris gives Marta the address of Mohsen's detective. 'Tell no one but him, otherwise these thugs will steal the money from you. Just give him this address which I have written here and tell him we are in the bottom basement level.'

Twenty-four hours pass and nothing happens. Marta returns the next morning.

'You ask too much. I can't do it. They will kill me.'

'They will kill you if you don't go . . . I shall tell the guard about the money you took from us . . . the cheques you cashed . . . the credit card you used. All these things have told the police where we are. They'll be here soon. It's your choice. You can be a millionaire, a heroine, everyone will praise you. Or you can go to prison for life, if the gunmen don't kill you first.'

'She'll go,' Sienna says. 'I feel it. I know it. It's going to work.'

40

When longed for events suddenly happen, it's hard to get to grips with reality. At eight p.m. the lights switch back on. Chris blinks and tries to see her watch, but it takes a second to get used to the light. This is it, she thinks. And then again . . . this is it!

Sienna jumps to her feet. Her eyes are wide and she's biting her lip. 'Listen . . . listen,' she whispers. 'What is it?'

Chris doesn't answer. They've invited this, but it might not mean their salvation.

'Didn't you hear something?'

Chris rushes to the wash basin to splash cold water on her face.

'Listen, for goodness' sake. There it is again.'

Chris is putting on her shoes. She feels naked without them.

Gun shots. Or a tyre exploding, and then hammering . . . at eight p.m.? Chris begins to tremble.

'Something is happening,' Sienna whispers.

They hear shouts above. Then the door slides silently open. David stands there looking wild and almost unhinged. He's pointing a gun at Chris. His expression frightens her more than the gun. He looks sorry for her, like a hunter faced with shooting his favourite horse.

'I warned you, Chrissie. Why didn't you listen

to me? I begged you. I never wanted to harm you.'

Her rage erupts and with it a surge of adrenaline. She yells and propels herself forward, leaping high, shooting her heel into his face, as he fires straight at her. She feels a burning sensation in her thigh, but it's nothing. Her rage is everything as her foot kicks out again and again. Three hammer punches in quick succession with the steel heel of her shoe.

His head jerks back and in that split second she goes for his gun. She's not going to get it out of his grasp, he's too strong for her. Instead she presses her finger over his, letting the bullets fly harmlessly down the passage while they grapple and fight. Six . . . seven . . . then empty clicks. He may throttle her, but he's not going to shoot her. She leans against the wall, feeling sticky wetness trickling down her thigh. She won't look. The pain must keep away.

David is dazed. He's rubbing his face. He looks at his hand which is covered in blood and swears. The lift is coming. As he turns towards it, she grabs the gun from his hand and smashes it over his temple. He falls back against the wall and she does it again . . . and again, with all her strength.

He's out on the floor. Chris is shocked to learn how easy it is to knock a man out.

Turning, she finds Sienna close behind her. Two of their guards rush out of the lift. 'Down the passage . . . both of you . . . fast . . .'

'Leave them,' the second goon says.

'We need hostages.'

They are manhandled down the passage to a door, which unlocks at the touch of the gunman's fingers. Surprisingly they find they're in the car park. They are pushed into the back seat of a BMW, which lurches forward with screeching brakes as they speed around the sharp bends up to street level. The driver turns right towards the Thames and Chris senses they are being taken somewhere where they can be disposed of. They are the only evidence of any criminal activity.

The goon is keeping them covered with his gun while he wipes his forehead with a dirty handkerchief. He has twisted half around to face them. The muzzle of his gun rests on the back seat. It's pointing right at Chris, who motions to Sienna to get down on the floor, but she can't see her chance to act.

Something behind them catches the thug's attention.

He swears. 'We're being followed. Go faster!'

The car weaves through the traffic, shooting across red traffic lights, leaving a trail of hoots and shouts. A police car with its blaring siren keeps up with them.

Chris sits tense and upright, every nerve poised for action if a chance presents itself. The car is dodging and swerving . . . the minutes pass.

Five minutes later, the police car draws abreast. 'Pull over to the left,' comes a tinny voice through the loudspeaker.

The goon grabs Chris by her hair, pulls her up and forward, ramming his gun at her temple. He gestures to the driver to fall back. The driver brakes and they surge on. Chris topples back on to the seat. They're moving towards Docklands. That figures. They will kill them there and dump their bodies, Chris shudders.

It seems hours later when they hear a helicopter hovering over the road. Their driver swerves. He rams a car that's suddenly appeared abreast of them and the car skids off the road. The gunman is leaning forward, peering up at the night sky. The muzzle of his gun has momentarily swung away from her.

Chris lunges forward and knocks the gun around, gasping for strength as she presses his trigger finger. The report seems loud enough to shatter her eardrums. The driver slumps over the wheel and the car skids out of control. Veering across the road, it mounts the pavement and crashes into a railing. Chris is flung head first over the front seat. She sprawls over the gunman and goes for his gun. She's failing badly, swearing, fighting, seeing the gun twisting towards her. There's pounding in her ears, and she's losing her grasp on the gun and reality as her strength fails her and the muzzle touches her forehead.

A sickening blast dazes her. This is it! But then she sees blood trickling from the man's mouth and the gun slips from his limp hand. Bewildered and frantic, she looks round and sees Sienna holding the driver's gun. She's shaking violently. Her mouth is open. She's trying to say something, but she can't get the words out. Chris lunges over the seat and grabs the gun from her, throwing it on the floor.

Dazed and shocked, she hears running footsteps and the roar of the helicopter landing nearby. She blinks several times and sees Jim, of all people, racing along the road. Sienna is shouting at her: 'Free . . . we're free,' but Chris' world is spinning off into oblivion.

★ ★ ★

Chris opens her eyes. She feels absolutely vile. A man in a white coat is bending over her and there's a strong stench of disinfectant all around them.

'Where am I?' Can he hear her whispered croak?

'Must we play this scene again . . . and again. You're in the recovery unit of the University College Hospital, Christine. I'm Tim Rose. Remember me? You have sustained a painful flesh wound, but the bullet was merely passing by. I've stitched you up. You're going to be fine.'

The male nurse is new. He wheels her to the lift in sombre silence. They wait for a long time. Eventually the lift arrives and they creep up to the fifth floor. Chris is wheeled along a beige corridor to a two-bed ward with a floral curtain hanging between the beds. Sienna is sitting there, huddled in a large overcoat. Chris can see her prison pyjamas sticking out below. She's wearing hospital slippers.

'Sienna, oh, Sienna,' Chris croaks. Her mouth is too dry to talk. 'Water . . . please.'

'Rinse your mouth and spit, dear,' the nurse says.

'Are you all right?' Chris croaks hoarsely.

'Yes. Thanks to you. I can't stay long. Father's waiting in the TV room. He sends you his love. He's coming to see you when you've recovered a little. He wanted to take me home, but I had to see you first. The goons didn't die, by the way. They're in hospital under police guard. The police have been here, too. They're coming back to take your statement later. I've done mine.'

Sienna rubs her cold hands. 'Dearest Chris! I've missed you so much. We lost touch. That was wrong. I never want to lose touch with you again. Promise me it will never happen. Not even after we're married. By the way, Hamid and I have decided to go ahead with a quiet marriage at my home.'

'Good for you,' Chris whispers. 'Hamid? Would that be Hamid Khan the bogus detective?'

Sienna giggles like a schoolgirl. 'Yes, but of course he was no such thing. He's my father's marketing manager and he was helping to find me.'

'Do you love him?'

'Yes,' Sienna flushes and then smiles.

'I'm so happy for you. Would you call the nurse? I feel terrible. My thigh's on fire.'

Sienna stood up and went outside. 'Please give her something for the pain,' Chris hears her say in the corridor.

Moments later she returns with the nurse bearing an injection.

Sienna is talking and Chris struggles to concentrate. 'The police told me that David Marais has been formally identified as Herman Visser,' she's saying, as the nurse injects the morphine. 'He's been arrested for kidnapping and for a 25-year-old murder. Your father brought all the evidence they needed.'

'My father?' Chris says wonderingly.

'Yes, he's staying in London. Everyone was here this morning, but the nurse told them to come back later. Look at your flowers. Your mother brought these. Aren't they lovely. I'll see you tomorrow. Come and stay with me for a few weeks to recuperate.'

'No chance,' she hears a voice from the doorway. 'I'm taking her far away from London. We're leaving for a long holiday.' Jim's voice.

Chris closes her eyes and smiles . . . and falls asleep.

★   ★   ★

It rains in the late afternoon. It always does at this time of the year: heavy, pulverising rain that revives the earth after the noonday heat. By six, the clouds have rolled away, the sun has not set, yet it's cool and fragrant. The leaves drip noisily and the glowing twilight suffuses the veld with a soft, golden haze. This is the time that Chris loves best of all.

Slowly, gently, with hardly a sound, the paddleboat drifts along the wide river. Hanging over the railing, Chris gazes at the graceful impalas grazing on the river banks. Four giraffe stand with their feet splayed, heads close together, staring curiously as the boat moves silently past. A bat-eared fox slinks through the grass and once again she sees the massive baobab tree she loved so much the first time she saw it. Elephants are herding their young into the water to bathe. Scores of twittering weaver birds are diving into their colony in the Acacia trees as they prepare for the night.

'Are you cold, Chris?' Jim pushes her stole around her shoulders.

He's become absurdly protective. She knows he feels guilty. In his view the rescue was a disaster.

'Let's sit down. You need to rest as much as you can.'

They sit on a bench by the rails, under a thatch roof, open on all sides, and watch the African bush preparing for the night. Soon the baboons make for their rooftop sanctuary, a hyena jogs past, swaying from side to side in its ungainly posture, preparing for the night's hunt.

'Jim, thank you.' She reaches for his hand. 'It's been wonderful.'

'It's not over yet, Chris.'

She watches the birds roosting and stares at the purple clouds piling up on the horizon.

'What are you thinking about?'

'I was thinking about Dad. Did you know that Mohsen Sheik persuaded him to go public with a minority interest in his new mine, so he can buy the equipment he needs? All the shares were taken up as soon as they came on offer. They were bought through various nominees, but I suspect that Dad and Sheik are partners.'

'Could be great for both of them.'

'There's so much I don't know, Jim. You promised to tell me all that happened while I was in the cell.'

'When you're better.'

'As you can see, I'm better.'

'Do you really want to talk about work on such a lovely evening?'

'That's what you always say. *Yes, I really do.*'

'Shall I start from the beginning?'

'It's as good a place as any.'

'All this talking makes me thirsty.' He grins and gestures to the barman.

'When you didn't arrive at work, I realised something was wrong. That was a bad time . . . the worst.' He places his hand under her shawl to fondle her shoulder. 'Nowadays I never stop saying: 'Thank God'. Rowan Metcalf told me you had called him the previous evening, but you hadn't arrived in London. I checked with British Airways and found that you'd arrived that morning. I went to the police and they made out a Missing Persons file, which wasn't going to get us far in a hurry.

'I decided that the diamond launderers were the most likely guys to have you, but I didn't know who they were. I called Petrus Joubert and he flew out to Kelly. Your father tried to remember everything you'd said and done in the last two days before you left. It was your flight to *Shimpuru-64* that intrigued Petrus . . . that and a statement you made to your father. Do you remember? Kelly asked you what you expected to find there and you replied: 'a derelict mine'.

'Petrus and Kelly got through to the Chamber of Mines and found that all of Kelly's old marginal mines were in Trans-Africa Diamond's portfolio. I faxed Kelly some photographs of Marais and he was sure he was Visser.'

'So quickly, and it took me two months.'

'We were following in your footsteps . . . that's all.

'Petrus felt that there wasn't enough evidence to entice the Met into raiding the mining house. Besides, if you weren't there, what was the point? They could have hidden you anywhere.'

Watching his face, Chris realises how afraid he was and how angry he still is. That's why he can't bear to talk about it.

'Petrus is the real star here. He got his superiors to reopen the investigation into the death of the skipper of *Rainbow's End* . . . and he did it fast. The next day, Petrus arrested Skoog for attempted murder and persuaded Skoog to turn State Evidence. Skoog gave a sworn statement that Visser had killed the skipper. He said Visser had knocked him out and left him to die when the boat sank. Only later, Petrus told me how much it hurt him to let Skoog escape justice. He wanted to get him back for what he did to you. He's waiting for the go-ahead to arrest him for trying to murder you. You have a real fan there, Chris.'

'I like him, too.'

Jim frowns at her, but soon thinks better of it.

'We had a breakthrough. Kelly remembered that some of Visser's possessions were left in his cottage near the mine they lost. He'd packed them in a trunk in the loft. Kelly had forgotten about them until Petrus asked. There were clothes, hairs on the clothes, a hairbrush . . . so at last we had Visser's DNA. David Marais' DNA proved that he and Visser were one and the same, so Petrus applied for his extradition, but still the police were hesitant. Evidently he is on the latest honours list.'

'How did you get David's DNA?' Chris asks.

'That was the easy part. I broke into his private bathroom and stole his hairbrush.'

'We had no idea where you were. I set up watches at various cash dispensers, in the area where your card was first used, but we didn't know who to look for. When the bank called the police about your cheque we guessed that you were in the Trans-Africa building, but we still couldn't get our act together.

'That was the moment when the Armenian woman, Marta, arrived at Mohsen Sheik's office to claim her reward. That was sheer genius on your part. She told the Sheik where you were, and that the basement opens only to fingertip controls. I must say, when the British police decide to act, it's pretty impressive. They were ready to break in that same night, complete with a computer expert to get them into the lifts and basement.'

'So that's how it was.' She sighs. 'I don't

understand how David realised I was on to him.'

'In his statement at Scotland Yard, Marais said that as soon as you found Skoog and escaped he realised the game was up.'

'What will happen to David?'

'He'll stand trial for kidnapping and attempted murder in London, after which he'll be extradited to Namibia to stand trial for murder, the sentences will run consecutively, I'm told. He's unlikely to get out of prison in the next twenty-five years. By the way, Freeman has been extradited to Liberia. He'll stand trial, but having defrauded the government, I doubt he'll ever leave prison. His sister has disappeared, but I have the greatest faith in Petrus Joubert. He'll get her.

'Heard enough? Can we put it behind us and get on with our holiday?'

'I guess so. The best thing about this investigation was meeting you, Jim.'

She leans over the table and kisses him on his mouth. 'I love you.'

Jim looks sad and happy all at once. 'I just have one question, Chris. I noticed that amongst all those flowers you received, the arrangement from Prince Husam was by far the costliest. A real extravaganza.'

'I wasn't aware that you'd seen it. I sent it home with Mum. She liked it so much and the ward was overcrowded.'

'Well . . . I've been meaning to ask . . . did you . . . or didn't you?'

'That's not the sort of question you should

ask me, Jim. It's classified. You have to take me on trust.'

He laughs at her. 'Touché.' Then he puts his arm around her. 'OK, you win. We're almost back. Let's go in to supper. I have a yen for an early night.'

We do hope that you have enjoyed reading this large print book.

Did you know that all of our titles are available for purchase?

We publish a wide range of high quality large print books including:
Romances, Mysteries, Classics
General Fiction
Non Fiction and Westerns

Special interest titles available in large print are:
The Little Oxford Dictionary
Music Book
Song Book
Hymn Book
Service Book

Also available from us courtesy of Oxford University Press:
Young Readers' Dictionary
(large print edition)
Young Readers' Thesaurus
(large print edition)

For further information or a free brochure, please contact us at:
Ulverscroft Large Print Books Ltd.,
The Green, Bradgate Road, Anstey,
Leicester, LE7 7FU, England.
Tel: (00 44) 0116 236 4325
Fax: (00 44) 0116 234 0205

Other titles published by
The House of Ulverscroft:

RIPPLES ON A POND

Madge Swindells

The well-heeled village of Temple Minnis presents a façade as smooth and calm as its deep, dark lake. But all is not as it seems. Simon Shepherd's marriage is a sham, his daughter running wild. When he awakes one night to the smell of woodsmoke, his fury at the thought of tramps, gypsies or immigrants on his land is fierce — until he sees the exotic and intriguing Bela who has taken refuge there. But Temple Minnis has a darker secret to hide. Thirty years before, the villagers conspired to plan and conceal a murder, but only their dying local novelist, Melissa, suffers from pangs of conscience. As the villagers face up to the past, love turns to fury and tragedy . . .

TWISTED THINGS

Madge Swindells

Rescued after hours in the freezing water clinging onto the wreckage of her yacht, Clara Conner wakes up in Dover hospital. Patrick, her husband, is missing, presumably killed by the explosion that tore the *Connemara* apart. Clara becomes convinced that Patrick was murdered and that she was attacked. As she sorts through Patrick's business affairs, she realises that her husband had led a double life. He was involved with criminals and owed someone a lot of money. So when a mysterious man appears to be following Clara's every move, her fears for her safety grow — and that of her twelve-year-old son. Could this man be the attacker, and does he want to finish the job?

WINNERS AND LOSERS

Madge Swindells

It isn't until her grandfather's accident that Samantha Rosslyn realises that Woodlands, the family-owned brewery, is in deep trouble. To raise cash, Sam decides to sell an ancient family title, but the proposed sale attracts a young American historian, whose presence brings unexpected complications. As Sam struggles to pull the company round, her sister becomes involved with a campaign to publicise the plight of animals kept in battery conditions, her grandfather teams up with some wartime comrades to fight off a threat to the brewery from organised crime, and Sam's best friend is desperately trying to avoid an arranged marriage.